Sarah L Steele

The Right Honourable Arthur Macmurrough Kavanagh

A biography

Sarah L Steele

The Right Honourable Arthur Macmurrough Kavanagh
A biography

ISBN/EAN: 9783337012069

Printed in Europe, USA, Canada, Australia, Japan

Cover: Foto ©Raphael Reischuk / pixelio.de

More available books at **www.hansebooks.com**

THE RIGHT HONOURABLE

ARTHUR MACMURROUGH KAVANAGH

A Biography

COMPILED BY HIS COUSIN

SARAH L. STEELE

FROM PAPERS CHIEFLY UNPUBLISHED

Does the road wind up-hill all the way?
Yes, to the very end.—CHRISTINA ROSSETTI

WITH PORTRAIT

London
MACMILLAN AND CO.
AND NEW YORK
1891

TO

HIS CHILDREN

AND

GRANDCHILDREN

PREFACE

ONE beautiful January morning, with the blue expanse of the Bay of Naples shimmering under our windows in the sunlight, I received a letter which changed all our plans for the year.

It was to ask me to undertake the Biography, now placed before the public, of my cousin Arthur Mac-Murrough Kavanagh.

It has been a labour of love,—of love both to the dead and the living,—and though I feel very deeply how inadequately I have portrayed that noble life, yet I have striven with all my heart to do it justice.

My object has not been to make an exhaustive Biography. It has rather been to show, as much as possible in his own words, how, deprived as he necessarily was of the usual course of education, his early life of travel, assisted by his own keen observation and self-reliance, made good that loss; how his character thus moulded gave him the high place he filled in the esteem of those whose opinion is of value; how his thoughtful work for his own people and for his country was unweariedly carried on through difficulty and disappointment; and how he strove for no other reward than the approval of his conscience and of his God.

I could never have undertaken the task but for the guidance and co-operation of my husband. From the beginning to the end his ungrudging help was always ready, and his deep appreciation of Mr. Kavanagh's rare qualities rendered it doubly effective.

My cordial thanks must also be given to those whose greater knowledge of various portions of Mr. Kavanagh's life and work was so loyally placed at my disposal. To Mrs. Kavanagh first, then to Mrs. Bruen, the Bishop of Ossory, the Bishop of Cork, Lord Courtown, Mr. Sweetman, J.P., Mr. J. F. Vesey-Fitzgerald, Mr. G. D. Burtchaell, and the Rev. G. W. Rooke.

My acknowledgments are also due to the Right Hon. W. H. Smith, the Right Hon. G. J. Goschen, and the Right Hon. J. Chamberlain, for valuable material they allowed me to publish; and, further, to my sister Mrs. Meredyth, Mr. T. E. Kebbel, and Mr. C. A. Cooper of Edinburgh, for incidental assistance.

Mrs. Alexander's beautiful verses which close the Biography need no comment from me beyond this word of gratitude for the privilege of publishing them.

I cannot conclude without expressing the earnest

hope that this imperfect record of one "of whom the world was not worthy,"—whose whole life revealed the humble submission of a Christian, united to the manly chivalry of a noble race,—may not have told its story in vain.

Sarah L. Steele.

Florence, *Christmas Eve*, 1890.

CONTENTS

CHAPTER I

CHAPTER II

CHAPTER III

CHAPTER IV

CHAPTER V

CHAPTER XI

CHAPTER XII

CHAPTER XIII

CHAPTER XIV

CHAPTER XV

CHAPTER XVI

CHAPTER XVII

CHAPTER XVIII

CHAPTER XIX

CHAPTER XX

CHAPTER XXI

CHAPTER XXII

CHAPTER XXIII

CHAPTER XXIV

CHAPTER XXV

ILLUSTRATIONS

THE RIGHT HONOURABLE

ARTHUR MACMURROUGH KAVANAGH

PROEM

His strength was as the strength of ten,
Because his heart was pure.—TENNYSON.

AMID all the beautiful scenery of Ireland, no lovelier view can be found than that from the ancestral home of the Kavanaghs.

Green levels of lawn and wood carry the eye to where in the distance the Barrow winds down to the sea, and on the left to the deer-park hill, where, among trees and fern and almost within hearing of the brook he loved so well, sleeps the noblest son of all that kingly race in a small ruined church, now consecrated as the family burying-ground.

His physical privations, overcome by sheer principle and pluck — two of his most signal characteristics— never debarred him from mingling with his fellows, and fulfilling all the duties of a resident Irish landlord.

For many years he served his country in Parliament —from 1866 to 1868 as member for the County of Wexford, and from 1868 to 1880 as member for the County of Carlow—from which latter he was unseated in circumstances which ever after painfully affected him.

From that time till the close of his life, though

shut out from the Legislature, he still assisted with his clear judgment and well-balanced mind in all schemes set on foot for the benefit of Ireland, chiefly in devising and working the Land Corporation, which, if properly supported, would have neutralised the Land League, and conferred untold blessings on the country.

The rehabilitation of the Church in Ireland also engrossed much of his time and thought. Indeed— while neglecting nothing for the best interests of his own tenantry—he spared no effort on behalf of the people at large.

And when the summons came to "go up higher," all knew that at this crisis of her history Ireland had lost the ungrudged and ill-requited service of one of the truest patriots she ever possessed.

CHAPTER I

No family in the British Islands can point to a more ancient pedigree than the Kavanaghs.

They can trace it back to the dawn of Irish history. Tradition, indeed, carries it far beyond that limit—to the legendary foretime, nay, even to the fabulous Feniusa of Scythia, coeval with the Tower of Babel, whose descendants, having wandered into Egypt, found their way back again to Scythia, and thence to Spain, from which country Heber and Heremon, the two sons of Gallamh or Milesius, crossed over to Ireland, reduced it to subjection, and divided it between them.

From them sprang lines of kings ruling over the five monarchies into which the island was split up.

" One branch of the descendants of Heremon eventually established themselves as kings of Leinster (writes the accomplished scholar and antiquary, Mr. G. D. Burtchaell), and from Murchadh, or Morrough, King of Leinster, in the eleventh century, the family became known as MacMorrough, or the 'Sons of Morrough.' The grandson of this monarch was Dermot MacMorrough, King of Leinster, surnamed na-nGall, that is, 'of the Strangers,' who invited the Normans to Ireland in 1167.

"Dermot, in order to secure the support of Richard de Clare, Earl of Pembroke, surnamed Strongbow, to re-establish himself in his kingdom, from which he had been expelled, agreed to give him his daughter Eva in marriage. On the death of Dermot in 1171, Strongbow claimed the throne of Leinster in right of his wife, and in defiance of Irish law and custom. He was soon obliged to renounce his pretensions to establishing himself as an independent sovereign, and surrendered his rights as such to King Henry the Second.

" Dermot, however, had left a son, Donell, surnamed Caomhanach, or Kavanagh, which means the ' Handsome.' His descendants claimed to be lawfully entitled to be kings of Leinster, and were from time to time successful in defying the English power and asserting their rights.

"Of these descendants the most renowned was Art MacMorrough, son of Art 'More,' or the Great, at whose 'puissance,' says the chronicler, 'all Leinster trembled.' He re-established the sway of his clan over the greater part of their former territories. In right of his wife he became entitled to lands in the County Kildare, which, however, were declared by the English Government in Ireland to be forfeited by reason of her marriage with an ' Irish enemy.' Art determined that he would merit this title, and became so formidable to the English power that Richard the Second came over in person to oppose him. An amicable arrangement was concluded by which Art accepted other lands in place of those of which he was deprived, and in consideration of a pension surrendered his rights to the King. He did homage, swore allegiance, and, together with the other kings of Ireland, received knighthood from King Richard's hands in circumstances of great pomp in Christ Church Cathedral, Dublin. The compact was very soon broken, and Art renewed hostilities. King Richard was obliged to visit Ireland a second time, but failed to make any impression on the Irish monarch, who vowed that not for all the gold in the world would he again submit. From that time till his death in 1417 he waged incessant war against the English colony, and helped to reduce the Pale within the narrowest bounds.

" After his death the power of the clan gradually declined, and Art More's descendants became divided into several rival houses.

" One of the junior lines was that of St. Mullins[1] and Polmonty. Art Boy MacMorrough, *alias* Kavanagh, of Borris and St. Mullins, County Carlow, and Polmonty, County Wexford, was father of Cahir MacArt, who succeeded in getting the English Government to recognise him as chief of his name on acknowledging himself an English subject.

" In 1553 he was rewarded by being created Baron of Ballyan for life—his eldest son Morgan receiving at the same time the title of Baron of Cowellellyn.

" The line was carried on by the Baron of Ballyan's fourth son, Brian MacCahir of Borris and Polmonty. He died in 1575, having married Elizabeth, daughter of Hugh O'Bryne of the County Wicklow, by whom he left several children.

" The eldest son, Morgan Kavanagh of Borris and Polmonty, was Member of Parliament for County

---

[1] Pronounced Mullins—the accent on the last syllable. Ryan (*History of Carlow*) spells it " Molines."

Carlow 1613 to 1615, and died 19th of June
1636.

"By his first wife Elinor, daughter of Edmund
second Viscount Mountgarret, he had sixteen children, of whom Brian, the eldest son, succeeded his
father.

"Brian Kavanagh was fortunate in being able to
preserve his estate from the general confiscation which
took place after the reduction of Ireland by Cromwell,
and died 1st December 1662. His second wife was
Eleanor, daughter of Sir Edmund Blancheville of
Blanchevillestown, County Kilkenny, and Lady Elizabeth Butler, daughter of Walter eleventh Earl of
Ormonde and aunt of the great Duke of Ormonde.

"His only son Morgan, the issue of this marriage,
succeeded, and died in the reign of Queen Anne. He
married Mary, daughter of Thomas Walsh of Pilltown,
County Waterford, by Ellen, daughter of John Lord
le Poer of Curraghmore, and was succeeded by his only
son, also Morgan, who was born in 1668, and died 22d
February 1722. By his first wife Frances, daughter
of Sir Laurence Esmonde, Bart., of Clonegal, County
Carlow, and Lucia, eldest daughter of Colonel Richard
Butler, the great Duke of Ormonde's brother, he had
three sons, of whom Charles, the second, entered the
Imperial army and died Governor of Prague in 1766.

"The eldest son Brian succeeded his father, and
died 22d April 1741, leaving by Mary his wife, eldest
daughter of Colonel Thomas Butler of Kilcash, a son
and heir Thomas."

Thomas married in 1755 Lady Susanna Butler,
daughter of Walter Butler of Garryricken, sister of
John seventeenth Earl of Ormonde, and died in 1790,
leaving several sons and daughters, of whom Thomas,

the fourth son, born March 1767, inherited the family estates.

Thomas sat as M.P. for the city of Kilkenny in the last Irish Parliament, and after the Union represented the County Carlow in the last two Parliaments of George the Fourth, and the first of William the Fourth. He married first, on the 24th March 1799, Lady Elizabeth Butler, daughter of John seventeenth Earl of Ormonde, and by her, who died in 1822, he had issue, Walter, who died in 1836, and nine daughters, of whom six died spinsters and three were married— the eldest, Anne, to Colonel Henry Bruen of Oak Park, County Carlow, M.P. (whose son was afterwards Arthur's colleague in Parliament from 1868 till 1880).

Mr. Kavanagh married secondly, on 28th February 1825, Lady Harriet Margaret Le Poer Trench, daughter of Richard, second Earl of Clancarty, and left at his decease in 1837 Thomas, who died at Batavia on a voyage to Australia for his health in 1852 ; Charles, also unmarried, an officer in the 7th Hussars, who died in 1853 ; Harriet Margaret, who died 7th May 1876, widow of Colonel W. A. Middleton, C.B., D.A.G., R.A., at the Horse Guards, and Arthur MacMurrough, the subject of the present biography.

A few words may here suffice for the Austrian branch of the family.

Among the archives at Borris House some old letters, written in German, very faded and hard to read, make mention of one Baron Kavanagh who was chamberlain to the " Empress - King," Maria Theresa, and of another Kavanagh who was chamberlain to her son, the Emperor Joseph the Second.

These are most probably General Dermitius (the Latinised form of Dermot) Kavanagh of Hauskirchen,

who died in or about 1750, and his brother-in-law,
Baron John Baptist Kavanagh of Ginditz in Bohemia,
to whom he left the Hauskirchen estates.

John Baptist died in 1774, and the property seems
to have been for some time without a claimant.

According to the letters above referred to, a Baron
Kavanagh towards the close of last century, when
on a tour in Carinthia and Styria, wandered into
a village churchyard and suddenly came upon a
monument erected to one of his name. He drew the
custodian's attention to the inscription on the tablet
and asked to which Kavanagh it referred. The man
told him the deceased had left no heir; that for a
quarter of a century the estate which had belonged to
him had remained without an owner; and that by
Austrian law it must at the end of twenty-seven years
revert to the Crown. Baron Kavanagh, who seems
to have been Maurice, only son of John Baptist, Baron
of Ginditz, and to have unaccountably permitted his
rights to lapse, investigated the affair. It was a
condition that the property must always be held by a
Kavanagh, and finding that, as the next of kin, he himself was the heir, he successfully vindicated his title.

Maurice, who thus became " seized and possessed "
of the estate of Hauskirchen, died unmarried in 1801
at Ofen in Hungary, a general of cavalry and com-
mander-in-chief in that country.

There being again no direct heir to the property,
it must have reverted to the Austrian Crown unless
claimed within twenty-seven years, when, in 1818,
Walter Kavanagh, Esq., of Borris, at that time
its rightful owner, renounced his title to it in favour
of his cousin Count Henry Kavanagh—an officer in
the Imperial army.

The legal instrument by which this renunciation was effected seems to have been vitiated by a technical flaw, in that the consent of the Austrian Government to the transfer had not previously been obtained. The renunciation thus became invalid, and as Mr. Kavanagh failed to assert his rights to the property, a nephew of the last possessor, Count Schaffgotsch, became the owner.

The representative of the Austrian branch of the family is now Baron Harry Kavanagh, who lives near Rohitsch in Styria.

Among the family relics preserved at Borris were the old crown and charter horn of the kings of Leinster. In the troubles of '98 they were removed for safe keeping to Dublin, and deposited in Trinity College. When tranquillity was restored and they had to be given up, the crown was not forthcoming. It had mysteriously disappeared, and no clue to it could be found. Years afterwards there was a report that it had turned up at Toulouse, but nothing more was heard of it, and even the report was not authenticated.

The charter horn, however—a large fluted cornucopia of ivory mounted in brass and resting on a brass eagle — was restored, and is still an heirloom at Borris House.

Mention should also be made of another relic, the Book of St. Moling, still shown in the library of Trinity College: a piece of Irish work of great antiquity, made of leather and mounted in silver, on the model of the ancient Egyptian book-satchels. It was long in possession of the Kavanaghs as Chiefs of Idrone, whose tutelary saint, St. Moling, gives his name to the Abbey of St. Mullins.

CHAPTER II

ARTHUR MACMURROUGH KAVANAGH, third son of the late Thomas Kavanagh, Esq., M.P., by his second wife, Lady Harriet Margaret Le Poer Trench, was born at Borris House 25th March 1831.

From the outset it was manifest that his upbringing must be different from that of other men, born, as he was, without limbs. But it soon became equally apparent that his was a nature that would rise above every disqualification and fit him to bear no common part in the battle of life.

In 1839 he was placed in the house of the Rev. Samuel Greer, curate of Celbridge in the County Kildare, for two reasons: first, that, being at Celbridge, he would be under the eye of Colonel Conolly of Castletown, his mother's cousin, on whose judgment she placed the fullest reliance, and, second, that he might have the companionship of the younger Conolly children—of Mary, now wife of the Right Hon. Henry Bruen of Oak Park, County Carlow; Fanny, who died unmarried in 1874; and Richard, whose death occurred in 1870 when attaché to the Legation at Pekin. With them his weekly half-holidays were spent, and the recollections of those boyish days sent me by Mrs. Bruen I cannot do better than transcribe, to show the early promise which was so nobly fulfilled in later life :—

"We first became acquainted with Arthur when he was put under the charge of a good clergyman of high scholarly attainments—the Rev. Samuel Greer, who was curate of Celbridge, the village at the gate of Castletown, my father's place.

"As well as I can recollect, it must have been about the year 1839 or 1840 when, on our return from Donegal, where we usually spent the autumn months, as my father was M.P. for that county, we met Arthur as we were walking with our nurse—my youngest brother, my sister and myself—in the grounds of Castletown.

" I remember well this first meeting with the merry-looking, very fair-haired boy, riding his pony, and in the most fearless way trying to get it through a very narrow gate. Of course he succeeded (as he usually did in whatever he attempted, even at that early age), to the admiration of us, his cousins, and from that day we became dear friends, drawn to him by his singularly engaging manner, so genial, so manly, so full of sympathy—a most delightful boy who came into the routine of our young lives like a sunbeam.

"So bright and full of fun was he that the days when we did not meet him in our walks were comparatively dull.

" I suppose he must have been placed with Mr. Greer partly in order to be within reach of the great Dublin surgeon, Sir Philip Crampton, whose rare professional skill, it was hoped, might devise some mechanism to make up for what had been denied him in physical development. This must have been a most trying ordeal to his fine unselfish nature, so light-hearted as he was, so grandly submissive in his sense of privation. Much pain, great discomfort, and continual disappointment were all that came of it, borne, however, so uncomplainingly that one must feel they were not the only result ; while the sympathy from us, his child-friends, so gladly and lovingly received by him, drew him nearer to us than aught else could have done. Even as children we could not but wonder at his cheerful submission to his many annoyances and discomforts, and indeed the continual consultations over his case must have been most trying to so manly a boy.

" His holidays were spent with us. He used to ride up to Castletown—a careful lad leading his pony, and his faithful nurse, Anne Fleming, in attendance. After our formal schoolroom dinner, presided over by our very strict governess, who kept us all four in great order, we were allowed to amuse ourselves in any way we liked in any part of the large house.

" Delightful were these afternoons ! Arthur led the games and was first in everything ! His personal influence was even then remarkable, and we were all so devoted to him as to be his most willing subjects. As though he were a king we would follow his will as law, and he often led us, or the children of his tutor, into the most ridiculous pranks, or predicaments, not always looked upon by our elders with strict approbation.

" From his upstairs room in Mr. Greer's house he would sometimes amuse himself by fishing, as it were, with a bait at the end of a long string for the ducks in the yard below, till one day a duck swallowed the bait! and then great was the excitement as he pulled up the string and landed the duck safely in his room, to be killed, plucked, cooked, and eaten in haste, lest the performance should be discovered by Anne Fleming, or by Mrs. Greer, who, kind and good to Arthur, ruled her household with a strict order—notwithstanding which he could induce the children to obey him in most of his wishes.

" He even persuaded Mr. Greer's eldest son to submit to having his ears bored as if for earrings! Arthur himself performing the operation with the greatest glee. And how often in after years he has described this, enjoying the recollection of it and wondering at the victim's meekness under so painful an ordeal!

"Often, of course, he was in disgrace for so entertaining himself and his young companions, but he was seldom long depressed at that time of his life. The sternest could not long be angry with him. His merry bright face and winning ways drew out every one's love and attached all to him, both high and low; and when in 1841 we left Castletown for Paris to spend two years on the Continent, the parting from him was most grievous to us all. His fearless undaunted spirit and pluck had made him a hero in our young eyes, and the friendship thus begun in childhood ripened in after life into the intimate and sympathetic intercourse that lasted to the end."

His education was then continued during a two years' residence at St. Germains with his mother and sister, and on a subsequent short visit to Italy.

Of his stay in Rome he retained a lively recollection, and often afterwards spoke of the apartments they occupied in the Villa Strozzi — now, alas! destroyed, like so many others, for the reconstruction of the city.

I cannot quite fix the date of my own earliest recollections of Arthur—of his pleasant visits to our schoolroom when he came to see us in Dublin, and would playfully supervise my weary struggles over simple sums—of our long sojourns at Borris, where one of our amusements was to harness his mother's pet spaniel "Prince" to a little cart, seated in which he would drive me about the entrance hall—and (not least) of the hymn, "Arthur's Hymn," as we used to call it, and all the dearer to us for that reason, which might seem to foretell his future love of the sea, and the steady trust that deepened with advancing life in a Father's guidance :—

> 'Twas when the sea with awful roar
>   A little bark assailed,
> And pallid fear's distracting power
>   O'er each on board prevailed
>
> Save one—the Captain's darling child—
>   Who steadfast viewed the storm,
> And, cheerful, with composure smiled
>   On danger's threatening form.
>
> "Why sporting thus," a seaman cried,
>   "While dangers overwhelm ?"
> "Why yield to fear ?" the child replied,
>   "My father's at the helm !"
>
> Christian ! From him be daily taught
>   To calm thy groundless fear ;
> Think on the wonders He has wrought ;
>   Jehovah's ever near.

VIEW OF BORRIS HOUSE

CHAPTER III

Ille terrarum mihi praeter omnes
Angulus ridet.   HOR. *Car.* ii. 6. 13.

In all the world no spot there is
That wears for me a smile like this.
        SIR THEODORE MARTIN.

THE old gray stone building, since 1570 the family seat of the Kavanaghs, commands from its position a widely-extended view over the fine woods of the demesne—across the valley of the "goodly Barow" to the blue mountains in the distance, Brandon, Mount Leinster, and Blackstairs. Turreted walls and the rich colouring of years attest its antiquity, and the chapel wing, added at a later period, consecrates the beauty of the historic house. Through the tangled ivy that veils the chapel the Gothic windows show their mellowed tracery, while, guarding like sentinels the narrow pathway leading to it, stand the venerable beech-trees that Sunday by Sunday have watched generations of worshippers wending their way from the village to what, in fact, is the parish church of Clonagoose.

But far other gatherings than that of a peaceful congregation has the old house witnessed. Stormy scenes have been enacted round its walls, rebel and loyalist contending for the mastery. Twice has it sustained a regular siege and twice driven off its assailants gallantly.   The first of these was during the great rebellion of 1641, when it was surrounded by the insurgent Irish, whom it kept at bay till they were finally put to flight by Sir Charles Coote of Castlecuffe in the Queen's County—an ancestor of the Cootes of Ballyfin.

Again, in the rising of 1798, it was attacked by the rebels and again defended by a Kavanagh—Arthur's father, who all through the insurrection bore a most honourable part.   In his *Memoirs of the Different Rebellions of Ireland*, Sir Richard Musgrave says of him that, having been distinguished by his devotion to the Crown and his energy as a magistrate, he was "peculiarly the object of rebel vengeance."   On the night of the 24th May, accordingly, Borris House was invested by a body of about five thousand insurgents, who, we read in Ryan's *History of Carlow*, were driven off by Captain Kavanagh's yeomanry corps, leaving behind them fifty men in killed and wounded.

Returning to the assault on the 12th of June, the rebels began operations on the village of Borris, lying under the demesne wall.   They burned the houses of the tenants, and followed up their advantage till they were met by a determined resistance at the house itself, which was garrisoned by twenty of the Donegal militia and seventeen of the yeomanry.   Commanded by one Kearns, a priest, who was afterwards hanged at Edenderry, the assailants attempted to batter down the walls with a howitzer, but made no impression on them, and were compelled to retire with considerable loss.

"One of the insurgents," says Sir Richard Musgrave, "who was wounded and could not retreat, proved to be a tenant of Mr. Kavanagh's who lived close to the house, and to whom he had been singularly kind. On being asked why he had embarked in this treasonable enterprise, he confessed that he was tempted to do so by a promise of obtaining a portion of the estate "—a promise not then made for the last time!

Round Borris, indeed, both house and village, there was a series of encounters with the rebels—the only encounters, it is said, in which the loyalists were decidedly successful during that memorable rising. In one of these at Kilcomney, a short distance off, the King's forces were commanded by Sir Charles Asgill, and, with a few discharges of artillery, put the enemy to rout. They retreated precipitately to the County Wexford through the Scollogh Gap, and were pursued by the regular troops for six miles, losing many of their number on the road, and finally abandoning their cannon, baggage, stores, and provisions.

But those wild scenes have long given place to others of a more peaceful nature, and in the early light of a summer morning from the windows of the old house nought can now be surveyed but the outlined hills and the dark woods, and the Barrow just suggested by the faint mist that the sun has not yet dispersed, while the lawn below is alive with rabbits, fearlessly sporting in the silence, unbroken save by the twitter of the wakening birds.

The demesne of Borris is skirted on one side by the Barrow, into which, under Bunahown Bridge, dashes the brook—a mountain torrent bright and rapid even in the hottest summer, reminding one, in places, of the Garry as it threads the Pass of Killiecrankie, with just the same brown pools lying clear and still between the mossy boulders rounded by the water, just the same

high banks, clothed with trees and underwood. The
Borris brook indeed is smaller, but, in its picturesque
course, not the less lovely, with the large clumps of
rhododendrons, scarlet and purple, showing brilliant
patches of colour through the dark green of fir and
beech.   Might not Coleridge have seen it or heard it,
in vision or dream, when he sang

> of a hidden brook
> In the leafy month of June,
> That to the sleeping woods all night
> Singeth a quiet tune?

Attractive enough as a trout stream, with its little
wooded islets and " fairy forelands " breaking the
current, it has yet other attractions which some may
prize still more—clear crystals and even pearls!

But for salmon the angler must turn to the Barrow,
the varied scenery of which as it winds majestically
past Borris down to New Ross recalls, not seldom,
Tennyson's

> slow, broad stream
> That, stirred with languid pulses of the oar,
> Waves all its lazy lilies and creeps on
> Barge-laden,

through fields

> browsed by deep-uddered kine,

till, as it widens between lofty, bold, and wooded banks
it might equally have suggested Sir Walter's

> Where through groves deep and high
> Sounds the far billow !

Many a time from the boathouse, near the bottom
of the old deer-park, has Arthur steered a gay party
out under the arch fringed with wreaths of ivy into the
broad river, then past Bunahown Bridge and through

the frequent locks that equalise its levels, past the ruined abbey of St. Mullins, where generations of his forefathers rest, and so down the gliding water beneath the romantic old bridge of Graigue to Drummond, where, half hidden by trees and half covered with roses, nestles the small slated house, built about thirty years ago, when the sporting instincts were highest. Now the little place is deserted save for an occasional picnic. But none who ever shared in them will forget the joyous parties round that informal board, at which the steersman of the morning, presiding as the kindly host, welcomed all to the dainty contents of the hampers. And after the merry luncheon came the pleasant ramble through the woods, dense with honeysuckle and ivy, till just in time to save the tide began the journey home through the still evening—not the least enjoyable part of an excursion, always one of the chief delights of those happy summer days at Borris.

CHAPTER IV

Es bildet ein Talent sich in der Stille,
Sich ein Character in dem Strom der Welt.—GOETHE.

A Talent moulds itself in quiet study,
A Character in life's eventful stream.

FROM the still life at Celbridge and afterwards at Borris, where, amid the scenes and associations just described, his education was carried on by tutors, we have now to accompany him on a tour, during the years 1846, '47, and '48, through Egypt, in the track of the Israelites, to the Holy Land.

Shut out from the discipline of a public school, he had the best possible substitute in foreign travel, with its special opportunities of observation and reflection, enhanced under the guidance of his highly-gifted mother.

A detailed record of this journey has been preserved in a series of letters, chiefly from Lady Harriet, and, in much fewer number, from others of the party, which included his eldest brother Tom, his sister Harriet, and their tutor, the Rev. David Wood.

About the middle of October 1846 they left Marseilles for Alexandria, and thence proceeded to Cairo, where they hired two boats, and, early in November, began the ascent of the Nile as far as the third cataract. Their experiences were mainly those

of every traveller interested in the past and present
of the great Nile valley, and, as described in the
letters, were thoroughly enjoyed by the whole party,
favoured as it was by ample leisure, and, as far as
concerned the young people, by a superintendence
and companionship advantageous from every point of
view.

Tutorial work, chiefly in Latin and Greek for the
boys, with regular readings in history, sacred and pro-
fane, filled up a portion of the day, the rest of which
was spent in sport upon the river banks, when not
occupied by visits to scenes now of easier access to the
archæologist and art student.

Of these expeditions Arthur, by this time in his sixteenth year, hardly missed one, whether its object was
a jackal hunt, a shot at an ibis, an ascent of the Pyramids, or an exploration of the ruins of Thebes. He
was his own master in all his movements, and enjoyed
a freedom which in any other so circumstanced or
poorer in resource would hardly have been safe.
Not, however, that he was invariably prudent.
Through all his life he had more than his share of
narrow escapes, of which the following, on the 14th
January 1847, was among the most providential.

The two dahabeayahs on which they were making
the voyage upstream were moored alongside each
other near the shore, between Luxor and Karnak.
He was sitting on the gunwale of one and leaning
over half asleep on the gunwale of the other, while
the rest of the party and all the servants were away
on an expedition or below in the cabins. Either a
breeze or the swell from some passing boat caused the
dahabeayahs to drift apart. He fell between them,
and they closed over him. An Arab on the shore

saw him fall and gave the alarm, so that he was rescued, though to all appearance drowned, and it was long before he was restored to consciousness.

Of this life—half sport, half study, and all pleasure —he grew so fond, that its renewal on the return voyage only heightened its charm for him, and it was with something like regret that he exchanged it even for the journey across the desert. No incident or experience was thrown away upon him; and it may be noted here that, though the youngest of the party, he was the aptest to pick up, and the longest to retain, the language of the Bedouin escort, insomuch that when necessary he could act as interpreter. At home in the saddle, on horse, camel, or mule, he rode across the desert, drinking in the melancholy fascination of its aspects, living or inanimate; and to the close of life he never lost the vivid and solemn impressions of Mount Sinai, Mount Horeb, and the wilderness between Egypt and the Promised Land.

The following letter to his brother Charles, then at Borris, will show how little, in point of observation and literary expression, the boy of sixteen had missed by not having been at a public school :—

"BEYROUT, 26*th May* 1847.

"MY DEAR CHARLEY—We have completed our Egyptian and Syrian travels, and have arrived at Beyrout. We do not know whether we are to leave for Constantinople and spend another year in our wanderings, or else to go direct home. The next letters will decide us.

"We have had a very jolly time of it. We crossed the desert in force, having joined with three other parties, making in all sixty camels. We went round by Petra and Sinai, and at Hebron we exchanged the desert camel for the Syrian horse. We enjoyed the desert immensely, but fully appreciate the difference between the parched and arid sands of Africa and the grassy plains, wooded mountains, and silver streams of the Land of Promise,

> Where the citron and olive are fairest of fruit,
> And the voice of the nightingale never is mute,
> Where virgins are soft as the roses they twine,
> And all, save the spirit of man, is divine.

"I bought a horse from the Governor at Hebron —a very nice little fellow. I have ridden him all the way from Hebron to here. He is generally well-behaved. His name is Dougal M'Tavish. We have another horse in the party of the same sex, with whom he fights.

"I am writing this letter at a window looking out on the sea, and while I was drinking a glass of sherbet it was blown off the table into the dirty street, but, as you see, I have got it back all safe.

"We have parted with all our Arab servants to-day, and are sending them back to Alexandria by steamer. We are going to take Ishmael, our drago-man, to Ireland. He is a very nice sort of fellow. I am sure you will like him. He has very long moustaches.

"Tom has got a Turkish dress all embroidered with gold for £13. Hoddy [his sister Harriet] has got a lady's dress, and I have got a Bedouin's costume. Tom has also got the carpet Mehemet Ali Pacha used to say his prayers on. It is white satin, all covered with gold. It cost £10. He has also bought an Arab gun, nearly sixteen feet in the barrel, all inlaid with silver. He and I have joined together and bought a brace of Arab horse-pistols all covered with silver, besides sabres, scimitars, daggers, and knives innumerable. I also bought a beautiful little horse-piece, inlaid with silver—what the Mamlouks use. We have also got shields made of giraffe and crocodile skin, along with spears and Nubian knives. I am sure you would enjoy the East immensely—the most delicious fruit and everything enjoyable.

> 'Tis the land of the East, 'tis the clime of the sun !
> Can he smile on such deeds as his children have done ?

" It would charm you to see their beautiful eyes—

> Those eyes' dark charm 'twere vain to tell !
> But gaze on those of the gazelle,
> It will assist thy fancy well.

" It seems as if it were a dream, a fairyland ! Picture to yourself gardens of apricots and pomegranates, vineyards and oliveyards, intersected with sparkling brooks and silver fountains, where the rose and the myrtle in full bloom send their fragrant scents to the cloudless heavens and perfume the balmy air with their delicious odours. I cannot help reciting Byron's beautiful lines, so striking for their truth and the beauty of their composition."

And here the letter closes with a transcript from memory of the familiar

> Know ye the land, etc.

In further illustration of the use he made of his opportunities I may give the following letter to the Rev. Ralph Morton, then tutor to his brother Charles at Borris.

" JERUSALEM, 30*th October* 1847.

" MY DEAR MORTON—It is a long time since I have written to you—indeed I believe not since I was at Marseilles; and I am sure you must have attributed my silence not only to neglect, but to entire forgetfulness of you and your former kindness. And although, certainly, my idleness would deserve such an interpretation, I must say this is not the case. The only excuse I will plead is my own idleness and the difficulty of finding an opportunity from constant travelling. The rest I will leave to your indulgence. . . .

"We are going to cross the short desert. We expect to meet the D——s in Egypt. We heard that they were going to spend the winter in Rome, so we wrote to them to come out to us instead; for I believe travel in Egypt is the easiest sort of travel.

" I am sure you would like these countries extremely (if I have lived long enough with you to be acquainted with your tastes). I even think that Charley—my patriotic brother—would find means for enjoyment. The best shooting, I believe, in the world is to be found on the Nile—birds of all plumage in abundance, from the large white pelican to the beautiful little green and gold humming-bird. There is also wolf and wild boar and hyena hunting, which is generally managed on horses with rifles; also coursing gazelles with beautiful Persian greyhounds. I have been out coursing gazelles sometimes here. We also ran a wolf with the dogs, but the poor fellow has very little chance, and gets pulled down in no time.

" I am very fond of the Bedouin Arabs—they are so good-natured and hospitable. We often got into their encampments, particularly on our way from Jerusalem to Damascus, and used to stop with them till our own tents came up, when we set to work to pitch and get ready for passing the night.

" The tents generally are pitched in half an hour.

We have three tents: one large one for the ladies, another small one for us, another smaller one again for the dragoman, cook, helper, and luggage. The instant we halt the cook sets to work to light his fire and get the dinner ready, while the dragoman and helpers are pitching the tents, making the beds, collecting the luggage, etc. For two hours our camp shows a very busy and lively scene. By that time dinner is ready, and we all sit down. The rest smoke their long chibouques or narghilehs (narghileh is a machine for smoking tombak, a strong tobacco, through water). After dinner we smoke until eight, when we go to bed, having always to be up at four. Then begins a busy scene. The tents are struck, everything packed up, we get our breakfast while they are loading the mules, and, in about an hour and a half, you would not know where we had passed the night.

"We lunch in the middle of the day, for, breakfasting at four and not dining until six, one feels the want of something at that time.

"We have bought our horses at Beyrout for this journey to Cairo—six. I have got a very nice horse indeed. I gave seventeen hundred piastres for him. He has a true Arab mark on his ear, and everybody I have shown him to says that if not entirely he is very nearly pure Arab breed. He stands about fifteen hands, has a beautiful head and fine ear, long nose, almost a milk-white coat shining like glass; his limbs are fine without a puff; his eye and the expression of his countenance fiery, yet sweet—an odd phrase to use about a horse, but I do not know any other which expresses what I want so well. He is the admiration of everybody here. Mamma even thinks he will be worth taking home.

" Now I must try to give you a description of
Jerusalem.

" The frontispiece in your small book of Palestine
affords a very good representation of the Jaffa gate as
viewed from the Bethlehem plain.   The town is walled
round, the walls being kept in a perfect state of preservation by the Sultan.   Some parts of them are very
curious, the stones being of immense size, some twenty-
seven feet long by ten broad—an evident sign of their
antiquity.   One side of the wall stands near the valley
of Jehoshaphat, but it does not overhang it, as drawings generally represent.   The streets are very narrow,
dirty, and badly paved.   There are four clergymen
here.   The Bishop is a Prussian, Gobat by name.
Before his appointment he was a missionary in Abys-
sinia.   Mr. Fisher, an Englishman ; Mr. Nicholayson,
a Dane, who married a Mrs. Dalton, an Irish lady.
The other, a Mr. Ewald, is a German.   They are all
very nice and good-natured, and have been kinder to
us than any people we have met on our travels.   There
is also here an English consul, a Mr. Hine ; and
English doctors, a Mr. Sandford and Mr. M'Gowan
—the latter at present in Jaffa.   They all treat us
more as if we were their near relations than mere
travellers passing by.   We have hardly spent an
evening at our house since we came, being invited
nearly every evening either to dine or to take tea, and,
in the day, making picnic parties to places of great
interest.

" There are very extraordinary things shown here
by the monks—utterly ridiculous and difficult even for
the most credulous to believe ; such as the stone that
would have cried out if it could, etc.

" We are going out to-day gazelle-hunting, and I

hope we shall have some success.   Tom and I are thinking of buying a brace of these greyhounds, if we can get them for a reasonable price.

"We start the day after to-morrow for Cairo by the short desert, across which we are going to ride our horses.   We shall then have traversed both deserts, having crossed the long one by Petra and Sinai coming here—a journey of thirty-six days, while this one is only twelve.

"I have plenty more to say, only I have neither time nor paper.   How is 'Prince'? and my hound?"

A letter from his eldest brother, who was one of the party, supplies details of the sport not given by Arthur himself.   It is dated at a farther stage of their journey.

"RHODA, *6th March* 1848.

" . . . Lord Morton, whom we met up the Nile this year, has lent Arthur a gun, with which he has shot a great many wild geese, ducks, and snipe.   He shoots much better than Mr. Wood, who began about the same time that he did, and can hit a bird flying quite well.   His shooting is quite as wonderful as his riding.   He is also the only one of the party who can speak Arabic, which he does perfectly.

"The other day, when riding through the bazaars, he encountered a number of Bedouin and Arab sheikhs whom he got acquainted with in the desert, and with whom he is a great favourite.   As soon as they saw him, they all ran up and kissed him on both cheeks."

Yet another letter of Arthur's, addressed to the Rev. Ralph Morton, may here be inserted.   It is dated Marseilles, 10th April 1848, by which time they had closed their wanderings in the East, had visited

Smyrna and the shores of the Black Sea as far as Trebizond, had explored Constantinople and its waters, and passed another winter in Lower Egypt.

" . . . In a former letter from Rhoda I mentioned that we were to go to Malta for our quarantine and then come home by Italy. We changed our plans and intended coming here and then starting for Algiers or the coast of Spain, as the North of Italy was too much disturbed for travelling. When we came here affairs were so unsettled that our intended trip to Algiers had to be given up. . . .

"We hear nothing now but the Marseillaise hymn and see nothing but troops patrolling the streets. The National Guard has been recruited, and the Civic Guard called out. A great panic has struck all commercial men. The bankers refuse to cash any bills whatever. The shops are all shut at sunset, because, there being no demand for their articles, they do not care to burn their lights for nothing. All public works have been stopped because the Government have no money to pay the workmen. There is general dissatisfaction on account of the elections being put off. So much for the good of a revolution! I think certainly not less than two thousand men have passed under my window to-day, armed with muskets and sabres, and commanded by officers of the line. . . .

"We are taking home an Arab servant. His name is Hadji Mohammed. Also two beautiful Syrian gazelle-hounds which we bought at Jerusalem. [They were called Lufra and Gwherda—the Arabic, I believe, for Rosebud; the former black, the latter white, deeply stained with henna.] I sold my horse at Cairo. Poor beast! I cried the day I left him—he knew me so well! He used to lick my face when I came out of the tent in the morning to see him, and at the luncheon-time in the heat of the day, when I used to sit under him for shade, he would put his head between his front legs to take a bit of bread, without moving, for fear of hurting me."

This fondness for animals of all sorts, and very specially for horses and dogs, was a strongly marked trait in his character. Indeed, his power over them was wonderful. He would speak to them in tones and terms of coaxing endearment—the animals listening as if they understood his wishes, and obeying, as if forced by his influence to give up their wills to his.

In 1848, after his return from Egypt, he was thrown a good deal into the society of his two nieces, daughters of Colonel Bruen of Oak Park, his companions in many a frolic, riding or driving. Anne's ponies or his own partly trained ones he would drive four-in-hand, she sitting beside him to help by pelting the leaders with little stones. Or he would himself drive over, tandem, to Oak Park, where he was always a welcome guest—to none more than to his brother-in-law, Colonel Bruen, who, though much his senior, regarded him with affectionate admiration.

But in his riding excursions he was generally quite alone. Once, in the old deer-park at Borris, his horse bolted with him, tearing round the park three times. He was just able to guide him when his strength began to fail; so, hoping to stop his mad career by facing an impossible fence, he turned the animal's head to the demesne wall. At that moment the girths gave way, the saddle he was strapped into turned and

he was swung round.   He remembered nothing more,
and was found lying insensible beside the horse.

Another very striking incident of that year should
be mentioned.   It was at the time of Smith O'Brien's
rebellion, and he was staying on a visit to his great-
aunt, then Dowager Marchioness of Ormonde, at
Garryricken ("Garden of the King"), near Slieve-na-
Man, where the unsuccessful rising took place.   To
reconnoitre the movements of the "patriots," he went
out by night to see their encampment on a favourite
hunter given him by Colonel Bruen.   He succeeded
in getting near their outposts, but was discovered,
and pursued by some of their "cavalry."   Only the
speed and cross-country powers of his good horse
" Bunny " saved him from being captured—their horses
being unable to take the fences, to which he fearlessly
put his own.

CHAPTER V

πολλῶν ἀνθρώπων ἴδεν ἄστεα καὶ νόον ἔγνω.—Hom. *Od.* i. 3.

Wandering from clime to clime, observant strayed,
Their manners noted and their states surveyed.—Pope.

As slow our ship her foamy track
  Against the wind was cleaving,
Her trembling pennant still look'd back
  To that dear isle 'twas leaving.
So loth we part from all we love,
  From all the links that bind us,
So turn our hearts where'er we rove
  To those we've left behind us.—*Irish Melodies.*

Shortly after they returned to Ireland in 1848 his brother Tom celebrated the attainment of his majority amid the congratulations customary on such occasions, and in the following year Arthur and he, again accompanied by Mr. Wood, started on a prolonged tour—once more to the East.

Their journey was to lie through Scandinavia, Russia, down the Volga and over the Caspian, to Northern Persia, Kourdistan, and, by the valley of the Tigris and the Persian Gulf, to the Bombay Presidency and the Province of Berar.

Of this expedition Arthur kept a journal, in great part preserved, which, both from its still fresh interest and the view it affords of him as an observer of nature and mankind, may be given in pretty full extracts.

To him the experience proved an education and discipline during the years which other young fellows spend at college, and—just as on the tour through Egypt and Syria—it called into play his powers and resources, mental and physical, developing both, and forming the habits and tastes which influenced so much of his after life.

Accordingly, on 4th June 1849, the small party left Kingstown on their long adventurous journey; and through Denmark, Norway, Sweden, and Finland, without much striking incident, reached St. Petersburg on the 28th July, and Moscow on the 8th August.

Of these towns and their neighbourhood they made a thorough exploration, and on the 24th reached Nijni-Novgorod, while the annual fair was in progress. There they spent some days laying in stores and enjoying the varied and picturesque aspects of the celebrated gathering. On the 4th September began the work of packing, as on the following day they expected to start on the steamer for Astrakhan. He says :—

" We were by way of travelling light, and, certainly, the length of journey and time considered, we were not overburdened with either luxuries or necessaries. When everything was packed the baggage list showed —six portmanteaux, two cases of sherry, one of brandy, one of tea, four gun-cases, three bundles of beds and cloaks, two carpet-bags, two hat-boxes, two leather bags of shot, and innumerable small parcels. The voyage down the Volga, it was supposed, would make at least one case of sherry look foolish, so, that excepted, the above list was our outfit for Persia. Three bundles of beds sounds large, but those consisted of air-beds and two couples of cloaks tied up into a very small compass, and were as uncomfortable concerns as deluded travellers ever tried to sleep on. When inflated to the full extent the floor was just as soft, and when I tried to make mine a little softer by letting out some of the air, I was shot out on the floor by the rush of the air going to the one side. I therefore gave up the contest, and remained satisfied with the floor. The amount of portmanteaux might well, I think, have been reduced. Gun-cases and shot, if we had been gifted with prophetic vision, would certainly have been left behind. But, allured by vivid expectations of every kind of sport, we would as soon have left the guns as Wood his collection of Murray's Handbooks, which, with a volume called *Family Medicine*, filled the book-box. Three pocket-knives and forks constituted our canteen outfit, and of everything else we had to take our chance."

After a false start on the 5th, they got off on the 6th in a steamer—the *Hercules*—which he describes as "a fine vessel, flat-bottomed, five hundred horse-power, and tremendous length. Every evening," he continues, "at sunset we lay to, and started at sunrise, a necessary precaution from the innumerable sand-banks with which the river abounded. Sometimes it looked more like an arm of the sea with the tide out, just leaving the sand visible. A little farther on it would narrow, passing the foot of a low copse-covered range of hills, running then through a small district of gardens and villages, where we usually (that is, when we reached such an oasis) stopped to take in wood, provisions, fruit, etc. It would widen again, and apparently lose itself in an interminable stretch of sand and water."

On the 9th they reached Kasan (ten versts from the bank of the river), when two boats they had in tow ran on a sandbank. After six hours they got off one, and were,

" 11*th September*,

" Still working away without any seeming chance of getting off the other. The weather was very cold and showery. Our condition was much improved by having got rid of all the passengers at Kasan, except one fat Russian. Our dinners were very bad, consisting alternately of patriarchal cocks and horseflesh, followed by pudding made of goodness knows what. The sherry and beer we got at Nijni turned out very satisfactory, and many a health to our absent friends was drunk in both of them. About 5 P.M., to our great joy and contrary to our most sanguine hopes, we succeeded in hauling the hulk off the sandbank, in which affair we had a grand specimen of the idleness, stupidity, and obstinacy of the Russian sailors.

" 12*th September.*

" Left the fatal sandbank at 6 A.M., having been delayed at it nearly forty-eight hours, and steamed on prosperously through the day, which was cold and showery. Stopped at 9 P.M.

" 13*th September.*

" Started early, and arrived at Simbirsk at 4 P.M. Very hot weather, with showers. Stopped at 7 P.M.

" 14*th September.*

" Started early. Weather sultry. Saw plenty of game—duck, wild geese, teal, widgeon, and cormorants—on numerous sandbanks. I also saw two brace of wild swans. On one side of the river the hills abound in partridge, and on the other, the low swampy bank covered with sally bushes, in wild boar. However, as the steamer would not stop for us, we had to forego the pleasures of the chase.

" 15th September.

" A beautiful day. Arrived at Samara about 9 A.M. Stopped some minutes to discharge passengers. Saw plenty of game, among them a brace of pelicans and some birds which, I think, were of the same species as those on the Bosphorus, called 'les âmes damnées.' Fired two or three shots with a rifle, but with no success. The heat, though great, was of that exhilarating kind, which showed us we were reaching the southern latitude. The banks seemed thinly populated. On an average we did not see more than two or three villages a day, and scarcely ever a cultivated field. Water-melons, apples, and pears abounded in the villages we happened to stop at.

" 16th September.

" Had service in the morning. Started at 2 P.M., having taken in a large quantity of wood. Had the captain to dinner. A lovely day.

" 17th September.

" Sailed early. Hot weather. The hills on the side of the river changed from being wooded to barren rocks, composed chiefly of chalk and sandstone.

" 18th September.

" Saratov. Left the boats there to discharge cargo, and went to a village farther down to take in wood, making thereby a tremendous row all night. Got rid of the fat Russian. Wood got his cabin to himself, and Tom and I and my servant slept in the other— not a very fair division.

                         " *20th September.*

" Very cold day. Stuck on another sandbank. Succeeded in getting steamer off, after a delay of nine hours. Passed Kamischkin at about 7 P.M.

                         " *21st September.*

" About noon arrived at Tzaritzin, a large town, where we stopped to take in sufficient wood to last us to Astrakhan. Got some grapes, the first I saw in Russia.

                         " *22d September.*

" Started at 6 A.M. Hot weather.

                         " *23d September.*

" Had service in the morning. Passed immense quantities of pelicans and several encampments of Calmuc Tartars, their huts consisting of branches of trees stuck in the ground. They live entirely on fish and their flocks.

                         " *24th September.*

" Stuck on a sandbank. Passed a man riding a camel. I never knew before that camels were in use so far north.

                         " *25th September.*

" Arrived at Astrakhan at 9 A.M. The part of the river under the town where we lay was crowded with shipping from the Caspian, some of them with two masts oddly rigged, carrying a sort of lateen and a mainsail. Their poops were raised to an extraordinary height, and very gaily painted—something like the pictures one sees of the ships used by the old Romans.

There being no rooms to be had in the town, we were obliged to stick to our quarters on board and go to a café for our food—it being contrary to law to have fire on board any ship lying there. Even candles and smoking were forbidden under pain of a thirty rouble fine. Thinking, however, that the two latter clauses of the law were too ridiculous, I broke them both.

"Took a drive through the town, but found nothing worth seeing. It lies very low and is straggling. The streets are wide and not paved but covered with deep sand, which of a windy day makes it very disagreeable. The inhabitants seem to be chiefly Calmuc Tartars and Persians. We found capital grapes and melons of every sort in great abundance.

" *26th September.*

"A severe frost in the night. Finding the route to Tiflis by the Caucasus out of the question, we took our passage in a Russian Government steamer bound for Baku. On board we were introduced by the captain to several German engineers and inspectors of the port, who were very civil to us and helped us a good deal. Among them a Mr. Holst spoke English very well. To brighten our present gloomy prospects, we were told that the yellow fever was raging at Baku, and generally carried off its victims in six hours. Returned on board the steamer at 11 P.M., where our quarters consisted of two beds in the mess-room, which my servant and I occupied, and a cabin for Tom and Wood.

" *27th September.*

"Sailed at 3 A.M. The deck was covered with Persians and Circassians. Our companions were Petersen the engineer, the first, second, and third lieutenants, and an artillery officer, who spoke French, returning to his quarters at Kisliat. The cabin was dirty and dark and always filled with a cloud of tobacco smoke. Our meals were as follows: Petersen supplied us with breakfast and tea; at dinner and supper we all messed together. These meals consisted of cabbages boiled in oil for soup, beef and potatoes fried in oil, and a water-melon. At 4 P.M. stopped for the night at a fort on the mouth of the Volga.

" 28th September.

"Started early. A heavy swell. The wind due north. Arrived at Tarki. Lay there three hours, but it being too rough for a boat to put out, the artillery officer who was to have landed there was obliged to come on, in hopes of being able to go on shore at Derbend. A gale blowing in our favour, a very heavy sea running, and the deck being badly caulked, every wave that washed over made a regular shower in the cabin. The wind being fair, we set all our sails hoping to reach a dangerous part of the sea before sunset. However, the wind falling, we were disappointed. By 9 P.M. the captain, although it was a moonlight night, deemed it prudent to turn back for six hours, so as not to reach the dangerous place before sunrise.

"At supper we were foolish enough to produce a bottle of brandy, on the strength of which the first lieutenant got drunk. The night being rather rough, the captain and second lieutenant, who was the officer of the watch, were deadly sick, and the third lieutenant in bed. The consequence was that when the sun rose on the morning of the 1st October they could not tell where they were. They had no chronometer on board, and always came to us to know whether it was time to take their observations. As our watches all went differently, they were sometimes sadly puzzled.

"Arrived at Baku at 9 A.M. Called on the Governor, who generously gave us and the artillery officer rooms in his house. Both he and his wife spoke French. The town, which seems very old, is built on the side of a hill. The roofs are all flat, and the most outstanding object is the minaret of a mosque. The bazaars are miserable and the population almost entirely Persian. Dined with the Governor, who entertained us very well after the Russian fashion, and produced some capital English porter after dinner.

" Hired horses and went with Petersen to see the Fire Worshippers, a distance of fifteen versts, the road lying through fields totally uncultivated. The Fire Worshippers are well worth seeing. Their fire consists of naphtha-gas issuing from the earth. Their court or mosque is strongly walled round, with four fires inside it and about forty outside.

" *3d October.*

" Dined at the Governor's, and instead of going to Tiflis decided to go by steamer to Enzeli and Reshd, and thence to Teheran. Our friend the Russian officer left us for his quarters. We parted with regret, for he was exceedingly good-natured, gentlemanlike, and in every way anxious to help us. Tom and Wood went to tea with the General, and I went on board with the luggage.

" *4th October.*

"Sailed at 5 A.M. Tom and Wood lost their cabin, the wife and child of a Russian officer occupying it.

" *5th October.*

"Anchored at Lenkoran at 8.30 A.M. It is beautifully situated, the mountains very high and thickly wooded. Although the last town on the Russian frontier, it has a much more European aspect than Baku. Lay to all day. Started at 8 P.M. Stormy night. Found ourselves in the morning blown far away from Enzeli and obliged to go on to Astrabad.

" *8th October.*

"Arrived at a small island with a Russian settlement. Spent the evening with a Russian officer, who spoke French very well, and treated us most hospitably.

" *9th October.*

"Engaged a Persian who spoke Russ to go with us first to Astrabad and then to Teheran. Left the island at 9 A.M., the Captain giving us a champagne breakfast. Arrived at a Russian factory at the village of Gazaw, and then bade adieu to the *Couba* steamer. Petersen, etc., lodged in a small room in the doctor's house, and were fed by the people in the factory. In the night the jackals kicked up a great row.

" *10th October.*

"Started for Astrabad about a quarter to 9 A.M., taking nothing with us but our guns and beds. The road lay through jungle and forest, said to abound in tigers, lions, wild boar, and every sort of game, of which we saw nothing except a few pheasants, hares, and jackals; and from the covert found it utterly impossible to get a shot. Trees of every sort, from the gigantic oak to the beautiful acacia, grew in the greatest luxuriance. The wild or rope-vine entwining itself among the trees, in places forming an immense net, made the covert perfectly impenetrable. We

passed wild pomegranates and figs in the greatest pro-
fusion, and halted about noon.   Not having brought
any provisions, we shared a pilau with Hadji Abbas.

"At 4 P.M. halted half an hour for their prayers,
and at 5.30 P.M. stopped for the night at a small village
about two hours distant from Astrabad—the Hadji
declaring that from the Turcomans the road was too
dangerous to travel in the night, and that a Persian
had been killed by them on the same road the night
before.

"Put up in the Khan, a sort of shed with a large
dusty room smelling very strong of bats. About a
quarter of an hour after our arrival, he brought us in
the leg of a chicken and a small plate of rice—rather
scanty fare for four hungry fellows. A very cold
night.

"*11th October.*

"Off a little after daybreak. When about half an
hour from Astrabad the Hadji pulled up and showed
us in the distance a line of horsemen, who, he said,
were Turcomans. So after having cursed them as
sons of dogs, and children of the Evil One, he set to
work most vigorously to tell his beads, thanks to
which precaution, I suppose, we rode unmolested about
9 A.M. into the village—a walled miserable sort of
place. The inhabitants, a bigoted tribe, received us
most inhospitably.

"On entering the gate, one of the dogs which had
followed us from the factory, being nearly as hungry
as ourselves, killed a chicken, which occasioned not a
little stir, and led to our being caged up for the best
part of the day in the middle of the only square, and
pelted diligently by the inhabitants with rotten eggs
and bad oranges—soft things, no doubt, but not the

less trying to the temper. We were put up for the night in the cock-loft of the worst caravanserai (it not being allowed for Christians to enter the better ones), and there got a sort of breakfast which we sadly wanted. Left Astrabad about 3 P.M. Halted 6 P.M., and put up at a dirty mud hut.

" 12th October.

"Started at 6 A.M. No breakfast. Stopped for an hour in the middle of the day, and arrived at the factory at 2 P.M. Bathed about 9 P.M., after which, being nearly dead with hunger, we attacked and consumed sixteen eggs.

" 13th October.

"Off by 8.30 A.M. for Teheran, with ten horses, five for riding and five for luggage, and stopped at noon for an hour. Halted about sundown and spent the night in an open shed.

" 14th October.

"Daybreak found us on the road. Arrived at Ashraf by 9 A.M. Stopped at a beautiful orange grove. Three dogs accompanied us from the factory: a water-dog I called "Diver," a large rough one named "Tiger," and our friend whom we styled "The Chicken," who much to my delight (for I was nearly starving) succeeded in catching another fowl for us, together with which, and some meat and eggs which we fortunately secured in the bazaar, made up the first good feed we had had since we landed in Persia. Fruit was rather scarce, we found, but succeeded in getting two melons and some wild grapes. Left Ashraf by 11.30 A.M., having found the inhabitants more hospitably inclined than those of Astrabad. Halted

for the night, and having no house slept under a tree
—very damp.

"15th October.

"Started by daybreak.   Arrived at Sari, where we
changed our horses, which were miserable, and the
Hadji left us.   We had every reason to be satisfied
with him.   He was strictly honest, active, and obliging.
He delivered us into the hands of a Persian who also
spoke Russ, and came with him from Nijni, a watch-
maker by trade.   Put up at the caravanserai, but were
cursed by swarms of mosquitoes.

"16th October.

"Although up and packed by 6 A.M. we could not
start our new muleteers and man—Gabbett by name—
until after 10 o'clock.   We found the inhabitants very
uncivil.   The town, though large, was filthy.   Halted
at 4 P.M.   Slept out.   Rain in the night—all our
things wet.

"17th October.

"Off by 7.30 A.M., and began the passage of the
mountains.   A wet evening.   The scenery was beautiful, but the road villanous, in some places absolutely
impassable to any but the native beasts, who were well
used to tumbling through such passes.   The path,
sometimes about a foot broad, and very slippery from
the rain and mud, ran along the side of the mountain
—the rock rising abruptly on one side, a precipice of
five or six hundred feet on the other : a very grand
picture to look at, but very far from pleasant to travel.
Twice my horse slipped one of his hind feet over the
side, and only that he recovered himself in a miracu-
lous manner, he and I were dashed into a thousand
pieces.

" Halted in a farm shed, which was deluged in the night by the incessant rain. Bought a sheep for four dollars, which was seized on by the muleteers, who were too bigoted to eat anything we touched, and we saw very little of it in consequence.

" 18th October.

" Delayed till 10 A.M. by floods of rain. Leaving the wooded mountains, our path lay sometimes over rocks covered with thorny underwood, sometimes by the bed of a river rendered almost unfordable by the rains. Halted at 4 P.M. at a shed large enough only to contain Wood and Tom, while I slept by the watch-fire. Having seized the sheep's head, we made a capital porridge of it, and had the first good breakfast since our arrival in Persia; for I, not drinking tea, got only one meal in the twenty-four hours, consisting of a greasy pilau when we halted.

" 19th October.

" Off at 8 A.M. Very windy. Halted at 4 P.M. at a large caravanserai filled with travellers, and got a place with difficulty. We were nearly smothered with smoke, and the donkeys, horses, dogs, and men kicked up a fearful row during the night.

" 20th October.

" Very cold and foggy morning. The country through which we went was a complete desert, abounding in conies, one of which we killed. Halted in another caravanserai.

" 21st October.

" I shot a grouse. Halted in a small village.

" *22d October.*

" Off by sunrise, and in about five hours rode into Teheran and put up in a large caravanserai, where we were most unmercifully mobbed—the natives trying to break in the doors, climbing up on the roof and throwing dirt and stones at us through the holes."

CHAPTER VI

Aspera multa
Pertulit, adversis rerum immersabilis undis.

HOR. *Ep.* I. ii. 21.

He braves untold calamities, borne down
By Fortune's waves, but never left to drown.

CONINGTON.

" 23*d October.*

"FOUND the British Minister had left before for Tabriz. Tom and Wood called on Messrs. Reid and Thompson, the attachés. They kindly gave us rooms in the Embassy, and told us we must be their guests at dinner during our stay. Met at dinner a Mr. Burgess and a Mr. Hector, a Bagdad merchant, who offered to take our heavy luggage with him to Bagdad. My servant William was attacked with fever.

" 25*th October.*

"William worse. Attacked myself, and very ill till 4th November. Hired two servants—Ali as cook, Charum as general servant.

" 8*th November.*

"William and I improving. To try the merits of our new cook, gave a dinner to Messrs. Reid, Thompson, etc., which turned out more respectable than I anticipated.

"*10th November.*

"The doctor considering William and me strong enough and change of air desirable, we left Teheran about 3 P.M. Rode into Kend about 7 P.M. and put up at the Shah's house. Very cold. William very weak and complaining.

"*12th November.*

"Had a long day. Put up in a small room at a dirty village.

"*13th November.*

"Off two hours before daybreak. Wet, cold, and windy. Arrived at Kazvin drenched, after ten hours' ride. Put up in a very fine caravanserai.

"*14th November.*

"Found the ground covered with snow, and, as William threatened to die if we went on, we were obliged to make up our minds to stop.

"*15th November.*

"Started with thermometer below 15° F. Piercing cold wind. Halted in the mountains at a very small village, where we had a room and fireplace of the tiniest.

"*16th November.*

"William again pleaded his inability to go on, declaring we should have to bury him on the road, so we decided to stop again. We, however, threatened to send him back with Charum—a sulky fellow, who spoke no English; upon which, having eaten a great bowl of rice-milk, he jumped up and promised to delay us no longer.

"*17th November.*

"Off early, thermometer below 11° F. Halted at a good village, where again I had a threatening of fever.

"*18th November.*

"Arrived at Sultania, where we found a Colonel Sheil and his bride, Dr. Dickson, and Thompson's brother. The dinner and champagne were both too good, for in the morning I found myself in a regular attack of fever. However, after an eight days' journey, of which I can remember only the misery (being hardly able on some days to sit on my horse), we rode into Tabriz on the 26th, where Mr. Stephens most hospitably received us as his guests. On our arrival we put William under the care of a doctor, a Maltese, who spoke English perfectly. He found that from the intense cold William had got frost-bitten in his toe, and was in danger of losing it, but that otherwise he was pretty well. We decided, however, on sending him home by Trebizond and Constantinople.

"*27th-29th November.*

"Spent in trying to recover from an attack of diarrhœa, in hopes of being able to accompany Tom and Wood on an expedition to Tiflis.

"*30th November.*

"Went out hunting with Malichus Mirza, a Persian prince, son to Fat-Ali Shah, but saw nothing. We found him a very nice fellow, quite civilised in all his ways and ideas, and a great sportsman. We dined with him—the dinner capital, served in European style. Champagne, etc., flowed like water.

> " *1st December.*

" Tom and Wood started for Tiflis, while I, finding myself much worse, was obliged to stay behind. Mr. Stephens's kindness to me I shall never forget, and also the doctor's. All the days passed alike, sometimes getting better and sometimes worse.

> " *15th December.*

" Breakfasted with the Prince, and in the evening got a violent attack of dysentery and liver complaint.

> " *25th December.*

" Between sickness, loneliness, etc., I spent the most miserable of Christmas Days.

> " *26th December.*

" Better. Wood and Tom returned. Got a relapse in the evening.

> " *1st January* 1850.

"Got up for the first time, but fell ill in the evening.

> " *2d January.*

" Better. Moved to Malichus Mirza's house for change of air, and remained there till the 15th."

[His life under the Prince's roof he long afterwards described to Mrs. Bruen, who has kindly communicated to me the following details. He was semi-unconscious when the move took place, and, on coming to, he found himself lodged in the harem, where he was nursed by an old black slave who became devoted to him, insomuch that when to a certain degree convalescent she would convey him for recreation into the ladies' apartments. There he met with every kindness, and was entertained by the stories of the former lives of the inmates, many of them most touching in their descriptions of how they were carried off from their homes.   One of them—a beautiful fair-haired Armenian—awoke his deepest compassion by her pathetic longing for her own relatives and home.]

"The evening of the 15th I started alone for Sheshuan, the Prince's country-seat.   Tom and Wood having arranged to come after post, the consul and the doctor accompanied me a part of the road.

"I certainly ought to remember the hospitality and kindness I received in every way and from everybody—more especially from the doctors who attended me in the kindest manner during my long illness.

"In all the books of travel on Persia, Tabriz is described as the most beautiful and healthy of cities. To me it appeared far different.   I never could find out anything interesting either in or near it.   The town itself is large and straggling, situated in a barren plain at the foot of a large red hill.   I believe all the hills round it are of the same colour, but as I never saw them unless clad with snow I cannot tell.

"On our arrival at Tabriz we bought three horses which belonged to Colonel Farrant.   Tom chose a thoroughbred Arab, Wood a fat hack, and I a pony—an obstinate little brute but a capital walker.   They all, however, broke down before we got far.   We also bought an octave of port wine, and having discharged Charum—a worthless lout—we engaged another man, Pierre, who spoke a little French, to come with us to Urumiah.

"After two hours and a half arrived at Sardarud. Quarters bad.   Windows without glass—not pleasant on a snowy night.

E

" 16th January.

" Off at a quarter to 7 A.M.   Dreadful day of snow and wind.   Arrived at Gogan—quarters very good. Started at a quarter to eight, and rode in seven hours into Sheshuan, where I found the Prince, who received me kindly.   Had a *tête-à-tête* dinner with him on rather doubtful dishes for one recovering from dysentery.

" 18th January.

" Spent a stupid day, having seen nothing of the Prince until dinner.   He said he had passed his day in the bath, previous to his starting for Teheran, to escape the myrmidons of the Governor, Hanza Mirza, who had followed him from Tabriz, and then infested his house, in the name of the Government, to recover sixteen thousand tomaums, which it was said he had misspent during his period of maladministration.   This, however, he always denied, and said the Government owed him thirty thousand tomaums.   Hearing all this was but poor satisfaction for me who had waited for him the whole day, as he had appointed me to be ready at an early hour to go out hunting with him.

" 19th January.

" About 1 P.M. Tom and Wood arrived.   In the afternoon the Prince brought us into his garden, a large enclosure of about forty-five acres, to hunt hares.   The chase was conducted in the following manner.   He collected all his servants, fifty or sixty, and a large number of greyhounds, which he posted in different parts of the garden.   The servants then began to beat. After some time a hare was found which might have afforded a good chase but for the number of dogs and men.   Another hare afterwards appeared, which the

Prince, in the most unsportsmanlike manner, shot. The hares were something rather larger than ours, and formed a capital dish at the champagne dinner he afterwards gave us in one of the apartments of the harem. At dinner he insisted on our tasting a specimen of all his Persian preserves, which were numerous, and some of them certainly most delicious.

" 20th January.

" Had prayers in the morning and sent our horses on by Achmed to Urumiah—the Prince having offered us a boat to cross the lake of that name, which was by way of being a voyage of only a few hours, and therefore a short cut. He also gave us leave to have a few days' shooting on the island which lay about half-way across the lake, and to which he said he had sent on tents and everything to make us comfortable.

" 21st January.

" Saw the Prince in the morning for a few minutes before our departure. He told us he had settled everything for us—which we found was either a great fib or that his servants cared very little about his orders. We had the greatest difficulty to get mules to convey our luggage—a distance of about eight miles— to the boat, and did not reach it till about 3 P.M., where, instead of the nice little craft he had promised, we found a heavy passage-boat, crowded with people, and heavily laden with corn. The wind being contrary, they could not sail until it changed, which they expected it to do at sunset, so we settled ourselves on a heap of corn on the deck and piled our boxes round us to try and shelter ourselves from the bitterly cold wind. Fortunately we had brought a large quantity of bread with us, as provision for the time we expected to be shooting on the island. On this and a bit of sausage we made a miserable dinner and turned in, lamenting our fate at being obliged to spend the night in such cold quarters.

" 22d January.

" The wind having changed in the night, we awoke to find ourselves anchored within a stone's throw of the island. The wind blowing a regular hurricane ahead, we told the men to land us, and to our great disgust were informed that it was utterly impossible to move until the wind changed or fell. Neither of which it did until 2 P.M. of the 23d, when it became quite calm, and, by dint of three hours' punting and pulling, we reached the island, thoroughly sick of the whole expedition.

" The boat in its shape resembled a square tub with two masts and sails, rather than anything else. We reckoned that, sailing her best, she progressed about two miles an hour—the possibility of tacking or sailing with a side-wind seeming never to have entered the sailors' heads. Having discussed our bread and ham, we lay down, determining to have a good day's shooting the following day on the island, which the Prince described as swarming with game of all sorts, deer, wild sheep, partridge, etc. A bitterly cold night.

" 24th January.

" On awaking we found nature wearing her most disheartening aspect. We were covered with snow about an inch thick, and it was still snowing hard, with every prospect of its continuing. However, having eaten our bad breakfast, we started in different directions in search of game, and of the Prince's tents, where, in case of our chase being unsuccessful, we hoped to obtain some fresh water and provisions. I saw several coveys of red-legged partridge and a few wild sheep, but failed in getting either, and at length returned on board, nearly frozen to death and more disgusted with the island than I had previously been with the boat. Tom and Wood returned soon after, equally unsuccessful and cold, but our hearts were cheered in about two hours by Pierre making his appearance with fresh water, a large bowl of thick cream, and a live sheep. Having got the provisions on board, we ordered them to sail for Urumiah, but were told it was impossible, the wind being unfavourable.

" *25th January.*

" Found ourselves in the same position—a bitterly cold wind blowing right ahead, accompanied with showers of sleet and snow. The sheep, however, afforded us a good breakfast and dinner, and with some arrack and port wine, which we had in our stores, we managed to keep the vital spark alive. Towards evening, the wind having fallen, they rowed out and anchored a few hundred yards from the shore, in case, they said, of a good wind in the night.

" *26th January.*

" The good wind having sprung up in the night lasted only long enough to blow us half-way across, where we found ourselves anchored, tossing about in the most disagreeable manner, with a cold head-wind and the lake washing over us, so as to spoil the remnant of our bread and render our position most uncomfortable. The water being nearly as salt as the Dead Sea, left us when it dried in a complete incrustation. No fish can live in it, but its banks swarm with wild fowl of all descriptions.   To better our condition, when we asked for breakfast Ali informed us that they had eaten the rest of the sheep, and that there was no meat left.   During the day, the wind having changed, we sailed for about an hour, but soon again it became unfavourable.

" 27th January.

"Our provisions and water failing, we set vigorously to work to stir up the crew, and after five or six hours' hard punting and pulling we reached the shore, where we found Achmed and our horses waiting for us.   Remounting, we set off to a neighbouring village to procure quarters for the night and mules to bring up our luggage.   Heartily congratulating ourselves on our escape from the boat, we all unanimously agreed that it was the most disagreeable voyage we had ever made—tossed about for six days on the deck of a small boat, and the weather intensely cold.   The warmest night that we spent on board, the thermometer was below 15° F.   Our stock of fresh water was frozen so hard that, in trying to break the ice to get a drink, the jar that contained it was broken and the ice remained as hard as ever.   I certainly think that— humanly speaking—we owed our lives to our Russian fur cloaks and four bottles of the Prince's best arrack, which we were fortunate enough to bring with us.

" 28th January.

" After breakfast we started for Urumiah, and found the road very difficult from the quantity of snow.   The plain was certainly the best cultivated and, except the province of Mazanderan, the most fertile part of Persia I had seen.   The town, enclosed like Tabriz and

Teheran with a deep fosse and mud walls, is surrounded by gardens.

"We arrived there about 3 P.M. and were most kindly received by the American missionaries, particularly by Dr. Wright, who assigned us two rooms, and made us his guests. At dinner we met his wife, a kind amiable person. The dinner was very good, but being a temperance community they drink nothing but water, which I thought rather a bad plan in such cold weather.

"29th January.

" At about 8.30 A.M. we were summoned to prayers, which—much to our edification—were conducted in Syriac. First a hymn was sung, then a chapter in the New Testament read, verse about, and then one of the native priests gave an extempore prayer. There were about fifteen or twenty Nestorians present. At breakfast we were introduced to Dr. Perkins, the head of the community, and another missionary who had ridden down from a neighbouring village. Afterwards they introduced us to two Nestorian bishops, one of whom had been to America with Dr. Perkins and spoke a little English. They then conducted us through their book-stores, printing office, etc., which is very cleverly managed. They have printed a great many copies of the New Testament and other books in Syriac, and are at present preparing to print the Old Testament. They also publish a weekly journal in the same language for the benefit of the natives. At dinner we met the rest of the community.

" 30th January.

" After breakfast Tom and Wood started to see a village where Dr. Perkins and Mr. Studdert resided with their families.   In the evening two trays of sweet-meats arrived as a present from the Prince-Governor.

> "*31st January.*

"Spent the morning receiving visits from the principal men of the city.

> "*1st February.*

"Breakfasted with Mr. Stocking—a grand spread. Met all the community.   Pierre not being able to accompany us farther we engaged a German servant— John by name—very highly recommended by Dr. Wright.   His former history was certainly extraordinary, and his adventures rather different from what one would suppose should befall a man bearing so high a character for honesty as he did.   However, we were fully repaid by confiding in Dr. Wright's recommendation.

"Started at half past 2 P.M.—Messrs. Wright, Stocking, etc., accompanying us part of the way. They certainly form a community of as kind people as I ever met.   We rode four hours into Ardishei, and put up at Mar Gabriel's house.   He received us very hospitably, but we were immensely bothered by the curiosity of the natives.   The road was very muddy from the thawing snow and the rich quality of the soil.

> "*2d February.*

"Snowing hard, and the country almost impassable. Started at twelve o'clock.   The small irrigation canals being swollen to a great height, two of our mules fell into the stream, and we found to our dismay that the mule that carried our store-box or larder was one of them.   We were particularly disgusted at its occurring then, as one box was full of dainties provided for our journey by Mrs. Wright's kind forethought—such as chicken, mince-pies, and European bread and butter. The snow-drifts we encountered were tremendous— neither horses nor mules would face them.   As soon as they perceived them they turned their backs on them, we lying down on their backs to escape the cutting wind.   Arrived at a quarter past three o'clock at Kermi and found very fair quarters.

" 3d February.

"Off at a quarter past ten.   Crossed a large river by a bridge.   The road was good, lying along the side of the lake.   Fine morning.   Arrived at Garkan —a village built on a promontory stretching into the lake.   Quarters pretty fair but bitterly cold.

" 4th February.

"Off at 9 A.M.   The road at first lay along the side of the lake until 1 P.M., when it turned west, crossing a small chain of hills.   As long as we kept on the lee of the latter we were very comfortable, but as soon as ever we reached the top and began to descend the weather side, we were exposed to a fearfully cold west wind which nearly shaved the skin off our faces.   After descending the hills and going through a miserable hour's ride in the plains of Sulduz, we reached a small Kourdish village, where we were obliged to stop on account of the river being impassable from the ice.   At first the inhabitants were inclined to be uncivil, but soon finding that we intended to pay for what we got, they lodged and treated us well enough.   The men are a fine independent-looking set, the women in general well-looking—some very pretty. The plain is almost entirely sown with wheat. I do not remember seeing a single garden. The villages are surrounded by large mounds of ashes instead of manure, as the inhabitants use the dung of their cattle for firing.

" 5th February.

"Off at a quarter to 10 A.M. The road for two hours lay over the plain leading us through thick jungles of bulrushes. We kept a sharp lookout for game, but saw none. Having at length found a place to ford the river, we joined the regular road and arrived at Vasjé Bulak by 7 P.M. The cold was intense. There being no room in the good caravanserai, we were obliged to put up with a very small one, so we had to go without our dinner—both which circumstances went far to sour my temper."

CHAPTER VII

And thus they made entry into Kourdistan. . . . And as they
were bivouacking there the snow came down heavily, insomuch that
it shrouded their accoutrements and the men as they lay ; and it be-
numbed the beasts of burden ; and great was their reluctance to rise.

" 6th February.

" TURNING out with fearful appetites we made a
clean sweep of the rest of our ham and fifteen eggs,
and then sent our letters of recommendation to the
Governor, who forthwith despatched his ferash to
move us and baggage to his house. We were received by him in his judgment-hall, a considerable-
sized room. We found him and a lot of Kourds
sitting round a large charcoal pan. His Highness
was seated in an armchair, while all his followers
squatted on their hunkers. When we entered he
immediately stood up, and motioned us to sit in arm-
chairs that were placed at his side. We were then
served with *kalcouns* and tea. The judgment ceremony lasted three hours, during which time, as out of
respect to our host we were obliged to hold our
tongues, we had ample leisure to study his face and
costume and those of his companions.

" They were all fine-looking men, but he was by far the handsomest man I ever saw. Their splendid costumes, in my eyes handsomer than either Turks', Arabs', or Persians', showed off their fine manly countenances to great advantage—immense turbans of silk, striped white and brown silk kaftans, confined at the waist by a strap fastened by a richly-embossed silver clasp, and over all a cloak, lined, according to their rank, with sheepskin or fine fur, and all of course armed to the teeth.

" After the important business of the judgment-hall was over, our host turned and salaamed to us with great courtesy, insisting on our remaining his guests during our stay in the town—that is, until we could find mules and decide on which route to take. He also volunteered to do everything in his power to help us on the road.

" We found it very difficult to ascertain anything about the routes, each man we asked giving a different report. One said he had attempted the short route by Leggan, but had been obliged to turn back. A second said that even the long route by Suleimania was impassable. A third said that if we would wait five days for his mules he would take us the short way. The Governor strongly recommended us not to attempt it; but, having made up our minds to face every difficulty, we determined to accept our third friend's offer.

" After sunset, dinner was brought in on three trays, which were placed on the floor, one before our host, a second before Tom and Wood, and a third before me. We accordingly set to work, Tom and Wood slobbering away with their hands. I had fortunately a camp-knife and fork in my pocket and got on passably, first attacking a very rich-looking mess; but having swallowed one mouthful was obliged to desist, feeling very much the worse. The dish consisted of rotten cabbage, stewed in vinegar and oil, flavoured with a very nasty sort of spice. I next attacked a greasy pilau. Knowing that it always contained something in the shape of meat inside, I set to work to burrow, and at length succeeded in hauling out the back of a lamb, which I began to eat—but, the Governor having finished, etiquette obliged me to come to also. In vain I waited for another tray to make its appearance. The washing of hands followed, and I had to consider myself as having dined.

"In the evening we endeavoured to amuse the Governor by showing him different things. He was much surprised at the daguerreotype of Hoddy [his sister Harriet]. He expressed great admiration and said, How happy would a man be with such a wife! He left us about 8 P.M.

" 7th February.

"Unsuccessful in our search for other mules. About 3 P.M. the Khan made his appearance and showed us his chain armour, which was certainly very handsome. Greasy dinner followed by a stupid evening.

" 8th February.

"In the morning word was brought that the Khan was sick and wished one of us to see him, so Wood went and found him labouring under an attack of greasy dinner. He gave him some medicine which, in the evening, on being sent for again, he found his Highness would not take, because it smelt nasty. Wood, however, managed to coax it down his throat.

His illness gave us a long day's peace, in saving us from his visit, which, although good-naturedly intended, was an atrocious bore.

" 9th February.

" Khan better.   Started at 1 P.M. on a duck-shooting expedition along the banks of a good-sized stream which runs close to the town.   After some trouble and a good freezing we succeeded in killing a brace.   On our return we found the Khan quite recovered. Wood's revolving pistol was exhibited for the fourth time at his usual visit, and at 9 P.M. the Khan left us, heartily sick of his company.

" 10th February.

" Wet day.   Had prayers in the morning.

" 11th February.

" Got ready to start to see some antiquities, but, the day coming down wet, we were obliged to put it off till some more auspicious time.

" 12th February.

" The day being as fine as we could expect, we set off, and after a canter of about twelve miles arrived at the place.   It was a large square tomb, sculptured out of the solid rock, something like the tombs of Beni Hassan on the Nile.   Coming home we went along the riverside in hopes of getting some game, but were unsuccessful.   In the evening Tom got an attack of fever lasting to the 16th.   The man's mules having come in, he was in a hurry to be off, but Tom not being sufficiently strong we made him wait in his turn.

" 17th February.

" Had prayers in the morning. Tom being much better, and the day much warmer, we took a ride to some curious soda-water springs about three miles from the town. The water bubbles out of the solid rock, and is very good to drink, but rather flat.

" 18th February.

" Sent for the muleteer to load, Tom being quite recovered, but he refused to go, saying he had to shoe his mules—a lie, of course. The truth was, he wanted to stay for another large caravan which was to start the next day.

" 19th February.

" Got off at about 10.30 A.M. The first part of the ride was pleasant enough, but when we began to ascend and get into the snow it became bitterly cold, and our difficulties began in earnest. The large caravan, which consisted of seventy horses laden with iron, having gone before to beat down the snow, made the first part of the ascent tolerably easy—at least when compared to what followed. But when we got near the top, our mules being more lightly loaded, we had passed the caravan, and were obliged to chalk out the road for ourselves ; there was not a track to be seen—nothing but a sheet of smooth shining snow gradually ascending till it was lost in the clouds, which, to better our condition, were gathering fast on the mountain - top we had to pass over. Our horses were wading up to the saddle-girths, and sometimes falling into a ravine which had been filled up by a snow-drift, when nothing was visible but our own heads and sometimes the horse's nose and tail. It certainly was the most disheartening business I ever went through.   However, as there could be no going back, we had to put the best face on it we could.   At last we reached the top of the hill, where the snow nearly blinded us.

" Then began the descent, which was much quicker work than the ascent—sometimes rather faster than we wished.   Our horses being too wise to attempt to walk down, tucked their legs under them and slid down at a tremendous rate, the mules generally rolling down the best way they could.   Having at last reached the bottom, after an hour's easy riding we came to a small village, where we got a room and lit a fire, but the smoke soon obliged us to seek other means of keeping ourselves warm.   Our cook swore he was so cold he could not prepare anything, which, I believe, as he was very lazy, was only an excuse— although the thermometer was below 11° F.

" 20th February.

" Off about 9 A.M.   Sleeting hard.   Got wet through. Cleared up at noon, and the wind rising froze our clothes on us, making them as hard as sheet-iron. At 3 P.M. got into snow again and lost our way. The mules soon got thoroughly done up with wading in it, and we were obliged to come to ; so scooping a hole in the snow we ensconced ourselves among our horses and boxes.   Luckily, having a cooked chicken and some bread with us, we did not starve, although it was a small pittance for ourselves and three servants.   Getting two bottles of port and one of arrack, we drank deep healths to our friends at home, wishing that they might never find themselves in such a plight.   We then wrapped ourselves in our wolfskins and chose our respective places.   I got under my horse as a sort of shelter from an approaching snowstorm. However, as he was rather uneasy in the night and trod on me several times, it would have been better to have borne the brunt of the weather. My clothes also thawing, I had to undergo a trial of the water cure.

" 21st February.

" Wood's horse, getting loose in the morning, began fighting with my horse, and soon routed me out. Not caring to sleep again, I woke the others, and we made preparations for getting under way. Off a little after 9 A.M., floundering through the snow. Sometimes we got tremendous falls into ravines which had been frozen over and the hollows filled with snow-drifts. In such cases we had to dismount and pull the wretched animal out by the tail and neck, and then taking all our carpets and cloaks lay them across to form a sort of bridge for the mules.

" After seven hours of this work, during which we accomplished a distance of some four miles from the place where we slept, we arrived at the side of the mountain, and were lucky enough to find a large cave with plenty of firewood in it. We accordingly got in, picketing our horses at the mouth, and, lighting a large fire inside, the cave became so full of smoke as to drive us nearly mad.

" 22d February.

" The muleteers saying they must stop at least a day to rest their mules, Tom and I went out with our guns to try and get something for dinner, and were lucky enough to get a brace and a half of snipe. We were obliged to give the greater part of our stock of bread to the horses, for which we had no provender. We also sent one of the muleteers to a village about three hours off to engage twelve guides, as next day we had to cross a worse part than we had encountered, and also to bring some food for ourselves and horses.   He returned about sunset, fetching a pair of fowls, some bread, and a bag of rice for the beasts, there being no barley.   He said that the guides would meet us at the beginning of the pass next day.

"After dinner we were surprised by the arrival of a large caravan of about a hundred and twenty horses.   They described the pass as almost impracticable—sixty horses were obliged to leave their loads and make the best of their way forward without them. Shortly after two men were carried in insensible, and Wood was sent for to try and bring them to.   With one he succeeded, but the other was too far gone.

"*23d February.*

"Having fortified ourselves with a tolerable breakfast and a dram of brandy, we set out for the pass. About an hour from the cave we came to the spot where the muleteers had been obliged to leave their loads the night before.   Sixty loads all stood about in the snow, some of them half a mile off the right track.   There were large dogs left to guard them. Poor animals! they must have had a cold night of it. After a good deal of labour, tumbling, and rolling, we at length got into Riaz.   The road was much less difficult than I had expected.   It was bitterly cold— the thermometer never ranging above 15° F

"*24th February*

"When we wanted to start we found the courtyard gate locked.   On telling them to open it, they refused until we should pay them a considerable sum. We declined, and drawing our pistols, told the landlord that if he did not open it at once, we would blow his brains out. He saw we were in earnest, and that our pistols were not likely to miss fire. He began to growl, and said he would take half. A pistol was immediately presented at his head, which decided the matter, and the door was opened without more ado."

[Mrs. Bruen, from a conversation held years after with Arthur, adds : " The armed villagers still threatening to close the one outlet, he saw the danger, and suddenly forcing his horse into the open gateway, guarded it with his rifle, until every member of the party had safely left the yard, and then he quietly rejoined them."]

"We had not gone far when John found that they had stolen his coat. We forthwith returned and made them give it up. They had stolen Tom's rifle the evening before, but he recovered it by offering a reward.

" Had an attack of rheumatism in my chest. The scenery was wild and beautiful. Arrived about 3 P.M. at a small village. Beastly quarters — their cows being stabled with us.

" 25th February.

"Off by 9 A.M. Having got out of the snow, we went on comfortably enough. The road was very steep. Arrived at Roandoze at half-past one, and had good quarters.

" 26th February.

"Stopped to rest the mules.

"*27th and 28th February.*

"Went by a fearfully bad road, ending in worse quarters; rain pouring the whole time.

"*1st March.*

"Got into the plain.   Saw lots of gazelles and wild goats.   We were entertained by the sheikh of the village."

[It must have been about this stage of the journey that the party lighted on the track of the two Englishmen who had some years before ventured on the same route—Messrs. Conolly and Studdert—the first Europeans, they were told, who had come that way. Arthur mentions the incident in his book—published long afterwards—*The Cruise of the Eva*, from which I transcribe it, as here falling into its proper place.

" In Kourdistan I found poor Conolly's prayer-book, and was shown by an interesting Kourd the very tree to which he and poor Studdert were tied and foully murdered, the Kourd said, because they would not become Mussulmans. We had no intention of being turncoats either, but I expect we owed our whole skins to our poverty, possessing little more than our horses, rifles, and a change of clothes, one shirt off and another shirt on.   I don't mean to say that these were all we started with, but certainly they were all we had left, and the Kourds may have reasoned that it was hardly worth risking their precious lives in exchange for ours, the value of our possessions included.   They all dread the shining of a copper cap.   They saw the glare of our caps once, but to this day I do not know how we escaped."]

" 2d March.

"Left at 4 A.M. in hopes of being able to get over the river Zab and reach Mosul by night. Arrived at the river by sunrise. The mules were unloaded and swam across. We and our luggage were ferried over on a small raft, about the size of an ordinary dinner-table. The river was about a quarter of a mile in width, and the current tolerably strong. The raft had to make seven voyages, so that we were delayed till about 3 P.M., when, it beginning to rain, we were obliged to make for the nearest village, where we got a miserable hole as quarters. It being too late to cook anything, we bought some boiled fowl from the natives, on which we made a very scanty dinner.

" 3d March.

"Off at 10 A.M. Stopped at a village two miles from Mosul, and having killed a sheep, got a double allowance for dinner.

" 4th March.

"Wood and John went on in the morning to get a house, we following with the luggage. Arrived at about 2 P.M. We found that a house had been secured, but that we were invited to feed with Mr. Rassam. We were surprised to find so large an assemblage of English—Mr. and Mrs. Roland, Dr. Sandwith, Mr. Layard, and others.

" 5th March.

"Went out coursing and killed two hares. The ground about Coungak was splendid for riding. Spent the next two days buried in subterranean passages, seeing slabs, bas - reliefs, inscriptions, etc., which have been so well described that I need not waste my time in attempting what I could not do.

"*8th March.*

"Rode a distance of about eighteen miles to Nineveh, where I found Mr. Layard and Dr. Sandwith.   Dined and slept there.

"*9th March.*

"Went out coursing with Tom.   Two fair runs and two deaths.   Arrived at Mosul at sunset.

"*10th March.*

"Service in the morning.

"*11th March.*

"Dined with Mr. Layard. Met Mr. and Mrs. Roland.   Discovered Mrs. Roland to be a sort of connexion.

"*14th March.*

"Started at about 2 P.M. on a raft made of goatskins.   Our beds were raised on rude platforms, roofed with felt, more like beaver-huts than anything else.   Came to, an hour before sunset.

"*15th March.*

"Crossed the rapids over the bridge of Nimrod. Tom shot a brace of partridge, and I had one shot at a pig.

"*21st March.*

"Blew so hard from the S.E. that our raft nearly went to pieces.   We had to stop and land everything. Such a quantity of sand was driven up by the wind that everything was filled.   We were obliged to get under lee of the hill to eat such food as was not completely spoiled.   Having discovered during the day some spoor of lions and other animals, Tom and I went about a quarter of a mile to a place where the marks showed they came to drink, determining to wait there all night, but it coming on to thunder and rain, our powder was drenched, so we retired rather disgusted.

" *22d March.*

" The wind having ceased, we mended the raft as best we could, and got away.   About an hour after, the wind having sprung up again, we came alongside of an island covered with brushwood.   Tom having gone on shore, came back with word that he had seen seven pigs.   Accordingly we landed with guns and rifles.   I got a shot at a pig about fifty yards off, but missed him in a disgraceful manner. He, however, did not seem to pass the insult over unresented, but turned round and came at me.   I immediately seized my gun, which was loaded with swan drops, and gave him the benefit of them full in his face.   He turned tail and made off before I could reload.

"We set sail in the evening, and met the East India Company's steamer *Nitocris* coming up with Captain Jones, who was surveying the country.

"*23d March.*

" Arrived at Bagdad.   Kindly received by Captain Kemble, the acting Resident.   He advised us if we wanted to see Babylon to start at once that evening, and ride all night in order to catch a party consisting of his brother, Commodore Porter, commanding in the Persian Gulf, and Signor Casellani, the dragoman or secretary, who had started the day before.   We took his advice, and set off after dinner.   Rode till

2 A.M., when we arrived at a caravanserai, where we took a few hours' sleep, and then started once more.

"Such a stench as there was in the caravanserai I never smelt! For we unfortunately came in with a large caravan carrying Persian dead bodies to be buried in the holy city of Kerbola, as they believe that, if they do not die there, they must make their way to it after death. They have thus adopted the fashion of carrying corpses on mules to the aforesaid city by way of avoiding the trouble of a *post-mortem* navigation, to the great annoyance of travellers possessing olfactory nerves.

"We proceeded at 9 A.M., reached Hilla, and put up at a Jew's house, who gave us very good quarters.

"*26th March.*

"Having hired fresh horses, we started for Bes-fel Nimrod — by interpretation the 'Tower of Babel.' Reached it after two hours' cantering. It is a curious-looking heap of old burnt bricks, part of the fabric still standing. We got nearly to the top of it, and I thought we were much nearer heaven on the summit of the Pyramids. Having picked up some bricks, we cantered back after dinner. Then Tom and I rode all night, and got into the city of the Caliphs at 8 A.M. of the 27th."

CHAPTER VIII

Praesentiorem et conspicimus Deum
Per invias rupes, fera per juga,
   Clivosque præruptos. . . .—GRAY.

Our God to us yet nearer is
On trackless rocks, 'mid mountains wild,
   On brink of yawning precipice.

HERE occurs a break in the diary until

" 23d April.

" Leaving Bagdad we joined a party of Russians, and got on our way. Found it dreadfully hot. About two hours after dark we reached a middling-sized town.

"25th April.

"Off at 9 A.M. By 3 P.M. the thermometer marked 120° F. in the tents, and when bathing the water was above blood-heat.

" 26th April.

"Started with party of Russians about 2 A.M. to a steep mountain pass of about four hours. The road was dreadful, the scenery picturesque. Arrived at the caravanserai at 9 A.M. (the others of the party came in about 11 A.M.), and rested the remainder of the day.

" 27th April.

"Off at 5 A.M. Crossed another pass, not so bad as the former. Breakfasted at a small village, and halted about two hours ; then started for Kazeroum at sunset.

" 28th April.

" The Russian colonel and Wood started early for the ruins of Shaipoor, while Tom and I, wishing to spare ourselves and our horses, proceeded quietly to Kazeroum.

" 29th April.

" Left Kazeroum about 2 P.M., and got into a very pretty station at the source of a river, in time to pitch our tent before dark.   Rode over to an Arab encampment, where I bought a nice little mare for fourteen tomaums.   Crossed what is called the ' Old Woman's Pass '—reckoned one of the most dangerous in Persia. It is of an immense height.   From one of the highest ridges the Bay of Bushire can be seen, although three days' journey distant.   The road was dreadful in the ascent—the side of the mountain almost perpendicular, and the horses having no footing, except small holes cut in the slippery and perfectly glazed slabs of rock. My horse, ' Jack,' carried me over with only two falls—more than any of the horses which were led, with nothing on their backs, could boast of."

[It was doubtless about this stage of the journey that he had the terrible experience recorded fourteen years afterwards in *The Cruise of the Eva*, from which I transcribe the following account of it :—

" I remember once going through the very agonies of death. . . . It was in Persia, in the year 1850, on the march from Bushire to Shiraz, where the track— for I cannot call it a road—leads over one of the grandest mountain passes it has ever been my lot to cross.   I must here correct myself, for I am wrong in calling it a mountain pass; the country lies in plateaux, rising, as you go inland, like the Ghauts in the Deccan. When you start from Bushire, you march along an extensive level plain, towards what appears to be a blue line of hills on the horizon; as the distance decreases, the softness of the outline disappears, and the blue line assumes its true shape.   When you get under it, a perpendicular wall of almost polished rock towers over your head, bounding the lower plain on which you are, as far as the eye can reach, with apparently an insurmountable barrier; the path leads on along the base, till a dark cleft or fissure in the wall of stone, too narrow to be dignified with the name of valley, opens to your view.   Into this the path leads, and here this wonderful ascent commenced.

" Hewn, or worn out of the solid rock, is a narrow causeway barely wide enough for a laden mule, with holes worn into regular steps, like a cow-track in soft ground, by the feet of thousands of beasts of burden that have trodden it from ages past, and leads you, at no very gentle gradient, up the side of this ravine.   A sheer perpendicular wall of rock above, high enough almost to shut out the sight of day; a sheer perpendicular precipice of rock below, losing itself in the shades of a dark and terrible abyss, and no parapet to save you from the effects of a single false step.

"Although it is fourteen years ago, I remember it now as vividly as if it was but yesterday.   I was just rallying after a fourteen months' bout of jungle and intermittent fever—those who have suffered similarly will understand better than I can describe the state of one's nerves after such training.   I was as weak as a cat; my strength—artificial, derived from the daily dose of sixteen grains of quinine. With a splitting head, I was glad to be let go through the daily march in the middle of the caravan, with my horse's head tied to one of the baggage mules. Luckily for myself, I had heard before of this horrid ravine, and determined to take the management of my own beast to myself. We were getting tolerably high up, when a halt occurred, occasioned by one of our number losing his head, as it is called—by-the-bye he had never had either fever or quinine to upset his nerves! However, he declared his inability to proceed : his firm conviction was that he should throw himself over the brink. I have heard of giddy nervousness assuming this form, the sufferer being seized with an irresistible longing to rush upon the very fate he quails at. He was taken off his horse, and had to be supported during the remainder of the ascent by a muleteer on each side. The mule in front of me was laden with two deal boxes, which contained our canteen effects, and although not heavy, were rather a clumsy load, as the boxes were three or four inches wider than was customary.

"I do not quite know how it happened, but going round a projecting angle of the hill, the poor animal stumbled and struck the corner of the box against the rock ; the shock staggered him, and I fancy I can see the unfortunate beast now, and hear his cry of agony as he fell over the brink, the echo of the crash at the bottom being the last we ever heard of him or his load! It lasted but a minute, but in a second you may live an age ; it would have been a relief to screech were it not for very shame; but the rear part of the caravan pressed on behind, and on I went, filling up the gap in our ranks, to make way for those that followed."]

" Our road lay for the next hour or two through a beautiful valley covered with fine oaks. Had a long chase after a wild goat and at length caught him—he having got his horns jammed between two rocks. He was of immense size and must have been the patriarch of the flock.

"After crossing the valley, we began to ascend once more. When we had got about half-way up the second ascent, we reached a caravanserai, where we stopped a few hours to breakfast and rest the mules and horses. Started again at 3 P.M. Completed the ascent and descent, and, riding across a level plain, arrived at the station by 9 P.M., when, taking a hasty dinner, we turned into the only lodging we could get.

"May Day.

" Off early. Met numbers of nomad tribes changing their winter quarters. Encamped by the side of a river. Arrived at Shiraz at twelve noon. Were received by Hadji Gowam the acting Governor, who let us have a fine house and a beautiful garden. He also placed a company of soldiers at our disposal. The news of the surrender of Meshed had just reached the town, to testify their joy at which the bazaars were illuminated and numerous fêtes came off.

" 3d May.

" Spent in receiving visits—a species of entertainment I cordially detest, especially when the visitors are Persians. Their compliments and never-ending lies are enough to disgust any man who claims common sense.

" 4th May.

" Rode out in the morning to see the Palaces, Gardens, and Tombs of Sadi and Hafiz. We reached

Shiraz at the best time to see it, when all its roses—about which Persians rave—were in full blow. The gardens certainly were beautiful—at least, compared with the surrounding desert.

" 5th May.

" Passed in making purchases of the Shiraz productions, such as enamelled boxes, etc.

" 6th May.

" Intended to have started, but our new tent being still unfinished, and the Russian colonel not having concluded his arrangements till the next day, we packed up our purchases and sent them to Bushire.

" 7th May.

" Rode five hours to a good-sized village, and put up at the caravanserai. I had often heard of the plague of locusts, but never believed they could do such mischief till now, when I saw the ground absolutely black with them. The whole country for miles had been sown with corn, not a single blade of which was left; even the straw was eaten level with the ground. The sheikh of the district predicted a famine, as that was the part of the country on which Shiraz chiefly depended for its supply of corn.

" The Russians arriving late, breakfast and dinner were turned into one. Had a touch of fever.

" 8th May.

" Off early. The road led through a marsh. Saw lots of game, and killed some teal in spite of a terrible headache. Arrived at Takht-el-Yamsheed, or Persepolis, by noon. Set about exploring the ruins, which were certainly the best worth seeing after Baalbec that I had ever come across.

" 10*th May*.

" Started at sunrise—some of the party taking a circuit to see the tomb of Darius, while Tom and I proceeded quietly on our march for four hours.   Jack's back being sore, rode the mare.

" 11*th May*.

" Off before sunrise.   Bad mountain pass.   Found the mare safer than I expected.

" 12*th May*.

" The whole party—myself excepted—started to see where Solomon's mother was buried.   As for myself, having an attack of fever, I was very glad to get a day of rest.

" 13*th May*.

" Eleven hours' march brought us to a village near Persepolis.

" 14*th May*.

" Parted with the Russians.   Saw Darius's tomb on the march.   After eight hours reached the station, and pitched our tents in the gardens which surrounded it.

" 15*th May*.

" Off before sunrise.   Rode four hours through a fine mountain pass to a small village in the heart of the mountain, where, there being no room to pitch our tents, we got into the surrounding gardens.

" 16*th May*.

" Sunrise found us on the road.   Joined by a troop of cavalry, going to meet the Prince-Governor of Shiraz, who was coming from Ispahan to assume the reins of office.   The captain of this respectable troop, a very civil fellow, showed us some hawking. The road was very bad. After three and a half hours' ride, reached the plain where we encamped. Rain all day and night, making everything wet.

" 17th May.

" Off early. Found all the villages deserted. The inhabitants, having heard of the Prince's approach with his troops, had fled into the mountains to avoid being plundered. Encountered a tremendous hail-storm. On arriving at the station we found there the son of Klaku, one of the Bactrian chiefs, also going to meet the Prince. In the evening he came down to our tents by way of returning Tom's visit; but, I believe, only to get some wine, for which, unlike a Mussulman, he had a great predilection. I feigned sleep to prevent being bothered, and, in feigning it, it came over me, so that I did not awake until every one had turned in, thus missing my dinner, of which I was very far from glad, as I had had only a crust of bread for breakfast.

" 18th May.

" Started before sunrise—the Khan starting at the same time. Tom and Wood went on with him, while I remained behind with the caravan. It rained a good deal during the day. Arrived at the station an hour before sunset—Tom and Wood nowhere to be found. Sent the muleteer to look for them, halted the caravan, and pitched the tents. About an hour after a man rode in, bringing a note from Wood, saying that the Khan had invited them to dine and spend the evening with him, and they wished me to proceed there with the caravan immediately—a distance of about two hours. I wrote back that the tents were pitched and dinner ready, and that if they intended to dine or sleep in their own camp that evening, they had better return as soon as possible, as I did not mean to strike the camp that night. In the course of the evening they returned. The Khan arrived about 7 P.M. on the 20th.

" 20th May.

"As we passed the Khan's camp, one of his servants came out and seized a dog I had bought the day before from one of his own men. He insisted that the dog was his, and I of course refused to give him up, as I had bought him. We both got furious, and I ended the matter by applying to the Khan, who declared that the dog was his, and that the man who sold him had no right to do so. He insisted, however, on my taking him as a present, at the same time returning the money I had paid for him.

"Had two runs after gazelles. Rode nine hours into the Ezd Khouran—an extraordinary village built on the bank of a deep river.

" 21st May.

"Rode four hours into a fine caravanserai.

" 22d May.

"A dreadfully hot ride of six hours, into Koomisheh—a good-sized town, but bad quarters. Hadji Gowam's son, with all his train, overtook us on the road, on his way to meet the Prince.

" 23d May.

"Off before sunrise, and after four hours' ride arrived at a large caravanserai, where we found the Prince-Governor, Ferouz Mirza, encamped. He had just arrived from Ispahan. He travelled in a small *calèche*, of which an English farmer would be ashamed, surrounded by a lot of retainers on horseback, who made dust enough to smother an ordinary man ; but, as 'pride feels no pain,' His Highness endured it. Stopped there till after dinner, then started and arrived at Ispahan by 7 A.M. of the 24th."

CHAPTER IX

παρεμπίπτει γάρ τις ὀρεινὴ τραχεῖα καὶ ἀπότομος μεταξὺ τῶν Σουσίων
καὶ τῆς Περσίδος, στενὰ ἔχουσα δυσπάροδα καὶ ἀνθρώπους λῃστάς.

STRABO, c. 728.

For it is a mountain country, rugged and precipitous, that lies between the Susii and Persia, abounding in passes difficult to thread and in men who are robbers.

" 24th May.

" THE first sight of Ispahan was extremely beautiful. Met by Joseph, whom we had sent on, after a letter from the agent, to get us a house in Halfa. · Got fair enough accommodation. The agent and his son were Armenians, who had been educated in Bombay.

" 26th May.

" Had a severe attack of fever, which lasted on and off till the 12th of June.

" A few days after getting better, went out on a shooting expedition for change of air. Killed nothing, and being obliged to sleep out, brought on another attack of fever, till a few days before we started.

" 24th June.

" Having found mules, and getting ready our large tent, we started, bringing our friend Glen with us as our guest. I never left any place with such delight as Ispahan. Except going out once coursing, and once to see a celebrated 'shaking tower' and a mosque, I spent my time in bed with fever, or lolling about the house too ill to do anything.   Left at sunset and rode five hours into Kejjufabad.   Put up at a very fine house—splendid gardens all round the town.

" 26th June.

"Started two hours before sunrise.   Arrived. at Teheran by 9 A.M.   Could get no house, so put up under a tree in the town.

" 27th June.

"Off three hours before daylight.   Pitched tent near Askaran.   Very hot.

" 28th June.

"Off early.   Saw lots of small buzzards, and killed about six brace.   Stopped at a small village for breakfast, and during the heat of the day.   Started again at 4 P.M.   Arrived at Dumbeneh by 9 P.M.   Cold.   I slept on the roof, the house being too thickly inhabited by vermin.

" 29th June.

"Got into Chonsar by 1 P.M.   A very pretty town surrounded by gardens.   Put up in a caravanserai.

" 30th June.

"Started at sunrise.   Rode two hours through the gardens, and four more into Gookayou.   Put up in a fine house.

" 1st July.

"Started in the middle of the night.   Rode six hours into a good-sized town, and six hours farther into a small village—a pretty place for encamping. Slight attack of fever.

" 2d *July.*

" Long and hot ride through a village, where we put up in a house of refuge for criminals. Left very ill.

" 3d *July.*

" Four hours' ride into Burudshird, where we got a very nice house in a garden outside the town. Immediately on arriving had a bad attack of fever, which lasted several days. Being tired of getting fevers, I proposed going home by Tabriz, at which Wood was very indignant.

" 15th *July.*

" Off early. Got to the encampment after eight hours. Dreadfully hot ride. Were visited by two sheikhs whose property had been confiscated by Suleiman Khan for robbery. They asked us to speak a good word for them, and treated us very civilly. Having sent the caravan on (only keeping our own beasts), we were surprised at seeing it before us after only two hours' ride. Arrived at Haroumabad by mid-day. Dreadfully hot. Pitched in a garden. Had a row with the muleteers, who refused to take us on to the Commissioner's encampment according to their agreement. This delayed us, naturally.

" 18th *July.*

" Having got mules, we started after sunset, and rode six hours to the foot of the hills. During our stay, the son of Suleiman Khan, the Governor of the town, and Mirza, the Prince-Governor, behaved very civilly to us, giving us a company of soldiers to protect us from thieves, for which the town was notorious. However, they were not of much use, for during the night a saddle-bag was stolen from under Wood's head, without awakening him.   A fellow also put his hand under my pillow, but not being so heavy a sleeper, I awoke and was about to give him the benefit of a pistol-ball, when, hearing me move, he got away.   As I was sleeping under mosquito-nets, I could not see where he went, or I should have fired after him.

" *19th July.*

"Off early.   Rode five hours to a very pretty encamping-place, in a small valley at the junction of two rivers.   The scenery through which the road passed was beautiful.   On the road two of the mules strayed—one laden with our big tent and another with some of Wood's luggage.   We immediately sent back to look for them, and they were found about midway from the last stage some half-mile from the road. Killed several red-legged partridge and woodquests.

" *20th July.*

" Off early.   Rode four hours into Nazar-el-Khan. Instead of pitching tents, spread our beds under a fine oak.   Lots of scorpions, devil's coach-horses, large spiders, and all sorts of disagreeable beetles.

" *21st July.*

"Started at sunrise across a bad mountain pass. Sunrise splendid.   Stopped to breakfast at 9 A.M., and it being dreadfully hot remained till 3 P.M., then started again.   Lost our way.   Wandering about till near midnight, when we found the luggage mules.   To comfort us, we heard they also had lost their way; neither muleteers nor guides could tell where we were. Very little water and less dinner.

" 22d July.

"Stopped till 10 A.M., when the guide whom we had sent on to reconnoitre brought back word that they had found the road. Loaded and started, and wandered about the greater part of the day, missing our way every hour. At length about 3 P.M. we reached Kurki, a small village in a deep valley. Coming down the hill, Tom and I discovered a well of clear water in the shade. Stopped there two hours and bathed. Started again, but found it almost impossible to join the luggage, the inhabitants having set fire to the dry grass, and before we could get through, the whole hillside was in a blaze. However, we had nothing for it but to push our horses as hard as they could go, for the flames were closing in all round, and the large dry oaks had already caught fire over our heads. The heat was suffocating. The poor animals, frightened to death, were frantic, and dashed madly on, rushing through the blazing thickets, for we could not see the path. At length unexpectedly we came on a river, plunged in, and, having got across, put up to rest the almost exhausted animals. Had a look at the scene of conflagration. The thermometer 152° F.

" 23d July.

"Tom and I started three hours before sunrise with a guide to make our way by a short cut to Monghea, instead of going two days round with the luggage. We were told that we could get there in four hours, but that the road was too bad for any beasts of burden. After going along the valley for two hours, where the road was certainly bad enough, we arrived at a sort of cleft or opening between two mountains, through which a stream flowed.

" Up this we began to toil. It certainly was the most dreadful piece of work I ever went through. Most of the road was a series of stairs, or rather natural projections of solid bare rock, over five or six feet in height, up which the horses had to jump, without anything to prevent them, if their feet slipped, from rolling into the valley beneath. Sometimes the path ran along the bottom of a ledge of rock higher than one's head, the track being sometimes not wider than half a foot, and sometimes where the stones were broken away the horses had to step from stone to stone, like crossing a ford on stepping-stones, the precipice beneath ending in a river.

" Occasionally we came to places where, I think, a wild goat himself would have felt ill at ease. Notwithstanding, ' Jack ' walked on as unconcernedly as if he were traversing a level plain.

" Tom was nearly going headlong, horse and all, over the precipice. His horse, being frightened, made a mistake, and in trying to recover himself one of his forefeet went over the side.

" About 9 A.M., having performed half the ascent, we stopped for breakfast under the shade of a large walnut-tree.

" Starting again in about half an hour, we commenced the second ascent, which was a good deal steeper than the first, but the soil being soft the horses had better footing. About 2 P.M. we sighted the camp, pitched on the high ridge of the opposite mountain, and with about four hours' tremendous descent ultimately reached it.

" Mirza Jaffa Khan's camp was pitched nearest the top, the Russians next to him, and the English on another ridge lower down, and about four hundred yards distant, separated by a rather deep valley, through which lay the dry course of a river. All round the Russian and Persian camps the wild pomegranate grew in great abundance, and the side of the valley which separated the English from the other camp was covered with thick groves of myrtle. The English tents, being lower down, lay in a regular forest of fine oaks.

" Behind all the camps rose a precipitous wall of barren, scraggy rocks of a grayish-white colour, shutting us in on the N.N.W. and N.E., while the prospect to the south commanded a wide irregular valley until close to the mountains over Dizful. When we arrived we stopped at the Russian camp, as the road came in that way. They made us promise to live with them until our caravan should arrive. Before dinner we went down to see Colonel Williams [afterwards of Kars] and his party. Found all well except Wood, who was dangerously ill from an inflammatory sore throat, caught from bathing while too hot.

" *24th July.*

"About noon the luggage arrived, and I went down to choose a place for our encampment. Fixed on one about three hundred yards to the east of Colonel Williams's camp, beside a small tank of water. Dined with Colonel Williams.

" *25th July.*

" Employed in pitching our large tent and unpacking, and on the following days in arranging for kitchen, stables, etc. Altogether we had a shed of about seventy feet in length and twenty-eight broad, built along the side of a ridge, so that, looking over, one could see the valley some hundreds of feet below.

The kitchen occupied one end of the shed, the hen-house and servants' dormitories joined it, the pantry and store-box apartment next, then came our sitting-room and dining-room all in one. The whole affair was built of the branches and leaves of the oak trees, all the sides being left open to give us the benefit of any air that might be stirring, except the eastern side, which I closed with the curtain of our small tent, to keep the morning sun off my bed. Tom and Wood slept in the large tent, which was pitched on a terrace about ten yards distant. The stable was built on the same terrace as the tent, close to the kitchen.

" About a week after our arrival, when we had got well settled, we sent John to Dizful to buy such things as we could not procure from the camps, such as candles, spices for curry, flour, sugar, coffee, etc. He returned in about a week, and got an attack of fever, the fright of which did him more harm than the illness itself.

" 10*th August.*

" Had a slight attack of fever myself for a few days. The accounts of Wood were sometimes better, and other times worse. Heat tremendous. Just before sunrise, the coolest part of the day, the ther-mometer was 95° F. Found the natives, of whom we had heard very bad accounts, very civil, well mannered, and far less given to lying than their neighbours the Persians. When first we arrived we found it rather diffi-cult to get provisions from them, but afterwards, when they saw that we paid for what we got, they supplied us regularly with grapes, figs, milk, masta-curds, cheese, sheep, barley, beans, and now and then a wild goat. Eggs, rice, and chickens were very scarce, and we were obliged to send to Dizful whenever we wanted any.

"As far as I could make out, our numbers altogether—reckoning all the troops, soldiers, etc.—did not fall short of two hundred and twenty souls, besides two hundred and forty mules and horses, so that, considering the sort of country we were encamped in, we could hardly be surprised if, towards the end of our sojourn, provisions—particularly barley—became both scarce and dear. It certainly was the most miserably stupid summer I ever spent.

"The Russian camp being about half a mile off, and the road leading to it being too steep to travel, except before sunrise or after sunset, we saw rather little of them, and Wood being so ill in the English camp, we saw nothing of them either. The doctor, who came down nearly every day to play whist with Tom, sometimes dined with us. In the early part of Wood's illness I used to go every day and play chess with him—an amusement he seemed very fond of. However, it was soon declared to be too exciting for him in his weak state, so it was given up.

"Having read all our books, there was nothing for us to do but to smoke and try to sleep, which the flies by day and the mosquitoes by night made rather difficult. It certainly was a hell upon earth. The heat and glare reflected from the rock-salt round sometimes nearly roasted us alive. The only breeze we ever got was from the south, which, as the rocks above sheltered us from the north-west and east, came thoroughly heated from the Dizful and Shuster deserts. The valley was famous for its breed of scorpions and snakes. One of the Khan's servants, while bathing, was bitten by a snake, and died in two hours. Scorpions were innumerable. We found two large ones devouring one another in Tom's bed, both of which I deposited in a bottle of spirits for future exhibition. All the servants were more or less bitten. We also saw lots of immense spiders, said to be more poisonous than scorpions, 'Lutinis'[1] by name. We killed two larger than a full-grown mouse, and another smaller one on Tom's coat, which I preserved as a specimen.

" Thus flowed on our lives, with no difference or manner of change—Wood still continuing in the same doubtful state, until the 8th September, when, he being reported nearly out of danger, the Russians struck their camp. We were sorry to lose them. The colonel was a very nice fellow, a Russian who combined polish and sincerity.

" *16th September.*

" All the large tents struck. Colonel Williams told us that he had changed his plans, and instead of going to Susa as he intended, had decided on starting for Ispahan. We were sorry for this alteration, as it prevented us from seeing Susa, where we expected good sport. We therefore resolved to accompany him as far as Kirmanshah, thence striking off to Bagdad. The colonel and all his party dined with us. He engaged our little Indian cook and gave us his head cook, an Armenian, in exchange, at the same time telling us that we must join his table as long as we should remain with him—a proposal we were too glad to accept, being heartily tired of our *tête-à-tête* meals.

" *17th September.*

" Spent in making arrangements for starting, viz. selling all our useless traps. The Colonel took our large tent and the Khan our tables and chairs.

---

[1] Probably a local term.

"Post arrived from Bagdad, bringing us a budget of home letters.

"Employed in devising means for the conveyance of our servants and luggage to Haroumabad, as we heard that mules were not to be had for love or money at Dizful; so we sent round to all the neighbouring encampments to hire bullocks and men.

"Hearing that a lot of mules had come for the Khan, I sent up to his camp to try if I could persuade him to let us have some. He good-naturedly gave us eight, which saved us a lot of trouble.

"Up at 3 A.M. Got our caravan under way about six, and arrived at Scoderere by 10 A.M. The road was pretty fair. One of the Colonel's mules fell over a precipice and was killed. The young Khan joined us at breakfast, which we discussed in a cave. In the evening we had some fishing in the tanks, which are very large, and said to be of ancient date.

"Off at 5 A.M. Went through a beautiful pass. Road very dangerous. One mule killed and several severely injured. Arrived at Goolam by 11.30 A.M. Very hot; thermometer 125° F. in the tents. The Khan dined with us, as he was going next day to Dizful. He was rather a nice young fellow, and spoke French after a sort. The Colonel christened him 'Plaît à Dieu,' from a propensity he had to use that phrase.

" *26th September.*

" Off at 3 A.M. Arrived at our station by half-past ten. Encamped by the side of a nice river. Very hot. Fished in the evening, but caught nothing.

" *27th September.*

" Started at 4 A.M. Got at twelve noon to a very pretty encampment on the Haroumabad river. Discovered an antique balcony cut out of the solid rock, about ten feet from the ground. Made our beds there, and slept till sundown, when we had a bath in the river.

" *28th September.*

" Off at 4.30 A.M. Marched to 10 A.M., then halted at the top of a high mountain pass for the mules to arrive, but discovered that we had outmarched our station by about two hours. Breakfasted, and then marched till 3.30 P.M., when we got into a very dirty station, with only salt-water springs.

" *29th September.*

" Got to Nazr-el-Khan.

" *30th September.*

" Encamped in a pretty small valley at the junction of two streams.

" *31st September.*

" The road was steep but very pretty, something like travelling through an English park. Encamped on a small hill in sight of Haroumabad.

" *1st October.*

" Off at 6.30 A.M. Dressed in full fig. Met Golumjeer, elder brother of ' Plait à Dieu,' with a crowd of horsemen outside the town. They went through the jereed exercise for our entertainment. Some of them did it very well. At length we arrived, thoroughly dusty and tired. We were very well lodged in the Prince-Governor's house, a very fine place with a large garden and an immense tank of water. We got lots of the finest grapes and melons we ever tasted, besides apples, pears, pomegranates, quinces, etc., in the greatest abundance.

" 2d October.

" We went to the bath, escorted by a regiment of soldiers to protect us from the mob.

" 3d October.

" Hired mules and donkeys to carry us to Kirmanshah.

" 4th October.

" Off at 9 A.M., and on

" 5th October

" Arrived at the encampment, which was pitched in the plain of Aleshtan, celebrated in Persian records for the number of fine horses and mules bred by the inhabitants. We were therefore surprised that during a ride of two hours, to the place of our encampment, we saw only a few wretched-looking horses and young mules, half-starved from having lost their mothers before they were able to cater for themselves. Accordingly the Colonel sent for the Khan of the district to solve the riddle, who said—

" In the former spring the Government had sent their tax-gatherers to collect the taxes, but owing to a scarcity which prevailed, their corn having suffered a severe blight, they not only refused, but plundered the tax-gatherers. The Government, for a wonder, taking the upper hand (for the tribe is a powerful one), sent a lot of soldiers to punish their audacity by driving off all the animals that were worth having, to the number of ten thousand mules and eight thousand fine mares and horses. The people, naturally enraged at this, were then in open rebellion against the Government, and instead of the Colonel being able to increase his stock, he was afraid that the people would try in a measure to pay themselves out of our caravan for the loss they had sustained by carrying off all our beasts to the number of eighty head. He added, moreover, by way of comfort, that it would be no loss to us, as the Government would easily make it up by giving us an equal number of the beasts which they had carried off from the people, and that, as theirs were much finer than those they proposed to take from us, we should on the whole profit by the exchange. However, as we were blind enough not to perceive the great advantages which were to accrue to us in case of such an event happening, and not relishing to remain there until the Persian Government should send us the means to move, we told him as much and parted—he promising to do his best to protect us.

"Accordingly, about two hours after, eight ragged-looking cut-throats came down armed with matchlocks, and along with them a donkey-load of melons, as a present from the Khan. Caring little for the threatened danger, and seeing that the guards did not run away or hide, which they would have done had there been any chance of an attack, we turned in at 3.30 A.M. of the 6th, and found everything right.

" 6th October.

"Off at 5.30 A.M. Got in at twelve midnight. Found next morning that clever thieves had been at work, getting into the cook's tent without awakening anybody, and had stolen nearly all our kitchen-furniture.

" *7th October.*

"Off at sunrise. Got in, half an hour before sunset, having hunted all the country for Ali Khan, with whom we were to encamp, but without success. We were met on the road by different chiefs, with lots of horsemen, who escorted us through their different districts.

" *8th October.*

"Ali Khan arrived in the morning from his camp three hours off. Starting after breakfast, he escorted us a good way, his followers—of whom he had about fifty—playing the jereed and going through a sham fight. Arrived at mid-day at a good-sized village with beautiful gardens, where we had a great feed of fruit. Reached our station at sunset.

" *9th October.*

"Under way by sunrise. The Colonel and his party went straight to Kirmanshah—Tom and I making a detour to see Bezitoun and Taki Boustan. The latter place was well worth seeing—a curious arch cut out of the solid rock, from under which flowed a large stream of cool clear water. The former did not strike me as at all worth the trouble of the ride. It is merely an inscription cut in the face of the rock about eleven hundred feet from the ground.

"Rode into Kirmanshah about 5 P.M., and were lodged in one of the Governor's palaces—a fine roomy house with an immense garden, where we remained till the 13th, when we started alone for Bagdad.

H

"We were very sorry to leave the Colonel and his party, from all of whom we had received the greatest kindness. Indeed, Colonel Williams himself treated me more like a father than a mere friend. After four hours' scorching ride, we arrived at a dirty caravanserai, where we put up.

" 14th October.

"Off at 5 A.M.—the muleteer making a grievous complaint about our killing his beasts by travelling in the heat of the day. Marched six hours into Haroum-abad, where, the caravanserai being full, we had to put up at a mud cottage—beastly dirty quarters.

" 15th October.

"Started at 2 A.M. Rode seven hours into Kirind. Good quarters.

" 16th October.

"Off at daybreak. Rode four hours into Meuntaz —very bad quarters. In the evening went to see the gipsies. Some of the girls were very pretty.

" 18th October.

"Marched into Kasiri - Shireen. Visited and bothered by the commander of the troops on the frontier. However, he gave us fifty men to escort us.

" 19th October.

"Started at 2 A.M. Marched into Hairiki by eight. Put up at the Consul's house. The Consul and all the inhabitants were in great trouble about the Kourds who were robbing the villages about. Visited the Pacha, who asked us to let him take advantage of our escort to send his despatches ·to the Governor of

Bagdad, which, of course, we agreed to, and started our caravan in the night.

                                         " 19*th October.*

"Owing to the Pacha's things not being ready, we were delayed until the evening. Rain during the day. About 4 P.M. we started. The Pacha accompanied us about five miles, and then, with many apologies for not coming farther, he left us to the mercy of our escort, which consisted of about fifty Arabs, all mounted."

CHAPTER X

Θάλαττα, θάλαττα.—XEN. *Anab.* iv. 8.

The sea, the sea !

Thy towers, Bombay, gleam bright, they say,
Across the dark blue sea.—BISHOP HEBER.

HERE the diary breaks off somewhat abruptly. The travellers continued their journey apparently with little that is noteworthy, until on the 23d December of the same year it is thus resumed :—

"Left Bushire. Weighed anchor at 7 A.M. After leaving the roads, set the square canvas. Light breeze from north-west. Light swell, in which the vessel—250 tons—rolled tremendously. She seemed as if she were built entirely for that sort of amusement, having rather little breadth of beam in proportion to her length. She was schooner-rigged after a fashion. Half of the after-cabin was portioned off as a harem for the female Persian passengers.

"The Captain did *maître d'hôtel*, making a very generous arrangement with us—more so, indeed, than we liked ; but as he was rather given to taking offence, we had to consent. His cuisine, however, was far from the best. At two bells in the forenoon, breakfast was to be seen spread in filthy disorder on the table in our dormitory. In the main cabin at eight bells, tiffin and grog were served. Either there or on deck, at eight bells of the afternoon watch, the repast called dinner made its appearance. Heaven help the epicure, or the delicate jaws of any fair lady, who should have to choose between starvation or masticating the patriarchal cocks on board the *Sir Charles Forbes!* Last, though not least, at 8 P.M. the joyful sound of 'pipe to grog' resounded through the ship, after which we had a smoke, and then stowed ourselves away in our respective berths for the night.

"24th December.

"Smooth water. No wind. Very strong current setting up the gulf. Making only two and a half knots an hour.

"25th December.

"Passed Bassadore. Saw the *Constance* and *Tigris* lying in the roads. Double allowance of grog to distinguish Christmas Day.

"26th December.

"At 2 A.M. let go the anchor at Bunder-Abbas—a curious-looking town, under the government of the Imaum. A lot of natives, half Persians and Arabs, came on board to inspect the wonders of the steamer. Got under way at 2 P.M. Passed the island of Ormuz before sunset, about which Moore has written such a false description, as he has of all Persia. The remains of the town and fort were barely visible, and all that could be seen of the island was a series of concave mounds, composed of divers coloured sands or soil, which looked more like the production of some submarine volcanic eruption than the lovely and flourishing island described in *Lalla Rookh.* A slight breeze from the south-east.

27th December.

"Breeze increased to a gale. The vessel barely making headway. Heavy sea rolling her paddle-boxes under. At noon eased away two points. Got the stay, trysail, and reefed mainsail close hauled. Four and a half knots leeway. About 2 P.M. the gale changed into heavy gusts, coming down with heavy rain. The first gust blew the staysail into ribbons. Shortly after, the main-forestay was carried away, coming against the funnel with a sharp crack. Saw a waterspout on the starboard quarter. Heavy black clouds gathering about twenty miles to leeward over the land.

"About 8 P.M. took in the mainsail, but before it was well furled down came the squall which had been gathering in the north-west. It began with torrents of rain such as one sees only in Eastern climes. Then came the wind rushing along the water and covering it with foam. It struck us on the port bow, and, as the ship heeled over, everything below went adrift— tables and chairs, boxes, portmanteaux, beds off the locker. Our crock of butter came down with a run, leaving the floor in a nice state for those who liked sliding. However, that was washed up by the streams of rain-water which emptied themselves into the cabin through the chinks in the skylight. Everything was noise and confusion until the helm was put up, and immediately paying off, she righted, and went along for some minutes in apparently smooth water. The squall soon settled down into a steady breeze from the north-west—the fairest wind we could have. Set the foretop and foresails, and made from seven to seven and a half knots during the night.

"*28th December.*

"Fair breeze; smooth sea. Arrived at Muscat at 7 P.M. Found two French vessels lying in the bay.

"*29th December.*

"Lay there all day discharging cargo, etc. An extraordinary-looking place, built at the end of a small rocky bay upon cliffs of rock. The houses are all white, and apparently clean, for a wonder, and the rocks, being of dark reddish brown, give the place altogether a rather curious appearance. Over the town, and at each side of the entrance to the bay, batteries were perched, also built of white stone, accessible only by steps cut out of the solid rock. One of them, which was built nearer the water's edge, resembled on a small scale the Castle of Chillon.

"*30th December.*

"In a dreadful mess all day, taking in coal. An English vessel arrived just before we sailed at 7 P.M. Course east by south. Fine night.

"*31st December.*

"Beautiful weather. Light breeze from the southeast. Carried square sails, besides fore-and-aft canvas. Passed Ras-el-Hadd.

"*1st January* 1851.

"Light breeze from the south-west. Course east by south. Six and a half knots an hour.

"*2d January.*

"Fine weather. Course ditto. Light breeze from the east. Saw lots of flying, and a shoal of black, fish. Calm night. Seven knots an hour.

" 3d January.

" Freshening breeze from north-east. Kalliwar coast eighty miles distant on the weather-bow.

" 4th January.

" Breeze steady from the same point. Saw a shark and a few sea-snakes. Very heavy dew at night.

" 5th January.

" Fresh breeze dead ahead until noon, when it calmed. Put on full power, and the wind coming at 4 P.M. from the south-west and by west, carried fore-and-aft canvas—but all our efforts were in vain to get in before dark. Reached the outer lightship half an hour after sunset. Bombay at 8 P.M. About half an hour after, we were boarded by the Custom House officers, which reminded us that we were once more under English government.

" 6th January.

" Up early. Wood started before breakfast to engage rooms for us at the Hope Hall Hotel. About 10 A.M. started with the luggage for the Custom House. While there I got into a palki, and went to the post-office, where I received a budget of letters. Arrived at the Hope Hall for tiffin, then taking Colaba Point.

" 7th January.

" Got into better rooms. Went out early to leave letters of introduction. Romaine got a letter from Sir E. Percy, inviting him to go and live with him, which he immediately accepted. He returned in the evening, saying he had been introduced to a Colonel Brooks, who was about to start in a few days for Lahore, and that he had joined him, thinking it a good way of getting to Cashmere.

" 8th January.

" Decided on accompanying Romaine. Dined with Sir E. Percy.

" 9th January.

" Hard at work all day getting our outfit.

" 10th January.

"Wood succeeded in getting a horse—a large, strong brute, eight years old, which had been ridden by a lady, and therefore suited him to a T, for four hundred rupees. In the evening I concluded for a four-year-old, cob build, for the same money.

" 11th January.

" Bought a tent for a hundred and sixty rupees, a pony and buggy for the servants for three hundred, and a large well-bred charger from Colonel B. for eight hundred. Wood declaring that he was going to turn out a great sportsman (Heaven save the mark !), and must have another horse also, closed for an old horse for four hundred rupees.

" 12th January.

" Went to the dealer's stables before breakfast, and closed with him for three horses—an iron-gray for Romaine, a bay for Tom, and a light gray for myself, all of them under four years old, for seventeen hundred rupees. Tom and Wood went to church, and I went down to Romaine, who rather astonished me by telling me he had given up the Cashmere expedition, and was going to sell his horses and take the steamer for Calcutta immediately, on hearing which I countermanded the hackeries and gave up the expedition. Dined with the Commodore. Met Colonel B——, Captain Jenkins, Captain Heatly, Mr. Jones, Colonel Ogilby, etc. Got home at 4 A.M. of the 13th. Obliged to get out of my engagement to visit the Caves of Elephanta with Captain J——. Romaine changed his mind about going to Calcutta, but we remained firm, spite of all Wood's splendid representations. Romaine dined with us.

" 14th January.

" Rode down to Romaine to bid him farewell, but he was gone.

" 15th January.

" Tom and Wood went to a ball at Government House. As we had got our horses and outfit we determined to make an expedition to Nuggur for sport, and afterwards to the Caves of Adjunta and Ellora. Wood made tremendous preparations for killing game, getting enough bullets moulded to shoot all the tigers in India, and also getting a boar-spear, his reason for which I could not make out, as he seemed to find it difficult enough to sit on his horse without any such encumbrance.

" 16th January.

" Completed our arrangements about servants, of whom we had a precious lot, viz. butler, second servant, third ditto, cook and helper, bheestie, and seven ostlers, besides John and Badal.

' " 17th January.

" Tom and Wood went to a soiree at Sir E. Percy's.

" 18th January.

" Applied to Sir John Grey for Billy's [his cousin, William Bookey's] leave, who kindly granted it. Wrote to him to come down to join us. Went to look at two terriers, but two hundred rupees was more than I cared to give.

" 19th January.

" Dined with the Commodore, and got home about midnight.

" 20th January.

" Up early. Hard at work getting ready for the start. Went into town after breakfast to get money. Called on Sir E. Percy and Mr. Basset. Started from the Hope Hall Hotel at 5.30 P.M.

" My party consisted of myself, fifteen flunkeys, five led horses, and six hackeries. All the flunkeys walked except Badal and the butler, who went in the buggy. Rode my new horse 'Sir Roger,' who did not at all like the exchange of his idle comfortable life in the hotel stables for the fatigues of a marching one. About an hour after dark crossed the causeway connecting the island of Bombay with the mainland, and shortly after that, the commencement of the Poonah line of railroad, and then, taking leave of villages, cottages, and gardens, we marched through the jungle until half an hour after midnight, when we arrived at Tannah.

" Put up at the Traveller's Bungalow—a species of hotel built by the East India Company for the accommodation of all gentlemen travelling in their dominions, and as I considered myself one of that number, I took possession of a fine clean airy room, furnished with three arm-chairs, a mahogany table, and a bedstead. Put up the horses in the stable. Stowed my bawarchi in the cook-house, and filled the enclosure with my hackeries—altogether making myself at home. The carts arrived about 2 P.M. of the 21st, when, having seen that the horses were all right, I stowed myself away, much to my own satisfaction, as I was dreadfully sleepy.

"Awoke about 8 A.M., and to my joy discovered a bath-room, and breakfasted at 9 A.M. Dined at 2 P.M.; very much satisfied with the cook, who fed me like a fighting-cock. Started at 3.30 P.M., and had an hour's delay getting the things ferried over an arm of the sea. Rode 'Sir John Grey,' who was at first very much inclined to be rebellious.

"The first part of the road was good and the scenery beautiful, but as soon as ever light deserted us, we commenced a passage over a lot of sea-bogs, in which the buggy and its contents disappeared. Two hackeries also sank as if they were never to rise again, and were with difficulty hauled out by the natives of the neighbouring village. As soon as the moon rose our troubles ceased, and we had a spell of about four hours through low jungle. On my arrival at Panwell found the Collector of Tannah in the bungalow, and with difficulty succeeded in getting a room. Had an encounter with a tremendous rat, which I killed with Wood's spear. Reached next stage at 2 A.M. of the 22d, but the hackeries did not come till five hours later. Saw the serpent-charmers and jugglers. Got the carts off at a quarter to four in the afternoon, and myself at a quarter to six. Rode into Chukun at 8 P.M., sending the hackeries on. Halted there with the horses until 4 P.M. of the 23d, and then marched in three hours and three quarters into Kappooly.

"Road good, but filled with hackeries carrying soldiers' baggage. Indifferent bungalow. Had a lovely ride of about two hours up the Ghauts. The scenery was beautiful. The variegated foliage of the trees, and the rich plumage of the paroquets, parrots, and humming-birds, as they flew screaming from tree to tree, made me realise that I was at length in the long-looked-for, long-wished-for India.

" On reaching the top ridge a most extensive view broke on me. I could see plainly over the top of a smaller range of hills Colaba Point and Bombay Harbour, and on turning to the right I saw laid out before me the line of road on which I had been marching for the last two days.

" Reached Kandala at 5 P.M., a small place beautifully situated, and put up at the bungalow. Hackeries arrived at 7 P.M. The temperature very perceptibly cooler.

" 24th January.

"Started at 4 P.M. Road a little hilly—afterwards through large plains of rice and wheat. Marched into Carly at 6 P.M. and sent hackeries on. Stopped at Carly with the horses until 4 A.M. on the

" 25th January.

" Passing Nagotna, arrived at Poonah at 7 A.M. on the

" 26th January.

" Put up at the Sirza bungalow for breakfast, sending the butler out to hire one by the day. He returned in about an hour with word that he had found a very nice one with stables and lots of room, into which we moved and found that it in every way verified Baloo's description. Sent to the post-office to see if Wood or Tom had kept their promises—'Pie-crusts' again! There not being stabling enough, we had to pitch our tent for two horses. An unpleasant day, cloudy, with hot wind and plenty of dust. The house infested with mongeese.

" 27th January.

" Having succeeded in hiring an immense unwieldy machine of a carriage, drove to the 10th Hussar mess-room and left my card for Stopford Blair, and also called on Captain Studdert of the Bombay engineers.

" 28th January.

" Got word from the landlord that a certain captain wanted to take the bungalow, and in more express terms got 'notice to quit' on or before the 31st of the month—at which I was mightily enraged, considering it altogether a very shameful proceeding.

" 30th January.

" Rode to Captain Studdert's to inquire about a bungalow I had heard of. He was not in. Coming home, my horse threw me into a prickly-pear bush, from which I emerged very sore. At breakfast Captain Studdert appeared, inviting me to go and live with him until the rest arrived, and gave me another bungalow for the servants and baggage. I accordingly went down to him, and found myself very comfortably established. Met Captains Wells and Cooper.

" 31st January.

" Up before daylight and rode to the Brigade parade, where I was introduced to General Armisty. About 2 P.M. Tom and Billy arrived, and I went up with them to the bungalow. Dined with Studdert. Wood arrived at midnight.

" 1st February.

" Rode up from Studdert's in the morning and had

my things moved. We dined at the mess of the 1st Fusiliers.

" 5*th February.*

" Bought a fox and had a run with terriers after Reynard—five minutes without a check, and a kill in the open. Dined with Studdert.

" 6*th February.*

" Left Poonah at 5 P.M., Wood stopping behind. Marched five hours and then found we had gone ten miles wrong. I then got into the buggy, and reached Lunee by 2 A.M. of the 7th, seldom having had such a fearful shaking. Halted the hackeries. Tom and Billy arrived at ten, had supper and turned in. Intended stopping the day, but hearing there was nothing but hares to be got, we packed up and started at 4 P.M. Marched into Kondipory at 9.30 P.M., and got some rumbled eggs and anchovy toast as an apology for supper.

" 8*th February.*

" Started at 5 A.M. Reached Seroor at 9 A.M. After breakfast, sent our cards to Major Tapp, the Commander of the Poonah Irregular Horse, asking him to admit us to his garden, Captain Studdert having told us not to leave Seroor without seeing it. His answer was very civil, inviting us to lunch with him.

" 9*th February.*

" Tom not feeling well, Billy and I started and reached the hunting-ground by daybreak. The jungle was very thin and we found no game in it. Saw hares, but, being more ambitious, we let them go their ways in peace, and leaving the covert we struck through the cornfields until we reached the side of the mountain, up which we toiled, and gained the summit just as the sun rose. We were disgusted at finding nothing except a few herds of buffaloes tamely grazing near their owners' huts. We then determined to separate, Billy to persecute the hares and partridge, and as I had only my rifle I continued to search for deer. '*Fortuna favet fortibus.*' I descended the other side of the hill, and, getting into the dry bed of a river, had not proceeded far when I perceived in a field, where the Indian corn had been cut, four deer of the black buck species, about five hundred yards distant, gazing at me.

"I was rather disconcerted when I saw they had discovered me, but as they did not seem to take it much to heart—I suppose they took me for a native—I advanced towards them without altering my pace, until I had shortened the distance to about two hundred yards, then away they went and I had to risk a running shot, which at that distance of course missed. I fancied that the hindmost one staggered a little after I fired, but that was all I had to comfort me. Then loading, I sent the coolies round one side of the hill, while, in hopes of intercepting their retreat to the jungle, and getting another shot at them as they dashed past me, I galloped to the other side, but all in vain—I saw no more of them. Billy had been equally unsuccessful, so we returned to the bungalow empty-handed.

"Major Tapp called after breakfast. Tom and Billy lunched with him. I took a ride in the evening with the Major and the English of Seroor.

"*10th February.*

"Wood arrived at 4 A.M., just as we were getting on our horses for the jungle. Spent the day in ex-

citing but unsuccessful deerstalking.   Paid our adieux
in the evening to the Major and others, and at 8.30 P.M.
Billy and I cantered into Tufa after three hours'
ride, when, having no servants or beds, we were
obliged to throw our coats over our horses, and,
fastening the reins round our waists, did our best to
go to sleep.   The ghora-walas arriving about midnight, and relieving us of the horses, we divided our
bedstead between us, and slept till 8 A.M. of the 11th."

CHAPTER XI

Frater, ave atque vale !

CATULL. ci.

Farewell to thee, Brother, farewell !

And we know that all things work together for good to them that love God. ROMANS viii. 28.

"*12th February.*

"Started about 6 A.M. and reached Nuggur at 9 A.M. Breakfasted in the Sirza bungalow, sending the butler to look for another. We succeeded in getting Mr Tucker's, by far the finest I had seen.

"*13th February.*

"Billy and I went out deerstalking.

"*15th February.*

"Ditto—and had our joints shaken to pieces for eight hours, and saw nothing.

"*16th February.*

"Took a ride round the fort in the evening, and

"*17th February*

"Went to see some tombs.

"*18th February.*

"Received deputation from some rich natives.

" 20th February.

" Left Nuggur at 6 A.M. and arrived at Doggerajan, or the ' Happy Valley,' at nine. Put up at a Hindoo temple. The valley was very pretty, shady and cool, very small, precipitous and deep, but so filled with different sorts of trees that from the bottom it was almost impossible to see the sky. Started at 3.45 P.M. and rode an hour and a half into Imaumpore. Saw a few deer and some partridge.

" 21st February.

" Started at 5 P.M. and rode down the Ghauts into Rushampore. Lost our way.

" 22d February.

" Left at daylight. Rode four and a half hours into Toka. Saw a large herd of black buck, and at 9 A.M. Mackenzie and his wife and daughter arrived, and we were obliged to turn out and make room for them,

" 23d February.

" Started at sunrise, and immediately crossing a large river, which, however, was nearly dry—the boundary of the Nizam's dominions—we cantered into the next halting-place by 9 A.M. During the day I got a very good specimen of a kingfisher.

" 24th February.

" Off by daylight, and got into Aurungabad for breakfast, then went in search of a bungalow, and succeeded in getting a tolerably respectable one.

" 26th February.

" Went out at daylight to see a review of the Nizam's Irregular Horse, a very fine body of men, commanded entirely by English officers. On returning home we got a message from the native commanding officer asking us to dine at the mess.   It was a pleasant dinner, and a tolerable display of fireworks, manufactured by the natives, took place afterwards.

" *27th February.*

" Started alone in a bullock-gharry to look for deer at about 4 A.M.   Just as the sun rose I came in sight of a herd.   Got about two hundred yards from them ; then, as they began to move off, I fired, and after more unsuccessful shots returned home disgusted with my exploits.   On reaching the bungalow, found Wood and Tom had gone out to breakfast.   On going into Billy's room he shouted out " A tiger ! " and then told me we were to go to a jungle about six miles off, where a tiger had killed a bullock the evening before, and had been marked in by the shikarris.

" Accordingly we started off, joining the three Orrs. We cantered across the plain, then, passing through a steep ghaut, we found the elephants, and proceeded across a small range of hills, when we came upon a small steep valley, the sides of which were covered with thick prickly jungle, where the tiger was said to be lying.   The party was then divided.   There being only two elephants, Tom and Brigadier Twemlow went on one with Mr. Orr ; Wood, Dr. Orr, and I on another.   The others proceeded on foot, taking up the position on the top of the hill which best commanded the jungle.

" The elephants then commenced beating the cover, the one which I was on going first.   After proceeding for about five minutes in the jungle, we espied the tiger lying between a large rock and mimosa bush, but before we could fire he gave a loud ' roo-of,' and dashed away down the valley, exposing himself to a hot fire from the hill, and at length took shelter in an almost impenetrable jungle of wild prickly-pear bushes.   We then turned the elephants, and descending the hill, posted ourselves under the bush in which he had taken shelter, while the coolies on the top of the hill rolled down large stones into the thicket to try and dislodge him—but all in vain.   The only means which then remained of turning him out was to get one of the elephants up to the ledge of the hill and drive it through the jungle, for which service the beast on which I was, being the stauncher of the two, was chosen.   Accordingly we set off, and making a slight détour we reached the top of the ledge, and, entering the cover, proceeded for some minutes without any interruption, when all of a sudden the elephant halted, and began to trumpet, refusing to proceed farther.

"After vain endeavours to get him on, we were obliged to get him up another ridge of the mountain, on which he proceeded for a minute, then stopping, began to trumpet again.   We knew that we must be close to the tiger, and, expecting him to charge every minute, prepared to repel his onset, when, uttering a loud roar, he charged up the hill to where F. Orr and Frank Suter were standing; but receiving two balls, one through his left fore-leg and the other at the back of his shoulder, he turned tail and retreated into a thicket close to where we were.   Wood gave him one barrel, which hit the ground close to his head, the only part of his body visible.   I then took a pot-shot at him, and was fortunate enough to send my ball in behind his left ear, at which he sprang out of the bush and made his way to another lower down, after receiving four more shots.

"We then descended the hill until we got below the jungle in which he was and began beating up, when we saw him lying about fifty yards ahead of us. W. Orr giving him a shot, he charged down at us, but being too badly wounded, he rolled helplessly into a bush about five yards from us, where we gave him the contents of our rifles and polished him off. He was a fine young tiger, not quite nine feet from the tip of his nose to the end of his tail. He had received fifteen bullets all about his shoulders and head ; and after tying him on the back of an elephant we set off to our several destinations. I went with W. and J. Orr to Dowlutabad, where I found our camp, and dined with the Orrs. The rest returned to Aurungabad.

" 28th February.

"Set off at sunrise to see the fort—very curious old place surrounded by three strong walls, a fosse, etc.— after passing which, the ascent is made by a subterranean staircase, tunnelled through the solid rock. At the top of every landing-place there was a furnace and trap-door for the purpose of pouring down hot pitch upon the assailants, with various other amiable inventions. The top of the hill was surmounted by another strong battlement, and a temple to the presiding deity. Within the outer walls the jungle is pretty thick, and affords shelter to panthers, cheetahs, and peacocks. Wood, Billy, and Tom arrived.

"Word was brought that a tiger had killed a bullock close to the camp, so we all sallied forth and were conducted to a garden of castor-oil plants, which were almost impenetrably thick. Some of us were posted round it, while others began to beat. On coming on the spoor we found it was a panther, and, after fruitless endeavours to discover him, were obliged to give up the attempt.

"Struck camp at 4 P.M. Marched up a very steep ghaut and arrived at Rosa about sunset. Took possession of a gentleman's bungalow, who, luckily for us, happened not to be at home.

" 1st March.

"Started at sunrise to see the Caves of Ellora. Inspected three or four of the best, and then, having had enough, returned to breakfast. Struck camp at 4 P.M. and rode into Dowlutabad. Put up in a temple.

" 2d March.

"Rode into Aurungabad to breakfast, where we remained till the 8th, and pitched our tent under a thick grove of mango-trees.

" 9th March.

"Rode into Kinolo. Country wild and jungly—tolerably well stocked with game of the small kind. Found the tent pitched under a small grove of mangoes. A thunderstorm came on and we took shelter in a temple. Very hot.

" 10th March.

"Started at sunrise. Much cooler, cloudy sky. Rode three hours into the station—a tolerably pleasant encampment by the side of a stream. Found the jungle fairly stocked with peacock, hares, quail, and partridge, and made a good bag.

" 11th March.

"Off at six. Arrived at Adjunta by 9 A.M. Breakfasted in a caravanserai, which was so beastly and so Persian-like that I almost fancied myself in fever again. About twelve the tent arrived, and we had it pitched outside the walls of the town, under the best tree we could find, which was bad enough, affording us little or no shade, and consequently making the tent very hot. Sent out my two shikarris to look for sport, with orders to meet us next day at the caves.

" 12th March.

" Started early. Rode one and a half hours to the cave—the road down by the Ghauts being almost perpendicular. The shikarris arrived, but said they had seen nothing but one elk.

" 13th March.

" Went out at sunrise with Tom to a jungle about two miles off. On arriving there, a pig got up, to which I immediately gave chase. On riding through the dry bed of a river after him, all of a sudden I came on the fresh trail of a tiger, and shortly after on the skeleton of a horse. I immediately made my way to a rock, and getting my rifle, the coolies, of whom we had about thirty, formed in a body and began to beat, putting out nothing but a few peacock. We afterwards went to another jungle, where we saw a few pea-fowl and killed nothing. Sent the shikarris about six miles off to see what they could find there.

" 14th and 15th March.

" Spent in pursuit of game.

" 16th March.

" Returned to Aurungabad.

" 18th March.

" Off at dawn. Reached the station at 7.30 A.M. At dinner inspected the performance of a native rope-dancer. In the night three hyenas came to the water to drink, near my bed. I fired at them, but, the moon being clouded, missed.

"*20th March.*

"At Aurungabad and its neighbourhood, making almost daily sporting expeditions, till

"*13th April.*

"Arrived at Chickapore by 9 A.M. Started again at 4 P.M. Rode down a very steep ghaut in the province of Berar.

"*14th April.*

"We started at dawn. Arrived at Peepre by eight, where we found our party, consisting of Dr. Orr, Hughes, and Suter. The only sport they had had was the day before, when they had killed two cheetahs. The shikarris having brought in the report of a tiger, we started — Suter and I on the young tusker, the doctor on his own elephant, and Billy on Hughes's. The scene of action was the bed of a river partially dry, with patches of thick jungle on the banks. After beating up and down for some time, the doctor suddenly stopped by a thick bush and fired. We asked what it was, and he said, ' It is a tiger, and he is dead '; and so it turned out. The ball had entered above his eye and killed him without a kick. We then set off to look for a tigress and her cubs, which were reported to be higher up the river, but after a long search we gave up. A spotted deer was the next thing that fell to the doctor's lucky rifle.

"On our way home we overtook the camel which was carrying the tiger's body to our camp, when one of the most ridiculous scenes I ever saw took place. The camel as he walked along turned his head, now to one side, now to the other, to inspect his strange burden, and seemed far from satisfied with what he saw. At length he mustered up courage to smell the body, which he had no sooner done than his panic was complete. He kicked violently, broke from the man, and set off at a pace to which fox-hunting was a joke. Soon the pack began to turn, and all that was visible of the royal beast was his tail and hind-legs swinging about in the air; and the camel, getting doubly frightened by the fore-claws and head of the brute dangling against his own hind-quarter, redoubled his exertions to rid himself of his load, which he soon managed to do. Notwithstanding, he ran for about five miles farther without pulling up.

"*15th April.*

"Marched into Chitaum. I came in with a large herd of nilgai. After a tolerably long stalk, I got a very fair shot and wounded a large bull. After I fired he fell, and I thought I was sure of him, but before I could get my carbine he managed to get up and escaped. While we were at dinner a large herd of pigs passed close to the table. Orr and Suter got on their horses and started after them with their spears. I went to a place where corn was stacked to sit up for pigs, but did not get a shot. At 3 P.M. went out to beat some heavy jungle—saw some spotted deer, pigs, etc. Bag: one pig, one rock-pigeon, five partridges, one hare.

"*17th April.*

"Marched eight miles into Aleghaum. About five minutes after we arrived, word came in of a cheetah. Went out without breakfast and had a long troublesome beat through thick willow jungle before he came to light. When he did, he behaved in such a cowardly manner that he showed us little sport. Bag: one cheetah, two pigs.

" 18th April.

"Went out in the morning. Had a long chase after a large ape, and having brought him to bay, shot him. At breakfast news came that a tiger had killed one of the hackeries near the jungle. We went out, but did not find him.

" 20th April.

" Marched into Chikelgaum. Just at sunrise we came across a herd of nilgai. Orr and Billy went after them. A few minutes after, a young cow, having missed the herd, charged right through us, knocked down my ghora - walas and shikarri, coming right against my horse, and at length, getting clear of us, set off to join the rest.

" 21st April.

" Started at sunrise. Beat for half an hour, when two shots from Orr and a cry ' He is dead ' concluded our sport. The animal was a tolerable-sized tigress. The ball went in at the ribs and, I fancy, lodged in the heart. Hearing of another tiger at a place called Lunee, after some discussion the elephants were despatched and we followed on our horses. Reached the spot after two hours and a half, beat about two hours, and at length gave it up and commenced returning, when Orr (always in luck) pushed his hathy through a small thick bush, out of which the tigress jumped, receiving at the same time a ball in the side. She then came across the plain with her tail up and roaring a little, and would certainly have settled an unfortunate coolie who was right before her, had not a volley from Hughes and Suter pulled her up. She then raised herself up on her hind-legs and commenced growling and making faces at us, when I sent a ball

in through her eye.   Reached camp at sunset.   Bag :
two tigers.

" *23d April.*

" Off at sunrise with hathies, etc., to beat.   Orr
broke the leg of a spotted deer, had a run after him,
and at length pulled him down in the jungle.   I killed
another buck.   Beat the jungle for some time, when a
shot from Orr did for another tigress.   Bag : one
tigress, five spotted deer.

" *28th April.*

" Marched four hours and a half into Maun.   After
breakfast, started for the jungle there.   Bucklawar
Sing said there were three tigers.   The scene of
action was the course of a river, with light jungle on
the banks.   After beating up for about ten minutes,
we saw the tiger sneaking up our side of the river.
The tusker was immediately put about, and we gave
chase.   We soon came within seventy yards and gave
him a volley, but without effect.   He then cantered
on, sometimes turning round and showing his teeth
and lashing his tail, and at length came to, behind
a small bush, at which we immediately went.   When
we got about a hundred yards from him, he came at us,
roaring magnificently.   Suter fired and hit him, but he
came on.   When within about ten paces of us, our
huge elephant rushed at him, knocking him down.
However, he managed to get out behind him, and
charged one of the shikarries who was walking after
us.   He cut like lightning, the tiger close upon him.
Our elephant was hopping about at such a pace that
we could not fire, and were every minute expecting
to see the poor man killed, when the tiger fell dead
into a bush.

" Before we had well time to look at him, we perceived some scouts in a tree waving to us, so we set
off, and getting across the river into the island, we
soon put up a brace of tigers.   They crossed the river
—we after them.   They then separated, and we soon
came up with one, which Orr shot dead in a bush, and
then led after the other.

" After following him some time I marked him
into a bush, which we surrounded.   When about ten
yards off, he sprang out at us.   We fired, but as the
elephant chose to charge, he not only knocked us out
of our aim, but into the bottom of the howdah.   Orr
then followed him into another bush.   Out he came at
him, when to his disgust he found that all his guns
were discharged.   The beast then stood up on his
hunkers, and began to claw at the elephant, when the
mahout hitting him a clip in the face with his auchush,
he retreated into a thicket.   By that time we had
come up, having loaded our guns, and despatched him
with a volley.   Hughes and Billy killed a bear, and
wounded another tiger, which was afterwards found
dead, and brought in.   Bag : four tigers, one bear."

With this satisfactory record of a day's sport, the
extracts from the diary may close.   Mere notes of the
daily bag—and little more—form the remainder until
the 8th June 1851, when the entry under that date
stands thus :—" I left for Aurungabad "—there, as we
know, to join Tom and Mr. Wood.

He was afterwards left alone by them on different
occasions, and Tom during one of these absences having had two attacks of hæmorrhage of the lungs, it was
decided that for the benefit of his health he should
embark on a voyage to Australia.   With that object,

accompanied by Mr. Wood, he left Bombay on the 18th December 1851. By the time they reached Java the invalid had become much worse, and he died at Batavia at the close of January 1852.

Mr. Wood then continued his journey to Australia by himself, but, shortly after arriving there, he too died from the effects of an accident.

So of the three who, full of hope and anticipation, started from Borris in 1849, only one survived to return.

Man is immortal till his work is done,

and Arthur's life-work was still in the future.

Left alone in India, with none but the friends he had made for himself, and with only thirty shillings in his pocket, it became absolutely necessary for him to earn his living. Tom's sudden illness had evidently incapacitated him from making any arrangement for his brother to whom he was deeply attached, and, by some unfortunate mischance, the remittances due from the property not reaching him, Arthur was forced to search for immediate employment. Meanwhile, his newly-made friends generously came forward to assist him, but he could not bear to trespass on their kindness beyond what was actually necessary, and for that reason, and to eke out their timely loans as much as possible, he often restricted himself to one meal a day. At length he was given the employment of carrier of despatches between one part of the district near Aurungabad and another—a responsible post, necessitating long weary rides at full speed, and all for a very low, well-nigh nominal salary.

After a time he accepted a subordinate berth in the Survey Department of the Poonah District, under the East India Company, at £400 per annum. In this situation which he filled for about a year, when he was recalled to Ireland, he gave such satisfaction to his superiors that they offered to keep it open for him—promising a rise in it if he would return to India.

Then it was when, still the youngest son, depending solely on his earnings, and one might think disqualified from advancement in almost any career, that he made the following resolution :—To attain in public life the same distinction as his father, both as Irish landlord and as member of Parliament.

One of the last things he did before leaving India was to buy a silver filigree card-case which he set apart " for his wife." This was his first gift to the cousin whom he afterwards married, and is now her most valued possession.

On his return home in 1853 he was appointed under-agent to the property, and discharged his onerous duties with the vigilance and conscientiousness that he carried into everything he undertook. But none, even among those who knew him best at that time, could discern how the varied trials he had surmounted, and the experiences he had passed through, were preparing and maturing the large-minded politician and the large-hearted country gentleman.

CHAPTER XII

IN 1854, by the death of his brother Charles, Arthur, or, as he must now be called, Mr. Kavanagh, succeeded to the family estates. He was then twenty-three years of age, and the cares and responsibilities inseparable from his new position were aggravated by the serious financial difficulties that confronted him. These had arisen partly from mismanagement during the long minority of his brother Tom, but chiefly from the distress caused throughout Ireland by the failure of the potato crop and consequent famine of 1848, the effects of which lasted for many years—if even now they can be said to have ceased.

In these circumstances, when he first took possession of the property, he felt that to bring it into order again was well-nigh beyond his power. Nevertheless he set himself loyally to the task, and worked early and late to fulfil it—in this, as in all things, making his duty to God and man his first aim. And this went on without intermission till the land legislation of 1870 and 1882 so revolutionised the relations between landlord and tenant, and introduced such uncertainty as to what further changes might be projected, that it became hopeless for even good landlords to persevere in improving their property.

In 1855 he married his cousin, Frances Mary, only surviving daughter of the Rev. Joseph Forde Leathley, Rector of Termonfeckin, County Louth, by his wife Frances, daughter of Sir Daniel Toler and Lady Harriet Osborne, and by her had seven children, four sons and three daughters.

The ceremony was a very quiet one, performed at ɩ Mountjoy Square, Dublin, the residence of his aunt —my mother—Lady Louisa Le Poer Trench. Few were present at it, and of those few all but three have now passed within the veil.

Shortly after his marriage he set on foot various schemes for the improvement of the picturesque village of Borris, which lies under the demesne wall—improvements which have made it one of the prettiest villages in Ireland. According as the long leases fell in— and the existence of such old leases explains what the landlord, powerless in the matter, often gets the blame of, viz. the ruinous condition of buildings in otherwise prosperous towns—he replaced at a merely nominal rent the tumble-down thatched cottages by others, roomy, well-slated, and comfortable. He himself drew the plans, and received the medal of the Royal Dublin Society for the best cottage at the lowest cost.

By Mrs. Kavanagh's thought and care these new houses were soon adorned with creeping plants, to which the little town owes the impression it makes of a neat English village. But its outside ornamentation was not her only care. Years before her marriage her mother - in - law, Lady Harriet, had brought from Corfù specimens of old Greek lace which, modified by her taste and skill to suit the fashion, she taught the village women to copy. Every single pattern was traced by her own hand and given out every week to the workers—poor women in their cottages—who were thus enabled to add to the weekly family earnings.

All this was afterwards taken up by Mrs. Kavanagh, and by her unwearied superintendence brought to such perfection that "Borris lace" soon became well known for its beautiful designs and delicate workmanship, not surpassed in its own style by any of the "cottage industries" of Ireland.

Not content, however, with the partial rebuilding of Borris, Mr. Kavanagh aided most materially in giving it the advantages of railway communication. In 1858 a branch line was opened from Bagnalstown to Borris by the enterprise of an English gentleman, Mr. Mott, in conjunction with some others, and to him Mr. Kavanagh made a gift of fourteen miles of land for the purpose. Unfortunately the necessary capital for continuing to work it was not forthcoming. Mr. Mott broke, and the railway had to be closed. And closed it remained for a year, till, seeing the many advantages the neighbourhood would derive from it, especially if the original project for its extension to New Ross in connection with the Wicklow and Wexford line could be carried out, he assumed the whole management of it, and at a loss of £5000 worked it himself, until it was finally taken up by the Great Southern and Western Railway Company.

But Borris was not the only village he undertook to reconstruct. Another on his County Kilkenny property owes even more to him—Ballyragget (the "Town of the Raggets"). The name to English ears may sound uncouth, but to many a lover of scenery it will pleasantly recall the broad Nore gliding silently through the rich pasture-land, the avenues of magnificent lime and beech trees, the ilex grove suggesting the beauty of an old Italian villa, and, towering over all, the well-preserved ruins of the gray feudal castle—its former strength attested by its ivy-covered turrets and walls.

It dates from the sixteenth century, when it was built—like every other stronghold in the county, according to tradition—by Margaret, a Geraldine married to a Butler. This heroine, the " Mairgread Geroit " of popular story, lived oftener at Ballyragget than at any other place of strength in Kilkenny, and after her it was for a time, it is said, the home of her granddaughter, Anne Boleyn, in her yet untroubled girlhood.

Elected in 1857 one of the guardians of the New Ross Poorhouse, Mr. Kavanagh entered on the duties with his usual energy, and, till the close of his connection with the Board, fulfilled them with judgment and perseverance. And they entailed a weekly drive of thirty Irish miles, there and back, on an outside car, in all weathers; but the work so interested him that he rarely allowed anything to prevent his attendance.

He found much to do. Great negligence in its administration demanded searching inquiries, and a general reform, which he directed all his efforts to carry out. In November 1861 the following entry in his diary describes the state of things — " Found a very bad way of business going on. No stock ever taken. Nothing ever checked. No wonder the rates are high."

The graphic account sent me by one of his largest tenants, Mr. Sweetman, J.P., shows that his services were not wholly unappreciated by the other members of the Board :—

"One evening riding home with Mr. Kavanagh, after a day's hunting, I said to him, 'Now, Mr. Kavanagh, I hope you will take what I am about to say in the spirit I intend.'

"'Oh,' said he, 'say what you like.'

"'Well, then, I think you do yourself and others great injustice in hiding your bright intellect under a bushel.'

"He replied, 'You think more of me in that way than any other person.'

"'Well,' said I, 'if you will take your proper place in public affairs, I will be much disappointed if you do not make a name for yourself. The annual election of chairmen to boards of guardians will take place in a few days. Will you allow me to propose you as Chairman to the New Ross Board ?'

"He replied, 'They would not elect me.'

"'Well, leave that to me. I will not subject you to a defeat, but, if you are elected, you will act ?'

"'Very well. Do as you like.'

"After some opposition he was elected, and I now unhesitatingly say, a better president of a public board could not be. He was most painstaking and just, and in his decisions in any case that came before him his religion or politics could not be discovered."

In proof of this I make another extract from a note sent me by Mr. Sweetman. The perfect liberality it evinces is especially remarkable in a country unhappily the scene of so much religious animosity :—

"For several years it was looked upon by the

Roman Catholic guardians as a great scandal that the Sacrifice of the Mass and other parts of Roman Catholic religious worship should be performed in the dining-hall, with the débris of breakfast and other meals piled up in its corners. For years efforts were made to alter this, but without success, and at length I got a resolution passed, asking the then Poor Law Commissioners to set apart a portion of the house for Roman Catholic religious worship. After a long correspondence, they consented, and it was then decided by the Board to build a small chapel. At that time there were from three hundred to four hundred Catholics in the house, and but five or six Protestants. After the usual red-tape delays, an inspector having been sent down to report, etc., tenders were advertised for, but, when put in, they proved so high (I believe from £300 to £400) that the expense was warmly opposed by a large section of the guardians.

"After it had been considered at several different meetings, the matter came on at length for final discussion, when Mr. Kavanagh, who took an active part in it, said—

"'Oh, never mind the expense! If we build anything, let us build something we need not be ashamed of.'

"This observation carried the day. The chapel was built, being the first of its kind in Ireland, and, when finished, Mr. Kavanagh came up to see it and was greatly pleased.

"I must say that all applications made by the chaplain, Mr. Kavanagh was always anxious to have attended to, and his action in this matter was much and favourably spoken of."

In 1862 the idea occurred to him of utilising for the benefit of his tenantry and the neighbourhood generally the water-power of the mountain brook which rushes through the demesne into the Barrow. This he did by erecting a saw-mill, to which after a time he added turning-lathes, and accepted extensive contracts for bobbins from cotton factories in England, supplying much of the material from his own woods.

A sketch of his ordinary life at home will be of interest in these days when so much is said (not always in the fairest spirit) about Irish landlords and their duties.

Up and out by six o'clock in summer mornings and by daylight in winter, he would either exercise his little pack of harriers (which he always hunted himself) or ride over the demesne to inspect the works in progress.

With all that pertained to the management of an estate, whether farming or forestry, his acquaintance was practical and minute. In the question of the re-planting of Ireland he took great interest, but other and more urgent calls on his attention prevented his developing any scheme for carrying it out. He was indeed in closer touch with the wants of the country than the majority of landlords, and this was of signal service to him both in dealing with the tenantry and in promoting their interests in Parliament.

From his early morning rides alone with his dog he would return in time for family prayers, conducted by himself, and, breakfast over, he would repair to the courtyard behind the house and take his seat on a stone bench surrounding the old oak-tree that stands almost in the centre. There, like a chieftain in the midst of his vassals, he would sit patiently listening to all who came from far and near, with their tales of perplexity or grievance, to seek counsel or redress. All were received, men and women alike, with the same unfailing sympathy, and many a curious piece of family history or story of impending feud could that old tree reveal! But it could also tell of the invariably just decision, given with the cheery sympathetic smile and words that robbed even an adverse "ruling" of all sting. Nor was it only in matters of dispute that he was consulted by them, or his mediation sought. Many a happy marriage between "likely" parties was planned and made up by him under the shadow of the old oak-tree.

That his intervention in their private concerns was, in those days at least, valued by his tenants, is shown by the name it procured him among them of the "Father Confessor," and was still further proved by the fact that many of them, on their death-beds, left their daughters to him as his "wards," knowing that their trust in him would be justified by his solicitude for their welfare and settlement in life.

When this patriarchal court under the old oak-tree broke up, he would again ride off alone across country to visit outlying farms on the estate, and inspect the improvements, almost in every case of his own making. Greeted on all sides by marks of affection and respect as he passed the men working in the fields, his cheery "God bless the work, boys!" would be responded to by "God bless your honour!"

Till 1880—when for a time the family broke up from Borris—it was his Christmas custom to have several animals slaughtered and distributed among his

workmen and the very poor people in the neighbourhood. Most accurate lists were made of the recipients,
and a just distribution ensured by his personal superintendence of the cutting up of the meat. Blankets,
suits of clothes, and flannel petticoats, were also among
the seasonable gifts : and as many of the poor people
for whom they were destined lived far away—some
in the mountains and some in parts of the estate
difficult of access—he used to have as many parcels
as possible tied to his saddle, and from the old
oak-tree he would joyfully ride off to bestow them,
never so happy as when giving pleasure to the poor
—"sending portions to them for whom nothing was
prepared."

That old oak-tree was a great rallying-point at
Borris, particularly on Sundays, when after the pleasant luncheon, lingered over as it could not be on
week-days, he would whistle to the little fox-terrier
that went everywhere with him and adjourn to its
shade. Then, mounted on his old brown mare " Miss
Nolan" (frequently with a favourite cousin seated
behind him), and accompanied by the house-party on
foot, he would make the round of the place—past the
saw-mill and along the brook to where, under the
shadow of the stone-pines, and wooded hill-sides, it
rushes down to the Barrow ; across Bunahown Bridge,
and on, on, past the wood lawn or through the old
deer-park, back to the old oak-tree.

He was the life of the party — full of fun, and
relishing with keen appreciation the humorous side of
everything. None who knew him only in later years
could realise what he was before disappointment first,
and failing health afterwards, had robbed him of the
bright spirits of early manhood, though never of the

charm of manner and sympathy that won all who came within their influence.

And as evening closed in, the hour came for service in the beautiful little chapel, approached from the house through a long passage leading into the gallery, used as the family pew, where, Sunday after Sunday, seated in his special corner, he would show by his reverential participation in the service that, with him, religion was no empty form.[1]

The spirit in which he undertook all his work is marked by an entry in his diary on the last day of his twenty-ninth year :—

"This is my last of the twenties; to-morrow (*D. V.*) the thirties begin. What a ten years to review! When I began them, a homeless wanderer in India; what mercies I have had showered upon me! Have I tried to use and not abuse them? Have I cared for the people committed to my charge? Have I tried to make myself useful, and duly to fill the position in which I have been placed? Hard questions to answer. I have tried: but have I looked to God to help me, to give me patience, to encourage me when I have been weary and disgusted, to make me thankful for what I had, and not longing for things I had not?"

In the same year, 1861, when on his return from a winter's cruise in the Ionian Islands he was welcomed back with hearty demonstrations of joy by the tenantry —bonfires, illuminations, and crowds assembled to cheer him—this touching comment appears in his diary :—

"*13th July.*

"Poor people! they must like me; but how I

---

[1] Appendix A.

have deserved that they should do so I cannot think.
God grant me grace to cherish their affection and to
guard it as a precious blessing—one I can never prize
enough, or guard too jealously."

Such were his deep humility, his simple piety, his
sense of duty.[1]

[1] Appendix B.

O God for as much as without thee we are not able to please thee mercifully grant
that Thy holy Spirit may in all things direct & rule our hearts through Jesus Christ
our Lord

Almighty God unto whom all hearts are open all desires known & from whom
no secrets are hid cleanse the thoughts of our hearts by the inspiration of thy thy holy
Spirit that we may perfectly love thee & Worthily magnify thy holy Name through
Jesus Christ our Lord

Thy will be done

My God My Father while I stray
Far from my home on life's rough way,
Oh teach me from my heart to say
     Thy will be done

Though dark my path & sad my lot
Let me be still & murmur not
But breathe the prayer divinely taught
     Thy will be done

Renew my will from day to day,
Blend it with thine & take away
All that now makes it hard to say
     Thy will be done

If thou shouldst call me to resign
What most I prize, it ne'er was mine,
I only yield thee what is Thine
     Thy will be done

And when on Earth I breathe no more
The prayer oft mixed with tears before
I'll sing upon a happier shore
     Thy will be done

Psalm of life"

Tell me not in mournful numbers
Life is but an empty dream
For the Soul is dead that slumbers
And things are not what they seem

Life is real, Life is earnest
And the Grave is not its goal
Dust thou art to dust returnest
Was not spoken of the Soul

Not enjoyment, & not sorrow
Is our destined end or way
But to act, that each tomorrow
Find us farther than today

Art is long & Time is fleeting
And our hearts though stout & brave
Still like muffled drums are beating
Funeral marches to the grave

In the world's broad field of Battle
In the bivouac of life
Be not like dumb driven cattle
Be a hero in the strife

Trust no future how'er pleasant
Let the dead past bury its dead
Act act in the living Present
Heart within, & God o'er head

Lives of great men all remind us
We can make our lives Sublime
And departing, leave behind us
Footprints on the sands of Time

Footprints that perhaps another
Sailing o'er life's solemn main
A forlorn and shipwrecked brother
Seeing shall take heart again

Let us then be up & doing
With a heart for any fate
Still achieving still pursuing
Learn to labour & to wait

CHAPTER XIII

Sanum hominem qui et bene valet et suæ spontis est oportet varium habere vitæ genus : modo ruri esse, modo in urbe, sæpiusque in agro ; navigare, venari.   CELS. *De Medicina*, I. i.

A soundly-constituted man, who enjoys good health and independent means, should vary his mode of life : sometimes frequenting the country, sometimes the town, and oftener the open fields. He should yacht and hunt.

SUCH was the Roman patrician's advice, even after eighteen centuries still valid, insomuch that no memoir of a "good landlord" can be complete without its chapter on sport. This is pre-eminently the case in Ireland. Even through Mr. Kavanagh's graver pursuits it will, I think, be seen that he had his full share of the national characteristic, though, unlike many others of his class, he never allowed his pleasures to interfere with his duties.

With his love of sport, he had a strong love of all animal life. Horses, dogs, monkeys, parrots, all knew his interest and felt his power, for over them he had a wonderful influence, which in their several ways they each acknowledged, as I think can be traced in the records of his travels.

"There are few things that I enjoy more," he writes in *The Cruise of the Eva*, "than, unseen, to watch the movements and habits of wild animals—to see them as they are among themselves, pursuing their various devices in unconscious security. I have often lost a shot by thus indulging my fancy, and in no single instance did I ever regret it.

"From hardly any sort of sporting have I derived greater pleasure than during the hot season in India, waiting through the night at a 'do' or pool of water, the only one perhaps within miles. The variety of game that one sees, each coming in his own peculiar fashion!—the timid deer listening for every sound, trying each breath of air for the taint of an adversary; the sneaking hyena; the wolf and jackal, with their slouching gait, on the *qui vive* alike for prey as for danger! The pig—first, perhaps, an old patriarch boar, with his gleaming tusks and bristly back—comes down to have a root and wallow in the mud, or perhaps a whole sounder, and the long lanky sows with their half-grown young ones, bent upon the same errand."

His fondness for nature, indeed, embraced the tangled forest and "various-vestured" hill-side as well as their wild inmates.

"Its very beauty was a drawback to the sportsman," he writes of an Albanian covert that arrested his gaze, "with the lovely Mediterranean heath eight to ten feet high covered with its snow-white bells—the rhododendron, laurustinus, arbutus, vying with each other in the richness of their blossoms; the Judas-tree with its bright scarlet twigs and leaves, the dwarf cypress, the jessamine, in some parts all bound together and interwoven with the sarsaparilla creeper."

He was once given a very young bear, not much bigger than a large muff, which in its shape it much resembled. It was chained up in the courtyard, and its little house was near enough to the old oak-tree to allow it to sit on the encircling stone bench beside its master, who would caress and play with it as no one else ventured to do, stroking it and talking to it, until it actually seemed to understand.

Never once when beside him would " Bessy " show any symptom of the untamed nature which, when she grew too big to be any longer a pet, forced him to send her to the 1st Life Guards, who in their turn and for the same reason sent her back to him, and he then most unwillingly had to transfer her to the Dublin Zoological Gardens, where she now is.

The little monkeys too, that from time to time he had as pets at Borris, were tended through their various illnesses with a care bestowed on few dumb animals. But the hero of this group was "Jack," of whose first appearance at Borris Mrs. Kavanagh sends me the following account :—

"In March 1863 Arthur returned home from the Ionian Islands, we preceding him overland. He sailed to New Ross, fifteen miles from Borris, and I drove to meet him. As the car on which he was drew near, I saw that on the driver's seat sat a very large ape, which filled me with dismay. Savage to all others, he was quite gentle with Arthur, and perfectly devoted to him. On one occasion he broke his chain and made his way to the nursery— nurses and children flying before him in terror. The ' Master ' was sent for to dislodge him, but, on arriving, it was many minutes before he could speak for laughing. There on the middle of the table sat Jack, one paw deep in the cream-jug, looking blissfully content. However, at one word from his master he quietly returned to his own quarters, to every one's relief. There he often received visits from strangers, who sometimes found to their cost that Jack was not to be treated with too great familiarity.

"One lady, heedless of warning, ventured to approach him, when Jack put out his paw and seized a string of real pearls she wore round her neck and put them into his mouth, and great was the trouble his master had to make him disgorge them."

But poor Jack met with a most tragic end. Though due to an accident, it was a real grief to Mr. Kavanagh, who was much attached to him. Jack was in the courtyard one day, at a time when the house party were going out for a day's shooting in the demesne. Among them was Signor B———, an Italian gentleman who, with his family, had settled in the country. Out into the yard stepped *il bravo cacciatore* ready for *le sport*, which he facetiously commenced by levelling his gun. It was unfortunately loaded, went off by accident, and blew off poor Jack's head, just missing one of the grooms, who, not a moment too soon, had moved out of line—I will not say out of aim—for aim there was none. It was purely an accident, which I am sure Signor B——— regretted nearly as much as we all did who were at Borris at the time.

I do not think, however, he was ever invited to join another shooting-party there!

Who that knows the garden at Borris can fail to remember the beautiful deodara that marks the resting-place of "Nelson"—dearest of dogs and gentlest of retrievers—unable to survive the parting when his master started on a lengthened cruise on which he could not be taken! Or the little fox-terriers that, one after the other, were his constant companions—I had almost said playfellows!

His horses too returned the affection, ay and the tender care he had for them. Even the half-broken ones, to which in his journeys in semi-civilised countries he was often reduced, would take him over ground where an unladen one could scarcely keep its footing. For they not only "knew their rider," but loved him, as by his voice he would encourage them, sympathising with their difficulties and sometimes even with their terrors.

"When on a shooting-expedition in Albania," writes Mrs. Kavanagh, "he was quite dependent upon the miserable horses of the country to carry him about, as no English horse could with safety have got over the hill-tracks, which were very steep and often slippery.

"At Avalona only one horse could be procured for him—and that a mere bag of bones. Starting on this wretched beast to a covert where pig were reported to be, he was accompanied by the Greek beater and the sailors, while I walked close behind him. It was most unusual for him to ride near the rest of the party, for generally he preferred to keep quite away from them, as by doing so he had a better chance of shots. We had not gone far up a very steep mountain-path, where every now and then the horse, ever responsive to his call, had to spring up rocky steps fit only for goats, when just as we reached a spot with a precipice at one side many hundred feet down to the sea, the horse attempted one of these jumps, failed, and rolled over the brink. A small cactus-bush about ten feet below checked his farther fall, and Arthur quite calmly called to the sailors to unstrap him from the saddle. This they did, being able to climb down where few others could have ventured, and hoisted him up to the path, while the poor horse rolled down and was instantaneously killed.

"This did not shake Arthur's nerve in the least, for next day he rode over a still more impracticable mountain, and distanced all his party, till at last I overtook him, though in doing so the sharp rocks had cut through the soles of my boots, and I was almost barefoot."

Commenting afterwards on this incident in *The Cruise of the Eva*, he says :—

" I daresay it would not have been a painful death, but there is something more than usually awful in it that I do not fancy—something peculiarly exciting to the nerves in looking down a dizzy abyss and then find you are going over into it."

Borris is within reach—but by no means easy reach—of some of the meets of both the Carlow and Kilkenny fox-hounds, and with them in early years he had many a good day's hunting. His riding across country was marvellous. Though often indifferently mounted, he rode as straight as any of the keen sportsmen with whom the country abounded. Indeed one of the best riders of them all told Mrs. Kavanagh "how at one more than usually large fence in the midst of a run the whole field actually pulled up in horror at seeing Arthur put his horse at it, and only breathed again when they saw him galloping away on the other side."

But as business and other cares grew upon him, hunting was given up—like almost all his other plea-sures—and in 1863 he sold off his hunters and his own little pack of harriers not without deep regret. Till the last year of his life, however, when at home, he rarely missed his daily gallop round the place.

Fishing was another very favourite pastime of his, both at home on the Barrow and also on distant excursions—such as to Lough Arrow in Sligo and the Westmeath Lakes, Derevaragh in particular, at the rising of the May-fly, and sometimes even as far as Russian Finland and the Arctic Circle.

These latter he made in the *Eva*, and from 1864 to 1866 (when he entered Parliament) he, with two friends, rented a lodge on the River Pasvig, beyond the North Cape, for salmon-fishing, a sport in which he delighted and was very successful.

The following account of one of these cruises, taken from letters sent home to Mrs. Kavanagh, shows the zest and ardour with which he entered into the pleasures and even the roughing of the voyage, and makes a fitting close to this sporting chapter :—

"Near BERGEN, *8th June* 1864.

"After three days rough weather in the Channel, on the fourth we took our departure from Cromer Head and steered for Udsire Light.

"On the 7th my watch was the morning one—flat calm. V. was on deck with me, and we were trying to fish in two hundred and eighty fathoms of water (at least that is the depth the chart gives), when we spied two white things skimming along under the bottom of the ship. I thought they were two skates or flat fish, but they turned out to be the two fins of a whale. He passed under us and, giving himself a tumble on the other side of the vessel, soon showed what he was. He gave another swim round us, coming then close alongside, so near that he could be touched with a boathook. He gradually let his tail sink down till he was in a perpendicular posture, with his head over the water. There he remained for nearly five minutes having a quiet look at us. It was flat calm, and the water quite clear, so that we could see his whole form quite distinctly—about twenty-five feet long, and big in proportion. I don't think he was a regular whale, but more of the black fish species. Certainly, if any one else had described such a scene to me, I should not have believed him.

"When the excitement of the whale was over we discovered that we were in sight of land, and, a breeze coming up, we were soon up to the island of Udsire, where we determined to come inside, and took a pilot. He brought us to the Bömmel Fiord up here. The scenery is certainly lovely, and the water even in the roughest weather (we came in when it was blowing a gale of wind) smooth as glass. I am sure you would enjoy it thoroughly, and (*D. V.*) we may have a summer out here yet. From hurrying up north we have been obliged to leave some of the finest scenery behind us, but even the straight route is beautiful.

"Lat. 62.40 N., Long. 5.15 E., 12*th June.*

" The first day's sail from Bergen we met nothing very wonderful in the way of scenery, through a labyrinth of rocky islands barren and low, the extreme wildness of which was their charm. We met lots of natives out in their jolly little prowes. In the calm they came alongside, and bartered lobsters for biscuit. Such lobsters! One party we met coming in from a bank about fourteen miles out to sea, where he had been fishing all day with only a little girl about eight years old in the boat with him. She was pulling the two stroke oars (sculls) by which these boats are steered, and splendidly she did it, pulling as long and steady a stroke as her father.   Poor little child!   We gave her a lot of sugar and some sweet biscuits, at which she was greatly pleased, and insisted on shaking hands with H. who gave them to her.

"It is now broad daylight all night, although we are still six or eight degrees south of the Arctic Circle. The second day's sail brought us into really grand scenery.   At mid-day we got into such a gorge! with mountains covered with snow towering over our heads, and a series of waterfalls from the melting snow falling perpendicularly four hundred and five hundred feet.   The end of this gorge was something too grand! —the fiord turning round the base of Hornehlen, which hung over our heads two thousand eight hundred and sixty-seven feet plumb from the water.   The fiord in the turn is not a mile wide.   We fired two or three cannon shots, and the echo was astounding.   I don't think I ever saw anything grander than that day's sail.

"*13th June.*

"We have passed Christiansand, and are now getting into the fiord which leads up to Drontheim. We had a heavy fog all last night till about two hours ago, and had ticklish work picking our way in among the network of rocks, but now it is quite bright and fine with a strong north breeze, so that she just lays her course, and we are spanking along at a great pace.

"*14th June.*

"We have had all sorts of weather since I left off writing: yesterday a heavy thrash all night, with just as much wind as we could carry our canvas to.   At 4 A.M., when I was called, I found the glass had gone down five-tenths, so I guessed we were in for something nice. It was flat calm when I got on deck and a screeching hot sun ; then came a puff from S.E., hot as any sirocco ; and then it began to pipe in style. I ordered up Caines (the skipper) and his watch, and double-reefed her fore and aft, and stowed the foresail. The water was quite smooth, as we were in the sound between Hitteren island and the mainshore, but the squall blew as hard as·I have ever experienced, laying the ship on her beam ends. This lasted till 10 A.M., when we got up to the point where the Drontheim Fiord runs inland, and down which the squall came as if through a funnel ; but as there was nothing for it but to put her at it, and finding we were making little way, we dragged her into a little bay, where we found very fair shelter, and next day (15th) got into Drontheim.

"Between calms, currents, and headwinds, it took us to the 22d to get to the west fiord between the Lofodens and the mainland, and we are now sailing along with a fair wind. The scenery all the morning has been very grand—black scraggy mountains with sharp peaks of every conceivable shape and form rising from one to three thousand feet out of the fiord, which is about a mile wide. All the valleys and crevices are filled with snow, which has hardly begun to melt at all yet. The sky is all clouded and wild-looking, which keeps up the sombre character of the scene, and the wind off the snow makes one's teeth chatter.

"Suddenly the fiord takes a turn, so that the sides of the hills are exposed to the sun, and the whole scene is changed as if by magic—hardly a vestige of snow to be seen. The hills sloping up from the water are clothed with the bright green of the young birch— first-rate-looking covert! A cascade here and there drains off the water from the snow that is melting.

On the top of the hill a settlement of wooden houses, a church, and the parson's house complete the contrast.

"We got into the Arctic Circle on the longest day of the year, and, had we had a clear horizon, would have seen the sun just dip and rise again.

"At Hammerfest by the 27th, after which a dead beat brought us to the Sorroe Sund. Here we had to go out to sea, and on coming in again two whales came about us. One came close alongside, and then, getting frightened, tried to dive under us, but missed his reckoning and came such a bump against our keel! —shaking the vessel fore and aft.

"*11th July.*

"The end of our voyage. On the evening of the 4th we got to the Kloster Fiord, into which the Pasvig river runs, at the mouth of which we are now lying, and, getting into the gig, pulled up the river to call on Mr. Klerk. His house lies about two miles upstream. He is the great man of the district—'lens man'; and, so far as we can see, nearly the only man in it—king and subject all in one. He is quite a gentleman in manner, and was eight years in the copper mines at Alten, where he learned English. He has a very snug sort of settlement, the only one within miles. He gave us every information about the fishing, which had only just begun, and we got back on board about 11 P.M.

"The mosquitoes were dreadful! As the evening was close, we found them in possession of every cabin, although we are anchored at some distance from the shore. One could only get peace either in a cloud of tobacco-smoke or under the mosquito-curtains. The accounts we heard of them were certainly not exaggerated. They are not so bad in other parts of Norway as they are here; indeed we met hardly any till we got round the North Cape, and it is a well-known fact that the farther north you go (short of course of the ice-fields), the worse they are.

"On the 6th we opened our fishing campaign, breakfasted at eight, and pulled up in the gig to Klerk's, towing the dingy after us. Picked him up and pulled on up the river, the fishing-part of which does not extend more than a mile above Klerk's house, as there you come to a fall up which the salmon cannot get. In the pools and rapids immediately below it lies our ground.

"The first day I was unlucky and killed nothing. H. killed four—one over forty lbs., all over twenty lbs. I fish out of the dingy, the others off the shore. Next day we went earlier to work. I killed four. Between us we killed twelve, and one grilse.

"I cannot call the climate pleasant, at least so far as our present experience of it goes. If the wind is southerly or the sun shining, it is a great deal hotter than the Mediterranean and the mosquitoes swarm. If a northerly wind, it is cold enough for flannel shirts and the warmest coats, even though you may be working hard, thrashing with a heavy salmon-rod, and sometimes there are two or three of these changes in a day.

"I don't think we have much prospect of shooting. Ptarmigan, white grouse, and black game exist, but in no very great number, and do not come in till after the frost and snow set in, when they come to feed upon the birch-pips.

"The scenery is nothing particular. The hills are

rocky and abrupt, but not high, and covered with birch-scrub wherever there is any soil. Inland, I believe, it is flat and swampy, with pine-forests.

"Seals are almost a myth. On the whole voyage we have only seen four or five. Our fishing-ground is in Russian Lapland, not in Norway. We cross the frontier every day we go to fish. On one bank of the river there is a Lapp settlement—a lot of huts built of logs, and a log chapel with some pictures and candles in it. The Russian Lapps are of the Greek Church. The whole population are down on the sea-coast fishing, and we have availed ourselves of their absence to appropriate one hut, where we have luncheon, and into which we retreat when the day is calm and the mosquitoes unbearable. Then we shut the door, light a fire of sticks, and keep our eyes shut till the smoke is gone.

"*17th July.*

"We have been fishing every day except two since the 11th, and up to yesterday evening have, among us three, killed seventy-seven salmon, weighing one thousand seven hundred and ten lbs., which gives an average of twenty-two lbs. for each fish. H. has as yet killed the largest—forty lbs. I come next to him with a thirty-six pounder. I have to keep the ship with my rod, as the others give all their fish to Klerk, and I try to lay in a store of dried fish for the voyage home. It is impossible to get meat here. We have been able to get only two lambs.

"Since writing the above I have had the best day's fishing I ever had, or, I suppose, ever will have. I killed eight salmon, weighing one hundred and sixty-six lbs., to my own rod.

"Our salmon bag is now made up, and, between us three, shows one hundred and twenty-three salmon, weighing two thousand six hundred and ninety-three lbs., average twenty-one lbs., which is not bad—at least for unsophisticated people who are used to Irish rivers."

[In the following year, the result of another short season of ten days was, to Mr. Kavanagh's rod alone, thirty-nine salmon,—average weight twenty lbs. three-quarters per day. Total weight eight hundred and twelve lbs.]

CHAPTER XIV

Θάλασσα κλύζει πάντα τ' ἀνθρώπων κακά.

EUR. *I. T.* 1201.

The sea-wave washes down all man's annoys.

BUT the outdoor pleasure that survived all others was the life afloat.

From 1857 he always kept a yacht, and in 1860 he built one himself—a schooner of one hundred and thirty tons—which he christened the *Eva*, after his eldest daughter, who bore that historic name.

Every year he made a short cruise, except when a more distant voyage had to be undertaken for a special reason, such as the health of his eldest boy Walter, which had caused Mrs. Kavanagh and himself the deepest anxiety, aggravated by what proved to be a needlessly alarming medical report. On this sorrow he wrote to his wife a most touching letter, which may here be given, as it preceded the winter cruise in the Mediterranean prescribed by Sir William Jenner :—

" I am very sorry, my own dearest, that you should write in so sad a mood, although I cannot wonder at it. The dreadful anxiety completely knocked me down. . . . It is very hard to place one's whole trust and confidence in God. I do not think *the trust* you should try to feel is that God will *avert* anything, but to trust implicitly that what He orders is for the best ; to feel that He is your nearest, dearest, firmest friend ; that when you are in trouble you can, as it were, put your hand out, and lean on His Almighty arm—*sure* that He is both able and willing to help you in every time of need. This alone can take the sting from earthly sorrow ; but it does take it indeed! Had I not felt it, I would not say so. So try to feel it, dearest Fuz—feel that Walter has a Father in Him who watches over him day and night, and without whose leave a hair of his head cannot fall. Trust implicitly in His mercy.

"Do not think that I am canting or that what I say is hypocrisy. Inconsistent as I am, I do feel in my heart that God hears my prayers. I have often been startled at their being so quickly answered, and sometimes so literally. I try to pray for every little thing that I want, and when sometimes the very thing came, or happened unexpectedly—trivial as it might be—I could not help thinking that it was sent as an encouragement.

"One of the greatest comforts is to feel that God sees every thought of one's heart. He knows the frailty of one's nature, and in His mercy forgives the bad, while the faintest shortest prayer breathed, or even felt in the heart, is seen also—seldom though it be. I cannot express exactly what I mean, but I often feel that it is so, and I think that the feeling increases one's trust in God. The 'dreadful anxiety' was almost unbearable until that feeling of trust began to come again, and, as I prayed, it strengthened until I believed that in His never-failing mercy He had again heard me. I still think and believe He has— for Jesus Christ's sake. 'Whatsoever thou shalt ask in

My name, I will give it,' is a promise, although centuries old, as strong and sure as the day it was made. May we all feel it!

"I don't want to preach, dearest; but I do *sometimes* feel really what I have written — too seldom indeed. Inconsistent, proud, often dissatisfied with what I deem a monotonous life, often forgetful of God, I still feel that He 'came not to call the righteous but sinners to repentance.'"

In 1860 the *Eva* was fitted out for sea, and started on December 1st for Malta. Mrs. Kavanagh and the two boys went by P. and O. steamer to join him there, after which the whole party proceeded to Corfù, and remained in those waters till July 1861.

Again, for Walter's health and also for the shooting on the Albanian coast, he sailed for Corfù in October 1862, and was joined at Naples by Mrs. Kavanagh and the children. This voyage lasted till April 1863, and is described in his *Cruise of the Eva*. In this book, written during intervals of the most prosaic county business, we can feel his "passion for the long lift of the wave," and admire the thoroughness with which he had mastered the "mystery" of navigating a vessel under every vicissitude of sea and sky. No fair-weather sailor, sharing only the enjoyments though not the hardships of the life, but taking his regular watches —four hours at night and four hours in the day—his volume teems with practical knowledge such as the mere amateur yachtsman seldom acquires—such, too, as would not be thrown away on those more kindred spirits who delight with him in what he calls the "daily work and progress of sea-going life." "To those," he adds, "who do take an interest in navigation, in that science which teaches the mariner with certainty to find his way over the trackless deep, there is no lack of employment, no day which does not bring its own amount of interest to keep the mind at work. For the speed and comfort of the voyage certainly, and the lives and safety of your crew possibly (under God, of course, for it is He who holds the mighty deep in the hollow of His hand, and it is at His word the stormy wind ariseth) depend upon your care, skill, and judgment."

Who but a born seafarer, with the rapture of a poet and the eye of a painter, could have written the following passage from *The Cruise of the Eva*, describing an impromptu race between his own schooner and a rival of larger tonnage on her way out to Malta?

"*16th November.*

"Strong westerly wind, squally, aneroid down to 29.6½. . . . . At half-past one the small schooner got under way, and a little after two we sighted our anchor, having first tied down a reef in the mainsail and got our small jib out, as it was blowing fresh. As we passed the *G——* she was just leaving her berth, but for some reason she made a tack in the roads, which gave us a start. Stood on starboard tack till we could clear Europa Point; then 'jibe oh,'—a critical job even in a large schooner when it is blowing hard; and in this case it nearly cost us a man, as he stupidly got foul of the mainsheet as it came over. I thought at least his leg was broken, but he providentially escaped with rather a sore bruise.

"The *G——* came round the Point about ten minutes after us, and, making a shorter reach, jibbed to windward of us. We then fell to work, hoisted the *Eva's* rags, set square sail and foresail; but the

G—— got her sails quicker than we did, and no doubt overhauled us.   The squalls came heavily off the Rock, convincing me, if I had a doubt, that the trysail, and not the mainsail, is the canvas for a schooner running when it is blowing heavily. . . .

"In the present instance we could not, for the honour of the *Eva,* have shortened sail, as long as our adversary carried all hers.   So we drove her into it, and merrily she went, skimming over the huge waves like a bird ; now on the top of a regular stunner, flying through the water like a racehorse ; then slower, as he passed on under her bows and her stern sank into the deep leaden-coloured valley, waiting for the next ; and he was an angry chap, but superbly beautiful in his anger—such an exquisite emerald hue as the declining rays of the old sun made through his bristling crest as he topples over, looking as if he must break upon our cross-trees !   But no !   She was not inclined to try that game.   Quick as thought, she was on his top when, in his baffled rage, with a deafening roar, he broke about her main channels.   On ! on ! again—as if exulting in her victory and showing her wild joy by her mad race through a sheet of creaming, seething foam, forward she went, surmounting the highest tops, frustrating the worst efforts ; her deck as dry as a chip, save for the frothy particles of foam that the increasing wind carried from the billows' broken tops.   The little dear !   How I wish I was on her deck now !

"By this time the *G——* had caught us up and was on our broadside, and here began the real race. For more than an hour we sailed neck and neck.   It was a pretty sight, for it was a fair sea-going race : none of your large jibs ; none of your big topsails ; but blowing a gale of wind, the whole sea covered with ragged streaky foam, the beautiful range of the Sierra Nevada in the distance, with its snow-capped ridge gilded by the rays of the now setting sun ; and these two frail-looking vessels, defying the rage of the elements, each to outvie the other. The *G——*, fair reader, is, I think, as pretty a yacht as I would wish to see ; and I would not deserve the name of even half a sailor, if I did not love and admire my own !

" It now came on to blow harder. ' Up main tack, ease down the throat and peak halyards a foot or so !' This manœuvre eased her considerably, and we began to draw ahead. We had arranged before we started that at eight o'clock we were to show a light each, to determine our relative positions then. Accordingly as eight bells went, we showed our light, and had the satisfaction of being answered by our adversary—well astern !"

In this rapid, glowing, picturesque style, none the less enjoyable for its lack of all literary pretension, we are made to accompany the *Eva* as she skims the Mediterranean to Palermo, where the recent annexation of the Two Sicilies to the kingdom of Italy is shrewdly commented on, and thence to Naples, where Mrs. Kavanagh and the children came on board. Quitting the blue bay beneath the burning mountain, they thread Scylla and Charybdis, and drop anchor in Corfiote waters, when the yachtsman on the high seas becomes the keen indefatigable sportsman in the happy hunting-grounds of Albania.

The book has long been out of print, and this might tempt me to extract from it some of the charming descriptions of coast scenery, of mountaineer life, of nature in her varied flora and fauna as they were scanned by the inner and outer eye of an observer whom nothing escaped. But I must limit myself to one or two more instances of the mingled sagacity and fun that enliven its pages:—

"The Albanian dogs are without exception as fine a race of animals as I have ever come across. Large, powerful, savage and half-wild, they are most formidable assailants; indeed, their attacks are the greatest danger one has to encounter in Albanian shooting: even in self-defence you dare not kill them, as their lives are rated far above a man's. If you shot an Albanian, you might get into a row, no doubt, but if you shot a dog you would never hear the end of it—it would be foolish to trust yourself in the same region again; and when one comes to consider how the shepherds are situated, one cannot wonder that they prize their four-footed allies so highly. Without them, the wolves, jackals, and foxes would very soon leave the shepherd a Flemish account of his flock; and yet under the guardianship of these fine dogs I don't think the denizens of the jungle often get a taste of mutton, even in the lambing-season.

"I have seen a whole flock of sheep with their young lambs left in the middle of a jungle, solely and entirely in charge of these dogs; perhaps twelve or fifteen dogs guarding two hundred sheep, and well they reward the trust reposed in them. They post themselves at various distances, forming a circle round their charge, and woe betide the stranger, be he man or beast, that dares to molest them.

"I am very fond of dogs, and these noble fellows excited my admiration immensely. I remember watching one hoary patriarch sitting at his post, the very picture of an old fellow who had pursued his dog-path through life uprightly and fearlessly. The scars and cuts about his noble head spoke of many a bloody battle, of many a hard-fought field. I am sure, if we only knew how he came by them, they would have been as clasps and medals and Victoria Crosses to the old hero. He seemed, while he sat thinking, as if his mind had wandered back to the adventures and scenes of his past life, which now, in all dog-probability, was near its close. He was disturbed from his reverie by a little lamb staggering up to him and falling against his shaggy side. He turned his great head round and looked at the little beast, licking his old chops as much as to say, 'I should like awfully to eat you, but I am in honour bound to defend you;' and to avoid temptation he got up and stalked away. Our chaps came up at the time, and as if to prove the good faith of his promise to the lamb, he went at them with all his might. Pick up a stone, of which they have a most wholesome dread, and show a fearless front, and they are not difficult to keep off.

" Sometimes, however, if you are alone, they will charge home, and then it does become serious. I have known of some severe accidents to happen, and have heard of many more. One officer who was with us was bitten twice, and so badly too that each time he was laid up for nearly three weeks. A reverend gentleman from the garrison also came in for a mauling; and ill-natured folks said that the dogs did not approve of clergymen shooting. Another son of Mars, although he was not hurt, came in for rather an unpleasant and ridiculous adventure. He was shooting in some place about Santa Quoranta, when coming, alone as he thought, upon a tempting-looking river, he determined (the day being hot) upon having a bath. Accordingly he peeled off his clothes, leaving them, naturally, on the brink with his gun, and proceeded to enjoy himself. He had not, however, been long paddling about when two savages, in the shape of two Albanian dogs, came down upon him. The water proved his protection, as they would not face it, but they took precious good care he should not come out, and posted themselves accordingly as sentinels over his clothes. How long he was kept there I do not know, nor will I vouch for the truth of the report that it was the women out of the village that rescued him, but so I have been told."

The enjoyment of the wild life in Albania was not restricted to the sportsmen. The ladies also had their share of it, as Mrs. Kavanagh pleasantly narrates :—

"We all liked the climate of Corfù, and the sport on the opposite shore of Albania afforded Arthur the keenest pleasure, in which we all participated, accompanying him as far as was possible, and when tired either resting on the ground or climbing into one of the splendid ilex trees with which that country abounds, where, out of sight and scent of the game, we often saw far more than the sportsmen. The interest of watching the wild animals when they fancied themselves unobserved was unfailing, and the return in the evening to the yacht was always pleasant. An excellent well-cooked dinner awaited us, and then music (which Arthur always passionately loved) closed the day."

A favourite amusement of his was photography, which he acquired before the days of prepared plates, and when it was far less common than it is now. On this expedition he often proved his skill in the art— now taking a group of Albanian women in their picturesque costume—now a view of some lovely land-locked bay—now of an imposing ship of the line at anchor—all of them even now unfaded, while many of them—reproduced in chromo-lithography—form the illustrations of *The Cruise of the Eva.*

The annexation of the Ionian Islands to Greece was at that time contemplated, and he, like so many others, felt it hard to acquiesce in a policy that gave that lovely group into foreign keeping. His prophetic fear was realised that, when on the 7th of March they left Corfù, they would never more see the Union Jack waving from the citadel.

The delightful holiday so much enjoyed was brought to a somewhat premature close by bad news from Ireland—the first distant rumbling of the coming storm : " Tenants were getting rusty because they could not enjoy their idea of tenant-right, which would seem to be living rent-free on their farms, and being supported as well."

And so the *Eva* set sail again for home, and 17th April saw " the old ship anchored in Irish waters." Then once more the harness was put on, and bravely worn — with never again so long a respite — till the end.

CHAPTER XV

THE time had now come for him to take his proper place before the world. His experience of local and county business qualified him for the larger sphere that Parliament offered, and opportunity only was needed.

That opportunity seemed ripe in 1862, when a vacancy occurred in the representation of the County Carlow. His wish then to come forward as a candidate was very strong, but, as Mrs. Kavanagh writes, he received no encouragement, and refrained from putting himself in nomination. "With the deepest regret," she continues, "I have to acknowledge that I used all my influence to keep him back. It seemed to me that, accustomed as he was to a life of constant exercise in the open air, the confinement of Parliament would be most injurious to him. How little one can judge for others! There is no doubt that the thirteen years he subsequently sat in the House were the happiest of his life."

Yet how well prepared he was for the great arena

of politics, and how thoroughly he understood its qualifications, may be inferred from the speech he made on the hustings in July of that year when proposing Captain Denis Pack Beresford, who had come forward in his stead to represent the county. And that he not only understood but also possessed those qualifications, his whole subsequent life, both in and out of Parliament, sufficiently proved. In this light the speech itself will not be without interest, setting forth as it does, though incidentally, his own aims and views.

Mr. Kavanagh said :—

"Mr. Chairman and Gentlemen—I beg leave to propose Denis William Pack Beresford, Esq., as a fit and proper person to represent this county in Parliament.

" He has come forward at the request of the gentry and constituency of this county, and the only sorrow I feel is that he has not found some person better fitted to introduce him to you.

" From his address, you are already aware that he comes forward on Conservative principles. You have read the address, and it is unnecessary for me to explain those principles to you.

" I believe that it is usual for candidates on coming forward on an occasion of this kind to explain their political opinions and give pledges of their political conduct, but I shall tell you what is more satisfactory than any pledges or explanations—the precedent of the past.

" He has been amongst us eight years. You have seen him fulfil all the duties of his station as a magistrate, a landlord, a grand juror, and a Poor Law guardian, and the many other duties of a country gentleman. It is from the manner in which these are performed that we can estimate a man's character and judge of his mode of action in scenes of a higher kind.

"It is an old and hackneyed saying that property has its duties as well as its rights (hear, hear). The duties of a landlord in this country are far from trivial. His responsibilities are great in many ways, and the duties he has to perform are very numerous, for the care of his tenantry and the poor, the increase of industry, and the suppression of crime, are all objects of a landlord's attention (hear). It is a fact that when the influence is extensive the responsibilities are commensurate. From him to whom much is given, much will be required.

"Captain Beresford has fulfilled all the duties of his station conscientiously—a fact which I can bear witness to, as his property lies adjacent to mine. That he has cared for the poor and forwarded his tenants' interests, not only I but many persons can bear witness to. It is to these facts that I refer to prove that with the same conscientiousness and diligence which he has shown in a private sphere he will fulfil and discharge the duties you will this day entrust him with (cheers).

"I know that it is customary to expect or ask of candidates on the hustings, political pledges. I am certain that what the present candidate pledges himself to do he will perform, but nevertheless I propose to send him free and unbound (loud cheers). I would ask him to lay aside all party feelings (prolonged cheering), to consider each measure proposed, and advocate or reject it as he thinks fit. I would leave his conduct to his own sense of right and justice (loud cheers). I would ask him to seek grace from Above to guide him as to the way that he should act, and I cannot leave him with a more friendly wish than that he may find that grace to guide him as to what he ought to do and give him strength to do it " (loud cheers).

By the spirit of this political creed his whole life was guided, both public and private. By it he may be judged.

In 1866 the opportunity at length arrived for him to carry his principles into the parliamentary arena, and they will be seen to have actuated him in debate at St. Stephen's as well as in the routine of home duties.

The sitting member for the County Wexford, Mr. George, Q.C., was appointed a judge in the Court of Queen's Bench, and the representation of the county thus vacated.was proposed to him in the way described to me by Mr. Sweetman, whose words I cannot do better than quote :—

" In the Board-room [of the New Ross Poorhouse] there happened to be present three or four leading *ex-officio* guardians who, after the transaction of business, fell to discussing among themselves who would be a suitable candidate for Mr. George's seat. I went over to them and said :—

" ' You want a candidate ? You need not go far for one.'

" And on my mentioning their chairman :

" ' Oh,' said they, ' he would not consent.'

" I replied :

" ' If an influential deputation will wait on him and explain matters, I will undertake that he will consent. But he will not otherwise come forward.'

" They at once grasped at the idea and went into

the town to consult others.   Meanwhile I privately mentioned to Mr. Kavanagh what they were about to do."

The deputation in due course waited on him and received his consent to contest the county, which he did, and was returned at the head of the poll against Mr. (now Sir John) Pope Hennessy, the numbers being 4523, and Mr. Kavanagh's majority 759.

About that time many changes of vital import for Ireland were looming on the horizon, and from the first his attitude with respect to them showed that he fully gauged their grave significance.

Some months after his election to Parliament the long unsettled state of Ireland had culminated in the Fenian rising, and so great and widespread through the country was the feeling of uneasiness, that he thought it prudent to put the old house in readiness to stand—if need were—another siege.   Night by night, as in the rebellion of '48, he would ride out alone to watch the secret drilling and manœuvres of the insurgents, and thus get some insight into their strength and probable movements.   He was no alarmist, but his intimate knowledge—gained at first hand—of the country and of the people enabled him to interpret the signs of the times; and how loyally he strove to sound the note of warning—often to deaf ears—will be seen farther on.   None knew this better than the rebels themselves, and, as his coming on horseback was naturally easy of discovery, his approach would be signalled from hill to hill long before he could reach their semi-military gatherings.

"Wonderful as was his riding in the hunting-field," says Mrs. Kavanagh, "where, as all know, excitement inspires both man and horse, it was as nothing to that on these lonely nocturnal expeditions across a country which any one accustomed only to an English sporting-county would regard with horror."

During his representation of the County Wexford, which lasted till November 1868, he was, as far as speech-making went, a silent member, but all the time he was quietly preparing himself for the future by the careful study of the procedure of the House and its then mode of conducting business.

To his exertions at this time, it may here be stated, is due the revival of the privilege formerly enjoyed by members of the House of Commons of having their yachts moored in the river under the House itself. Of this privilege he availed himself session after session, to secure on the "silent highway" a little rest and recreation, doubly welcome after the heated and stormy atmosphere of many an Irish debate.

Attendance in Parliament kept him much in London during that year, except for an occasional run down to Lymington. In August, however, he took a real holiday, and went in the *Eva* for a cruise round the coast of Holland. On his return he crossed from Antwerp, but before starting he was witness of the terrible conflagration that on the night of 14th September broke out among the shipping.

In a letter to Mrs. Kavanagh written the following day he describes the scene :—

ANTWERP, 15*th September* 1868.

" Last night we came in for a splendid fire. Three 'schuites' [that is, barges, varying in size up to 1000 tons], loaded with petroleum, lying alongside the quay, took fire about a quarter before eleven. For an hour they burned as petroleum only can burn. It was a grand sight—flames that lit up the entire town and river, and the volumes of black smoke that hung with inky density higher than our masts. It was just at the young flood that they took fire. I don't think we had swung up the river half an hour, consequently the schuites themselves with their crowd of unhappy neighbours were all hard and fast in the ground, unable to move, and it seems almost a miracle that every one of them was not destroyed. However, as the tide rose, between tug steamers, warping, pushing, and screeching, they got them off and sent them adrift up the river.

"In the meantime they had got two powerful steam fire-engines to play upon the burning mass, not knowing that thereby they were only making matters worse. Of course you know that, in the late experiments on this rock oil, it has been clearly proved that a jet of steam is required to create perfect combustion —which their stream of water at once. supplied. Before, although a fearful fire, it was lurid and heavy, mingled with dense clouds of smoke. The instant the jet of water touched it the red smoky glow was changed as if by magic into a clear, vivid blue, shooting almost to the sky.

"The wind had been blowing off the shore, rather towards us. Just then it changed, or rather a gust came from the opposite side and blew the flames on to the shore, on which there were, I suppose, over one hundred barrels more petroleum, besides bales upon bales of cotton, and half Antwerp, with eyes and mouths wide open, gazing in petrified horror.

"For a minute I certainly did think the whole business was in a blaze. Providentially, the wind changed again. If what was on the quay had ignited, I am sure hundreds of lives would have been lost.

"Meantime the schuites had burned down to the water's edge, and, the tide rising fast, we supposed that the whole thing would have been over. Every minute small globules of fire became detached and floated towards us, first one or two, then hundreds, till the whole river looked spangled—very pretty, such a curious sight!—but not pleasant in a ship built of wood.

"At last the tide got into the burning hulls, but, instead of putting them out, it floated the entire mass of blazing oil out of them, and up the tide it came like a great burning island, with flames eight to ten feet high, blazing, roaring, and hissing in the water. Then there was a general scurry; all were taken by surprise; so anchors were slipped, warps cut, and all drifted away where they could.

"A large iron steamer from Grimsby, laden with coal, was the first. Fortunate it was she was not wood, and they managed to cut her adrift before her cargo ignited, or we should have had another style of fuel added to the general blaze. She divided the fire; part came out and up the middle, the other part inside and under a landing-pier formed of wooden posts, which I need hardly tell you was in a blaze in two minutes, and demolished before much longer. However, this was providential, for that part of the oil got hung to the posts and things and was burnt out without moving, whereas, had it gone on, it would have swept the whole length of the quay, with five or six large steamers besides smaller vessels.

"The other island of flame that came outside concerned us more. Fortunately we were anchored

well over the other side of the river, so there was no
actual danger of its touching us, but, about fifty yards
on our own quarter, there was an American barque,
about 1000 tons, discharging petroleum into a schuite
alongside her, right in line of the drift.   Up it came,
and, right between their two bows, went the burning
mass.   That was a bit exciting, for, if the barque had
caught fire, I don't think we should have been burnt,
but roasted, to death.   They cut away everything, and
away went the schuite surrounded with fire.   As she
paid off round the barque's stern she caught fire, her
petroleum ignited, and there was another fearful
blaze.

"About thirty yards above the barque there was
another schuite riding at anchor, laden with apples.
Athwart her hawse came the one that had last caught
fire.   In a moment she was in flames, and, her rope-
mooring being burnt through, they all drove up
together, and we lost sight of them round the turn of
the river.   In all, five schuites and the wooden pier
were burnt—no lives lost.

"The river this morning is literally covered with
roast apples!"

[In the General Election of 1868 he was, on the 18th
November, returned along with Mr. Bruen, unopposed,
for the County Carlow.   United by ties of family and
friendship, as well as of party, the two colleagues, in
and out of Parliament, worked in perfect harmony
together—"model members for the Model County"—
until April 1880.]

CHAPTER XVI

Quid referam ingenium magnæque capacia curæ
  Pectora, custodem depositique fidem ?
Eloquiumque potens mandatis addere pondus,
  Comere res tenues, promere difficiles ?
                    BUCHANANI *Epigr.* ii. 20.

So full of purpose was his heart and head,
  So true his conscience to the trust imposed,
His words but added weight to all he said—
  The trite ennobled, the obscure disclosed.

'Ἤτοι μὲν Μενέλαος ἐπιτροχάδην ἀγόρευεν,
Παῦρα μὲν ἀλλὰ μάλα λιγέως, ἐπεὶ οὐ πολύμυθος
Οὐδ' ἀφαμαρτοεπής, ἢ καὶ γένει ὕστερος ἦεν.
                    HOM. *Il.* iii. 213.

When Atreus' son harangu'd the list'ning train,
Just was his sense, and his expression plain,
His words succinct, yet full, without a fault ;
He spoke no more than just the thing he ought.
                    POPE.

IT was not till 7th April 1869 that Mr. Kavanagh intervened in debate. Even through the several stages of the Bill for the Disestablishment and Disendowment of the Church in Ireland he had done little more than record his vote against the measure, though few were better able, from knowledge personal and historical, to place the defence of the Church on its true vantage-ground. But he preferred to leave that honourable task to others older and more experienced, if not more competent, whom he had certainly assisted in private, as he steadily supported them in public.

On the above date the Poor Law (Ireland) Amendment Bill came on for second reading — a Bill to procure for Ireland one of two things: either the old English law of settlement and removal, or the new English law of union chargeability. The second reading having been moved by Mr. M'Mahon (M.P. for New Ross), who said the Bill was identical with that which had been introduced by Mr. Sergeant Barry (Solicitor-General for Ireland), Mr. Bruen, Mr. Kavanagh's colleague in the representation of County Carlow, moved as an amendment that the Bill be read a second time that day six months. After Mr. Knight and Mr. Synan had spoken in a similar sense, Mr. Kavanagh delivered his maiden speech, the circumstances of which were so vividly described in the *Star*, Mr. John Bright's organ (then conducted by Mr. John Morley), that I shall give the *ipsissima verba* of the reporter, since known to have been Mr. Edward A. Russell, afterwards Member of Parliament, and now editor of the *Liverpool Daily Post* :—

" In the debate upon Mr. M'Mahon's Bill, which proposes to apply the principle of union chargeability with respect to the Poor-rate to Ireland, the heaviness with which the discussion hung upon the House was relieved by the peculiar interest which the maiden speech of Mr. A. M'M. Kavanagh, one of the members for Carlow County, excited. Seldom has the leader of the Government or Opposition been listened to with such breathless attention, or had riveted upon him so steadily the eyes of all his hearers, as was the case with Mr. Kavanagh. Although the hon. member for Wexford County had on a few occasions placed notices on the paper, and duly put his questions to ministers, he did not, up to the close of the 1868 session, address the House, nor had he done so in the new Parliament as Member for Carlow County until last Wednesday.

"When the House had been for some two hours listening rather lazily to the familiar and combative utterances of some three or four representatives from Ireland, one of the latter sat down, after delivering himself upon Union chargeability, and half a dozen other Irish members started to their legs, straining their necks to catch the eye of Mr. Speaker. But the right hon. gentleman in the chair, quietly nodding towards the Opposition benches said, ' Mr. Kavanagh.'

" The effect of the words was electrical, and in an instant every eye in the House was turned towards the back seat, almost under the gallery, where the hon. member for Carlow sat, cool and collected, his papers arranged before him on his hat, and his face turned towards the chair.

" Opening his views in clear, well-chosen language, the hon. gentleman dived into his subject, and, in the course of a speech of some twelve minutes' duration, exhibited an intimate knowledge of the question under discussion which, as an extensive Irish landowner, he would naturally possess, placing before the House his own experiences of the working of the Poor Law electoral system, and taking this comprehensive view of the Bill before the House : that it was only a fractional part of that larger and more important question which the Government should deal with, viz. national taxation.

" To his remarks the Speaker and the Premier [Mr. Gladstone], especially the latter, paid great atten-

tion, and as the hon. member took off the upper sheet
of his notes of reference from his hat and applied himself
to the next slip, encouraging cheers came from every
part of the House.

"At the conclusion of his speech Mr. Kavanagh
was loudly cheered.

"Judging by the matter of his first address, and
the manner in which it was received, it may reasonably
be predicted that Mr. Kavanagh, who belongs constitutionally to that type of men which wins in public
life, the men with the large heads, deep chests, and
faces full of force, will be often heard with advantage
in the House of Commons."

Though dealing with a somewhat dry subject, a
speech that won from the opposite side such generous
eulogy, to say nothing of the cordial appreciation of
the Speaker, will be read even now with interest, and
I give it as it appears in Hansard.

Mr. Kavanagh said : "That he supported the
amendment of his hon. colleague (Mr. Bruen) that this
Bill be read a second time that day six months,
because he thought the subject of Union rating was
merely a portion of that far larger question of national
taxation which was so ably brought before the House
a few weeks before by the hon. baronet the member
for South Devon (Sir Massey Lopes), and because he
held that the principle of this measure was unjust unless
it were considered in conjunction with that larger
question.

"He understood the First Lord of the Treasury
to promise on that night that, when other questions
which he regarded as of more importance had been
disposed of, the attention of Her Majesty's Ministers
should be directed to the consideration of that subject.

When that occurred he hoped that the taxation of Ireland in that respect would not be excluded from their deliberations.

"He was quite aware that this subject of national taxation was now before the House, and he would not, therefore, further refer to it than by saying that in his opinion it was a very great injustice that landed property alone was held liable for the relief of the poor.

"So far as he could gather, there were three main arguments used in support of the principle of this Bill —first, that the principle had been adopted in England, and should, therefore, be applied to Ireland; secondly, that Union rating would remove the encouragement which electoral rating held out to landlords to clear their properties of the labouring classes, lest they should be taxed for their support; and, thirdly, that the high rates on town electoral divisions, as compared with rural electoral divisions, were mainly due to the influx of the pauper population so cleared off the estates of the landlords.

"With respect to the first argument, his hon. colleague had sufficiently disposed of it; but he must be allowed to say that it was with no small surprise that he heard their argument used by hon. members opposite, whose general cry was that no analogy existed between the two countries, and who claimed legislation of the most exceptional sort for Ireland. Without going further, he need only refer on this point to the Irish Church Bill, and to speeches from hon. members opposite about the Irish land question.

"As regarded the second argument, he would say that if it were applicable in times past, it was not so now. He could not remember the year 1838, when— or in 1839, he believed—the Poor Law Act came first

into force in Ireland, nor could he from his own personal knowledge say much about the famine or those
terrible years that succeeded it. He believed, however, that it was dire necessity, and not the landlords,
that drove the people into the towns from the rural
districts. They fled from their dwellings, where
pestilence was rife, and starvation stared them in the
face, into the towns, where food was to be had. He
had both heard and read the accounts of those who
were engaged in endeavouring to alleviate the suffer-
ings of those unfortunate people, and from them he
gathered that the difficulties they experienced arose,
not so much from want of money, as from the almost
impossibility of conveying the food to the starving
multitude who were scattered about. The natural
consequence was that the survivors flocked into the
towns and workhouses, where the food was to be
obtained. But he thanked God such was not the
present state of affairs, and he firmly believed that, so
far from this argument being now applicable to Ireland, the present tendency was for landed proprietors
to build dwelling-houses and encourage labourers to
settle on their estates, for in many places the want of
labour had begun to be seriously felt.

" The third argument was the consequence of the
second, and if the one were not applicable, the other,
which was based upon it, could have no force.

" For argument's sake, however, he would admit
that an increase in the rates of a town electoral division was caused by the influx of the labouring class
to obtain employment. If such were the case, he
would ask, was not the very temptation which the
town afforded these people to come into it a very
substantial proof of its comparative prosperity ? Did

the town owe none of this prosperity to the district in which it was situated?   Was it not the centre of trade to that district, the market where the produce of the land was sold, the mart where the occupiers of the land obtained their different supplies, by which the trade of the town was created and maintained?   Did the inhabitants of the town possess no advantages over the country farmer?   Was not the value of his property in the town electoral division enhanced by its situation to an extent more than sufficient to counter-balance the high rating he complained of?

" The clearest way to come at the truth of this was to analyse the two cases.   Suppose a man living in a town electoral division to be owner of three acres of land, representing a value in the Ordnance valuation of £2 per acre, for which, on account of its vicinity to the town, and its consequently increased value, he received a rent of £3 per acre, and suppose that the poor-rates which he had to pay were at the rate of 4s. 6d. in the pound on his Ordnance valuation, amounting to £1 : 7s. on his three acres.   Then, on the other hand, suppose another man in a rural district, also the owner of three acres, of exactly the same description and quality, with an Ordnance valuation of £1 per acre, liable to a poor-rate of 1s. 2d. in the pound on that valuation, amounting to 3s. 6d. on his three acres, and that he received a rent of £1 : 10s. per acre.   Which of the two men would be in the best financial position?   The town-man would receive out of his three acres a net annual income of £7 : 13s. The rural man out of his three acres would receive a net annual income of £4 : 6 : 6.   The town-man, there-fore, after paying all these high rates—and 4s. 6d. in the pound was a very high rate—would be a richer man by £3 : 3 : 6 annually than the rural inhabitant, independent of other advantages — and they were many—which the owner of land in the vicinity of a town possessed over a country farmer.

"These were not exceptional cases got up for the occasion, but simple facts that had come under his own notice during the fifteen years that he had been connected with the Board of Guardians in the borough (New Ross) for which the hon. and learned gentleman was member.

"Was the town, then, he would ask, only to enjoy the advantages of its position, and not be responsible for the drawbacks consequent upon the mixed nature of its population, and which was by no means due to the influx of paupers from the country?

"No one who had any knowledge of these matters would attempt to deny that there were other causes of these high rates, with which the rural districts could have nothing, either directly or indirectly, to do.

"He was sorry to say that the great social evil occasioned in many town electoral divisions an important item in taxation.

"Again, if the town were a seaport, a class of people quite distinct from the rural element flocked in, and by sickness or other causes became dependent on the rates.

"Two special cases had been quoted as arguments in favour of the principle of this measure. One was the town of Dungarvan, and the other that of Gorey.

"In both cases only a small stream divided the town electoral division from the rural, and in both of them it was known that a migration of paupers did occur, and, by merely crossing these streams, became chargeable to the town divisions. But he maintained that these two cases were merely cases of boundary, and ample power existed in the hands of the Poor Law Commissioners to set those matters right.

" He had, he thought, said enough on the subject of town *versus* rural electoral divisions, and he would now, in a very few words, refer to what he regarded as a no less important consideration—namely, the relative positions of the rural districts themselves. In some electoral divisions there were mines, and why should they impose a tax on the other divisions for the support of the paupers coming from the mines ?

" He might remark that he did not think that implicit reliance could be placed in all cases upon the returns as to the rates in certain districts. The hon. member for New Ross had stated in his speech that some years ago there was a poor-rate of 3s. 6d. in the pound charged upon the rural electoral division of Bally-murphy, while at the same time on the town electoral division of New Ross the rate was only tenpence in the pound. He was not in a position, speaking from memory only, to question the correctness of the statis-tics which the hon. member had quoted, but, as the proprietor of that electoral division of Ballymurphy, of this he was certain, that he had never applied to the Board of Guardians of the New Ross Union to relieve him from that high rate by placing part of it upon New Ross or any other electoral division in the union, which was, in fact, the principle of the measure now before the House.

" Suppose an electoral division owned by an absentee landlord, who never looked after the poor upon his property, never tried to give them employ-ment or to ameliorate their condition, and that this electoral division has consequently become swamped by a large pauper population, who had come upon the rates for their support in the way of outdoor relief, and thereby increased the rating of that division to double that on another division in the same union where a resident landlord had looked after his people, built them houses, and perhaps often pinched himself to keep them in employment and keep them off the rates. Now, was it fair that the latter should be taxed for the shortcomings of the former ?

"The effect of this Act, so far as the rural divisions were concerned, would be to make proprietors careless about the condition of their poor, inasmuch as they would cease to be individually responsible for their support.

"The opinion of the Duke of Wellington had been already quoted, and it was useless to repeat it. But of this he was convinced, that a Union-rating Act would tend to increase the indiscriminate granting of outdoor relief, which was a very dangerous principle when carelessly administered.

"When the taxation ceased to be local, and was, therefore, only indirectly felt, a feeling of mistaken charity, or a desire of obtaining popularity, might oftener influence a guardian in obtaining outdoor relief for those very little poorer than some rate-payers who might be taxed for their support. It would also tend to make many guardians careless about attending. What was everybody's business was nobody's business, and it would end by putting increased expense upon the union by necessitating the appointment of paid guardians to carry on the business.

"He had great pleasure in supporting the amendment of his hon. friend."

His speech settled the fate of the Bill, for that session at any rate, and he had the gratification of receiving, hastily pencilled on a sheet of notepaper, the following testimony from the Speaker :—

"DEAR SIR—I offer you my compliments on the excellent manner and tone of your speech, which, as you will see, has made a very favourable impression on the House.—Yours sincerely, J. E. DENISON."

In the lobbies, standing about in groups or passing out on their way home, members of all parties might have been heard exchanging the remark—repeated often enough in after years—that " the speech of the night was Kavanagh's."

CHAPTER XVII

Νόμος ὁ πάντων βασιλεὺς
θνατῶν τε καὶ ἀθανάτων
ἄγει δικαιῶν τὸ βιαιότατον
ὑπερτάτᾳ χειρί.

PIND. ed. Christ. Frag. 28.

King of all things mortal and immortal, Law establishes with omnipotent hand the supreme constraint of Justice.

Ce n'est ni la force du nombre, ni la puissance populaire, ni la liberté même qui doit prévaloir : c'est une équité souveraine, analogue à la Providence divine elle-même.   VILLEMAIN.

There is no Nation of People under the Sun that doth love equal and indifferent Justice better than the Irish ; or will rest better satisfied with the Execution thereof, although it be against themselves ; so as they may have the Protection and Benefit of the Law, when upon just Cause they do desire it.   Sir JOHN DAVIS,
Attorney-General of Ireland under King James I.

MR. KAVANAGH took no part in any debate subsequent to that on the Poor Law Rating Bill until 1870, when the Right Honourable Chichester Fortescue, Chief Secretary for Ireland, introduced his Peace Preservation Act.

On this measure his views may be given at some length, as they will be read with profit in the light of events which necessitated more stringent legislation.

The scope of the Bill was merely temporary. Its provisions were to remain operative pending those remedial measures which were to put an end to the discontent of which agrarian crime was the expression. It was carried by an overwhelming majority, which included supporters of the Opposition as well as of the Government, and of course Mr. Kavanagh voted for it. But he did not do so without words of warning, which history has amply justified. He drew attention to the fact that no remedial legislation can effect the slightest diminution of crime when this proceeds from no sense of wrong on the part of a peasantry "plundered and oppressed by their landlords," but from influences arising from the perennial aspiration of so-called patriots to sever Ireland from Great Britain— plotters who by every art known to the revolutionist play upon the susceptibilities of the ignorant, the impressionable, and the impulsive, and treat all such legislation as but a grudging concession of rights unjustly withheld.

He asked how it came to pass "that, little more than a week having elapsed since a measure of an unquestionably exceptional nature had passed the second reading, guaranteeing to the Irish peasant security of tenure, they should now be engaged in devising means to ensure to the Irish landlord security of life?"

The necessity for some such measure as that before the House was, he showed, "unquestionable and urgent." In his opinion it had only been too long postponed. But in promising to give it his earnest support, he could not refrain from glancing at what appeared to him to be two of the principal causes which had brought about this present unparalleled crisis; they were—ceaseless, reckless, unprincipled agitation, and feebleness and partiality on the part of the Government in their administration of the law.

Having given as specimens of the agitation in question some extracts from incendiary speeches by Roman Catholic clergymen, he " would ask the Government if one man paid, or otherwise incited, another man to commit a murder, was the former not amenable to the law ? Was it less culpable, then, to excite to a general massacre of an entire class, than to an individual assassination ? If the law as it at present stood did not give the Government power to take notice of speeches of that nature, why did they not seek for that power which Parliament would gladly give them in this Bill ? But if the present law did give them the power, why had they not used it ? "

He asked, if the two reverend agitators had been ministers of the disestablished Church, would they be allowed with impunity to incite to such deeds ? " All he could say was, Heaven forbid they should ! He was sorry to be obliged to say it, but he believed it to be true, that such had been the policy of Her Majesty's Government since they came into office. The policy of the previous administration in some cases was very near akin to it. Fenian processions the noble Earl, now Governor-General of India (the Earl of Mayo), permitted unnoticed, or nearly so, while Orange processions were stopped by force, and their leaders thrown into prison. He was not an Orangeman. He deprecated, as strongly as any man could, such processions, or any act calculated to give offence ; but he did like even-handed justice. Without it, those whom they tried to conciliate would scorn and despise them, and in the minds of those who suffered from their injustice they raised feelings of bitter hate.

"He would conclude by asking Her Majesty's Government gravely to consider the vast importance of the present crisis, to remember that it was from no earthly Hand they held the power for weal or woe, and before more blood was spilt to do justice and fear not."[1]

Those impressive words, from the lips of one whose clear insight into both sides of the complicated Irish question enabled him to judge it fairly and in a states-man-like spirit, were not without their effect. But this, as usual, was evanescent, as the powers conferred by the Bill were to lapse within a limited period. While all such legislation has been fitful, the move-ment it seeks to arrest has been continuous, and in their journey down stream the brazen pot of agitation has invariably wrecked the earthen pot of repression. Nothing but a steady enforcement of the law for the good of Ireland, unswayed by party exigencies, can command the respect of the ill-disposed on the one hand, or the confidence of the well-disposed on the other.

Legislation in Ireland for the protection of the minority is very apt to be called "coercion" by those who feel it as a deterrent; but the plausible misnomer was so clearly exposed in a speech Mr. Kavanagh delivered on 22d March 1875, in the debate on the second reading of Sir Michael Hicks Beach's Peace Preservation (Ireland) Bill, that some extracts from it will not be inopportune.

He said, "That he should not have trespassed on the time of the House, but for some remarks of the noble Lord the member for Westmeath (Lord Robert

Montagu), who had denounced the conduct of this country towards Ireland as grossly tyrannical and coercive. That strain was taken up by hon. members opposite, and echoed and re-echoed until at last an hon. member found in the Irish famine the curse of British rule. The hon. member went further than that, and said the result of English policy had been to turn the population of Ireland into rebels. He (Mr. Kavanagh) thought the hon. member must have been carried away by his feelings, for he could hardly have remembered what the state of affairs was at that time; he could hardly have remembered that if it had not been for the charity and generosity with which England went to the aid of Ireland in that hour of need, the people would not have lived to be rebels, but would have perished with want. He had never yet heard it said that, with all their faults, the Irish people were wanting in gratitude, and the hon. member for Meath must have forgotten himself in making such a remark.

"He (Mr. Kavanagh) endorsed the old saying that 'Speech is silver, and silence is gold'; but they might be too silent, and he felt bound, on behalf of his constituents, to come forward now, and not allow the imputation to be cast upon them that they were either participators in, or sympathisers with, the crimes against which these acts were framed. His constituents regretted with him, sincerely and earnestly, the necessity which first caused the adoption of them, and which he regretted to believe made their continuance imperative.

"Against what was the law relating to murder framed? Was it not against the crime of murder? Who felt it as a restraint or coercion? Was it not those who committed murder ? . Who felt the law against the administration of unlawful oaths to be coercive ? Was it not the conspirator ? Who felt the law enacted against the writing of threatening letters as coercive ? Was it not the dastardly coward ?— and crime made dastardly cowards of all her votaries.

" Those laws were not felt as coercive or as restraints save by those who wanted to break them, and he believed that they could have no stronger proof of the necessity for their continuance than the fact that they were felt as a restraint. Those laws, to the well-disposed and peaceable inhabitants, were a protection, not a restraint ; and he thought that hon. members opposite paid their constituents a very sorry compliment by representing them as groaning under the oppression of laws that were directed against such crimes. . . .

" His constituents felt with him sorrow and regret that Her Majesty's Government, who were responsible for the peace of the country, should be obliged to come to that House to ask for such power ; but he emphatically denied that his constituents felt those laws either as a restraint or a coercion. He confidently asserted that, for the last four years, since the mad dream of Fenianism had vanished, no case either of arrest or prosecution had taken place in the County of Carlow. As far as that County was concerned, therefore, these acts were a dead letter, and he might say, on his conscience, that they might be repealed without the slightest risk, so far as regarded the County of Carlow, if the Government chose to show that mark of favour to a well-disposed and peaceable part of the country. . . .

" He wished from his heart that the same could be said for the other parts of Ireland ; he wished from his

heart that hon. members opposite, instead of exciting
the passions of the people by describing to them the
Peace Preservation Act as one of tyranny, would show
them how, if they ceased to desire to commit crime,
the law would cease to oppress, and the so-called yoke
to gall."

In May 1875 the "Sale of Intoxicating Liquors
on Sunday (Ireland) Bill" came on for second reading,
and it received his cordial support.   He had not
always approved of it, but he states the motives that
induced him to change his views on the expediency
of the measure, in a short speech so liberal in its tone
and so sound in its reasoning, that now, when the
subject of temperance is so much before the country,
it too may be read with profit.

He said, that, "in supporting the second reading
of the Bill, he felt constrained to assign some of the
reasons which had induced him to alter his opinion
on the subject.   He had hitherto resisted its passage,
on the ground that he thought it savoured of class
legislation, and that it was an interference with the
rights of the working man ; but further consideration
of the subject had led him to think more favourably
of it, and induced him to form the opinion, that when
society was unable to regulate its own actions in
accordance with the rules of propriety, then it was
time for, and the duty of, the Legislature to interfere.

" He had had brought before him overwhelming
evidence of the evils produced in Ireland by Sunday
drinking, and of the overwhelming desire of the
great body of the people that the Legislature should
deal with the matter as proposed by the Bill now
before the House.   He had heard many objections
urged, but he was not scared by the fear that the

passing of this Bill would lead to what some described as private and illicit drinking. He knew the people well, and he did not believe that, although easily led and prone to yield to temptation, their character was that of besotted drunkards. So far from it, the Irish people possessed many high and many estimable qualities, the standard of morality of the nation was considerably above the average, and, if we could provide or guard against two principal causes, Ireland might challenge the world for immunity from crime.

"The two causes to which he alluded were these— first, disloyalty and discontent, originating in past mismanagement, and now kept alive by unceasing agitation, with the crimes which had grown out of that cause. Government had been endeavouring to deal with it of late, and, he was sorry to say, had met with but qualified success, and for this reason, that legislation had been directed to lop the branch, and not to cut the root.

"The second cause of crime in Ireland was drunkenness, and in coming here that day to ask the House to pass that Bill, they were asking the House not to lop the branch, not to deal only with effect, but to lay the axe to the root, for he believed that Sunday drinking was the most prolific cause of the crimes which filled the Irish calendars, and Irish members came there with one accord to ask Parliament to mitigate that evil, and remove the temptation. . . .

"He should say no more, but give the second reading of the Bill his most cordial support."

In the same spirit he discharged his duties as Justice of the Peace, a position in which his absolute equity and determination to strengthen the hands of

Government by enforcing respect for the law were eminently conspicuous.

The Rev. George W. Rooke (precentor of St. Canice's Cathedral, Kilkenny, and for many years previously private chaplain at Borris) kindly contributes the following: " I can well remember the evening of a sad day when a murder had been committed in the village. From the circumstances of the case, it was very difficult to detect those who were guilty. But his judgment and his patience overcame every obstacle. Regardless, as usual, of personal ease, he remained at the Court-House till the small hours of the morning, examining witnesses and investigating every minute detail, till evidence pointed in the right direction. And it was mainly through his perseverance that the murderer was convicted and the ends of justice finally attained."

Again Mr. Sweetman sends me a characteristic anecdote, which he thus introduces :—

" Since his appointment as Lord Lieutenant of the County Carlow in 1880, all his recommendations for the Magistracy were based on an intimate knowledge of the requirements of the district and of the capabilities of those whom he recommended.

" As an illustration of what he considered to be the duty of a magistrate, I will mention a case that occurred at the Borris Petty Sessions many years ago. A man was summoned for trespass in pursuit of game. The offence was fully proved, but the Bench was divided in opinion as to the amount of punishment to be meted out to him—it having come to the ears of one of the magistrates present that he was a poacher although never before brought up on that charge. After some discussion,

Mr. Kavanagh said: 'Recollect, we are here to punish and not to persecute; and any amount of penalty you inflict on this man beyond that which the case now before us deserves would, in my opinion, be persecution.'

" I remember on one occasion," continues Mr. Sweetman, " telling him that I found great fault with his voting for the retention of flogging in the army and navy. His reply was: 'I am as much against flogging as you are, but, under existing circumstances, I did not like to be a party to removing that power from the authorities.'"

CHAPTER XVIII

Arthur MacMurrough Kavanagh, a landlord of landlords.

SIR CHARLES RUSSELL
(Opening Speech for the Defence before the
Parnell Commission, p. 257).

IN January 1877 his eldest son, Walter, attained his majority, but, for family reasons, its celebration was postponed till the following October.

A dinner and ball to the tenantry of the three counties — Carlow, Kilkenny, and Wexford — and festivities for the gentry heralded his assumption of man's estate. Surrounded by his family, then an unbroken circle, and welcomed by all, Walter took his position as heir to the " Chief of the Sept and Nation," and entered on its responsibilities amid the blessings of his father's dependents.

A deputation from the Carlow and Wexford tenantry waited on him with a congratulatory address, which was signed by the Rev. P. Carey, P.P. of Borris, and presented by him on their behalf.[1] In that address, couched in terms of admiration for the father and of fair augury for the son, it will be found that, with every desire to express the heartiness of their good will, they could frame no higher wish than that the son should resemble the father. Nothing

[1] Appendix C.

O

better or more hopeful for themselves could they conceive than the realisation of that wish—certainly nothing better for the object of it. And, in unison with this, at the dinner to the tenantry, Father Carey used the following words in proposing the health of Mrs. Kavanagh. Alluding to her loyal co-operation with her husband in his efforts for the good of the people, and especially to her establishment of the Borris Clothing Club, etc., he said—

" She has done all this and much more without any alloy or taint of bigotry. In this, as in many other social virtues, she resembles her beloved husband (cheers), for he is not only a good landlord—that is, he never raises the rent and never puts out a tenant who pays a fair rent (loud cheers)—but he assists and does good to his people, props the tottering tenant, helps the weak, and builds houses for the poor (renewed applause). May the prayers of the poor obtain for him blessings for time and eternity."

Two of Mr. Kavanagh's speeches at that dinner—the first to introduce his son in his new position, the second in reply to the toast of his own health—must be given in full, as conveying his hearty response to the good feeling shown by the people, as well as the strong grounds they had for their love and loyalty.

After giving the toast of Her Majesty the Queen, which was heartily honoured, he said—

" My friends, the next toast I have to propose is the health of my son Walter, on the occasion of his having attained his majority within the present year. It may seem somewhat singular that I should do so myself, and not, as would be perhaps more usual, have left it to be proposed by some one among you, as I am sure it would have been with all the earnestness and heartiness of your kindly nature ; but the occasion of our meeting here to-day is not one of ordinary occurrence.

"To my son, I need not tell you, it is an era in his life, and to you and me it is an event of scarcely less importance, considering the strong ties of mutual interest and, I hope I may say, of warm friendship which bind us all together.

"I need not now dilate upon the well-established fact of the identity of interest of landlord and tenant. I need not tell you that, even without that great tie of clanship which, if history speaks truth, has bound us and our ancestors together during centuries that are past and up to the present time, our interests are so interwoven, so identical, that neither prosperity nor adversity can touch the one and leave the other untouched. That is, I . think, a fact that must be apparent to you all : if any great calamity or pressure were to come on you it must fall on me too, and, on the other hand, if I get into embarrassed or needy circumstances, I lose the power of affording help to individual cases in the hour of adversity—I lose the power, no matter how much I may possess the will, of either protecting or advancing your interests in the many ways that only a landlord can. That is what I term our identity of interest, and it is, as bearing upon that, that I regard the occasion of our meeting here to-day, when I introduce to you my son, who will, with God's blessing, hereafter occupy my place and have charge of your interests, as an event of no mean importance to you all.

"It is, then, regarding it in that light that I have taken this part of the proceedings upon myself, and partly because I feel that on an occasion like the present there is no one more fitting to wish to another every blessing, temporal and eternal, than a father to a son.   That is my apology, boys, for perhaps spoiling the part and taking upon myself that which might have been performed in a more graceful manner and in more fitting terms by many others, and, having thus prefaced, as it were, what I have to say, I must bid you all a hearty welcome, and thank you from my heart for your kindness in coming here to-day.

" It is no empty phrase that I use, for I look upon your presence as an unmistakable token of that kindly feeling and affection which I most highly prize—not only prize as coming from yourselves now, but as the unbroken continuance of those feelings which have existed between your forefathers and my own for ages past, feelings the true warmth of which is seldom found save in Irish hearts and on Irish soil.   I am sure if those old mountains which bound our barony could speak to us their experience and recount to us the scenes that they have witnessed, they could tell of many a gathering such as this, when our ancestors met to rejoice together and congratulate each other upon some kind act of Providence.   It may have been on some signal victory as the conquerors on some hard-fought field— for, if history speaks the truth, hard knocks and broken heads were the custom of the day.   It may have been in more peaceful times, on some such occasion as we are met to celebrate to-day ; but the object matters not, the feelings that drew them together were the same, and I am thankful and proud to believe that the same feelings of kindly interest, of mutual trust and friendship, and, I think I may add, of warm affection, which existed between them, have been handed down to us, their descendants, unimpaired in warmth, unaltered by circumstances, and, more than all, untired by time.

"It is as a proof of this, one more among the many that you have shown me during the time I have been among you, that I thank you for your presence here to-day, and on my own part, need I assure you, that it is now what it always has been—a pleasure to me to meet you. I would ask, can any one doubt, can any one wonder that I should feel both pride and pleasure in finding myself surrounded by such an assembly as that which I now address? Surrounded by men, many of them old and well-tried friends, among whom I have passed the greater portion of my life in uninterrupted harmony and friendship, and by women too whose cordial greetings and kindly smiles have never been wanting to afford to me a hearty welcome when I went amongst you, the wonder would be, not that I should feel thankfulness and pleasure in this, the wonder would be if I did not, and if I did not, among all the rich blessings which God has poured upon me, prize as among the richest that which is the brightest jewel in a monarch's crown—a people's love.

"Time flies fast, and it is now some two-and-twenty years since I had the pleasure of meeting many of you on this same spot. I use the word many of you, because I cannot use the word all. During the lapse of that time, many who then met me here have passed away, and I miss from among your numbers the face of many a tried and valued friend ; but such is life ! and I must not now dwell upon the sad features of a retrospect. But, as I have said, it is now two-and-twenty years since I met many of you on this same spot. On that occasion it was my good fortune to have to introduce to you my wife. I told you then, if memory serves me right, that, as years rolled on, and as you came to know her, you would learn to love and value her for herself. I do not claim to be a prophet, but I think my words were true. You welcomed her then for my sake, but now I think she has gained for herself a place in your hearts that I could never give her.

" Now I meet you here to introduce to you my son on the occasion, as I have already told you, of his having attained to the age of manhood and responsibility, and in doing so I will use the same words which have already proved such a happy omen, and say that I hope, as years roll on, and as you come to know him really well, you will learn to love and value him for himself, and that he, on his part, remembering and realising to the full the immense responsibility attached to the position, which I trust God will spare him to fill, will try to deserve your confidence and win your love, and that, having won it, he will guard it as a prize that gold could never buy. I think I can promise that for him with every confidence. I think I can promise that, no matter what temptations the world may hold out to him, the old blood that runs in his veins will never let him forget the duty that he owes to his people, and that the real, the true meaning of the word landlord is the tenant's friend.

" I will say no more. His introduction to you now is, in a way, but a formal matter, for he is known to most of you, and has been brought up amongst you, and will, I hope, with the blessing of God, spend his life amongst you. I hope when his time comes, as please God it will, to enact the same scene which we are met to celebrate to-day, he will be able to pass on to his descendants and to yours, in unbroken love and unimpaired integrity, the trust, the confidence, and the affection of a happy, a prosperous, and a loving people."

To this speech, which was loudly applauded from point to point, and hailed with quite a storm of cheering at its close, Walter made a worthy reply, after which the toast of "Our Landlord," fittingly assigned to Mr. Sweetman, J.P., was proposed in these words—

"This toast requires no words of mine to cause it to be received by this assembly with affectionate and enthusiastic respect—Our Landlord. He has now been over us for upwards of a quarter of a century, and during that period I defy—I was going to say his enemies, but I really believe he has not one—I defy any one to show one single act of harsh treatment on his part towards any of his tenantry. On the contrary, his kindly feeling towards them, and his anxiety to promote their prosperity and to increase their comforts, are proverbial. If any of them gets into a difficulty, when brought before him, he will assist him, nurse him out of it, and, if the man deserves it, set him going again.

"It is a well-known fact that, when the cattle disease visited his estates, he in many cases replaced the stock lost by his tenants; but those feelings of kindness towards those under him are hereditary; they come to him from a long, long line of ancestors— royal ancestors—of whom history tells us of sacrifices made in olden times in protecting the interests of their followers and dependents. I have a vivid recollection at one time, in an assembly such as this, of hearing his princely father say, 'I am fond of my tenants,' so that, in point of fact, he could not be otherwise than what he is : he knows the duties devolving on him, and he performs them. But as all those acts are so well known to every individual present, it would ill become me to occupy your time, particularly in his presence, in dilating on them.   I will therefore call on you to drink to the health and long life of our good, kind, and just landlord."

With Mr. Kavanagh's reply to this speech, received as loyally as it was given heartily, I may conclude the account of the rejoicings at Borris.   His words were these—

" I am now to do what is perhaps the most difficult task of the day, and that is to try to return thanks— adequate thanks I cannot—but to express in words how deeply grateful I feel to my friend Mr. Sweetman for the kind way in which he has proposed, and to you for the warm manner in which you have drunk, my health.   I wish I could practically realise the truth that ' out of the abundance of the heart the mouth speaketh.' In my case it is nearly the direct opposite, for when I feel most I can say least, and now when I would much covet the gift of eloquence to try and express my feelings, I fail to find terms to thank you for the kindness you have done me.

" I wish, my friends, I could think I deserved the warm eulogy Mr. Sweetman has passed upon me ; but although I cannot claim all the credit he ascribes to me, I am not, believe me, less grateful to him and to you for the high compliment you have both paid me, and for the credit you have given me for endeavouring to do my duty towards you.

" It would be but a small part of the truth for me to say that I have, all through our intercourse, felt a real interest in you all.   Not only that, but I have always, as I could not help, learned to look upon and regard our welfare as identical.   But, my friends, no matter what efforts I might have made for your welfare, if they had not been seconded by you they would have availed little, so that I must not claim to myself the credit of all the success that God has been pleased to bless my efforts with.

"I believe, my friends, there are few—very few—in any country who have been blessed with the amount of confidence you have placed in me. Day by day and year by year, as I marked its growth, I felt how great would be the account required of me if I either slighted or abused it. I have been among you, as my friend Mr. Sweetman said, some twenty-five years. I do not allude to the time previous to that, for I need not say that I was born among you, but during the twenty-five years I have had the management of my property nothing but the greatest unity and good feeling has existed between me and my tenantry—the kindly greeting and cordial recognition when we met, and the hearty 'God bless and save you' when we parted. Therefore, my friends, what I have to do now is not only to thank you and Mr. Sweetman for your kindness to me in drinking my health as you have done, but for the warm affection, trust, and friendship of a lifetime which, believe me, is far more than an ample reward for whatever I have been able to do."

.   .   .   .   .   .

With the lapse of little more than two years all these relations were dissolved.

The tenants, apparently so proud of their landlord, seduced by promises—not to say threats—with every demonstration of ingratitude and vindictiveness, contributed to create the majority that returned a stranger to represent the "Model County" in Parliament.

The wound thus inflicted he felt most deeply, and it saddened his life till its close. It was for his people that he felt it, even more than for himself; but, bitter as was his disappointment, he never relaxed his efforts for their good, though the relations that had so long subsisted between them and him for the happiness of both, were severed—never to be renewed.

Never again could he place the old trust in their professions of regard—never again believe that, as he had stood by them, so they would stand by him.

An end was made of all that when the declaration of the poll at Carlow on 10th April gave the lie to their pledges, and proved that they had deserted him.

On the day of the election, before the result of the poll was declared, he had to go to the County Kilkenny to record his vote for the Conservative candidate Lord Arthur Butler. That evening there were bonfires and illuminations in Borris and the surrounding country to celebrate his own defeat. The following letter to his wife shows the spirit in which he endeavoured to face it :—

"*11th April* 1880.

"Many thanks for your dear letter.

"It would be folly to deny that the blow is a sharp one, but to me it was not unexpected, for I always felt how hollow was the ground we stood upon.

"The sharpest part of it is the belief that is forced upon me that the majority of my own men broke their promises to me. My confidence in them is gone, and a great interest and pleasure in home-life gone with it.

"That is the poisoned stab. If I could have believed them true, the actual defeat would be easy to bear, because I have nothing that I can see to be ashamed of in it. But to have to look forward to passing the rest of my life among them is almost more than I can do.

"I do not think more than forty of my fellows gave me a vote. But there is no good in brooding over it, and one must guard against the natural impulse to resent it, which God alone can help one to do.

" Do not, my darling, fret yourself for me. I look upon the defeat as God's will, and try to take it as such. That makes it lighter than I could have believed.

" The sting that rankles is the treachery and deceit of my own men—'my own familiar friends in whom I trusted'—but that feeling must be choked. I wish I could say or do something to cheer your own dear self. Believe what is the real truth : that it is all for the best. It must be, as it was ordered so." [1]

.   .   .   .

On the assembling of the new Parliament, Mr. Kavanagh's, like many another of the "old familiar faces," was missing.

The representation of Ireland was entering on new conditions.

The lowered franchise which five years later gave the illiterate peasant a vote (or rather multiplied votes for the parish priest to place at Mr. Parnell's disposal), flooded it with publicans, petty tradesmen, adventurers, and such like, who, holding their seats at the good pleasure of the "uncrowned king," made the clamour of obstruction their substitute for debate. Even when these men became Mr. Gladstone's supporters, of which of them—from their leader downwards—could he say : "A gentleman of whom I ever desire to speak with the greatest respect"?

This reference he made to Mr. Kavanagh at a

[1] Appendix D.

time when the absence of the ex-member for Carlow's experience, sagacity, and judicial fairness had become more and more felt by the House.

Irishmen of education, judgment, and experience, with but few exceptions, had now little chance of making known their views save from the platform or through the press, and among the numerous speeches and letters delivered or published from time to time, none were more opportune or statesmanlike than Mr. Kavanagh's. So anxious was he that the world should have an intelligent appreciation of the Irish Question and of the difficulties involved in its solution, that he was always ready to be interviewed by representatives of journals, American as well as British. Not only so, but he committed to writing, for circulation in official quarters, many statements of opinion and detailed memoranda, some of which—given in later chapters—will be found to have lost nothing of their value by their now, for the first time, seeing the light.

CHAPTER XIX

Ad majorem Dei gloriam.

Τοὺς θρέψαντας
. . . ναοὺς θεραπεύω.

EUR. *Ion*, 110.

I serve the Church that reared me.

IN 1869 the Church in Ireland — "the missionary Church which," according to her opponents, "had failed"! — was, by Act of Parliament, disestablished and disendowed, and the co-operation of the laity in the several dioceses had become essential to grapple with the many difficulties that confronted her, and so to re-organise her system, that, on the expiry of the life-interests of her clergy, for which alone the Act provided, her places of worship should not be closed, nor her ministrations cease throughout the land.

"Mr. Kavanagh," writes the Bishop of Cork, "was one of those who from the first recognised this necessity, and threw himself heartily into the work of re-organisation. The influence of his character, and the position which he held in his own county, made his help in every way most valuable.

"Immediately after the disestablishment of the Church he became a member of the Organisation

Committee, composed of the bishops and representative clergy and laity of each diocese, which drafted the
Constitution of the Church for consideration by a larger
body of representatives; and, as soon as the Constitution was adopted, he filled every important position
to which the suffrages of his fellow-churchmen could
elect him.

" He became member of the General Synod and of
the Diocesan Synod, and of the smaller executive
body, the Diocesan Council. Indeed, as he was connected by property with the three dioceses of Ossory,
Ferns, and Leighlin, not a few offices were laid upon
him.

" The patronage of the Church is administered by
Boards of Nominators presided over by the Bishop,
three nominators representing each parish, and three
nominators representing the diocese, to act in every
vacancy which may occur during their term of office—
a plan suggested by the late Bishop Selwyn of New
Zealand and Lichfield. Mr. Kavanagh was always
chosen to fill the post of Diocesan Nominator; and to
the discharge of the duties of the office he brought
that good sense and knowledge of character which
distinguished him in every relation of life.

" At the close of the year 1874 the Bishop of
Ossory, Ferns, and Leighlin, the late learned and
highly distinguished Dr. O'Brien, died, and from that
time all provision for the See from the funds of the
late Established Church ceased. It had been wisely
determined that, if possible, in order to secure permanence and independence, the incomes of the Bishops
should be provided from endowment. This object commended itself to Mr. Kavanagh. He took a leading
part in securing this provision for the united diocese

of Ossory, Ferns, and Leighlin, and never ceased his exertions—working quietly and systematically—until a fixed and sufficient income was provided for the future Bishops.

"In the year 1876 Mr. Kavanagh succeeded the late Viscount de Vesci as a member of the representative body of the Church of Ireland. This is the body entrusted with the management of the general financial concerns of the whole Church. He continued to attend the meetings of this body, of which he was a valued member, until his last fatal illness.

"His mind was eminently practical; and this showed itself in his work for the Church. He was ever characterised by deep religious feeling, and took a strong interest in all religious questions; but he was never influenced by that desire for change and alteration of the doctrine and discipline of the Church which marked some of the laity, and led to protracted discussions on the revision of the Book of Common Prayer. On these occasions, although he generally voted with his lay friends, it was his obvious desire to find a practical solution and to do what in his judgment would be most conducive to the interest of the Church.

"These characteristics, which a few years after placed him at the head of various organisations for the protection of the property of Irish landowners, made him ever welcome in the councils of the Church. With a large knowledge of the world he united an intimate knowledge of the people of Ireland, and of their modes of thought. Taking a practical view of every subject, his natural reserve and self-control restrained him from intervening prominently or hastily in discussion, but when he did, his wide experience, conveyed in clear and telling language, gave unusual force to the expression of his opinion, and placed him high in the esteem of those with whom he was brought in contact for deliberation or for work."

This able summary of Mr. Kavanagh's services to the Church is worthily supplemented by the following more detailed sketch furnished me by the Bishop of Ossory :—

"My acquaintance with Mr. Kavanagh began at the time that the Church in Ireland was disestablished and disendowed, and from that period until his death we were continually brought into close contact by means of the Church councils, synods, and committees in which from the first he took such a leading and prominent part.

"As the Church Act deprived the Church in Ireland of everything except the life-interests of the clergy and a sum to compensate for private endowments, it became necessary to form a financial scheme for its future maintenance, and to husband its small resources to the best advantage. In this matter his immense ability and capacity for business were of the utmost importance, and did much to enable us to pass through a most difficult crisis and to lay wise foundations for future security. He more especially concerned himself with providing an episcopal endowment fund for the diocese, and with the aid of a few like-minded with himself, he secured a permanent provision for the See of Ossory, Ferns, and Leighlin.

"More serious matters soon engaged the attention of our Church, as a new constitution had to be adopted, and fresh rules and statutes provided for its altered circumstances. Here his practical wisdom and strong common sense were most helpful, and it was soon manifest that in matters more distinctly connected with the Church's highest welfare, he was not only supremely anxious but far-seeing and judicious.

"Difficult questions arose both as to the formularies and canons of the Church, and in dealing with these Mr. Kavanagh exhibited that calm judgment, tact, and decision for which in other matters he was so distinguished. In 1870 a committee of clerics and laymen was appointed on the motion of the Marquis (afterwards Duke) of Abercorn to 'consider whether, without making any such alterations in the liturgy or formularies of our Church as would involve or imply any change in her doctrines, any measures could be suggested calculated to check the introduction and spread of novel doctrines and practices opposed to the principles of our Reformed Church, and to report to the General Synod in 1870.' Mr. Kavanagh was a leading member of that committee, and, being myself one of its secretaries, I had the fullest opportunity of knowing his opinions upon the subjects which at that time occupied the attention of the Church and afterwards came into full review when the General Synod, of which he was also a member, took up the wider subject of the revision of the Book of Common Prayer.

"The two things which struck me most in connection with his relation to this part of the Church's work, were, first of all, the pains he took to make himself master of the subjects under discussion, and, secondly, the moderate conclusions at which he generally arrived. It was striking and instructive to observe how, as a layman, in the midst of theological debates, and without attempting any elaborate arguments, he contrived, without parade, to throw light upon the subjects under discussion. Sometimes it was by asking a question which suddenly brought into due prominence a point that had been rather overlooked; sometimes by reference to a fact, historic or other, which gave a new complexion to the topic under review; sometimes by the exercise of that shrewd common sense which is often worth more than the most elaborate of theories.

"It was customary on that committee for the members to write papers upon special subjects. These were printed and circulated among the members and afterwards discussed. One of the most thoughtful of these was from Mr. Kavanagh's pen, and while it was marked by a firm resistance 'to all these innovations in doctrine and worship whereby the primitive faith hath been from time to time defaced and overlaid,' it nevertheless exhibited a strong repugnance to that spirit of intolerance which would force all opinions into one narrow groove and demand absolute uniformity in matters that were unessential.

"On the general subject of revision he took up no extreme or party position. He made it his rule (I use his own words) 'to distinguish between those points which were raised by the conscientious scruples of earnest deep-thinking men and the cavils of those who, having no real convictions one way or the other, gladly seize on every excuse for schism.' There were a few points in which, relying on this distinction, he advocated either slight changes or explanations in our liturgy, and it is worth noting that, in the final issue, some of these were adopted. But with regard to most of the passages objected to in the Prayer-Book his recorded language is, 'I prefer adhering as closely as possible to the old words, which are, throughout the entire book, unsurpassed for simplicity and beauty of expression.' He laid it down as an axiom that the teaching contained in a public liturgy should be, not only in doctrine, but in expression, 'no more than the Bible warrants and no less than it authorises.' And he wisely maintained that the pushing of extreme opinions did 'as much harm by exciting men's prejudices and driving them to the very opposite extreme, as by deceiving and misleading them.'

" I mention these things in order to show that in this remarkable man the Church of Ireland had a wise and trusty counsellor in matters affecting her spiritual character, as well as an able and judicious helper in her more secular concerns. But it was in these latter he was most widely known. During the twelve years that I have been Bishop he was by far the ablest and most helpful financier in my diocese ; never absenting himself from our councils ; weighing every statement in our documents and reports ; endued with a marvellous power of explaining involved and difficult accounts and making them clear to ordinary minds ; and always speaking with a strength of honest, calm conviction that carried weight and influence in all our discussions and debates.

" Of his generosity and liberality it is unnecessary to speak. As he was foremost in our councils, so was he also foremost with his pecuniary assistance. His purse was as fully at the service of his Church as either his tongue or his pen. In more senses than one it might be said that 'his house joined hard to the synagogue.' It was a treat to witness the way in which he conducted family worship, and it left behind it the impression of reality and devotion. The private chapel annexed to his mansion was always used as the Parish Church, and the clergyman received £100 a year, in addition to his salary as incumbent, for acting as chaplain to the household. It is deserving of record that, when after the passing of the Church Act a special Sunday was appointed in order to make collections in behalf of the disendowed and disestablished Church, the largest offertory in the whole of Ireland was contributed by the congregation at Borris. It need scarcely be added that by far the larger portion of that generous contribution came from the princely liberality of the lord of the soil. When the unhappy condition of the country made a serious alteration in the means of our gentry, he was one of those who never reduced his contributions towards religious objects or relaxed his self-sacrificing endeavours for the maintenance of his Church; and we all felt and knew that in this, as well as in all his other acts, he was influenced by the highest and most sacred considerations.

"There was one office filled by Mr. Kavanagh both in the diocese of Ossory and in that of Leighlin which brought out in a special manner his deep attachment to his Church and his earnest zeal for the best interests of religion. He was one of the Diocesan Nominators in each of those two dioceses, and his duty as such, in connection with the other Diocesan and Parochial Nominators and the Bishop, was to select and appoint suitable clergymen for vacant incumbencies. In discharging this duty he not only manifested the greatest conscientiousness, but he likewise took the greatest pains to ascertain the relative claims of the clergy and their fitness for the special requirements of the various parishes. With him it was a solemn duty to be performed with careful deliberation and with earnest prayer; and it was evermore a comfort and a privilege to the Bishop to feel that he had such a wise and true-hearted assistant in such an important work.

"One always felt assured that in Mr. Kavanagh's

esteem the spiritual interests of the Church were of more vital moment than the gathering in of its assessments or the investment of its funds. He carried that deep conviction with him even into cases that concerned individual souls. I have known him to be filled with such anxious concern for the spiritual state of a friend who was troubled with doubts and difficulties about revealed religion, that he went himself through a course of careful reading upon the evidences of Christianity in order that he might help that struggling spirit out of the quagmire of unbelief, and help to place the unsteady feet securely upon the Rock of everlasting truth.

"It was not often that he spoke in public about these sacred subjects which lay nearest to his heart, but when he did, it was with an earnestness and solemnity that left their deep impression upon all who heard him. At the last diocesan synod which he attended, after making an able and exhaustive statement concerning the position and prospects of the Church, he closed with some earnest and solemn words, in which he pressed home upon all who heard him their duties and responsibilities as Churchmen and as Christians. It is to be regretted that these words were not taken down at the time ; but they were words which, coming from him, could not easily be forgotten, and now that his lips are for ever silent they will be more and more distinctly impressed.

"It was the last time that he addressed us, and his heart was full to overflowing as he spoke about the recent death of the late Provost of Trinity College, the Rev. Dr. Jellett. The words he then applied to that illustrious man may now with all truth be repeated concerning himself. They were these—

" ' His death was a great loss to his country, to his Church, and, he might add, to every one who had the advantage of his acquaintance and the privilege of calling him his friend. For himself he happily had both, and he keenly felt the great void which his death had occasioned, both as a godly and wise counsellor to Church and State, and to himself as a valued friend.' "

CHAPTER XX

WITH the return of Mr. Gladstone to power the Irish Question was thrust into unexpected prominence, and Mr. Kavanagh's exclusion from Parliament brought him no respite from public affairs.

On the 29th July 1880 a commission was appointed to inquire into the working of the Landlord and Tenant (Ireland) Act of 1870 and of the Acts amending the same, with the purpose of improving the relations between landlord and tenant, and of assisting the latter towards the purchase of his holding. This was the well-known Bessborough Commission; and one of the five who sat upon it was Mr. Kavanagh.

Its report, issued in the first days of 1881, was signed by four of the Commissioners—by two of them, however, with a reservation; while Mr. Kavanagh refused his signature to it altogether, as he believed that the remedies it proposed would produce greater evils than those they cured—a belief more than confirmed by subsequent events. He therefore drew up a separate report upon the evidence heard before the Commissioners, and this, as constituting what in discussions on the Land Act of that year was repeatedly referred to as the ablest exposition of the landlord's case that had ever been put forth, I have thought right to give unabridged in the Appendix.[1]

In 1882 the Land Act became law. It would be idle at this time of day to enter on a review of that measure, with its creation of dual ownership, now seen to be intolerable. Like so many of its predecessors, it has shrunk into a mere stepping-stone towards that more statesmanlike enactment whereby the tiller of the soil shall also become its owner.

Meanwhile its administration was soon felt to be quite out of keeping with the professions and assurances that had expedited its progress through Parliament—to be, in fact, so charged with injustice to the landlords that their leading representatives summoned an "aggregate meeting" in Dublin to try and avert the loss, in many cases the ruin, it must ere long bring upon them. At the meeting, which was held in the Rotunda on the 3d January 1882, the speeches were of exceptional ability; but one of the very weightiest was Mr. Kavanagh's, who, after showing that Mr. Gladstone's words on the 7th April and on the 22d July 1881 meant—if anything—that the Act would certainly not effect a wholesale and universal reduction of rents, proceeded to answer the question, "Have we got a dispassionate and impartial Tribunal?"

Waiving all question as to the impartiality of the Head Commissioners, he passed a severe judgment on the Sub-Commissioners—firstly, for their decisions in themselves; secondly, for their almost uniformly with-

[1] Appendix E.

holding the grounds on which these were made; and thirdly, for the insufficiency of such grounds when they ventured to give them.

"It has been announced," he said, "that the rent is to be fixed, not according to the value of the land itself, but according to the capability of the occupying tenant to get value out of it. The extravagance of such a principle is too glaring to require comment. A holding may be of the best description, the land of the richest quality, with every facility for realising its productiveness. It may be that these very facilities were conferred by the landlord's expenditure. But, according to this new theory, if it be held by a drunkard, a thriftless, idle, or slovenly tenant, who fails to work the holding to profit, the landlord is to get nothing out of it. A direct premium is held out to all kinds of extravagance, by which it would not be difficult for the tenant to arrive at the stage of not paying any rent at all.

"Take another instance, and by no means an uncommon one in all parts of the country—the holding small and poor, the family large and soft, as the saying is. How would that be when the tenant applied to have a fair rent fixed? We had a striking case of such as that before us when I was on the Bessborough Commission in Galway. A witness came forward to represent his own case and that of his neighbours, and stated, as well as I remember, that there were eighteen families living upon fourteen acres of poor land. He did not ground his complaint upon excessive rent; that, I believe, was something nominal; but he declared that if he held the land for nothing he could not live on it. Now, if we follow this newly announced principle in this case to its logical sequence, it is clear that the landlord, instead of receiving rent, should pay the tenant for occupying the land.

"We have another announcement not a whit less extraordinary in the case of a tenant holding a rich bit of meadow-land in the vicinity, I think, of the city of Limerick. It was proved that the land had been of considerable value from its inherent fertility. But this went for nothing on the landlord's behalf, because it was proved for the tenant that by taking excellent crops off it, year by year, without putting a single bit of manure on it, he had entirely exhausted it. The rent was reduced to the value, I believe, to which the tenant had by his wanton and, I might almost say, his malicious conduct deteriorated it."

His whole speech made a marked impression at the time, but it had no appreciable effect on the administration of the Land Act. Nothing remained but to accept the position as created by law, and to try by what means the rights of property could be saved from still further infringement.

The Land League, formed in 1882, owed its first successes to its intimidation of the tenants—above all, to the vengeance it wreaked on those who paid their rents. To such a pass had its terrorism come that, like many another landlord, Mr. Kavanagh at dead of night received visits from his people, afraid of going near him in open day. Then, having paid their rent, they implored him to keep it dark, as they dreaded its becoming known to the League. Tenants even travelled to some distant post-office—fifteen or twenty miles off—and thence transmitted him their payments enclosed in a letter adjuring him to give them no receipt or acknowledgment of any kind, lest the League might get wind of the transaction. So terrorised, the

tenants came to feel that non-payers were, financially
at least, better off than those who paid, and there is no
doubt that the spread of this feeling recruited the
ranks of the League.   Then too arose on the tenants'
part the inevitable ill-will to the landlord he had
defrauded, in confirmation of the *odisse quem laeseris*
principle : you cannot wrong a man and not hate
him.

Against these demoralising forces counteracting
measures on the landlords' part were not wanting.

From the commencement of the struggle Mr.
Kavanagh had foreseen that in the not distant future
legislation would be carried out to the serious detri-
ment of the owners of property in Ireland, to meet
which he suggested the formation of a body called the
"Irish Land Committee," consisting of representatives
from each county, who were to devise means for
vindicating the rights of the landowner, not only in
Parliament and the Law Courts, but throughout
England and Scotland.   As one of its honorary
secretaries he worked with unceasing energy, and
it was chiefly through its agency that members of
Parliament and public speakers drew the information
which subsequently proved so invaluable.   Besides
this there were the Emergency Committee and the
Property Defence Association, with both of which he
was connected—the latter set on foot in the autumn
of 1880 at a meeting presided over by the Earl
of Courtown, to whose kindness I am indebted for
details as to its management.   For well-nigh twenty
years he and Mr. Kavanagh had worked together
on various committees, and during most of the later
part they were chiefly engaged in carrying out plans
for the relief of the threatened minority.   They first

met with this object on the Land Committee above mentioned, and again in December 1882, when under Sir John Whitaker Ellis (then Lord Mayor of London) the Mansion House Committee was formed to assist in the defence of property in Ireland. Of this Mr. Kavanagh was a member, and also its commissioner for supplying it with information, and for the transmission of funds to Ireland.

Carrying forward the work of the Property Defence Association and attending to the multifarious matters brought before it—some of these naturally belonging to it, others again devolving on him as one of the heads—entailed a mass of correspondence that pursued him even on his rare holidays, as shown by this extract from a letter to Lord Courtown, dated 9th October 1882, and written from the R.Y.S. *Water Lily*, Southampton :—

" Altho' when down here I am by way of being on a holyday, this letter is my forty-third since I got the post at two o'clock on Saturday, and I only left London on Wednesday night " (4th).

All this time the scheme of the Land Corporation was revolving in his head, and he was arranging its provisions concurrently with the business of the older society. That business was complicated — not the least by conflicting views and claims. There was also much financial pressure, consequent on the waning interest in the Mansion House Fund, which, after about a year of generously-afforded aid, ceased to contribute, and was finally wound up [1]—transferring its balance to the Irish Defence Union established in London.

Sundry changes in the staff of the Property

[1] Appendix F.

Defence Association, and the differences of opinion which led to them, gave both Lord Courtown and Mr. Kavanagh occasion for much thought and anxiety in addition to the responsibility their co-trusteeship involved. Conscientious personal investigation where such was practicable was, indeed, habitual with them, and guaranteed to the subscribers of the funds the fullest certainty of their upright management.

The bodies above referred to were especially useful in supplying men to serve writs in cases where the local bailiff had been intimidated from discharging the duty. A tenant owing rent was thus brought under legal process, and a sheriff's sale of his property would in due course ensue. The Land League having warned off any others from bidding at the sale, the tenant would himself be the sole bidder—bidding sixpence for a cow or a bull—and so the sheriff, in the absence of other bidders, was obliged to sell the animal for that sum. Such a sale, of course, could not satisfy the landlord's claims, and then it was that the above-mentioned associations would intervene, sending an agent of their own to bid against the tenant, and so raise the price till the rent owed, or a fair equivalent, was paid.

Blocked in their first game by this move, the League constrained the tenant to make a clean sweep of his effects, and so nothing was left to be put up but his right in his holding. The League boycotted the farm, and, as no man durst bid for it, it could not be disposed of. Here again the associations above referred to interposed, and by themselves becoming purchasers of the interest in the holding, prevented the sale from being turned into a farce.

But how to deal with the land so purchased was

the difficulty. Tenants hung back through fear. The land was in danger of lying derelict and running to waste, and to keep it so was part of the game of the League. Then Mr. Kavanagh came to the rescue, though it was not without reluctance that "he forsook the old landmarks of kindness and goodwill that had so long characterised the relations between most landlords and their tenants." But what with the inertness of the Government and the uncontrolled activity of the League, he had no alternative but— in his own words—"to replace the landlord by a Corporation which, proverbially, was without a body to be kicked or, in this case, to be shot."

In a prolonged interview he had with a correspondent of the *New York World*, who came from America to investigate the Irish difficulty from both sides, Mr. Kavanagh gave a full account of the circumstances under which he started the Land Corporation. As a powerful defensive weapon in the hands of the loyalists it could, he showed, achieve nothing but good, while it taught the Land Leaguers the salutary lesson that they could not have matters all their own way. It was also calculated to have a wholesome effect in dissipating the wild communistic visions that had been conjured up before the poorer peasantry. But there was another class to whom it did more direct and tangible good.

It was an aid to poor landlords. It intervened between them and their unscrupulous enemy, and saved them from ruin. There were, and still are, many families in Ireland, the lineal representatives of some of the oldest proprietors, reduced to the direst straits by sundry causes, such, for instance, as the famine years 1846-50, when they assisted their tenants to tide over the crisis—families who, though they surmounted that ordeal, have ever since had a struggle for subsistence. Others, from different causes not seldom beyond their control, were compelled to mortgage their small estates to an extent which left them but little margin to live upon. In the case of such estates, rents had not been raised for years. Guided by the old "live and let live" principles which have regulated the conduct of their class, such landlords afforded an easy mark to the Land League, which no doubt drew encouragement from its knowledge of their helplessness. To them the refusal to pay rent for two years, or even for one—and in some cases eight or nine years' rent was owed!—meant the foreclosure of mortgages, and therewith privation of the bare means of living in the present, and utter ruin in the future.

"To interpose between them and ruin," says Mr. Kavanagh, "was the first object I had in view, as it was of those who acted with me. In defending them we were defending the outposts of our own position, for, if they were conquered, further attack would have been facilitated and the position of the Land League considerably strengthened. This latter reason no doubt recruited our ranks with numbers not quite disinterested, and will," he added, with far too trustful anticipation, "if the combat continues and the necessity arises, enlist the wealth of the entire landed and vested interest of England in our cause.

"Only in quarters where the League had made it necessary was the Land Corporation, with its rigidly commercial working, to be substituted for the landlord, and opposition to it could take the form only of outrage. For this," said Mr. Kavanagh to his American interviewer, " we are prepared, not only by armed protection, but also from the fact that we are able and determined to recover damages for malicious injuries from the ratepayers of the districts in which they occur. This compensation is chargeable on the County Cess, a fund which is chiefly paid by the tenant-farmers, and we will therefore, by our claims against it, create in them a direct pecuniary interest in repressing outrages. This will have the good effect of rousing a reaction in favour of law and order throughout the country. It will teach the Land League that its fight with its peculiar weapons is over, that it is met on every hand and beaten. Agitation, of course, as of old, will continue in Ireland. But the untamed colt of the Land League has a bridle placed upon him by the Land Corporation."

I have stated above that the Land League was formed in 1882. The Land Corporation was registered on St. Patrick's Day, 1883. These dates are of importance, inasmuch as an attempt was made in Parliament to justify the starting of the former on the ground that it had become necessary as a defensive movement on the part of the tenantry against a combination of the landlords. The very converse is the truth. As Mr. Kavanagh reiterated to his American interviewer, the Corporation was purely defensive from the outset, and when the extermination of the landlord class was the openly avowed object of the Land League, it could hardly be called unwarranted. The names published in support of the Corporation were those of all the largest and best landlords in Ireland, with but few exceptions—men who never did a harsh deed, men whose tenants, by their own evidence before the Bessborough Commission, admitted that their estates were fairly and humanely managed. In Mr. Kavanagh's own words : "Their only complaint was that they had a feeling of insecurity, not knowing what manner of man the present landlord's successor might be, or how he might treat them. To give them this security, and on behalf of other tenants on differently-managed estates, they asked for fixity of tenure. They have got it. They asked for the right to sell their interest in their farms. They have got it. They asked for fair rents, and they have got a Court with the most arbitrary powers, formed almost exclusively of men whose leanings are towards their side, to which they can appeal if they feel themselves aggrieved. In fact, the tenant-farmers of Ireland hold their farms on exceptionally favourable terms which no other tenants in any other country in the world possess. The object of the Land Corporation is not to infringe these new rights which the law has given them, but to teach them to obey and look to the law for the enforcement of them rather than to the counsel of those who know that if peace and order were restored the hope of their gains would be gone."

The scheme alike in conception and practical working was Mr. Kavanagh's, and, had it received the countenance, not to say the support, it deserved, it would have gone far to settle the land difficulty and to spare the country those deeds of violence and vindictiveness that have darkened its history for the last eight years.

No move in the policy of the Land (or National) League escaped Mr. Kavanagh's vigilance. In 1887, after the announcement of the Plan of Campaign, he threw himself with all the weight of his experience and power into the "Anti-Plan of Campaign Association" ;

and again in 1889 he actively promoted the " Derelict Land Trust," set on foot to render assistance to tenants who took farms on estates which had become vacant from the adoption of the Plan.   These, like the other defensive associations already enumerated, owed much of the success of their working to his intervention, which only ceased when his last fatal illness made further exertion impossible.

The winter of 1882 was clouded by the heaviest sorrow he ever had to bear.   In the midst of anxious work—maturing and moulding the Land Corporation —came the mournful news that his second son Arthur, lieutenant R.N., had been invalided home from the South American station.   The news fell like a thunderbolt, for, except in a letter from his son saying he had " had an attack of bronchitis, but was better," no warning had reached him.

A young fellow of the highest attainments, loved by every one who knew him, and giving promise of a career worthy of his honoured name, he had passed far ahead of all competitors of his year in the very stringent examinations for his profession.   At the age of twenty he was already full lieutenant, and in passing for that step gained the coveted " three firsts."

But all the loving hopes centred in him were fated to be crushed !

When he returned to England in advanced consumption it was clear that the end was not far off, and in three short weeks the bright young spirit was at rest — " safe in the haven where he would be."

To his father the blow was overwhelming, not only

from his tender love for his gallant boy, but also from his natural pride in the rare abilities and high character he displayed. But the "silver lining" even to that dark cloud revealed itself, and with deep thankfulness he was able to record in a letter to the Bishop of Ossory his dear child's coming "in abject dependence and earnest faith to Him who alone can save," and the comfort to his own heart thus mercifully given. " From that hour the sting of the blow was taken from me, and what happened since was light to bear. The answer to prayer came, and the sting of death was gone."

One of his brother officers speaks of the impression he had made, of his "extreme amiability and kindness as a messmate, of his great qualities as an officer (which were in everybody's mouth), and of his manly devotion to sport—of his good common sense, his life as a Christian, and his patience under suffering," during his last voyage home.

Lord Charles Beresford, under whom he had previously served, wrote thus : " I had the greatest affection for him. He was one of the best officers in the navy, and he was a real loss to the country. There are not too many like Arthur Kavanagh."

In the private chapel attached to Borris House, Mrs. Kavanagh, " To the glory of God," and in remembrance of her sailor son, placed a stained-glass east window which, while it records the mother's sorrow, points to her "strong consolation"—her faith in her ascended Saviour.

I close this chapter with these touching verses by the Bishop of Ossory, which he has kindly allowed me to publish. They evince the deep sympathy which united him in unbroken friendship with Mr. Kavanagh, enabling him to speak the " word in season," alike in sorrow as in joy. They were sent by him to Mr. Kavanagh at this time.

" He asked life of Thee, and Thou gavest it him, even length of days for ever and ever."—Ps. xxi. 4.

> " We askèd life of Thee, O Lord,
>   Both life and length of days ;
> Thou heard'st our prayers, but answeredst them
>   In Thy mysterious ways.
>
> " Thou gav'st him life—the blessed life
>   That comes through faith in Thee ;
> And then the everlasting life
>   Of immortality.
>
> " We bless Thee 'mid our grief and tears ;
>   We bow and kiss the rod ;
> For ' through the grave and gate of death '
>   Our loved one passed to God.
>
> " The waves are passed, the storm is o'er,
>   For *him* the port is gained ;
> For *us* his blessedness assured—
>   God's mystery explained.
>
> " Lord, come Thyself and fill this blank,
>   Let Heaven the nearer be ;
> Be more to us for that dear child
>   Who has gone home to Thee."

CHAPTER XXI

He being dead, yet speaketh.

On the 9th of February 1883, addressing his Border constituents on the Irish Question, Mr. (now Sir) G. O. Trevelyan, then Chief Secretary, pointed out that the British public seemed unable to realise the fact that there are two Irelands—the Ireland of the intelligent, the well-educated, the law-abiding, and the comparatively prosperous, and the Ireland of the superstitious, the ignorant, the disloyal, and the poverty-stricken. Commenting on this remark, to the soundness of which he testifies, Mr. Kavanagh, in a paper written at the time but never given to the world, proceeds as follows :—

" This division exists in so marked a degree that it constitutes a characteristic distinguishing Ireland from any other nation, and unless this is thoroughly understood it is idle for any one to attempt to prescribe a cure for her condition. It is what I must call a sort of dual life ; no other words would describe it. We have two distinct classes constituting her population. The first or loyal class, already indicated, who would live and let live, and be only too glad to be left alone to pursue their avocations in peace, includes a far larger number from the poorer grades, such as tenant-farmers, labourers, small shopkeepers, and

tradesmen, than many would believe, and its numbers
would be larger still were it not for the dire system of
intimidation which has forced many of them, actuated
only by the self-preserving instinct, to join the other
ranks. This class is seldom or never heard. Its
members hold aloof from mobs and political meetings;
among them are not to be found the noisy elements of
the turbulent sections; indeed, they are too passive,
too quiet, and from the fact that they are so their
existence as a class is often doubted; but, for all that,
it is as certain as that their presence affords a glimmer
of hope for better times.

" I know the country well, and although many
here in England may doubt the assertion and say
that ' the tree must be known by its fruits,' the cheering
fact remains that there is a large and influential party
in Ireland (excluding the landlord class, whose interest
in the support of order, whatever their political opinions
may be, is too patent to be questioned) who are sick
unto death of this never-ceasing agitation and turmoil
which has resulted in so much crime and misery.
The agitation was aimed at the landlords, but, sorely
as they have suffered, it has come with even heavier
severity upon the poor, and has turned many among
the lower classes, who at first if they did not actually
approve at least watched its progress with interest,
into earnest well-wishers of the cause of order.

" ' You must never forget,' says Mr. Trevelyan,
' that there is an Ireland of men of all parties and
creeds and callings who, whatever else they differ
upon, unite in wishing to preserve law and order and
the right of every citizen to go about his business in
peace and safety. It is the gravest mistake,' he
adds, ' to underrate the numbers and the claim to

respect of the party of order in Ireland.' This is the cheering side of the picture, and though emerging only now from the shade, it shows a light ahead. As confidence begins to be restored, this party of order will, I confidently hope, take courage and cause its salutary influence to be felt. Even as I write the prospect lightens. The evidence given at the Kilmainham inquiry discloses the enormity of the plot ; but while it does, it shows that the Government have tapped the source of information, and when once the fear of giving evidence is overcome the chief safeguard of the conspirators is demolished. We see already that juries can be found again in Ireland to give an honest verdict even at the risk of their own lives. Their independence once more established, the most dangerous element in the reign of terror will have been removed, and the power of the law will again be felt.

" On the other hand, we have the dark and gloomy side still too plainly visible—the other party in this dual state, what Mr. Trevelyan calls 'the other Ireland, the smaller Ireland, as I firmly believe, of the men who foment and condone and sympathise with crime.'

" I wish I could agree with him as to its being the 'smaller Ireland.' He is undoubtedly correct, if the intelligence, education, and wealth of the party of order is to be given its proper position and counted in proportion to the responsibility which it represents. In that he has at once an overwhelming majority. But if the poll is taken by counting heads, I fear the numerical majority will be found on the side of what I designate as the 'second class,' which represents little that is estimable (even giving credit for mistaken fanaticism), and all that is cowardly, dishonest, violent, and disloyal. I might with truth prolong my list of such like qualifications until I had exhausted every evil term in the dictionary; but abuse is neither argument nor proof, and the history of the country during the last two or even three years will depict more vividly and truly than any words of mine could do the diabolical spirit which originated and supplied the motive and developing-energy to this Land League conspiracy. Started under the ominous title of 'Struggle for Freedom,' it soon assumed the direct weapons of tyranny, and did not shrink from the murder of its own employés, if suspected of wavering, to sustain its power and enforce its rule. Started plausibly to defend the rights of the poor, it soon established a reign of terror, in which none but the rich or independent durst disobey its laws. The social structure was subverted and, as Mr. Trevelyan says, 'instead of the law being a terror to evil-doers, evil-doers were a terror to the law-abiding and industrious.' He describes in his speech the state of affairs he found when he took office in Ireland. It is a plain, true statement of things as they were—not a word of exaggeration either as regards the dismally desperate conditions of the country or the danger or responsibility of the office he was called upon to fill. And, if he and Lord Spencer will allow me to say so, the admirable manner in which those onerous, distasteful, and most important duties have been discharged, has well earned for them the gratitude and esteem of every loyal subject of Her Majesty.

"This dual state, then, is the condition which must not be lost sight of in attempting to unravel the Irish tangle. Mr. Trevelyan in the same speech says: 'At this time the position, if not of Ireland, at any rate of the Irish government, is more critical than it has been at any preceding time, on account of the want of knowledge of a great many people of what Ireland really is. The cardinal division of Irish society is not, as is sometimes imagined, between Whig and Tory, between Protestant and Catholic, between the camp of the tenant and the camp of the landlord'; and then he describes what it is in the words I have already quoted. It may fairly enough be argued that Ireland is not singular in this dual condition— this division of classes; that in every country the same exists; in every country there are rich and poor, bad and good, industrious and idle, contented and discontented; in every country there are political differences of opinion more or less strongly marked. But in no country that I know of is there the same clearly defined palpable line of demarcation between the two antagonistic sections of the population that there is in Ireland, and that is what English people do not understand. It is difficult to find terms under which to designate them, but the nearest I can think of — those that most truly characterise the main principles of each—are loyal and disloyal.

" United under the former are differences in politics, creeds, and interests, Liberal and Conservative, Whig and Tory, Protestant and Roman Catholic. Some of all classes and all of many classes are drawn together by the common bond of loyalty. This is the party of order.

" Opposed to this we have the disloyal class; and it is in its particular composition and characteristics that, I believe, we may find the peculiarities which distinguish the case of Ireland from that of any other country. Composed of many sections forming, numerically speaking, I fear, the majority of her population, they are also held together by a common bond, and that is 'hatred of the British Crown and connection.' Unreasonable as this may appear to people in this country, various as may be the reasons which give rise to it, different as may be the objects which each have in view in fostering it, it is the bond of union and common platform which brings together and joins discordant spirits and men who would otherwise be rivals if not foes. Here we have ignorance and education, the atheist and the ecclesiastic, the communist and the business-man, hand in hand—truly a strange combination! Many of the poor and destitute are in it. Whether their want is occasioned by misfortune or by their own recklessness (but more especially the latter), having nothing to lose, they look for the possibility of gain by a revolution, and as their numbers are made up chiefly from the un-educated, their ignorance renders them an easy prey to the designs of agitators, whose never-ceasing story is that all their ills are the consequence of British government. Many of the farming class (and, con-sidering the special form the agitation took, this cannot be wondered at), as also shopkeepers and artisans, though not in actual want, are in it—men who can read and are, comparatively speaking, educated. In all of their minds the hope is no doubt more or less present that revolution might possibly bring some amelioration of their material circumstances. But, whatever effect that may have in influencing their conduct, one of the most active causes of their dis-affection is this : that the only source of information they possess, the only means within their reach of forming any judgment on public affairs, is through the medium of the Irish (so-called) 'National' Press.

"Since education has become more general in the south and west of Ireland disaffection has increased tenfold. Why? Because, first, as a general rule, in former times every National school teacher in these districts was a rebel, and took real care to instil his own principles into the minds of his pupils. Second, because, when the people learned to read, they could get nothing else to read than papers dyed with treason. No matter what party was in power, every action of the Government was misrepresented, whether wise or foolish, just or unjust, harsh or benevolent. It mattered little; it was twisted or exaggerated to support the popular views, as they were termed.

"The simple fact is this, that the lower classes of the population of Ireland have been reared and brought up in treason. These may be new and startling facts to the majority of Englishmen, but they are facts which no impartial man who knows the country can controvert.

"It is, then, to the adhesion and complicity of these lower classes that this disloyalty owes the numerical majority of its supporters, and it is this only which gives it any semblance of the right to call itself a national movement. But, although their co-operation gives it material power and influence, if we are to be just, in the circumstances I have described, we can hardly hold the people responsible for the line they have taken or blame them for their disloyalty. In order to put the saddle upon the right horse, we must look further into the ranks of this strange confederation, which although now an exaggerated growth is not of very new creation, and in them we find men on whose behalf no exculpatory plea of ignorance can be urged. We have both education and talent in the form of the political agitator—a character which has figured more or less in every page of Irish history since she has been endowed with the rights of constitutional government.   To the action of these political agitators, both in the present and in the past, we owe much of the existing trouble.   Charitably we might try to palliate their excesses by the excuse of patriotism, but, unfortunately, history would not bear us out.   Instances are not wanting of political agitators, wild in their patriotism, reckless in their eloquence, who when they had climbed up by the steep ladder of popular passion and excitement to office, the object of their aim, returned to their right mind and became powerful and consistent supporters of law and order. The history of many a brilliant ornament of the Irish bar would afford examples of such conversions, and, I may add, that some of those who now sit upon and adorn the Irish bench have helped to sow the wind from which they now reap the whirlwind.   Their case in the past is not very different from the actors on the political stage in the present.   Ambition, love of notoriety, self-interest in some form or other, whether the desire to pull down their superiors or to exalt and advance themselves, are the actuating motives which influence these so-called popular leaders—seldom, if ever, real patriotism.

"In no country in the world is the path so easy or the promise of reward so bright to the political agitator as in Ireland.   Under no government is the pursuit of that trade attended with so little risk.   Look at France : how did she deal with Prince Napoleon for issuing a manifesto which is simple child's play when compared to the very mildest of the incendiary harangues delivered by these agitators within the last three years?   How would America have dealt with such an agitation and reign of tyranny and terror as we have suffered from?   Freedom of speech and liberty of the subject are the valued and inherent rights of free-born men, and under no form of government are they so thoroughly possessed and enjoyed as under the British Constitution.   But when these rights are prostituted by reckless adventurers to forward their own ambition, the position is reversed, and the right of liberty is turned into an instrument of tyranny.   Thus, we see, in this confederation we have two influences acting and reacting upon each other.   We have chronic discontent, disloyalty, and ignorance among the lower classes, rendering them a fertile soil for the agitator's operations.   His trade or calling is constitutionally licensed and he not unnaturally makes use of this liberty to foment the discontent, to increase the disloyalty, and to darken the ignorance which are the origin of his existence and the mainstay of his power. Under circumstances such as these there is small room for hope to those who long for peace ; no apparent elements of the dissolution of the disturbing causes ; rather the principles of perpetual motion.

" There are other classes still to be noticed in this confederation of disorder.   I have put them in apposition as atheist and ecclesiastic, as communist and business-man.

" The atheist or infidel and communist are classes which I can afford to dismiss with brief notice, although from among them are probably drawn the tools with which the others work—the executive who carry out the orders of the inner circle.   I hope they are few, but we have no very trustworthy means by which to estimate or test their numbers.   Both communism and infidelity are importations from America, therefore we may not be very far wrong in assuming that most of those young men who have returned from there are tainted with them.[1]   How far they may have spread their doctrines among the farmers' sons when meeting them at public-houses and other places it is not easy to say ; but, no doubt, amongst such they have found willing listeners and minds already prepared to receive their teaching.   The farmers, as a rule—save in so far as this land-agitation has imbued them with a part of this principle—are not communists.   They have something to lose, and they fail to see the charm of dividing what they have among the labourers and their poorer neighbours.   With their sons it is different.   All they have is prospective ; and although we might have hoped that interest in their families' concerns and welfare would have tended to keep them steady, it is, I fear, too well known that the insidious teachings of their American friends and an unprincipled press have proved too much for them, and that from their numbers the ranks of the party of disorder are to a considerable extent recruited.   It is not a cheerful outlook for the future that the rising generation are more deeply disaffected than their forefathers ; but it would be folly to ignore it.   If the labourers had joined this move-ment, heart and soul, it could hardly, considering their wretched condition, have caused much surprise.   But I think they have been shrewd enough to see that they had not much to hope for from it.   They perceived that in the division of the spoil the programme was to leave them out and let them remain labourers still.

[1] After the bursting of the Fenian bubble large numbers of the farmers' sons fled to America.   A considerable portion of these have since returned, many of them attracted by the rising which the Irish-Americans confidently expected would take place.   A. M. K.

"The business-man is also a class over which I need not waste much time, and I do not believe that the party of disorder can number many among its ranks. With those who have joined it their motive has been, I must believe, one more of self-preservation —the fear of losing customers—than approval of, or sympathy with, its objects. If the report is true, we have in the last Mallow election an example of the kind of pressure brought to bear upon merchants and traders. There the account states that the farmers of the surrounding district assembled *en masse* before the election in obedience to the command of the Land League and told the shopkeepers who had votes that, unless the Nationalist candidate was returned, they would withdraw their custom and deal elsewhere. Yielding to temporary pressure such as that in a district like Mallow may be excused; but it is difficult to understand how educated men, brought up to business habits, which are certainly supposed to be based upon the principles of common honesty, can join hands with communists.

"Yet, much as this is to be wondered at, it is far more astonishing to see the ecclesiastic making common cause with the infidel. We have Archbishop Croke and Bishop Nulty disseminating as mischievous doctrines and using as violent and reckless language as ever distinguished the speech of a Land League agitator; and, when members of the hierarchy of the Roman Catholic Church not only countenance but promote this disloyal confederation, we need not be surprised if every one of its meetings is attended by priests, and if the curates, almost to a man, are enlisted in its ranks. To my mind it is simply incomprehensible how men occupying their position, with history to warn them, can fail to see the danger—to put it on no higher grounds—of prostituting the influences of religion to serve political ends.   It is a subject of no small congratulation that Cardinal M'Cabe has been spared and remains still to exercise the salutary power which his position and his well-known high character deservedly give him on the side of order.   His loss at this crisis would have been immense, for there has never been a time when the interests of his Church in Ireland more urgently required the guidance of his wisdom and steady hand than now.

" Those members of the hierarchy who have given their countenance to this movement and their encouragement to the lower orders of their clergy to co-operate with it have incurred a very grave responsibility.   It is the consequence, and only the natural consequence, of their own acts that their influence and power for good over their flocks have been weakened. Not one of them can deny the fact that the power of the priesthood over the lower classes of the Irish people has received a rude shock, and, in my opinion, the rulers of that Church have the unscrupulous license of their curates to thank for it.   Since even the comparative spread of education among those classes, their minds have received some enlightenment.   They perceived that there might possibly be some other test for right and wrong than the dictum of their curate. But when that curate announced from the stage of a public meeting, or, worse, from the altar of their accustomed and sacred place of worship, wild theories in excuse or palliation of murder and other crimes, their old landmarks in religion were blurred, if not obliterated; questions began to exercise their consciences, and their faith in the infallibility of their Church's teaching was shaken. With the ignorant and superstitious, when the old belief is once weakened, the passage to infidelity is not a long one. From outside, while this change was going on—while this doubt was deepening in their minds—they were, I may say, flooded with Trans-atlantic literature, ventilating every kind of socialistic and atheistic principles, which were further indus-triously disseminated and propounded by emissaries from America, and by the young men who had returned from there after the Fenian scare was over.

" This process has been gradual. To its actual commencement it is not easy to fix a date; but the first clearly-marked evidence of the weakening of the influence and power of the Roman Catholic clergy over their flocks was apparent during the Fenian agitation of 1866-68. Then, I believe, many of them, cer-tainly the majority of the hierarchy and parish priests, endeavoured to stay the plague, but even by that time they found that much of their power of restraint was gone, and since then its decline has been more marked and rapid.

" There are many, I believe, who think that this change is a subject more for congratulation than regret, and in this they are not without both ominous facts and weighty arguments to support them. As a broad rule, the general power of the Roman Catholic Church has been exercised more against than in favour of the British connection. As a strict rule, the influence of the lower clergy—I mean the curates—has with rare exceptions been exercised to create and foment discon-tent, to set class against class, to embitter differences, and to import religious fanaticism and violence into civil questions. But, notwithstanding all these con-siderations (and I fully appreciate their weight), I cannot agree with those who hold this view. I do not believe that the diminution of the influence of religion can be regarded as an improvement in the moral or social condition of any nation. What they mean is clearly this, that the diminution of the influence of the priesthood as now exercised would be a subject to be grateful for—not the diminution of the influence of religion. That I grant them. But I cannot see how, circumstanced as Ireland now is, it is possible to separate them. The question I ask myself is this, If religious feeling, and with it the influence of the Roman Catholic clergy (the one hangs on the other), were to disappear, what is to succeed it ? The people will not rise higher. They must sink lower. Socialism and infidelity would simply become general. I am not attempting to defend or justify the use—I might more fitly call it the abuse—which the clergy have made of their power. I am merely giving the reasons and considerations which influence me in forming the opinion I hold.

" It may seem that I am rather needlessly dragging the subject of religion into the controversy to complicate and embitter its discussion—that I have no warrant save some far-fetched notion for classing in this confederation the ecclesiastic and the atheist.

" I can but point to France to prove my position. What happened in the course of her Revolution ? When Socialism became triumphant was not Religion swept away ? And were not abstract definitions, coined to suit the popular whim, substituted for the saving truths of Christianity ? What did the ' Commune ' do ? Were not priests and bishops, venerable and venerated by their flocks when in their right mind, shot down in Paris in the open day ? Infidelity and Communism are inseparable !

" To pass over unnoticed the bearing of this movement upon religious interests would be to ignore the ominous warnings of the past. The clergy of the Roman Catholic Church—those, I mean, who have fallen in with this movement—may say that they join the others only on political grounds, in their desire for ' Home Rule,' and that it is unjust to mix them up with Communism and disloyalty.

" For argument's sake allow that it is so. What does ' Home Rule' mean? The answer required is not the specific interpretation given to the term by this or that theorist. But what does it mean as understood by the masses of the Irish people? On that point we are left in no doubt. It is too clearly and distinctly defined by their exponents to leave any room for question. It is separation from England. That achieved, what does any sane man expect would follow ? Probably the immediate consequence would be civil war, as the North would hardly submit tamely to be governed by the other provinces. If the North was overcome or only succeeded in maintaining its own independence, what would be the condition of the rest ? Can any one doubt it ? Anarchy and Communism ! A repetition of the French scenes, with no one can tell what ultimate result.

" There is no use in trying to shirk the real issue of the question. Let the clergy's excuse be such as I have suggested or not, they cannot throw off their weight of responsibility in the matter. No man who joins a movement has any right to try to shelter himself under the excuse that he did so with the impression that it had an object or meaning different from that which has been accepted and understood by the mass of those who supported it. The clergy knew perfectly well the light in which the people regarded it, and, whether they joined it from their own convictions or for the object of sustaining their popularity and of sailing with a tide they could not stem, their culpability remains the same.   By joining in it they were palpably lending their influence and the influence of their position to support the objects of the Communist, and so to bring about the inevitable consequences of his success.

"It is, then, with no desire needlessly to import the religious element into the consideration of this great question that I have dwelt upon the part the clergy of the Roman Catholic Church have taken in it; but simply from the fact that, both in the present and in the past, they have assumed so prominent a place in all political matters that to leave them out in describing the present complicated and deplorable condition of affairs in Ireland as regards these two great and antagonistic parties, or the causes which have produced it, would be to give a very imperfect and misleading representation of facts, upon the clear and true appreciation of which so much of grave importance hangs in the future.

"I have now stated as thoroughly and clearly as I am able what are, in my opinion, the component elements of this party of disorder; and the next important point which it is necessary that I should refer to is the nature of the present conspiracy, which has grown out of and been matured by it, and I think I shall have little difficulty in showing that it is in many important respects different from those which have preceded it."

CHAPTER XXII

"FROM time immemorial we have had in Ireland rebellious plots, conspiracies, and agitations of more or less gravity ; but, without underrating the importance of the crisis in 1798, or of any of the previous insurrections which resulted in an appeal to force, I think the present is the most deep-rooted and the most serious. All the prospects of success in the former attempts at revolution which assumed any magnitude or importance depended more or less on the promise and hope of foreign aid, which invariably failed at the critical moment. This, however, has been laid on different lines, and based upon the spirit of disaffection, the individual action, and the dogged and determined combination of the people. American sympathy and support was, no doubt, calculated upon, or Mr. Parnell and his friends would not have taken the trouble to cross the Atlantic to make the speeches we have heard so much about. But it was not upon aid from America as a State that these conspirators reckoned. It was upon the support, whether in the form of men or money, which it was thought the turbulent elements of her population would be likely to supply. In this they were not far wrong. Money they have got, and, had matters come to blows, I believe they would have got men too.

" This agitation practically dates back to the Fenian Conspiracy in 1866-68 ; for although that appeared to die out after the futile attempt at a rising in the spring of 1868, the organisation has been efficiently, although secretly, kept up, and the spirit which fed it has been always present.

" The originators, therefore, of the Land League Confederation had a matured organisation upon which to begin work.   They had a soil already well prepared in which to sow their seed.   At the commencement, and until that seed had time to take root over the whole country, they advisedly kept their ulterior objects dark, and restricted the movement to a political agitation within the bounds of the law.

" The passing of the Ballot Act aided them materially, and the result of the General Election which immediately succeeded that, although it brought about a change of ministry and put the Conservatives into power, gave them a parliamentary party sufficient to warrant their carrying the war into the legislative chamber.   The result of their unscrupulous policy upon the action of the House of Commons—the condition of " dead lock " to which their persistent obstruction almost brought the legislative machine— gave their supporters in the country fresh heart. They, for the first time perhaps, really saw a glimmer of hope that their dreams of separation from England would be realised.   The people further saw, as regards their own immediate interests, that the preceding agitation and turmoil—the Fenian rising, the Clerkenwell explosion—had got for them the disestablishment of the Irish Church and the passing of the Land Act of 1870 ; and they, not unnaturally, thought that persistence in that line would be productive of further concessions—sops to Cerberus, I might call them.   In this belief they were encouraged by the result of the General Election of 1880, which strengthened their parliamentary party, and brought back to power the same ministry who had showed themselves so sensitive to the influences of agitation and outrage.   It is indeed hardly possible that upon a people gifted with such quick perception when their own interests are at stake as the Irish are, the Midlothian speeches should have failed to produce some effect.

"Then, again, the main principles of the agitation of 1879 were devised with more than ordinary ingenuity.   They were framed with the purpose of appealing to the cupidity of every tenant-farmer in Ireland, and this they did most successfully.   Revolution, separation from England, and other extreme objects were, as I have said before, most cleverly kept in the background.   Tenant-right—the great principle of the North — and other two Fs (fixity of tenure and fair rents) were the ostentatiously-adopted mottoes, so that for the first time we have the tenants of the North drawn into and made accomplices in a movement, the real and ulterior objects of which would, if successful, have wrought their destruction.

"There came to pass also at this time a peculiar conjunction of circumstances which more or less directly tended materially to favour this agitation.

"It will be remembered that the Land Act of 1870 gave to the tenants a considerably greater legal interest in their holdings than they possessed before— an interest which was readily available as a security

for borrowing money or getting goods on credit.
This the shopkeepers, the petty usurers or "Gombeen
men," as they are called, and the local banks did not
fail to take advantage of, and an almost unlimited
system of credit was extended to the farmers, who were
rendered perhaps more than ordinarily careless or im-
provident by the good years and large harvests of the
five or six seasons preceding 1878.

"In that year there came a change. There was a
partial failure in the crops, and the money market
began to tighten. In the early part of 1879 there was
almost a financial panic in Great Britain, brought
about by various causes. The failure of the City of
Glasgow Bank and other large concerns occurred.
The English and Dublin wholesale merchants pressed
for payment upon the Irish retail dealers, and they, in
turn, came upon their rural customers for a settlement
of their claims. Added to this, the harvest was the
worst that had been known for years—the season a
most inclement one. Mr. Parnell was reported in one
of his speeches delivered at this time in the County of
Mayo to have thanked the elements for fighting on
his side. He well knew the lever the prospect of a
bad harvest and consequent poverty would give to his
agitation. The situation was simply this : all credit
was suddenly stopped and the peasantry over head and
ears in debt, with little or no prospect of being able to
pay. Then the Land League programme appeared,
affording a short and easy solution of the difficulties
under which the tenants found themselves. Thus
we see that the agitation which appealed directly
to the cupidity of the lower classes was brought
to bear upon them at a time when a combination
of indirect and most unfortunate circumstances gave

to it an initiatory force which it is difficult to over-estimate.

" Its history is well known.   It grew and flourished. At first a canvasser for support and adherents, it soon passed into the position of an omnipotent . dictator, forcing fealty and submission by terror, and punishing disobedience to its laws by death.

" I have already said that this agitation, although originated against the landlords and upper classes, has fallen with much more terrible severity upon the poor and the defenceless.   By specifying certain murders in the former classes, I do not imply that the others which I do not mention are less horrible and revolting.   It would occupy too much time and serve no purpose now to go through the details of the bloody list.   But there is a danger, and I would guard against it, that the peculiar circumstances and shocking incidents of poor Mrs. Smythe's murder at Barbavilla and the cold-blooded atrocity of the Phœnix Park butchery (I refer to them merely as a type of the others) may divert attention from the class of victims who are really the most to be commiserated—from the defenceless poor upon whom the cowardly tyrant's arm fell with im-munity from risk, and with wanton and remorseless cruelty.   In the case of every outrage committed against the upper classes, no matter how carefully pre-cautions have been taken and plans prearranged, a certain amount of danger has to be faced—a danger of resistance, a chance of being fired at again, of being identified and ultimately punished.   There-fore there always was more or less brute courage called into action in their perpetration.   But in the murders of the poor there was no such risk, and in their commission we have exemplified the true characteristics of the originators of the Land League.

"Mr. Arnold Forster in his letter to the *Times* of 16th February 1883 brings out this point so forcibly that I cannot do better than quote his words: 'Horrible as are the exploits of the "inner circle," as described by many witnesses and as exemplified by many hideous crimes, they are not, as some recent critics have declared them to be, the "worst crimes which have disgraced the present agitation." The instinct which led the Phœnix Park murderers to attack Mr. Burke, or which prompted the assailants of Mr. Field in their cowardly assault, was the instinct of wild beasts who, in attacking those charged with the administration of the criminal law, were merely trying to get rid of their natural enemies. It would be an insult to the brute creation to draw any such comparison with regard to the agrarian and Land League murders of which the Chief Secretary speaks. These murders, one and all, were perpetrated in almost every instance with one definite object—that, namely, of securing obedience to the rules of the Irish National Land League; and were intended either to procure or to avoid the payment of money. Mr. Trevelyan has done good service to the cause of order both in England and in Ireland by brushing aside the falsehood with which the Land League leaders and their supporters have invariably sought to cover the iniquities which were perpetrated in their behalf. Ninety-nine out of every hundred Englishmen when asked who were the victims of the Land League agitation, would reply that they were landlords or agents, who, according to what Mr. Parnell[1] called "the wild justice

---

[1] After Bacon: *Essays*, iv.

of revenge," had been shot down in pursuance of a rough system of reprisals. Mr. Trevelyan states in general terms that this was not so, and declares that the sufferers were the defenceless and the unoffending. I have been at some pains to inquire into this matter, and the result of the inquiry is certainly somewhat startling. Some time ago Mr. Dillon, in one of those flourishes with which readers of Land League oratory are familiar, declared that "there would soon be evictions and processes by hundreds and thousands, the result of which, he feared, must be bloodshed and massacre in Ireland, and," he added, in a tone of melancholy which by the light of the facts seems somewhat grotesque, that "the massacre would no doubt be mostly on the side of the Irish people." Mr. Dillon, as it turned out, was perfectly correct. The massacre did take place, and it was almost entirely on the side of the Irish people. But who were to be the perpetrators of the massacre Mr. Dillon does not mention. The following figures will throw some light on the question. I find that from the 1st of January 1880 down to September 1882 there were no less than 10,058 agrarian offences of all kinds reported. Of purely agrarian or Land League murders, not including the Dublin crimes, there were 57. Of the victims 25 were farmers or the sons of farmers, 10 were labourers or herds, 11 were persons of various occupations unconnected with the landlord class, 1 was a magistrate and murdered as such, 6 only were bailiffs' agents or process-servers, while 4 alone, out of the whole 57, were landlords. Again, there were 145 cases of attempted murder. Of the persons attacked, and the majority of whom were more or less dangerously wounded, 62 were farmers, 19

were labourers or herds, while 22 only were bailiffs'
agents or process-servers, and 10 only were landlords.
322 cases of firing into dwellings were reported, yet
only 33 of the occupants of the houses attacked were
of the landlord class or its dependents.   In short,
it was upon the poorest, most defenceless, most
thoroughly Irish section of the population, that the
Land League waged unrelenting war, and whom it
mutilated, murdered, robbed, and terrorised in the
interests of its miserable unwritten law.   These simple
facts the League and its supporters have always
endeavoured to conceal, and by perpetually affirming
their opposite, have succeeded in misleading public
opinion to an incredible extent.   There are no illu-
sions about these matters in Ireland.   There it is
known that the vast proportion of these outrages were
committed by and on behalf of the Irish Land League.
While the "inner circle" counts its victims by units,
the Land League counts them by scores.   The bulk
of the outrages were committed under the auspices of
the local Land Leagues, at a time when, to use the
words of *United Ireland,* "the plan of the campaign
was in the hands of the Land League, and whoever
moved without their order was a deserter—whoever
thwarted them by individual action was an enemy."'

"He then proceeds to show how Messrs. Parnell,
Sexton, and Dillon—the members of the central
League—were in constant communication with Messrs.
Brennan, Boyton, and Sheridan, were the avowed
friends of Devoy, and the pensioners of Patrick Ford
of the *Irish World*; and he concludes with these
words: 'As soon as the English public realise that
the Irish National Land League never would have
existed for a day, and never in fact did exist, without

the sanction of wilful murder, the better it will be. It will be a great mistake if we allow the dramatic circumstances of the tragedies in Dublin to divert our minds from the far more cruel, far more frequent, and far less excusable outrages which were committed by or on behalf of the Irish National Land League.'

"There is a further peculiar characteristic of this conspiracy which distinguishes it from those which have preceded it, and bears materially upon the main question. During the whole of its progress up to last autumn, there has been an impossibility of obtaining any information save the general report of outrages. As to the tactics or plan of action of its organisers, or any evidence which could lead to the conviction of the parties guilty of the crimes that had been committed, the whole community seemed to be bound under a common seal of secrecy, and practically of complicity. We have only to remember the verdicts of the different coroners' juries in the cases where the police and one or two others were tried for firing in defence of their lives, and in the discharge of their duty. If these verdicts had been allowed to take their course, many judicial murders would have been committed.

"As regards agrarian outrages this difficulty of obtaining evidence has always been present, but not at all to the same extent as regards other crimes. It would appear as if agrarian murder came more peculiarly under the code of the Ribbon Society, and was carried out under its directorate, and we have seen in what has passed very strong evidence for the assumption, if not belief, that the Land League, if not one with them, adopted their rules. However that may be, one important element which must not be lost sight of in endeavouring to understand the nature and character of this party of disorder, and to appreciate fully the great difficulty of dealing with them, is the deplorable circumstance that when an agrarian crime is committed in a district in Ireland, the whole population of that district at once become 'accomplices after the fact.' That is, I believe, the legal term: what I mean is, that all with one accord join in refusing to give information if they possess it, or, if they do not, they are as united in endeavouring to throw every possible difficulty in the way of discovering those who do.

" During my experience as a magistrate in Ireland I have had several investigations to conduct in agrarian murder cases, and have found invariably present the spirit I describe. In cases of other sorts of crime it has been quite different. Englishmen must not think that agrarian murder means only the murder of a landlord for evicting a tenant. In the cases that came before me the victims were tenants, and their crime, according to the Ribbon code, was trying by fair means or foul, it did not much matter which, to obtain the land of another.

" But I have digressed, and must return to my point, which is the strict secrecy observed by those implicated in the present movement. On every other occasion of a conspiracy of the same magnitude there always have been means of getting information as to what was at least likely to happen, and as to the general, if not the particular, tactics of the organisers. In 1798 the Government had full information on these points, as also in 1847, and in the Fenian conspiracy of 1866 to 1868. Then, I well remember, I had no difficulty in getting information. I was warned of the intended rising at Caherciveen a week before it took place, and sent what I knew of it to Lord Mayo (then Chief Secretary for Ireland), as also of the Dublin *émeute* which followed almost immediately afterwards.

" But during the present crisis, the usual attendant on an Irish conspiracy—the Irish informer—has been conspicuous by his absence. It may be thought that no information of a rising or open insurrection was to be had because none was intended. It is very hard to say what were or were not the intentions of the prime movers. I believe there were divided counsels, but of one thing I am certain, that some movement was confidently expected. Whether this expectation was general or not I cannot say. I can only speak of those parts of the country with which I am connected. At first it was reported that it (whatever 'it' was) would take place in the early spring of 1881. Some will remember how full the streets of Dublin were of Yankee-looking strangers at that time. Then it was fixed for the night of the 31st December 1881, and again for some date, which I do not remember, in February 1882. The rumours were very vague as to what form it was to assume. The commonest report was that it would be a renewal of St. Bartholomew's Day—a general massacre of the Protestants. I have no doubt myself that something of the kind was intended, and that it was only averted by Mr. Forster's foresight in filling the country with troops.

" The question, however, of what was or what was not intended is of little moment now as bearing upon the point I want to make clear, and that is, the secrecy which attended this movement—which distinguished it from all other similar movements, and which gave it its peculiarly ominous and dangerous characteristic—connected it clearly with the Ribbon Society, and with the spirit which ruled it.

"At the commencement there seemed to be a split between the Fenian party and the Land League faction. It may have been put forward as true for a purpose. But whether pretended or real, the Dublin revelations show that they very soon healed their differences, and joined hands for the common object which I may summarise as this—the destruction of the landlord-class as the first and principal redoubt before attacking the connection with England. That the latter was the real and ultimate object of the organisers is clear from the words used by Mr. Parnell in his speech at Cincinnati on 23d February 1880, as reported at the time. 'None of us,' he says, 'whether in America or in Ireland, or wherever we may be, will be satisfied until we have destroyed the last link which keeps Ireland bound to England.' This declaration was of sufficient breadth and force to enlist the Nationalist or Fenian element. Thus, by the conjunction of these two principles, all the parties of disorder in Ireland were, for the first time known in history, united under one flag, and the most formidable and deep-laid conspiracy organised that ever threatened the peace of the country.

"The League once extirpated root and branch, the reign of the Uncrowned King and his power for evil, in its present form at least, will be at an end. In this there is, I trust, a hope for peace, if not a permanent one, then for a few years of quiet, until some fresh form of agitation is invented, based of course upon the elements of disturbance ever present, and the rich promise which legislation in the past holds out to agitation in the future.

" The past is gone and cannot be recalled.   It is only in so far as affording a guide and a warning that a review of it can now serve my purpose, and it is with that object alone that I have endeavoured to give a general account of what has happened, and to bring into prominence the circumstances and facts which, in my opinion, are the main causes of the condition in which we are now placed.   This conspiracy, with all its evil consequences, has been a warning to us ; but, unless we understand rightly and thoroughly its real origin, the warning will be of no use, perhaps do more harm than good.

" By its light, however, I hope, if I have described it correctly, we may be able to form a right judgment as to the merit and value of the various remedies prescribed, which I have now time to mention only cursorily.   Among these, on the one side, we have Mr. George's essay, *Progress and Poverty*, the full bearings of which I have not been able to master, but, so far as I have, his prescription would appear to be identical with Mr. Davitt's doctrine.   He brings us back to first principles—to the first chapter of Genesis as it were, and the second verse of the history of Ireland ; it, Ireland, was without form and void—and Mr. George proceeds to shape it.   We have Mr. John Morley's treatise in the *Nineteenth Century* of November last, which, without any disrespect to him, I think I can show displays, on many points, that English ignorance of Irish affairs to which I have referred, as well as prejudice and distorted judgment on the whole.   We have Dr. Posnett's letters advocating the lowering of the franchise, parliamentary and municipal.   We have Mr. O'Brien's exhortation to the Government—as their legislation has so crippled the landlords that they cannot continue their improvements—to undertake the reclamation of waste lands, arterial drainage, planting, and other works, to give employment at the public cost, and so to supplement what the landlords did and can now no longer do. And we have, the most ominous of all, the announcement which Mr. Gladstone is reported to have made at Cannes, that he now believed that the real cure for Ireland was decentralisation. I presume that means abolishing the Local Government Board in Dublin, and placing the administration of local affairs entirely in the hands of the people. From among all these proffered blessings it is not easy to choose. All, except Mr. O'Brien's, point practically to the same end. I fear, however, unless Mr. Trevelyan's good sense and judgment are allowed their due influence and weight, that, whatever is done, we shall again experience what is now becoming a very common result of party government: that the measure will be devised with a view to strengthen party-power, regardless of the requirements of the case or the benefits it may confer on Ireland.

"On the other side, we have many and carefully-calculated schemes for the gradual formation of a peasant proprietary, without either robbery or confiscation. We have schemes for relieving by emigration the poverty-stricken districts of their surplus inhabitants. I should much like to have attempted, by a careful review of these, to show where I thought them wrong and where I thought them right; but I felt that it would be simple folly to try to discuss a remedy without first endeavouring to describe the nature of the disease (as I understood it) for which it was suggested as a cure. In doing that I have (I hope not uselessly) occupied so much time, that I must not trespass further, although I would be glad of the opportunity of pursuing the subject to the end.

"I may, however, be allowed to add one word in conclusion as an indication of the direction which I think should be followed. If the trade of the political agitator is stopped—in that I include the action of the so-called 'National' press—there is no reason why Ireland should not become as quiet, prosperous, and contented a country as there is in the world, and a pleasanter one than most others to live in. The characteristics of the people (when let alone) are the best—generous, warm-hearted, with, strange as it may seem to say so, the true instincts of real loyalty inherent in them, if they were afforded a chance to develop them—their great, their national fault is their being so easily influenced and led; and it is by the action of those who have obtained the lead over them that all their evil qualities are brought to light and their good ones concealed. But as, in the present state of public feeling while this wave of democracy is in the ascendant, it is not likely that the political agitator will be interfered with, we must look for the most probable means of establishing order, despite his efforts.

"To find such, it is only a common-sense axiom to say that we must try to enlist as many as we can on the side of order, and in the present condition of affairs I can see no other way of attaining that result with the same likelihood of success as by the establishment of a large class of peasant proprietors.

"Once you give a man a proprietary interest—something to lose—it is only the logical inference that he will become opposed to anarchy and lawlessness.

To give a lower franchise now, under existing circumstances, is not really to give increase of political power to the people as a people, because they are not free to make an independent use of it.   Its only effect would be to give increase of power to the political agitator, to the disturbers of the peace of the country, and to the enemies of England."

CHAPTER XXIII

But the record fair,
That memory keeps of all thy kindness there,
Still outlives many a storm, that has effaced
A thousand other themes less deeply traced.

COWPER.

Οἶος πέπνυται. τοὶ δὲ σκιαὶ ἀίσσουσιν.

HOM. *Od.* x. 495.

Alone he keeps his head, while, shadow-like,
The others waver.

COWPER's lines above quoted indicate the feeling which brought Mr. Kavanagh's tenantry once more into sympathy with the old house, when, in the July of 1885, the family vault was reopened to receive his mother.

Full of years, loved and honoured by all, Lady Harriet died at Ballyragget Lodge, which had been her residence for well-nigh a quarter of a century. There, as in former days at Borris, her time was spent in doing good to every one who came within the sphere of her refining influence.

She was a woman of high culture and of unusual artistic power. During the years—the many years, I might say—that she spent abroad, her sketches and water-colour drawings assisted the records of her graphic pen in reproducing for the benefit of those left behind the beauties of the scenery in which she delighted. Egypt, Palestine, the lovely island of Corfù (endeared to her by many ties), and the scarcely less lovely Neapolitan Riviera—all enriched her portfolio, till it became a very magazine of bright impressions and happy recollections.

Failing health—for the closing years, a "calm decay"—had confined her entirely to Ballyragget. But when the end had come she was brought back to Borris, to the old home, for one night, on her way to her last resting-place : the picturesque abbey overlooking the Barrow.

In the early morning the mounted tenantry from far and near assembled to escort to St. Mullins the remains of her who was so long and so well known to many among them. The striking convoy accompanying the hearse slowly passed down the sloping street of Borris, where the closed shops and hushed bystanders attested the widespread sorrow for the gentle lady. Memories of kindly words and deeds, and the tears of those she had befriended in the dark hours of desolation and poverty, welled up as the procession passed on to lay her in the old Abbey—there to rest in "sure and certain hope" till the morning of the Resurrection.

In the September following, Mr. Kavanagh, on his return from one of his brief holidays, found Ireland in a state of rampant lawlessness on the Nationalist side, and of grave disquietude on that of the loyal and well-disposed. By personal interviews and through the daily post he received ample confirmation of this impression from gentlemen belonging to nearly every part of the country, and he was strongly advised to call together a meeting in Dublin to represent emphatically the uneasiness felt by the minority, and the prevailing sense of urgency for the adoption of measures to check the Land (now become the National) League.

This advice he refrained from following, as he was unwilling, directly or indirectly, to embarrass Lord Salisbury's newly-formed Government or to prejudice its position, rendered doubly difficult by the circumstances bequeathed by its predecessor. He took occasion, however, to make known his views on the condition of affairs, and in a letter which he wrote on the 2d October, and which even now, except in a few passages, must be withheld from publication, he commented strongly on the widespread boycotting and terrorism, as proved not only by the reports of the constabulary and divisional magistrates, but also by personal observation and by facts received at first hand.

"I do not believe," he says, "that the country was ever in a more deplorable condition. . . . It is reported that the 'Coercion' Act, as it is called, will not be renewed, on the ground that the ordinary law is sufficient to govern the country.

"This is, of course, a point upon which country gentlemen like myself are not competent to offer an opinion. But, if it is a fact that the ordinary law is sufficient to deal with the existing crisis, the present condition of Ireland would prove that it is not put in force.

"That, I may say frankly, is the main apprehension of a large number of the loyal classes, and I cannot too strongly emphasise the great danger of allowing the action of the National League to go on unchecked."

Again, writing on 14th October, he says :—

"I accept the statement, but, I must confess, not without some misgiving, that the ordinary law will prove sufficient, and I am thankful to be assured that, in cases where it is applicable, it will be vigorously applied.

"I trust, however, that I shall be forgiven for saying that in my opinion prosecutions at Petty Sessions, directed against comparatively unknown persons, adjudicated upon by local magistrates, and resulting, probably at most, in the inflicting of trifling punishments, although in themselves necessary, will go but a short way to re-establish order and to check crime, if in notable cases no proceedings are instituted.

"All experience in this country shows that, to meet and defeat conspiracy, it is at its chief instigators that the blow must be struck, and I very much fear that the effect upon the public conscience of such proceedings against those who are, in reality, but tools in the hands of others will be of little avail, if meetings are permitted to be held throughout the length and breadth of the land, where resolutions are adopted, not only encouraging systematic boycotting, but, in several instances, naming the individuals who are to be singled out for attack.

"I claim sympathy not so much on behalf of those who are, comparatively speaking, in a position to defend themselves, as for those who, while legal proceedings are pending, are being absolutely and irretrievably ruined by the action of the League."

The late autumn of the same year witnessed the General Election on the recently-lowered franchise, and Mr. Gladstone, it will be remembered, appealed to the constituencies for a substantial majority, on the express ground that it would make him independent of the now greatly-augmented Parnellite vote. The response was more than dubious; but it brought a decisive change in his policy.

Early in 1886 the new Parliament met, and Lord Salisbury's Government, having been defeated on Mr. Jesse Collings' Amendment, was succeeded by Mr. Gladstone's. Once more the Irish Question was thrust into the foreground. Mr. John Morley was appointed Chief Secretary, and the misgiving soon became general that the unhappy island was again to become the victim of experimental legislation. How sorely unfit she was for any such ordeal may be gathered from a paper written by Mr. Kavanagh in the late spring—a paper never published, but strikingly prescient, as the following extracts will show, of the dangers ahead and of the one mode of averting them.

" If either party, Conservative or Liberal, had possessed the courage to proclaim the Land League and renew the Crimes Act, or pass some other Act for the prevention of crime and boycotting, their action would have been welcomed with silent gratitude by hundreds of thousands of the farmers and labourers in the country. None save those who have lived in Ireland and had personal knowledge of what has taken place during the last six years can form any idea of the grievous tyranny to which the people have been subjected, or of the range and manner in which the powers of the National League have been exercised.

" It is a great mistake to suppose that there is any difference, save in the slight change in name, between it and the Land League, which was suppressed by Mr. Forster as an illegal combination. The head offices are the same. It is worked by the same men. Its sources of support are the same. Its objects are the same. Its means of enforcing obedience are the same.

"It is a well-known fact that in many districts the law of the land is superseded by the law of the National League, and its members boast of it. With the Supreme Court, or Court of Appeal, they have minor courts established throughout the country. In their organs, from the *Skibbereen Eagle* to *United Ireland*, I have seen their decrees published inflicting fines or ordering boycotting for breach of rules or disobedience to their mandates. The graver kinds of punishments by which their authority is enforced, such as murder, personal violence, burning of house or offices, maiming of cattle, and other phases of outrage (the latest invention being holding a girl while a dog tore her legs), are not named in those papers, but they are quite as well understood.

"That the objects of the new and the old League are identical is evident from the decrees issued on the land and on the rent questions. As to the first, there are the same punishments for, and denouncements against, the taking of 'evicted' farms, or 'land grabbing,' as such is popularly termed; and, as to the latter, almost the same 'no-rent' manifesto was issued as before. Although the effect was less general, every effort was exerted to make it equally so. That there was no real general unwillingness on the part of the tenants to pay their rents I know from my own case. Many of my tenants have come privately to me within the last few months saying that they were quite ready and willing to pay, but that they dared not do so, lest their houses should be burned, themselves or members of their families injured, or their cattle maimed. Others have come asking to be served with writs or processes as an excuse for paying. One very peculiar case that I heard of was that of a poor woman, after she had

paid her rent, begging to be served with a process
which she might show as a proof that she had not
paid! But such is the state of the country that I
regret to say only too many well-authenticated instances of such facts can easily be given.

"There is, however, this difference between the
old and the new League : the former was proclaimed
before it had much time to develop, the latter has been
allowed to grow unchecked till it has gained enormous
power, established branches in every part of the land,
and extended its action to interference with every
undertaking in public or private life. The working
of Acts of Parliament, no matter how beneficial, has
been interfered with. The Land Purchase Act has
been rendered practically inoperative. The application of the Labourers' Dwellings Acts has in many
districts been limited to building houses only for
members of the League, for others distorted into a
weapon for injuring 'obnoxious' individuals, which
simply means that, by their loyalty, they have brought
themselves under the ban of the League. No public
company or institution is too great to be above its
aim : instance the attempt to ruin the Bank of Ireland,
the attack on the Cork Steamship Company, the
attempts to boycott National Schools. I believe there
are over sixty of such instances, but the particulars
and numbers of them can easily be ascertained by
reference to the Education Office. It would be a
return well worth moving for.

"No act of private life is too trivial to be beneath
the ken of the League. A farmer cannot hire or discharge a servant, buy or sell his stock, or do any act,
no matter how common, in carrying out his lawful
business, without rendering himself liable to be called

to account.   No more can a labourer or a shopkeeper.
And it should be borne in mind that the rules of these
district branches of the League are as often framed
with the object of indulging the private malice of the
ruling spirit as of enforcing any intelligible principle.   Under circumstances such as these it can
be no matter of wonder that the people should
look for relief by the re-establishment of the authority of the law and the restoration of their personal
liberty.

" It is in shrinking from giving this relief that I
think both the great parties in their turn are most
seriously to blame.   The weakness, and I may say
cowardice, which they have thus displayed have
immensely magnified the difficulties of the future
government of the country, and have confirmed in the
minds of many the previously fast-growing belief that
the real power has passed from the British Government
to the Nationalist leader and his party.   It is certainly
true that, according to the rules of party warfare,
appearances favour this opinion.   Mr. Parnell, as
parties are now in the House of Commons, certainly
holds the balance in his hands.   But it seems to me
almost beyond belief that a party of eighty-six, whose
avowed object is the destruction of the Empire and
the ruin of England, should be allowed to rule over
the rest of the House of Commons, the majority of
whom, it is to be hoped, love their country and are
jealous of its honour.   Under ordinary circumstances,
the mere supposition that such could be the case would
be absurd, but under those to which I have referred it
would be hard to say what might not be possible.   It
is that doubt which makes me say that, bad as our
present condition is, the future, humanly speaking, is

even more gloomy.   Were it not that the issue lies in higher hands than ours, there would seem to be but little chance of light.   Feeling this, I cannot yet bring myself to think that all is hopeless—that all our public men have lost the sense of right, or that the English people, when they understand the true issues, would ever consent to hand over Ireland to the confiscation, anarchy, and ruin which the Nationalist programme would involve.

" I would hope that the result of this crisis would be the formation of a coalition, consisting of those members of the two great parties, who, seeing the imminence of the dangers threatening the Empire, will sink their party differences and unite in one strong body to avert disaster.   If they do so, the crisis will have been, I believe, productive of real good ; but, until this great problem is solved, it seems to me but waste of time to speculate on the future, or to endeavour to discuss the questions which may then arise.   The whole fate of this country practically hangs upon the question of the restoration of law and order. If the Union is to be maintained, the National League must be suppressed, and the laws of the Empire enforced.   Until this is done, we are in no position to consider future legislation, because it is idle to talk of making laws which would be inoperative when passed ; and if the Union is not to be maintained, the sooner the loyalist inhabitants are made aware of the fact the better, that they may have an opportunity of escaping with their lives."

It was to the manipulators of the Irish-American conspiracy, miscalled the " National League," flushed with past successes and approaching triumph, that Mr. Gladstone proposed to commit the destinies of the industrious, the educated, the law-abiding minority, Roman Catholics and Protestants alike ; and it was by the unexpected and tardy intervention of such a coalition as Mr. Kavanagh indicated that the attempted revolution was to be frustrated.   But I anticipate.

CHAPTER XXIV

Hoc caverat mens provida Reguli
Dissentientis condicionibus
  Fœdis, et exemplo trahenti
    Perniciem veniens in aevum.—HOR. *Car.* iii. v. 13.

This had his prophet-soul foreseen,
Prompt to reject the compact mean,
  With its train of woes that, in future ages,
Must on the Empire supervene.

To the surprise and dismay of the constituencies, Mr. Gladstone capitulated to the Separatist leader against whom he had so lately courted their help. As his newest panacea for Ireland, he had adopted Home Rule! This policy he unfolded in two bills, concurrently brought forward—one to exclude Ireland from representation at Westminster and to concede to her a Parliament in College Green; the other, as the condition precedent of its companion, to buy out the landlords, and so relieve her of what—on the threshold of her " new departure "—she must have found a difficulty fraught with risk, if not disaster.

The fate of those bills—" those insane bills," as Mr. Goschen characterised them—was settled after six weeks' discussion. They were rejected in a full House by a majority of thirty—rejected, moreover, by that very coalition of loyal Liberals and Conservatives which had commended itself to Mr. Kavanagh. A

General Election ensued, with the result that the country reaffirmed the verdict of the House four times over. It raised the majority of thirty to well-nigh one hundred and twenty, charged with its mandate to maintain the unity of the Empire.

It would serve no useful purpose to review Mr. Gladstone's stupendous "rhetorical misadventure," to show the inconsistencies of his scheme to grant Home Rule to people whom his legislation had been treating as imbeciles or minors, unable to make or keep a contract! Equally idle would it be to dwell on the cruel wrong it must visit on Ireland by withdrawing her representatives from the invigorating friction—the education, in a word—provided by the Imperial Parliament. The reader is too cognisant of the characteristics of Mr. Gladstone's bills to require more than this reference, from which I now pass to what will be perused with present interest: Mr. Kavanagh's "Few suggestions for consideration as to a future Policy of Government for Ireland."

This paper, written in the Carlton Club just after Mr. Gladstone's defeat at the polls, has hitherto been read by only a few political friends; but from its author's experience and fair-mindedness, it will be welcome to all who have at heart the permanent good of Ireland :—

" I must preface what I have to say by a few words as to the condition of the country.

" At the present moment it is, perhaps, comparatively quiet, because those who really rule it have, on grounds of expectant policy, given the mandate for a temporary peace. When this object ceases to have weight there is little doubt that the same condition of things will reappear which existed but a few

short months ago, and the effects of which exist
still.

"That condition was simply this: that, save in
times when it was in open rebellion, it never was in a
more unsettled state and seldom in a more threatening
one. Even now no one knows from day to day what
to expect. Trade is paralysed. All confidence in the
support of law and order has vanished. Civil contracts
are practically worthless. In some districts the Queen's
writ does not run. In some even the fundamental
laws of every civilised state 'for the protection of life
and property are powerless; the mandates of an ille-
gally constituted body, the National League, being
alone regarded.

"These are facts which are too well and widely
known to render it necessary for my present purpose
to dwell upon them.

"For the causes which have produced this condition we have not far to look. It is a case of history
repeating itself, and of Ireland being made, as of old,
the battleground of English party strife.

"The British Constitution is a grand one, guaranteeing to every subject the greatest amount of
freedom consistent with the safety of the commonwealth. The system of party government is also as
near perfection in its theory and conception as any
human device can hope to reach. But for either of
these to have a fair trial there are conditions absolutely
needful, and they are: that those who hold the helm
of the State and lead the parties should have a conscientious regard for the first principles of right and
wrong, and make ambition subservient to patriotism.

"An impartial review of the history of this country
for the last twenty years will show, I fear, how these

conditions have too often been ignored ; how the love of power, the desire for place, have perverted mighty minds, and how the sacred trust of the destinies of a great nation has been prostituted for the furtherance of personal ambition.

"We have had during the period I have named, more especially within the last few months, instances too palpable to be questioned of words eaten, pledges repudiated, policies which were declared to be outside our planet's sphere, not only brought 'within measurable distance,' but as warmly advocated and adopted as they were before, by the same lips, stigmatised as immoral, denounced and condemned. But invariably this sudden change of opinion has been in the direction of bidding for the support of whatever political section appeared most likely to be in the ascendant or even to hold the balance of power, regardless of ultimate consequences as of present honour.

"No constitution could stand such a strain. In England, with the old constituencies, the majority of whom were educated thinking men, it might have had a chance. But with the newly-enfranchised masses that hope seems vain.

"Encouraged by the example of a great popular leader, numbers of adventurers are ready to step into the arena as devoid of principle as of any material stake in the country, and, instead of trying to lead or direct the masses whose trust they seek, they bid for their votes by playing upon their cupidity and pandering to their passions.

"Even in a country like England such a course can, I fear, only result in disaster and disgrace. But in Ireland, with an excitable population peculiarly open to the influences of agitation, the numerical majority reared in disloyalty from their cradles, whose only source of information or means of forming an opinion upon the questions of the day are derived from the Nationalist journals and other treasonable and un-scrupulous publications, the consequences are a hundred-fold more dangerous, and have already brought us face to face with the existing crisis.

" Bad as the present is, the future prospect appears to me to be more gloomy, and if the weak and waver-ing policy of the past year is to be followed, I can see no other result possible than anarchy and civil war.

" On the other hand, I believe that if the Govern-ment once showed a firm front and an unmistakable determination to restore and maintain order and to punish crime, and showed, further, that they regarded that as their first and paramount duty, and did it because it was right, there would be little difficulty in the task. They would have with them the sympathy and respect of a very large number of the people—a very much larger number than many would suppose.

" I have no doubt that both parties, Conservative and Liberal, have, in their turn, shrunk from the policy of firmness and adopting the means necessary to restore and maintain order from the fear of losing popularity and being charged with 'Coercion.'

" It is a very grave mistake which many English-men of both parties are under to suppose that the majority of the rural population in Ireland (I do not speak of the towns) are really sympathisers with crime. It is quite true that since the establishment and spread of the Land League the people are in such abject terror that not one in a thousand dare raise a voice against a system from which they suffer more acutely than any other class.   But that is not from sympathy with crime or from any love of the yoke under which they groan, but from the utter absence of all moral courage. That is a national characteristic, and constitutes the main difference between the inhabitants of the two islands.

"Believing that the circumstances I have named are the chief causes of the present condition of affairs, I must put the restoration of law and order—involving, as I believe, the absolute necessity of the suppression of the National League—as the first and most important duty of any government.

"It may be found that to facilitate, or even render possible, the efficient accomplishment of this task, the granting of additional powers to the executive may be necessary. In that event their application should be extended to the United Kingdom and their duration made permanent.

"With the large Irish population under the direct influence of the Fenians and other types of rebels now living in many parts of England, the general application of these extended powers may be found not only desirable, but absolutely necessary, for the protection of the loyal inhabitants of the country. Making such permanent in character would do away with the difficulties and heart-burnings of their periodical enactment. Neither could be objected to, save on the ground of sentiment, and I confess I have little sympathy with that kind of sentiment which calls the prevention of murder and outrage 'Coercion.'

"Next in importance to the restoration of law and order, and indissolubly connected with it, comes the Land Question.

"There can be little doubt that it, with the majority of the people in Ireland, underlies the Home Rule cry.

With ninety-nine out of every hundred of the agricultural population who follow Mr. Parnell it is the question of the land that influences them. If that was settled, the force would be taken out of the agitation, and it would in the future be supported only by the roughs and scum of the towns and country, who will go on plotting and agitating to the end of time—no matter what the condition of affairs.

"The system of dual ownership created by the Land Act of 1881—although previously existing in Ulster, where 'tenant-right' has hitherto been a legalised and acknowledged system—has, in the south and west, produced a condition of affairs that is simply intolerable.

"The enormous injustice of giving to the occupiers in those provinces a vested right in holdings which they neither inherited nor bought has naturally led them to believe that, as this was extorted by agitation, persistence in that course must ultimately result in gaining for them, on like terms, the fee-simple of their holdings. It will be impossible, I believe, while 'party government' exists in this country, to convince them of the contrary, and while this belief remains, agitation with all its inseparable evils of poverty and crime will be the consequence. We cannot change the system of government, and, in that condition of affairs, we must therefore look for other remedies.

"In my opinion, the only practically efficacious one is, by the development of the scheme on which the Purchase Acts are based, to establish a large and yearly increasing class of yeoman-proprietors, so that in course of time the majority of those having the franchise will be, in the support of their own individual and vested interests, ranked on the side of law and order, and thus rendered fit to be entrusted with larger powers in the administration of their own local matters, for which they are now eminently unfitted.

"The advantages offered to the tenants by the Purchase Act of 1885 are so material, that this end ought not to be difficult of attainment, but now the tenants will not of their own accord come forward as purchasers, because those who lead them and whose interest it is to keep up agitation, knowing that it would settle the question and quiet the country, use their influence to dissuade them ; and, further, because they have been so demoralised by concession after concession, that they would rather look to the chance of what may come than avail themselves of what is now offered.

" There are only two ways that I can see of meeting the difficulty : one is to convince them of the finality of the present legislation ; the other to introduce an element of compulsion into the Purchase Scheme.

" The first I believe to be impossible.   The second I do not like on principle.

" I think the tendency of legislation during the past twenty years has been far too much of what some would term the 'paternal system of government'—the 'meddlesome' I would call it.   As an instance I may mention interference with the right of private contract.

" As an extension of that principle I would, if it were possible, avoid making purchase compulsory, and be in favour of applying pressure by indirect means.

" Another objection that I have to the introduction of direct compulsion into the Purchase Scheme is that its effect would be general and too sudden.

" As to its generality, I think it would be most unwise to force all the small holders in Ireland to buy their holdings.   One of the real evils affecting Ireland is the chronic poverty of large masses of the people. There are districts in the south and west where the population is so large and congested that the land on which they depend entirely for their support is incapable of yielding it.   To force such as these to buy would be to perpetuate and increase the evil instead of alleviating it.   In these cases, if compulsion is to be applied, it should be in the direction of a generously-devised scheme of emigration.

" As to its suddenness, it would be nothing short of a revolution, and although for a good object and devoid of the main objections usually consequent upon such occurrences, I must say that I think these violent and sudden changes should where possible be avoided. The adoption of indirect means might meet this point.

" It is difficult, I admit, in the face of facts before us, to devise efficacious means to induce tenants to purchase their holdings when the advantages held out to them by Lord Ashbourne's Act failed to do so.   At even twenty years' purchase on the present rents, a substantial reduction on his present payments would be secured to the tenant buying under it, and he would become the owner in fee after a certain number of years.

" The reasons which, notwithstanding the advantages offered, prevent the working of the Act I have already stated.   There is, further, a very general, and, I fear, growing belief in the minds of the tenants, based upon some speeches of the late Chief Secretary for Ireland (Mr. John Morley), that the power of the State will not be much longer used to enforce payments of rent ; consequently, that the obligation to pay will cease; and that, by obtaining money from the State to purchase their holdings, they would be exchanging a liability which they would be forced to meet for one which they would not. The firm administration of the present law would no doubt do much to disabuse their minds of this idea and turn their attention to the Purchase Act. If they were convinced that it would be persevered in, it would have great effect. But, with the always possible chance of a change of Government and a change of policy, too much cannot be counted upon from it.

"Another indirect means of inducing tenants to purchase would be to enact that the holding of any tenant who refused a fair offer of sale under the Act should from the date of his refusal be placed outside the provisions of the Land Acts of 1870 and 1881. This plan of indirect pressure should certainly be applied in all acute cases—by such I mean cases where the tenants, having had judicial rents fixed, refuse to pay them without a further allowance, more especially when they enter into a combination to extort it.

" I am inclined to think that if indirect means such as these could be adopted the Purchase Acts would no longer remain a dead letter, that by degrees the object of establishing a large class of yeoman-proprietors would be accomplished, and that the objections to an arbitrary, general, and sudden change would be avoided. But, while I say this, I am bound to add that the gravest difficulty still remains, and that is, under the present plan of party government, the almost practical impossibility of convincing the Irish people that there was real finality in any legislation connected with the land. Unless that is done, it is clear that no purchase scheme could work; and, having regard to the difficulty of doing it, I admit that compulsion pure and simple may be found indispensable. I have stated my objections to it, but I believe that under the present exceptional condition of the country the adoption of the policy of the Land Purchase Acts is so imperative that the advantages it would confer would far outweigh the objections I have raised.

" The important question of providing the required money has been considered already by many much more competent to give a sound opinion than I am. All I would say about it is that I believe it could be arranged without any financial risk to the State. The price of the land bought could be paid by consols or land debentures. The State would not be asked to pay money, but to give its credit as security, and for doing that it would have, so long as the real power was retained by the British Parliament, ample security against loss.

" In the first place, it would have the fee-simple of the land bought. In the second, it would have the value of the tenants' interest, evidence of which is afforded by the enormous prices still paid for 'tenant-right.' People who would lightly forfeit the possession of land would not be so eager to acquire it as the prices they pay for it prove them to be. As each succeeding instalment was paid to the State by the occupier, his acquired interest in the land would be increased and he would be the more unwilling to lose it by default. If the occupiers were satisfied that a speedy and irredeemable eviction would follow the non-payment of the yearly instalments, the necessity of the State having recourse to such would, save in very exceptional cases, at once cease. To provide against these I would suggest a system of mutual responsibility, so that all living within a certain area would become mutually responsible for each other's payments ; all sympathy with defaulters would thus be put an end to, and the other occupiers of the area affected would in their own interests endeavour to find a solvent substitute or purchaser for a holding rendered vacant by the action of the State in enforcing payment. The most powerful weapon in the Land League policy would thus be made inoperative.

"Great stress has been laid by agitators on the depression of prices of agricultural produce and consequent inability of the tenants to pay their present rents. If this was a fact, it might undoubtedly affect the position of the State as creditor in the way of being security for the repayment of the purchase money. But it is only a fact with regard to wool, butter, and wheat (the last is not now a factor in Irish agriculture). In all other items the prices are now higher than when the majority of rents in Ireland were fixed, many of which have since been materially reduced by the arbitrary action of the Land Court.

"Looking at the question from the commercial point of view—the practical one from which the British taxpayer should regard it—I am convinced that it is not only the most effectual but the cheapest solution of the present difficulty. Unceasing agitation is the main cause of crime and of the difficulty of governing Ireland. It is a direct and most potent factor in producing the present depression. It has paralysed trade of all kinds, destroyed confidence, and checked enterprise alike in commercial as in agricultural matters. This stagnation and stoppage of the normal circulation of money has most seriously crippled the means of all classes of consumers, with, as must be the case, a like detrimental effect upon the interests of the producers, whether merchants or farmers. General poverty has been the only possible result, naturally increasing discontent, and rendering the sufferers more open to the designs of agitators whose chief interest it is to foment it. Thus the main results of the agitation go on acting and reacting upon each other, and will continue to do so in an increasing ratio while the cause remains.

"I believe the adoption of the Purchase Scheme would remove this cause. It would certainly take from the agitator the cry which has most force with the people. Agitation stopped and confidence restored by the firm administration of the law, prosperity would by degrees return, and, as it did, the general poverty would be proportionately lessened. As this change progressed, the benefit would be felt by the exchequer in the form of increased products from taxation, which are invariably affected by the prosperity or the reverse of a nation, and as the country became pacified it would be relieved from many of its present burdens. Considering all these facts, I think I am warranted in my assertion that the Purchase Scheme is the cheapest solution of the present difficulty. In stating them I have also given my reasons for believing that it is the most effectual one, and I can only say in conclusion that I look upon it as the only one by which finality is attainable.

"The Irish tenantry have been demoralised by an unceasing series of concessions, each pronounced to be the very last. First the Land Act of 1870, then the Act of 1881, quickly followed by the Arrears Act —the most demoralising of all. The Purchase Act of 1883 succeeded it, and that was followed by the Act of

1885 ; and now the tenants look for the realisation of the most revolutionary hopes engendered by the wild utterances of a Prime Minister to buy the support of rebels.

"Not until the Irish tenant is the owner in fee of his holding, with no creditor but the State, will he feel that the limit has been reached, and that there is no further object in clamour and disorder.

"Law and order having been established and the Land Question fairly and permanently settled on the lines, or some such lines as, I have endeavoured to indicate, I should no longer hesitate to entrust the occupiers (who would then be on what I may call the high road to become the owners in fee of their holdings, and who would thus become individually responsible for the payment of the rates) with the main control of the expenditure of those rates, for then the proper administration of the rates would be their own direct and individual interest. As matters are now, the manner in which they are administered proves that a large majority of the ratepayers regard the power they have over them more as a means for giving effect to political objects and party animus than as a grave trust for the relief of the poor or for their due application to the object for which they were levied. To put it shortly, I regard direct individual responsibility for the payment of rates as an essential qualification for the possession of control over their administration, and I believe the extent of that control should be commensurate with the amount of rate paid.

"The process of the conversion of occupiers into owners or quasi-owners (such as have agreed to buy) under the Land Purchase Act must, I believe, be gradual to obviate the delay of bringing about that condition which, I have said above, I regard as indispensable. Merely by the action of the Purchase Act, I would suggest that the payment of all rates should now be thrown upon the occupier, and that the rent payable to the landlord should, from the same date, be reduced by the average amount of rates allowed by him for a certain number of years.

" Under these changed conditions I believe that a large measure of local government ought to form a part of a future policy with regard to Ireland, and should, so far as practicable, be on the same lines as for England and Scotland.

" This part of the question is of too large and grave a nature for me to do more now than merely touch the fringe. It is full of difficulties involving conflicting interests and consequent jealousies, but, notwithstanding, there is no insuperable obstacle that I can see to a fair and just settlement. The desire of a capable citizen to have a direct voice in the control of purely local administration is in itself a healthy one, and should be rather encouraged than suppressed.'

CHAPTER XXV

Oh, think how to his latest day,
When Death, just hovering, claimed his prey,
With Palinure's unaltered mood
Firm at his dangerous post he stood.—SCOTT.

ABOUT this time his health began to fail, and he had no doubt contracted the seeds of the malady that three years later closed his earthly life. In thought and action, however, he still lived for Ireland—lived for her with all the devotion and vigilance of his best days.

In the foregoing chapter he expressed his conviction that with law vindicated and order restored, with the Land Question fairly and permanently solved, and with the occupiers made responsible for the payment of all rates (an equivalent reduction in rent being given in lieu of the increased charge thus thrown upon them), there need no longer be any hesitation as to entrusting them with the main control of the expenditure of those rates. He regarded direct individual responsibility for the payment of rates as a condition precedent to the right of controlling their administration, and further, he believed that the extent of that control should be commensurate with the amount of rate paid.

Subject to these paramount conditions, he had thought out a system of local government which might, in his opinion, be safely and beneficially given to Ireland. This, however, he had not, so far as I can find, committed to writing, and a few jottings on the subject are all I can lay hands upon.

From these I conclude that he would have put an end to the Castle government of Ireland, and replaced it by a permanent government—independent, that is to say, of the vicissitudes of party changes. Its tenure of office would, therefore, have remained unaffected by these, and in this way a continuity of policy could in some degree have been secured.

"If," he says, "in carrying out this suggestion, an arrangement could be made by which a member of the Royal Family would fill the post of Representative of Her Majesty, with a permanent residence in Ireland, it would have, I am convinced, a most powerful and salutary effect.

"Under this arrangement, the administrative functions of the Lord Lieutenant and his Secretary could be discharged by two secretaries for Ireland— one, either a peer or a commoner, with an ex-officio seat in the Cabinet, and the other with a seat in the House of Commons. Further, in this direction, I believe the Irish Privy Council could with advantage be utilised after being strengthened and having a representative element introduced into it.

"But in making these suggestions I feel that I am going into the details of a part of the subject rather outside my present purpose, which is simply to give my views upon what I consider to be the two most important problems of the Irish difficulty. In venturing to offer them, I do so more with the object of exemplifying the main lines of the policy that I am in favour of, than of attempting to define the practical means of carrying it out."

At this point the paper, itself a fragment, ends abruptly, and I do not know whether he proceeded further with his suggestions. That he fully contemplated completing them I have no doubt. But the incessant calls on his time and energies seem to have postponed it till it was too late.

Among them the agricultural state of Ireland occupied much of his attention—particularly the deterioration, becoming daily more serious, in the breed of cattle. On this subject a letter to the Right Hon. G. J. Goschen, kindly lent to me for publication, explains his views. Now that, owing to various causes, grazing is so largely replacing tillage throughout the country, his practical suggestions will come with special weight.

"BORRIS HOUSE, BORRIS,
" 18th December 1886.

" MY DEAR MR. GOSCHEN—Lord de Vesci has sent me your letter of 14th inst., with enclosures from Mr. Milner and Mr. Le Hunte.

" The latter is an old friend of mine, and I fully endorse all Mr. Milner says about him.

" The facts that they both state I look upon as indisputable—the connection of poverty with agitation ; the greater the former, the more easy to work the latter.

" That the depreciation of prices of agricultural produce in a country like Ireland must not only increase but create poverty is also self-evident.

" The cattle trade is our main branch of agriculture, and that the quality of our cattle has deteriorated, and is yearly becoming worse, any one who knows the country can testify to.

" I believe that Mr. Le Hunte is quite right—that the main cause of this is the absence of good bulls. In that fact alone there is tremendous change in this country. I can remember myself that ten years ago the country was full of good bulls, and now, save in some very favoured districts, you would have great difficulty in finding *one*.

"We used to have in every county Agricultural Societies with annual shows at which prizes were offered for the best sires of all sorts, and they were keenly contended for by both landlords and farmers. Now these have all disappeared. The landlords could not afford to subscribe to keep them up, and the farmers were told to boycott them (although that word was not invented then). They were told that such were landlord institutions and that they should have nothing to say to them.

" With these the breed of good bulls has practically disappeared, and consequently the young stock now reared in Ireland has deteriorated in a most marked degree, and *must* each year become worse as the good blood becomes more and more diluted with the coarse country breeds.

"Consequently our stores when sent to England are not in demand and cannot command the prices that they used.

" I believe that if the *quality* of our store cattle had been sustained, the foreign stores would hardly have been looked at. The Yankees are wide enough awake on this point, and do not grudge the highest prices for pedigree bulls to improve their breed, and that is now beginning to tell.

" It may be said that the landlords are to blame for this. No doubt the *immediate* cause lies at their door, but their line of action arose from inability to pursue their former course, not from unwillingness. They were forced by the political changes, the action of agitators, and the people, to discontinue their subscriptions to these local societies. They could not give the high prices for well-bred sires that they used to do; and no one, I think, can blame a man for discontinuing a course which he no longer can afford to pursue. Many are ruined altogether, and the strongest are only struggling to make the two ends meet.

"Those are the causes, and Messrs. Milner and Le Hunte have very truly described the effect or results.

"I have said all along that I believe *firm government* was the first and most essential element in the effort to remedy our ills, but I thoroughly agree with Mr. Milner that 'remedial legislation' should accompany such.

"I need not repeat his cogent reasons for saying so, and I also as fully agree with him that the true direction of such would be a wise liberality in fostering the material resources of the country. It is difficult, I am ashamed to say, to prescribe for Ireland a practical and *safe* way of doing this, because 'remedial legislation' has so often been perverted, and I may say prostituted, by jobbery. We cannot forget the enormous jobs that were perpetrated under the late 'Seed-rate Act' or under Relief Works. These are so fresh to my mind that I am almost afraid to advocate any course.

"If jobbery could be guarded against, I feel confident that it would be difficult to find a more practical and efficient way of materially benefiting the country than the endeavour to improve the breed of cattle, and thus bring back the character and quality of our stores to what it was.

"The proper mode to do it is the difficulty. I cannot agree with Mr. Le Hunte as to the Boards of Guardians being the proper means. They administered the seed-rate to which I have already referred, and I firmly believe if this was entrusted to them that we should only have a repetition of the same kind of proceedings. In fact, I believe, if they had the carrying out of such a scheme, no loyal man would be allowed any advantage from it, and I have no doubt the coarsest kind of bulls would be bought, if they only belonged to Nationalists, and the price paid would be in proportion to the political achievements of the owner, irrespective of the value of the animal.

"It is a humiliating opinion to have to give of one's own country, but I cannot help it, and I hardly know what means to recommend to carry out such a scheme.

"There is one association that might I think be utilised for that purpose. The Royal Agricultural Society of Ireland and the Royal Dublin Society decided on Thursday last to amalgamate and to apply for a new charter. The Government in granting the charter might make it a condition that they should carry out this trust.

"The Royal Agricultural Society did an immense deal in past days in keeping up good sires—bulls, stallions, rams, and boars—by holding their shows all over the country and offering large prizes.

"The Dublin Society also worked in the same line, holding a winter show every year in Dublin and also giving prizes.   It continues to do so still, I believe.

"The first, the 'R.A.S.,' was mainly a landlords' association, and almost collapsed from the reasons I have given.   The amalgamation was carried out to prevent its entire collapse.

"The latter, the 'R.D.S.,' was never a purely landlords' association, but was and is composed of men of eminence in all the professions.

"I believe Lord de Vesci has already suggested to you the adoption of this body.   He did so to me, and I racked my brains to try to think of any other, but I cannot.   Every other plan that occurs to me is full of objections, but I think that with care this might meet the want.

"I am ashamed to trouble you with such a long hurried scrawl, but I am much pressed for time just at present and could not manage to compress what I had to say into shorter limits.—Yours very truly,

" ARTHUR KAVANAGH."

Correspondence on practical subjects like the above, attendance at innumerable meetings in various interests, ecclesiastical, political, and magisterial — to say nothing of the several patriotic and defensive associations with which he was connected—sufficiently filled up his time.   Amid all these preoccupations his opinion on Imperial affairs was still in request—even on the part of those who held high office in the State.   Early in the autumn of 1888 an important correspondence passed between him and the Right Hon. W. H. Smith on the Irish Land Question.   One of his letters, by Mr. Smith's courtesy, I am now permitted to make public.

"Borris House, *September* 1888.

"Dear Mr. Smith—In further reply to your letter of the 19th inst., which I simply acknowledged when it reached me, I think it was about two years ago that I sent you my memo. about the Land Question which you referred to.

"The state of the country was then much worse and the prospects for the future more gloomy than they are now, but this fact (which I am thankful to admit) does not cause me to change the opinion I then expressed, which was, as nearly as I can remember, that the restoration of law and order should be the first object of the Government, and then the gradual creation by purchase of a large class of peasant-proprietors.

"This opinion was based upon what I must call the political vicissitudes of the constitution under which we live.

"Much of the present improvement is due to better prices, a most favourable season, with the prospect of an abundant harvest, which has in many places been already realised. But I believe the main cause is the firm and impartial administration of the law under Mr. Balfour's rule.

"Neither of these causes can we count upon as permanent. Nothing is proverbially more changeable than the weather, and experience proves that political affairs are fully as uncertain.

"We have, therefore, the same contingencies, notwithstanding the improvement, to guard against that we had two years ago, and I still believe that the course I then advocated is not only the only sound one, but it is the only course that possesses any reasonable prospect of success.

"Mr. Chamberlain, in a conversation I had with

him last June, expressed the opinion 'that considering the nature of the majority which supported the Government in the House of Commons, and the fact of the democracy now practically holding the reins of power, it was impossible for the Government to go on simply upon a policy of repression ; that in order to preserve the confidence and support of their present followers, they were bound to take some step in the line of remedial or progressive legislation ; and that the only step which appeared to him under present circumstances to meet the case was extension of local government in Ireland. It was with the object of preparing the people of Ireland for the discharge of this duty, or to fit them to be entrusted with it, that he advocated the Purchase Scheme. He believed that extension of this power to the people in their present irresponsible position would be madness ; that they would use it for objects of tyranny over the loyalists, giving effect to personal spite and party feeling, as demonstrated now by the way they use their power on Poor-Law Boards and such other local matters over which they have control.'

"In this I thoroughly agree with him, and believe that the only way of achieving this end is by the continuance and extension of the Purchase Scheme, thereby making the majority or a large number of the present occupiers responsible for the payment of the rates and taxes, over the expenditure of which they would be given the control.

"Further than this, the creation of peasant-proprietors is, I believe, the only course which has any reasonable prospect of success in attaining the object of raising the present occupiers above the influence of agitators, who are the curse of the country.

"Each year, as the scheme progresses, a larger number will acquire a direct or a yearly-increasing interest in their holdings, with an ultimate prospect of becoming the owners in fee. They will then, it is natural to suppose, become the supporters of a system which secures to them such advantages, and be ranked on the side of the loyal and peaceable members of the community.

"We have clear evidence that these results will be the certain consequence of the success or extension of this system, from the action of the leaders of the National League in doing all in their power to prevent the tenants from purchasing their holdings. They, whose interest it is to foment discontent and keep the country in turmoil and trouble, know well that, with the increase of the purchase system, their power for evil must decrease. Their knowledge of that fact, demonstrated by their action in trying to prevent purchases, is the strongest evidence we could have of the power for good which that scheme possesses. You have, I am sure, noted the avidity with which the agitators endeavoured to make capital out of the apparent refusal or unwillingness, on the part of the Government, to advance more money last summer for the purposes of Lord Ashbourne's Act. . . .

"I am not in a position to know the exact facts of all the sales which have taken place, but, from all I have heard, I believe that, so far as the Act has gone, the results have been most satisfactory.

"It is no doubt true that the effect of the Act is to place a man who has availed himself of its provisions in an advantageous position as compared with his neighbours who had not. . . . There are no cases of purchase in this neighbourhood, I am sorry to say;

therefore no such cases come under my notice. But I should say the man who did not buy had only himself to blame, and that, by extending the Purchase Scheme, the best opportunity would be afforded him of remedying his error. But even as the case stands I do not see that he has any injustice to complain of, nor have I heard of any such being made.

"As to the danger of allowing farms to remain derelict which have been bought and which the Government have been obliged to evict on account of non-payment of the instalments, I fully appreciate the grave importance of it, and see what a tool might be made out of the fact by those who oppose the Purchase Scheme. . . .

" I can only hope that there may not be many cases of that kind to be dealt with. I ground that hope upon what I think is about the most cheering mark of the improvement in the times. It is this: the National League are losing their power to prevent the people from taking evicted farms. In the Land Corporation we have had during the past year many instances of this fact. On the O'Grady estate, where we are fighting a fierce battle with the Plan of Campaign, we have, within this last month, scored a great victory—a tenant having taken one of the principal farms, paid *all rent and costs*, and agreed to all our terms, which were less favourable than those offered by The O'Grady in the commencement of the struggle. This is, I believe and hope, only the prelude to a general give-in on that estate. On Brooke's estate (Coolgreany), another test case of the Plan of Campaign, three or four of the evicted farms have been let during the past summer. . . .

" I have read Mr. Hurlbert's book with much

interest.   His object in writing it was to influence American, not English, politics, but I think such an exposition of the action of the National League coming from his pen ought to do good.   If it could be circulated among, and could be read by, the masses who now form the English constituencies, it would show them that, in the eyes of an American Republican, the so-called coercion of the Irish Executive was of a far milder form than would be meted out to offenders on the other side of the Atlantic.

" I agree with him that the ' three Fs ' now necessary for Ireland are Fair Dealing, Finality of Legislation, and Fixity of the Executive.   Their absence constitutes the backbone of the Irish difficulty.   The fact that party exigency may at any moment produce fresh legislation, and that the turn of the electoral wheel might as suddenly substitute a vacillating for a firm executive, is at the bottom of that absence of security and confidence without which prosperity and material confidence cannot exist.

" It is this condition of affairs which, I feel, constitutes the chief difficulty in trying to answer a question which has been put to me—' What I would endeavour to do if I were responsible for the conduct of affairs ? '

" It is not easy for me to realise such a position, nor do I know anything of the wheels within wheels now running in political circles.   But I would say that I regard the maintenance of the Union, and, as a *means thereto*, the preservation of the Unionist party, as of the first importance.   Next to this, though hardly secondary in importance, I must put the firm administration of the law.

" Nothing could be better than Mr. Balfour's rule.

If it can be continued either by himself or by some other equally firm and impartial man, we can desire no improvement.   I believe in this the main political difficulty lies, as Mr. Gladstone and his followers use the prosecution of the agitators to make political capital out of.   How far such tactics may tend to shake the allegiance of Liberal Unionists or to influence the opinion of English constituencies I cannot tell.   But I believe any relaxation of the firm attitude which Mr. Balfour has adopted would now do incalculable mischief, and I believe that the efforts of our public speakers and political associations could not be better directed than by instructing the English constituencies as to the truth on this point.   In this way I think Hurlbert's book will be of great use.   If I were responsible for the conduct of affairs, I would certainly regard the maintenance of order as a *vital point.*

" The Union being preserved, and the law firmly and impartially administered, I would extend the Purchase System.   It is not one that can work any great change suddenly, and it is the better for that.   As it developed, and as year by year a large number of occupiers were converted into quasi-owners of the land, we have every reason to believe that they would become orderly and peaceable members of the community, and fit to be entrusted with larger responsibilities.   According as that change became apparent and developed, I should have no hesitation in entrusting them with, first, under-powers in local government matters, and ultimately, as the scheme was completed, with entire control over the rates and taxes which they had themselves paid—always assuming that my first two conditions, the ' Union and Law,' were maintained.

" I do not believe that the British taxpayer would

run any risk in making the advances required for the purposes of Lord Ashbourne's Act.   After a few years there would be no necessity for an *actual* fresh advance, as the repayments would afford means for carrying on the Act.   In my opinion, the fact that the scheme must work gradually is strongly in its favour. Any great radical change like it which was sudden and sweeping in its effect would be little short of a revolution, and be. a dangerous experiment upon a people with the temperament of the Irish race.

" There are, of course, in working out this scheme many suggestions which might be made, but I do not regard your letter as inviting such, and, until the main question is decided as to the continuance of the Purchase Scheme, details would be premature.   But, if I understand your letter rightly, I do not think you would care to be troubled with such questions at present.

" I shall be quite ready to go into. the minor matters I have referred to if my doing so can be of any use to you.—Yours very truly,

" ARTHUR KAVANAGH."

The last two or three years of his life were spent in frequent suffering and consequent depression, though, now and again, the old bright spirit would revive.   The political outlook was such that, except in the continuance of Mr. Balfour's guidance of Irish affairs, he had but little to hope for in the future, seeing so clearly as he did the danger to the country of a feebly-administered government.   Still, with sinking powers and breaking spirits, he never failed, to the very last, to attend all the meetings and boards in Carlow, Kilkenny, and Dublin, for the despatch of business connected with land or Church, just as he did in full health, just as regularly, just as conscientiously. The one recreation he continued to allow himself, and that grudgingly, was an annual trip in his yacht the *Water Lily* to the coast of Holland for duck-shooting.

His last summer on earth was spent mainly at Borris, and by that time the change had become very apparent. In July he took a small party of cousins in the *Water Lily* to see the great naval review off Spithead, in honour of the Emperor of Germany. Thence he went to the Dutch coast, where he was soon joined by Mrs. Kavanagh. There the fatal illness of which the seeds had been so long developing made such rapid progress that he was forced to return to London for medical advice.

October, November, and the greater part of December were passed in rapidly-increasing illness and suffering, bravely borne with silent unmurmuring resignation to God's will—and on Christmas morning he died.

Not to the sound of the weird singing of the Banshee, that tradition assigns as herald to a Kavanagh's death, but to the music of the Christmas anthems before the throne, he entered his Father's house, to hear the welcome words : "Well done, good and faithful servant!" [1]

1 Appendix G.

EPILOGUE

Cui Pudor et Justitiae soror
Incorrupta Fides nudaque Veritas
Quando ullum inveniet parem ?

HOR. *Car.* i. 24.

Where shall be found the man of woman born
  That in desert might be esteemed his peer,—
Sincere as he, and resolutely just,
So high of heart, and all so absolute of trust ?

SIR THEODORE MARTIN.

So lived, so died, Arthur MacMurrough Kavanagh.

His was a life of high aspirations, of noble deeds, of unconscious heroism.

To those who loved him the loss is beyond words—the steady loyal friend, the wise counsellor, gone ; the music of the full-toned gentle voice hushed.

But to her—his best and dearest—who for more than thirty years, in joy and sorrow, "in sickness and in health," shared his life and was (what those who wished him well would have sought for him) a loving helpmeet—seeking nought in which he could have no part—making his aims and objects hers—who can tell what it is ?

And to Ireland, for which he toiled so long and so patiently, the loss of his clear sense and unbiassed judgment will be felt in the dark hours she may yet have to pass through.   Well for her if those who then sway

the councils of the Empire seek their guidance where
he sought his, and follow it as earnestly.

I feel that my pen has but feebly sketched this
most interesting character and career. The physical
privations which would have crushed the fibre of a
weaker nature served but to crown his moral complete-
ness. This was shown in all the manifold vicissitudes
of his life—in the lonely midnight watch in the northern seas—in the yet more lonely midnight ride through
the Indian plains—no eye upon him save the All-
seeing One of his " great Taskmaster "—and still more
in the life he entered on at home of patient self-
denying toil for others—toil for his people, for his
country, for his God.

His political career may safely be left to the judgment of posterity, who will gauge with true perception
the import of his chief work—the " Land Corporation
of Ireland."

But I, who had the great happiness and privilege
of knowing him intimately all my life, may tell of what
he was in private. Of the " light address "—the fun
that charmed and never wounded, of which flashes
appeared to the last—of the musical voice so rare in
any one inured to an outdoor life—and of the ready
cordial help in any and every difficulty—I think I,
more than most, can speak in loving remembrance.
For his manner invited a confidence which the result
always repaid; and many besides myself will gratefully
recall the sympathy and help received in times of
anxiety and perplexity from him who now lies sleeping
in the little ruined church on Ballycopigan—"until
the day break, and the shadows flee away."

30TH DECEMBER 1889.

Lay him down, lay him down in the full eye of Heaven,
    Beside these grey walls in the fields of his home,
Where Princes, perchance, of his line have been shriven,
    And peasants for prayer and for comfort have come.

Lay him down—in all Erin no temple so fit is
    To cradle the bravest and best of his name ;
The soft winds of even shall sing his *Dimittis*,
    And stars for his lyke-wake at midnight shall flame.

Meet resting this spot in its wildness and beauty
    For the Patriot true in a nation's despite,
The man that was faithful to God and to duty,
    Whose judgment unerring still held to the right ;

Whose soul was so grand in its simple reliance,
    Who stedfastly purposed and patiently wrought,
Who feared not opposers, nor quailed at defiance,
    And smiled at the honours that found him unsought.

Devoted, heart-true to the people who scorned him,
    Who craftily injured and cruelly spoke—
Unable to value the gifts that adorned him,
    Or fathom the love of the heart that they broke.

Ingrate and forgetful—Ah ! tenderly leave him ;
    The Arms everlasting around him are cast—
No chiding can chafe or ingratitude grieve him,
    Who sleeps in the Lord when his labour is past.

C. F. ALEXANDER.

x

APPENDICES ·

A, p. 137

In illustration of the remark in the text, the Rev. G. W. Rooke writes :—

"A very striking feature of his character was his cheerfulness. In my intercourse with him this often impressed me as very remarkable. And to those who looked for it the source was not hard to find. It sprang, I believe, from a feeling of Christian contentment and happy thankfulness to Almighty God.

"I recollect as if it was only yesterday the solemnity and the earnestness of his sonorous voice repeating the beautiful 'General Thanksgiving' of our Prayer-book, those first Sundays when I officiated as chaplain in the chapel attached to Borris House."

B, p. 138

For many years the two hymns and collects that are given in facsimile of his writing, headed every new diary that he commenced.

C, p. 193

ADDRESS

TO

WALTER MACMURROUGH KAVANAGH, Esq.

We, the tenantry of the Carlow and Wexford estates, tender you our heart-felt congratulations on the occasion of your attaining your majority.

You have bright prospects before you—youth, with all its charms—wealth, with all its influence—and you have the name, the fame, and prestige of an ancient, illustrious, and, we may add, a royal family.

Cast on the ocean of life, you cannot go astray, for you have a safe pilot in your esteemed father, and his acts are your chart.   He is a good landlord, a benevolent gentleman, particularly kind to the poor, and perfectly free from bigotry or exclusiveness in dealing with his tenantry.

Goodness must come to you by inheritance, for you have all the blood of the MacMurroughs in your veins and expanding your heart.   May your voyage through life be prosperous, may you escape the perils of the deep, and may it be very many years before you arrive at that haven or bourne "from whence no traveller returns."

That God may grant long life and happiness to Walter MacMurrough Kavanagh, Esq., the heir of Borris House, is the prayer of all his tenants.

Signed on behalf of the tenantry,

P. CAREY, P.P., Borris,
Chairman.

10th October 1877.

REPLY

GENTLEMEN—Deeply gratified as I must feel at the warm expressions of congratulation and regard conveyed to me in your address, I fear that I am totally unable, in a few words, to return you sufficient thanks, and also to express all the feelings which must naturally arise on such an occasion as this.

In your allusions to my father you have anticipated my own sentiments, and you may rest assured that I will, to the best of my ability, follow so good and thorough an example.

The occasion which has called from you so kind an address has for me its responsibilities as well as its pleasures, but I hope you will find that your best interests will be ever at my heart, and I trust that the more we know of each other the better friends we shall become.

In conclusion, gentlemen, I must once more thank you for the kindly spirit and affectionate wishes contained in your address, and I shall always connect it in my remembrance with the Carlow and Wexford tenants.

(Signed)   WALTER MACM. KAVANAGH.

D, p. 203

Not always, however, did he continue to express even that inadequate degree of blame for conduct so base.

The Bishop of Ossory says that in later years his invariable reply to any one who spoke to him of the ingratitude of his tenants and dependents was : ' If the poor people had been let alone they would not have acted as they did; they were forced to it by others.'

E, p. 216

BESSBOROUGH COMMISSION

SEPARATE REPORT BY A. MACM. KAVANAGH, ESQ.

I cannot agree in the draft report submitted by the Chairman, as I dissent from some of its propositions and the manner in which they are presented. I have therefore endeavoured to draw out a short statement of my views upon the evidence we have heard, as a more satisfactory mode of proceeding than by attempting to move amendments to those portions of their

report with which I do not agree. I do not attempt
to put this statement forward as being at all exhaustive
of all the different questions brought under our notice,
but as enabling me more explicitly to express my
opinion upon those points which appear to me to be of
the greatest moment.

The weight of evidence has, in my opinion,
undoubtedly proved—that the properties of the
majority of extensive landowners, which comprise the
largest portion of agricultural and pastoral land in
Ireland, have been well and humanely managed.

That on them the lands are let low, and the rents
rarely raised.

That evictions on title have been very rare, and,
although in many cases the power of ejectment has
had to be used for the purpose of obtaining the payment of rent, in comparatively few instances have they
resulted in the ultimate displacement of the occupiers.

On the other hand, it has shown that the Land Act
of 1870, while conferring considerable advantages upon
the tenant-farmers of Ireland, has not been altogether
successful in affording them such adequate security as
was expected, particularly in protecting them in all
cases against occasional and unreasonable increases of
rents.

Evidence has been given that on several properties
—some purchased as speculations, others belonging to
owners who have had no real tie to either the land or
the people, save that of deriving their income from it
—rents have been unduly raised to what has been
described, in some instances, as an exorbitant extent,
not only upon the value of the lands themselves, but
upon the improvements effected by the tenants on them.
And it is contended that in districts where such cases
of injustice have occurred the feeling of fear and
apprehension has spread, even among those not likely
to be affected by them. In the North and those
districts where tenant-right usages prevail, this raising
of rent has been stated in several cases to have almost
destroyed the value of the tenant-right, and I believe

a careful study of the evidence will show that one of
the effects of the Act 1870 has been on the whole
more prejudicial than beneficial to the tenants on
several of the properties subject to these usages in this
particular respect.

In the other districts of the country not subject to
clauses 1 and 2 of the Land Act, the evidence has, I
believe, proved that the beneficial effect of the Act has
been much more generally felt. Evictions on title—a
power seldom used and never unwarrantably on the
great majority of large and well-managed estates—has
been most materially checked where before it was
unjustly exercised, although instances of it still remain;
and of the great number of complaints of raising of
rents which have been made during the course of our
inquiry, some of which have been simply childish and
others bearing on their face their own refutation, the
majority—as the evidence will, I believe, show—date
previous to its passing; but sufficient instances have
been shown to have occurred of what would appear to
be the unjust exercise of both these powers, since 1870,
to prove that even in these districts the Act has failed
to be altogether effectual in preventing abuses.

The weight of evidence has, however, proved that
the question of rent is at the bottom of every other,
and is really, whether in the North or South, the gist
of the grievances which have caused much of the
present dissatisfaction. I think that the evidence
suggests the conclusion that the Land Act, as now in
force, does not afford sufficient protection to the tenants
against the unjust exercise of the power to raise rents
in unscrupulous hands; and, although I admit that in
adopting the suggestion of a system of arbitration for
the settlement of disputes as to rents and other matters
of valuation, I am endorsing an interference with rights
of property and freedom of contract open to grave
economical objections, and which to the great majority
of landowners who have not abused their powers
will, I have no doubt, appear unwarrantable; yet,
having regard to the mischief which the unjust exercise

of the power has occasioned, I can come to no other conclusion than that, in any proposed alteration of present rents, whether at the instance of landlord or tenant, when the two parties cannot agree, the question should be left to arbitration, with final reference, in the event of the arbitrators being unable to agree upon an umpire, to a Land Court or Commission which should be appointed for that and other purposes. It will, I think, be apparent that, if the Government see fit to interfere in the question of rents, they are bound to substitute for the landlord's power which they displace an impartial tribunal which will command the confidence of the public, and that they are further bound, as essential to the fair settlement of the rent question, to have a new general valuation of the country. If anything has been clearly established on evidence during this inquiry, the fact that the present Government valuation is not a dependable standard for the settlement of rents has been most thoroughly demonstrated. Fair as it may have been for the purposes of taxation in the years when it was made, the evidence shows that even then it was considered as below the fair letting value of the land ; and this fact is corroborated by the written testimony of the late Sir Richard Griffith, who was head of the Commission, as well as by the evidence of many other trustworthy and independent witnesses.

I must add that I am opposed to the attempt to draw out any rules for the guidance of arbitrators in their task of determining what a fair rent may be, further than the general instructions which are in justice too apparent to require mention, that the improvements effected by the tenants should be fully credited to them, as well as that any expenditure made by the landlord for a like purpose should be put to his account.

The evidence has, as might be expected, proved that the great desire of the tenant-farmers is for fixity of tenure and free sale. It is urged in favour of these that the first exists in practice on all the large well-managed estates, and that the second is only a logical sequence of it, that in fact the Land Act in clause 3 gives an interest, and that a vendible interest, and that therefore no very great practical change in the circumstances now existing on the largest portion of the lands in Ireland would be the result of the concession. It is further urged, on the grounds of the importance of giving to the tenants full security in the enjoyment of, and compensation for, the improvements they have made ; and this argument is, in my mind, the only one of real weight in this matter, backed up as it is by instances of hardship and oppressive action on the part of some of the small proprietors, to whom I have already alluded. In the shibboleth of agitation, "Fixity of Tenure" and "Free Sale" are coupled together as if they were one term, but I cannot regard them in that light. The Land Act, while giving compensation for disturbance which some call an interest, leaves the sale of that interest subject to the landlord's power of eviction, and it is idle to assert that, because a landlord from right feeling gives to his tenants the right of continuous occupation, so long as they discharge their obligations towards him, he thereby conveys to them the right to sell their holdings. To give fixity of tenure by law, although a very considerable and arbitrary interference with landlords' rights, would not, it is true, involve any great practical change as regards the majority of large landowners (provided it was given to the tenant under certain approved conditions) in their present relations with their tenants ; but to extend at once to all parts of the country the right of free sale would be in those districts not now subject to clauses 1 and 2 of the Land Act a very important change, and a very material and practical interference with the rights of property, and therefore it appears to me simpler to try to deal with the two questions separately.

First as to fixity of tenure. It is contended that the Land Act in clause 3 admits the principle in the case of certain holdings by giving the occupiers a claim for disturbance if turned out by the act of the landlord for any other cause than non-payment of rent ; the fact is clear that it does so within a certain limit of duration. But it does not give interminable fixity of tenure, and the proof of this is to be found in the Act itself. A lease of thirty years is made the equivalent of a disturbance claim, and the landlord by giving that can free himself at its expiration from the penalty on the recovery of the possession of his own land. It is therefore, I think, clear that any Act of the Legislature giving to the tenant perpetual fixity of tenure would be foreign to the principle of the Act of 1870. Those who advocate its extension as an existing principle would be, in my opinion, much more logically correct in adducing as their example or warrant for this argument the numerous cases on the old estates, where the tenants are never turned out so long as they pay their rents ; but whether it is right or just to deprive good landlords of a right which from good feeling they seldom if ever exercise, because some bad ones abuse it, is a question I must leave Parliament to answer. However that may be, the change would not be one, as I have shown, which would practically interfere with rights often used—this has been in fact admitted by the majority of large landowners who have given evidence before us, and the advisability of the general extension of the principle has been endorsed by not a few of them, as also by many agents of great experience on behalf of others, as well as by County Court Judges and other independent witnesses ; in short, there has been much less disagreement on this point than I was at all prepared for, and if I was only acting for myself, and if my own interests were alone at stake, I should have no hesitation in agreeing to their recommendations. But, on the other hand, we have a number of the largest landowners whose estates have been always managed on the very best principles, whose opinions are fairly represented by the evidence of Lords Lansdowne and Dufferin, who, while never arbitrarily exercising their power, entertain the strongest objection to legislative interference with it. In this view they are supported by the evidence of Mr. Ferguson, Q.C., County Court Judge, who, while wishing to extend the principle, considers it would be destructive of ownership and difficult to compensate the landlords for it ; and although my own opinion is what I have stated, I cannot disregard the unmistakable weight and truth of such evidence, and what I believe to be the fact, that had it been possible to receive further evidence on the subject, many landlords would have come forward to endorse it—the circumstance that they had not that opportunity I regret the more as I may naturally enough perhaps be held responsible for it.

Under all these circumstances, I am not prepared to recommend the general extension of fixity of tenure. My opinion on the most material point remains unchanged—that the Land Act, as it now stands, does not give sufficient security to the tenant, and that it is both just and expedient that this security should be increased. But it seems to me that there is another mode of attaining the same end, and of giving practical security of tenure to the tenant, without such a direct and sweeping interference with the rights of property as the first would involve ; and that mode is to stand by the principles laid down in the Act of 1870. By some of the County Court Judges it was recommended to increase the penalties on eviction in clause 3, and by others to abolish all limit, leaving the amount of the penalty to be inflicted altogether to the discretion of the Court, and, where they deemed the justice of the case required it, to refuse to give a decree for possession. This, it was asserted, would have the effect of giving practical security of tenure to all tenancies coming within the provisions of that clause. Some substantial extension of this power I am quite prepared to recommend, so far as residential occupiers are concerned, believing that, without conveying to the tenants a direct share in the property of the landlords, which granting "fixity of tenure" undoubtedly would do, it would confer upon them that practical security to which the majority, from the peculiar circumstances of their positions, are fairly entitled. But I am bound to add that, although I recommend its application only to existing residential tenancies and not to *bona fide* new lettings, there is no concealing the fact that the recommendation, if successful, will practically deprive the landlord class of the rights of both reversion in and control over the majority of holdings on many properties—for the arbitrary interference with which by the State it is only just that they should receive fair compensation.

As to the extension of free sale, although the majority of the evidence of tenant-farmers has been in favour of it, there has not been the same unanimity of opinion on this as on the former point. Some—few, I allow—looking farther than the present, have objected to the tax which the universal extension of free sale would impose upon those anxious to obtain land in the future, and in this view they have been supported by the evidence of both the landlords and agents who have had the most experience in the working of the different phases of the Ulster custom ; so that even in the North, where the custom of sale exists already, the wisdom of removing such limitations as are now in force is not unquestioned ; and when we come to the proposal to make the extension universal—to create it *de novo* in districts where no trace of it has ever existed —the difficulty, if justice or fair play is to be considered, is most materially increased. It is further shown by those whose views are not solely limited to the benefit of the present occupiers, but who consider the prospects of the future, that such a general extension would not only limit the future possession of land to those who have capital, and thereby preclude a very considerable portion of the population, whose only capital is their labour, from the possible chance of its acquisition, but would saddle all future tenancies with a rackrent, no matter how liberal or indulgent the landlord might be, as the rent reserved to him would only be a portion, and it might be only a small portion, of the true annual charge to which the holding would be subject, as the interest on the sum paid for its acquisition, although a voluntary imposition on the tenant's part, must necessarily be added. I am bound, therefore, to say that, having regard to the future, I fail to see that its general extension must necessarily convey the unmixed blessing to the commonwealth which some anticipate. That the general evidence of the tenant-farmers is in favour of it is only natural, as they are in the status of present occupiers whose position would necessarily be much improved, and cannot therefore cause surprise. Evidence was given by one or two labourers and by some other witnesses on their behalf, and the tenor of it was, if I remember right, opposed to the farmers' claims, with whom they seemed to have no great common interest; but to pursue this subject now would be to go into the great question of the over-populated and poverty-stricken districts, which I must reserve for another part.

On the other hand, the evidence in favour of its extension has been based upon the assertion, which is, I believe, a fact, that on the majority of holdings the improvements, if such they can be called, if not altogether have been chiefly made by the tenants, and that, without the right of sale, in the event of their leaving they would not adequately be compensated for them.

It was further urged in favour of its extension that the custom already exists on many estates outside of Ulster—those of Lord Devon, Lord Portsmouth, and Lord Portarlington, were specially named; and on them it was proved that it worked admirably, stimulating improvements, producing contentment, and rendering ejectments almost unnecessary for the recovery of rent. Some landlords and not a few agents, believing that these results would be the natural consequences of its further development, advocated it, and in this they were supported by the evidence of many of the County Court Judges. Other landlords, regarding it chiefly from the point of view of affording to them increased security for their rent, and as a possible temporary sop to agitation, were inclined to acquiesce, yielding more perhaps to the present pressure than to what they deemed the justice of the case. But with very rare exceptions all classes of witnesses agreed that where no payment had been made, either by the occupying tenant or his predecessors, for the acquisition of the good-will or improvements, the landlord should receive adequate compensation for the transference of the right; and it was as generally admitted that the landlord should have a right of veto to protect himself against the intrusion of objectionable characters upon his estate. Except by some few graziers themselves, the extension was not advocated to those kinds of holdings. As regards them it was asserted that a man's capital was all required to stock his farm, and that it was not desirable that it should be absorbed in the purchase of the good-will; and as to improvements on them it was asserted that, in the real permanent sense of the term, there could be and were none; and it was further stated that even if the right was extended to those, or indeed to any very large class of farms, the price they would fetch would be small, as the competition was limited.

I have now, as shortly, as fairly, and as clearly as I can, given the *pros* and *cons* which were adduced by either side on this great question, for I regard it as about the gravest and most difficult that was submitted to us. For my own part I must say that I entertain no disinclination whatever to extend this right to the majority of holdings on my own property, although I have spent very large sums myself in the improvement of them; and I must confess that strongly as I was opposed to its general extension before I entered upon this inquiry, the evidence I have heard, and done my best to sift, has convinced me that doing so would confer more advantages on the present occupiers than disadvantages on me. I can say, moreover, that I would be glad to see its application made general, if it could be justly done, believing that it is the simplest and most efficacious way of giving that perfect security to the tenants which I do think, where the improvements are all or mainly their own, they ought to have; and giving that would, I am of opinion, be such general advantage to the country that the landlords might be content to make some sacrifice to attain it. In those districts where the improvements have all been made by the tenants, the difficulty or injustice, so far as the landlord's rights are concerned, is not so glaringly apparent, provided the power of using a veto on their part is preserved against an objectionable incoming tenant; but in other districts where enormous sums have been spent by the landlords in improving their properties—on some few properties it has been proved that the English system exists in its purity, the landlord having made all the improvements—and on holdings where tenant-right formerly existed and has been bought up by the landlord, instances of which have been proved, its extension or re-establishment would, in my opinion, be simple confiscation, and an unwarrantable and arbitrary interference with rights of property which the circumstances could in no sense justify. I am therefore, on these grounds, not prepared to recommend its absolutely general or universal extension, so far as those special districts to which I have referred are concerned, without the free consent of the landlords themselves. The majority of the witnesses who advocated its extension to those districts where it did not already exist coupled their recommendation with the condition, as I have already stated, that the landlord should receive adequate compensation for the transference of the right. This principle, I maintain, is strictly a just one, and it is only subject to it that I am prepared to recommend the extension of the right of sale to those holdings now coming under the provisions of the Land Act, where the tenants have made all or the chief part of the improvements.

With these three safeguards which I have now recommended, *i.e.* the check upon raising rents, giving increased power to the Court in reference to evictions, where such apply to residential occupiers, extending to all holdings now under the Land Act upon which the improvements have been made by the tenant the right of sale, I believe the position of the present occupiers, or their representatives, would be such that they would have nothing to fear from the action of any landlord, no matter how harsh or unscrupulous he might be. But, on the other hand, I am bound to add that, although in weighing the evidence I have endeavoured to eliminate all revolutionary proposals, my three recommendations do involve very arbitrary and material interference with the rights of landlords, to which many would entertain, and with every reason, the strongest objection; and that if the Government see fit to adopt them, or to propose legislation in their direction, that proposal should be accompanied in fair justice by an offer of purchase at a fair price guaranteed by the State from those landlords of either the whole or such portions of their estates as they objected to have such made applicable to. And I think it will be admitted that my position in urging this is much strengthened by the fact, which in my opinion is proved in the evidence, that so far as the management of the large estates is concerned— and it is of importance to remember that they comprise the greatest agricultural and pastoral area in the country—no change in the present law would appear to be called for.

On the subject of the " North," and the different customs existing there, much evidence was given, as distinct from the question of the extension of the right of sale to those districts where such does not now exist. In my opinion it was shown, as I have already stated, that the exercise of the power of raising rent on the part of the landlords, where unduly used, was the grievance most severely felt, and that, I would hope, the proposal for the settlement of disputes with regard to rents, by means of arbitration, would fully meet; but still, as is only natural in a system so complex, there were other points brought under our notice, such as office rules, which, although distinct from the rent question, affected more or less directly the value of the interests involved. The most important named was the custom existing on many large and well-managed estates of limiting the price to be paid for the tenant-right. On this point there was a great conflict of opinion, those in favour of it asserting that it afforded most material and salutary protection to the incoming man, keeping the price to be paid from reaching the exorbitant amount which it was often proved to do on account of the reckless competition (especially in the case of the smaller holdings) for the acquisition of land. Instances of almost incredible sums thus paid were freely given. The natural consequence was also dwelt on with much force—that in the absence of some limitation a purchaser had often not only to spend all his own capital, but had to borrow largely, thus starting with a load of debt about his neck. To my mind the economic principle is indisputable, and the rule a most salutary one. But, on the other hand, I am bound to admit that the weight of evidence was clearly in favour of its abolition ; and by the weight of evidence I do not refer to numbers— some landlords and many agents of the greatest practical experience, admitting the wisdom of the principle, condemned its working as almost impossible. It was asserted, indeed I might say proved, that where a limit was attempted to be enforced, sums of money were invariably paid outside the office in an underhand way, and the limit utterly disregarded. It was further shown that the attempt to enforce a limit was a source of an immense amount of soreness and discontent among the tenant-class. It was contended on their behalf that a man could only sell what he had, and that any attempt to lessen or limit the value of that was most unjust. On Colonel Forde's estate especially, and on some others, what would appear to be a most satisfactory system of settling this point by means of arbitration was shown to exist, and, perhaps, the proposal for settling disputed rents might be found applicable generally in this case also. If it did command

the confidence of the parties interested, it would certainly appear to me to be the wisest course, in the
interest of the tenants themselves, to adopt; but if it
did not, and the feeling of discontent and soreness was
likely to be continued, I think, in the interests of the
landlords, it would be better that the rule should be
abolished.

The question of the method of sale, "public
auctions *v.* private sales," was also one upon which
there was a good deal of difference of opinion ; and on
this I think the weight of evidence, even in the
tenants' interest, was more against than for the public
sale.   It was urged, and I think with great force, that
the excitement of public competition, sometimes increased by fictitious offers, often induced buyers to
make bids which in their cooler moments they would
never have done, and recklessly to incur liabilities
which most materially embarrassed their future; and it
was further shown that the highest *bona fide* price
could always be obtained by either private sale or
what is termed a private auction—a species of sale
which it appears is customary among them,—neither of
which are open to the objections urged against the
other.   On these grounds I am clearly of opinion that
the landlord's right to forbid public sales by auction
should be retained.   Another point was as to the landlord's right of selection of the incoming tenant.   By all
sides it was admitted that he should have the right of
veto, to protect himself against the introduction of
objectionable characters or insolvent tenants upon his
property.   But it was further urged that he should
have the power of giving the preference, if so inclined,
to a tenant on his estate.   This would appear to me to
be a very reasonable and natural discretion to give
him, and provided, but only on that condition, that the
value of the tenant-right was not lessened thereby, I
would be in favour of the preservation of that right.
There may have been other points referred to in the
course of the evidence relating to the Ulster custom,
but as I do not pretend to make my report an ex-

haustive one, I have only attempted to touch upon those which appeared to me to be of real importance; and of those there is, I believe, only one more that I need mention, and that is securing to the Northern tenant resident on his holding the continuous occupancy, or security of tenure, which I propose to give to tenants under the same condition in the other districts; and that, I believe, would be achieved by the Act as it stands, with the extension of power that I suggest should be given to the Court under clause 3. The Act, in clauses 1 and 2, gives to the tenants under them the right to claim under any other sections of the Act, which would clearly allow them, in the event of an eviction, to come before the Court under the extended powers in clause 3, when the Court could leave them in possession by refusing to grant a decree.

Having by these recommendations, as I believe, thoroughly protected the interests of all the present occupiers now coming under the provisions of the Act of 1870, and their representatives, I am most decidedly of opinion that for the future all *bona fide* new lettings, whether within or beyond the same scope, should be subject to entire and absolute freedom of contract.

Powerful evidence was given to show that in the present lawless state of affairs, the fairest and justest landowners were not sufficiently protected in the enforcement of their most obvious rights, and in any change of the law increased facilities should be given for the assertion of just rights, and for the summary punishment of those who by terror or otherwise interfere therewith, or retake the possession of lands which have been legally given up to the landowner. If the evidence shows that under the existing land code tenants were not sufficiently protected from some hardships, it also demonstrates that under the same law landlords have been unable during the past few months to assert any rights whatever.

I do not feel called upon to discuss the present agitation, or the proper mode of dealing with the prevailing anarchy, or whether it should affect the selection of a period for legislation in reference to land, or to speculate upon the effect which any such legislation might. have upon the present critical state of affairs. These grave topics demand the earnest consideration of Parliament, but appear to be outside the scope of our reference. It must be borne in mind that the present development of the agitation is not reflected by the evidence given by tenant-farmers some little time ago before us, and that the proceedings of the Land League meetings give a representation of opinion in favour of the most extreme, communistic, and revolutionary views, which no legislature can fulfil or satisfy.

To every one who has either heard or read the evidence it must be apparent that there are circumstances existing in some parts of the country requiring both stringent and immediate remedies, which satisfying the popular cry for the " Three Fs " would not touch. Evidence of the strongest nature was given during the inquiry of a condition of affairs existing in the West and other over-populated districts, which the establishment of fixity of tenure, even coupled with free sale, would, in my opinion, only perpetuate, without alleviating. It is contended that by the granting of the right of free sale these small holdings would be ultimately absorbed, and so the present evil would be removed. But inasmuch as the whole population of these districts are paupers, I fail to see who would be the purchasers, unless the purchase by outsiders is contemplated, which would only have the effect of making a change in, not lessening, the population, or establishing a class of middlemen, which has been unanimously condemned ; but even if there was this local absorption assumed, the process would be so slow that the country would have to undergo many of its past trials before the remedy could be efficacious. In my opinion, the circumstances of these over-populated districts can only be dealt with by State interference, in the way of a liberal and humane scheme of emigration, by sending the people out in charge of their ministers to the large and fertile districts of unpopulated land in Western

Canada, where homes and the means of acquiring their living could be provided for them, such as they could never have in this country, and opportunities would be afforded to enlarge the holdings of those who remain behind.

A scheme was proposed, and strongly advocated by some witnesses, that these crowded districts should be relieved of the surplus population by transplanting the people to the tracts of waste land in different parts of the country, where they should be paid as labourers by the State until these lands were sufficiently reclaimed to support them ; but I must say it is a recommendation that I could not take upon myself the responsibility of endorsing. I believe, if they are to be moved (and I can see no other cure for such cases), emigrating them to good lands is a much wiser course than migrating them to lands as bad, if not worse, than those they left.

Much evidence was also given as to the labouring class, and the condition of many of them shown to be bad, both in respect of their dwellings and means of support ; but no practical suggestion that I can call to mind was offered for their amelioration. The giving to them gardens and dwellings, which some suggested the Church Surplus Fund should be devoted to, would only be planting them on plots insufficient for their support, without placing any more certain means for earning or gaining their subsistence within their reach. They (the labourers) are not incorrectly described as small farmers without farms ; and I fear a change in the present land law, which makes the possession of a certain amount of capital a *sine quâ non* for the possession of a farm, will not do much to improve either their present position or their future prospects. In my opinion, the reason of their poverty and want in many districts where small holdings are in the preponderance is the fact that small farmers are simply labourers with farms, who do not require extraneous aid to till their farms. And, therefore, save in the seasons of seed-time and harvest, in such districts the labouring classes who depend on labour only for their support must always suffer more or less acutely from the want of employment. One of the effects of the Land Act of 1870, as shown by the evidence before us, was that it had stopped many landlords from spending money in improvements on their estates, and I greatly fear that the further interference with their rights now suggested must, if adopted, have a much more marked effect in that direction, and, insomuch as it has, the future prospects of the labouring classes in the way of obtaining employment must be injuriously affected. It is only another, although a less extreme, phase of over-population, and I can only see relief in the same, although a less extensive, application of the emigration scheme.

Peasant-Proprietors

This subject has been touched upon by almost every witness, and the evidence has been as conflicting as voluminous. While originally in favour of it when I entered upon the inquiry, believing that in the common-sense view of the matter an owner of property of sufficient size to afford to him an adequate subsistence would be opposed to revolution, and anxious to preserve what he had, and that by creating such a class in Ireland we should be adding to the ranks of those interested in the support of law and order, and diminishing the numbers who are now at the beck of every agitator, no matter how wild his theory or communistic his principles, I must admit that considerations of a very weighty nature have been urged against the scheme by those who view it from the point of its possible, if not probable, results, and their opinions, it is only fair to say, are formed from the experiences of the past. As illustrations of their views the examples of the old perpetuity leases have been given us in evidence, where the lessees holding on grants for ever at a nominal rent, have been, so far as the question is practically concerned, in the same position as owners in fee; and the condition of those properties now have been cited as exemplifying what the result of peasant-proprietors would be, and if they can be taken as a fair example of what the result of a future experiment in that direction would result in, I think that even the most ardent advocate of that scheme would not consider it as encouraging. By the evidence it is shown that very few of the representatives of the original lessees are now in possession. Ruined by idleness and extravagance, their grants soon passed into the hands of mortgagees, who, looking only to gain, let and sublet, divided and subdivided their lands, till over-population with its consequent ills of never-ceasing want and periodical famine were stereotyped in those districts; and even in the few instances which remain of the representatives of the original lessees still continuing in possession the condition is no better. It is shown that as occasion arose for each owner to make provision for his family the same course was adopted, till the successive increase of each generation reduced the holdings to a size utterly inadequate to the support of those depending on them for even a bare subsistence. The difficulty, almost impossibility, of preventing subdivision under such a system has been dwelt upon by many witnesses, while the danger of it has been admitted by almost all.

The condition of those who have already become purchasers of their holdings under the Church Commissioners, and the Bright clauses of the Land Act, has also been the subject of very conflicting evidence; by some the present position of many is described as worse than before they bought—the late bad seasons —the small area and bad land of some of the holdings —the high prices which were paid—the large amount of costs, especially of purchases made under the Bright clauses—the high amount of interest charged when the amount to be paid down by the purchaser had to be all or partly borrowed, being among other causes given as the reasons, and it certainly does seem a reasonable assumption that when a purchaser has to borrow all, his position cannot be improved by the change.

On the other hand, it has been shown that many have prospered well, and that in such cases the sense of contentment and security has resulted in a very marked degree in the great improvement of their allotments. As might naturally be supposed, this satisfactory condition is almost entirely limited to those who, having money of their own, were saved from the necessity of going to the money-lenders to provide the amount required by the Acts to be paid down, and their success would clearly seem to be due in a greater degree to their own thrift and industry, which enabled them to save this money, than to the fact that they were saved the high rate of interest to which others had to submit.

Varied, however, as the opinions have been upon the subject, the weight of evidence has most unmistakably gone in favour of, subject to certain safeguards and limitations, what may be termed a gradual scheme for the establishment of tenant proprietors in suitable localities throughout the country. The proposal which some very few, I admit, advocated, for the Government to buy out all the landlords in Ireland, in order to re-sell the lands to the tenants, was one which was almost unanimously condemned, not only as unpracticable, but in the highest degree injurious, and is in my opinion altogether too wild even to admit of discussion.

The suggestions as to limitations and safeguards in carrying out the gradual scheme were many, but may, I think, be summarised under a few heads. First, subdivision was admitted by almost all to be the great danger to be guarded against; the great difficulty, almost impossibility, of its prevention was urged as an insuperable objection against the scheme at all, and it must be apparent that great difficulty does exist in the future. So long as any of the instalments of the purchase-money advanced by the State remain unpaid, the provisions of the Acts are stringent and cogent enough to prevent it, and it is only after that when, under the present law, all State control would cease, that the danger would arise. On this point it was suggested that the difficulty would be met by making these sales to the occupiers grants from the Crown subject to a nominal perpetuity rent (which would warrant a small reduction in the first cost to the purchaser), and to a condition against subdivision or subletting ; in fact, against alienation of any part less than the whole. It was further suggested on this point, and I think wisely, that the purchaser should not be prevented from mortgaging or selling his interest, so long as he dealt with the whole ; interference with either of these rights would certainly appear to me to be both unjust to the purchaser, and in no way necessary for the security of the State. If mortgaged before the instalments had been paid off, their priority would not be interfered with, and if sold, the same conditions that were binding on the original purchaser would continue so on his successor.

Second, as to fixing a minimum limit to holdings that were to be sold to occupiers, a considerable amount of evidence was given, and varied opinions expressed as to the smallest quantity of land upon which a family could subsist. Some witnesses were of opinion that 10 acres were sufficient, but the majority named the minimum as between 20 and 40 acres ; others maintained that sales should not be made to holders of less than 50 acres, and others named 100. The question is a difficult one, but of not the less importance to the well-being of the country, if the scheme of a peasant proprietary should be seriously entertained by the Government. It would, in my opinion, be worse than a dangerous experiment to establish owners on plots of ground which were not of either sufficient size or quality to support them ; it would only be tending to perpetuate the misery and want which now exist in many districts. Its only recommendation is the chance that in the future these small owners would be obliged to sell, and that gradual consolidation would ultimately remedy the evil. But to establish a system the only recommendation for which is the chance that it might die out is hardly a commendable policy. As to the other class of holdings, of from 20 to 40 acres, I certainly would be in favour—where thrifty, industrious men could be found able to provide the necessary proportion of the purchase-money themselves—of affording them facilities to purchase their holdings, subject to the safeguards I have mentioned—when estates were brought into the market, provided the sale of the remainder was not thereby prejudiced, or where landlords of themselves were willing to sell. But while I would afford facilities to them, I must confess that it is the establishment of the larger class of holders, of from 100 acres upwards, that I would most strongly approve of, and it is from men of that class that, I think, the most material benefits to the community would be derived.

A modified scheme of establishing a peasant-proprietary was dwelt on with much force by some witnesses, in which they recommended that the State should advance money to tenants to purchase long leases or perpetuities from the landlords at the present or reduced rents, and in favour of it I must admit there is a good deal to be said. It would facilitate and encourage a lasting agreement between landlords and tenants which would remove their relations out of the arena of dispute, and would contribute to the peace of the country. Many landlords, I have no doubt, would be willing (where they had the power) to grant long leases or perpetuities, at reduced rents, if they received any fair consideration for doing so, and others, whose rents are admittedly now much below the value, would be ready on a like condition to do the same. The case of limited owners would be easily dealt with, and the interests of remainder-men secured by law. It might, moreover, be found to be a very valuable alternative to offer to landlords who, not wishing to sell their properties, objected to the other interferences with them which have been suggested. The suggestions on other points were many, as might have been expected from the number of witnesses examined—such as to the further facilities which it would be advisable to afford to those desirous of purchasing their holdings, as to the removal of limitations and restraints existing under the present law, or under rules made by the Board of Works, and other matters.

As to the first, it was contended by many that the larger proportion of the purchase-money recommended in the report of Mr. Shaw Lefevre's Select Committee might safely be advanced by the State, more especially in the North, where there would be the additional security of the value of the tenant-right.

By others it was submitted that thrift and industry should be made a necessary qualification to entitle would-be purchasers to aid from the State, and that no advance should be made to those who could not provide out of their own resources the amount required to be paid down ; and, although it is not easy in a case of this kind to devise a hard and fast rule which would not be subject to objections, it does seem to me that some test or qualification of this sort would be of use.

A considerable amount of evidence was given as to the different systems of purchase under the Church Temporalities Commissioners, and the Bright clauses of the Land Act, carried out under the direction of the Board of Works ; and the latter was shown to contrast most unfavourably with the former, which was stated to be much cheaper and simpler in its method. It was further asserted that many who were most anxious to purchase were debarred from doing so by the expense, complications, and delay which purchases under the Bright clauses entailed. These, with other suggestions, which I do not touch upon, are minor points of detail with which the Legislature can have no great difficulty in dealing. To me it would appear as hardly admissible that, if the main principle and object of the proposal is right and sound, and I believe it is, a fault in the machinery should be allowed to prevent its success.

I am, however, of opinion that, to carry out a peasant-proprietary scheme successfully to any extent, the appointment of a Royal Commission or a Special Board would be absolutely necessary.

I have thought it right, in referring to this proposal for creating peasant proprietors, to place the objections which have been urged against it plainly in the foreground. As being myself still strongly in favour of it, I wished to guard myself against the charge of prejudice, and I have therefore, perhaps, given more than due prominence to its possible dangers. But to me the proposal appears to possess the advantage of being far more free from that arbitrary interference with the rights of property which the other proposals involve ; and as I have already stated that I regard the adoption of the suggestions as to rents, tenure, and sale as only in justice admissible where accompanied with fair compensation ; or, if they preferred it, the offer of sale to the landlords at a reasonable price ; the extension of this principle (the Bright clauses of the Land Act) would afford to the State the means of disposing of estates, which would in this way come upon its hands, with only a very trivial, and quite possibly without any loss ; and on this ground, as well as on its own merits, I am prepared most strongly to recommend its favourable consideration.

10th January 1881.

F, p. 220

At a meeting of the Mansion House Committee held 7th November 1882, the Right Hon. Sir John Whitaker Ellis, Lord Mayor, presiding, it was moved by the Lord Mayor, seconded by Viscount Folkestone, M.P., and carried with acclamation—

" That the thanks of the Committee of the Mansion

House Fund for the defence of property in Ireland
are eminently due and are hereby conveyed to A.
MacMurrough Kavanagh, Esq., who upon the invita-
tion of the Committee and at much personal sacrifice
of time and labour undertook the very difficult and
responsible position of Commissioner for the due
application of the funds to secure the very important
ends for which it was raised.   The loyal, fearless, and
able manner in which these arduous duties have been
performed by Mr. Kavanagh entitles him to the very
hearty acknowledgment, not only of this Committee,
but of all interested in the preservation of law and
order and the restoration of peace and prosperity in
the sister kingdom.

"That this resolution be suitably emblazoned and
framed and signed by the Lord Mayor

" J. WHITAKER ELLIS."

G, p. 300

EXTRACT from the SERMON by the Lord Bishop of
Ossory, preached at St. Canice's Cathedral, Kilkenny, at Morning Service on the 29th December
—the first Sunday after Mr. Kavanagh's death.

"We have lost a great and a good man, one who was
indeed a tower of strength, and whose removal is not
only a private but a public loss.   I shall not dwell at
any length upon his public life; it lives in the annals
of his country, and has received a generous and
appreciative notice in the press.   Gifted with great
mental power and firmness of character, he overcame
difficulties which would have overwhelmed any
ordinary man; but by the sheer force of his worth
and character he won among the foremost a foremost
place.   He held by birth and ancestry a unique
position, which linked him on to the early history of
his country, and gave him a rank ·beside which most

patents of nobility seemed to be things of yesterday. But he had something nobler than birth and lineage. He was the very soul of honour, and had a supreme contempt for everything that was base and mean; and better still, he had a conscience enlightened and guided by Divine Truth.   He was not a man to make a display of his religious feelings, but he was not a man who would ever venture to conceal them.   He lived and acted in the fear and love of God, and sought to regulate his life and conduct according to the Divine will.   Born to wealth, and with great capacities for enjoyment, he lived no life of selfish ease.   If he had an ambition, it was to live and die at home, to be the friend and benefactor of his people, and to render his life serviceable to them and to his country.   In the Imperial councils of the nation his voice was always listened to with respect and confidence, because of his wisdom, his prudence, and his thorough conscientiousness.   And those who differed from him had even to acknowledge that, if he was a formidable opponent, he was always a fair and generous one.

" What he was to our Church, both by his ability and his liberality, is known to us all.   Wise in counsel, and specially able in all matters of finance, we shall miss him from our councils, and especially from the representative body of the Church, of which he was an honoured and most diligent member.   Ever since our disestablishment he held a most important position upon our Boards of Patronage, and I can bear witness that to him it was no formal discharge of a mere function, but a careful and prayerful investigation of each case that came before him, and an earnest desire to seek for good and suitable men to fill our vacant parishes.   He viewed his office as a solemn trust committed to him by God, and he endeavoured most faithfully to discharge it.

" Those who knew him in the intimacy of his private life can bear witness that he was a loving husband, a tender ·father, a considerate master, and a

kind and courteous friend.   It was something never to
be forgotten to witness how he conducted the family
worship of his household; the reverent way in which
he read the Holy Scriptures; the earnest and devout
manner in which he offered up prayer and thanksgiving at the Throne of Grace.   Strangers, and
sometimes those of another creed who had the
privilege of being present at these devout services,
have acknowledged how much they were impressed
by them.   But, better still, the whole life and conduct
of the man harmonised with these devotions.   The
truth was that all this useful and noble life had its
roots deep in his strong and simple piety.   His was
the attitude of a lowly heart that had come to Christ
for mercy, and a trusting heart that ever looked to
Him for grace; and so when trials and anxieties came
upon him he was calm and immovable; and when he
was misjudged and ungenerously treated he exhibited
a noble patience, a generous forbearance.   He could
well leave his character to be its own defender, and his
memory will be honoured and loved when that of
his defamers is forgotten, or remembered only with
virtuous indignation.   A standard-bearer amongst us
has fallen, and the world is all the poorer for the loss
of such a man.   As the true type of a Christian
gentleman, he has left a legacy for imitation to those
who hold positions anything like his own; and to us
all he has left an example to do our duty in that state
of life to which it has pleased God to call us.

"It is just three years ago this very week that
I consecrated a new burying-ground in his own demesne for the use of his family; and vividly do I recall
how, as I stood beside him on that occasion, he joined
in the solemn service with uncovered head and with
subdued voice, while he prayed God would 'soon
accomplish the number of his elect' and hasten his
kingdom.   How little did we think that he would be
the first to occupy that consecrated soil!   We would
have wished for the sake of his country, his Church,
his family, and his friends that the evening of his day

was far distant from him still. But our Heavenly Father has ordered it otherwise, and we can only say, 'Even so Father, for so it seemed good in Thy sight.' Thus Christmas morning came this year, and while we were joyfully celebrating the birth of our and his Redeemer, one of the best of wives was mourning the loss of one of the best of husbands, and his dear children were lamenting, as well they might, the removal of a beloved and loving father.

"May the God of all consolation be in their midst. He alone can fill up with His Own Presence the blank that is left in their heart and home. If human sympathy can lessen grief; if the respect and love and honour felt for their departed one can give consolation, they have sources of comfort on every side. But they have better consolations than these. They know in whom he believed; they can feel assured that he has eternal rest; they can look forward in 'sure and certain hope' that they shall see him yet again in the home where death and parting can never come. 'Mark the perfect man, and behold the upright, for the end of that man is peace.'"

Among numerous letters of sympathy the two following were received by Mrs. Kavanagh—one from a private friend, who although differing from her husband in politics was for many years a loyal fellow-worker with him in the cause of Ireland; the other from one of the many public bodies with which Mr. Kavanagh had been associated.

"26th December 1889.

"MY DEAR MRS. KAVANAGH—Your letter received this morning prepared me for the letter which came by the next post from Mrs. Meredyth. I hardly know how to write to you in your great sorrow. It is difficult to realise the loss, not only to you and all those most nearly related to him, but also to those who had the high honour of being intimately acquainted with him ; and yet again to the country at large, and Ireland in particular.

" I know that all those who like me had been thrown much with him will agree that no finer character ever lived, or one who worked for the common good with a higher ideal.

" I think you will find that the remembrance and consciousness of this must surely be some comfort and consolation to you and your family.—I am always, yours most truly, —————"

County Kilkenny Grand Jury, Spring Assizes 1890

Vote of Condolence

Proposed by Hon. L. Agar Ellis, seconded by E. L. Warren, Esq.

" We, the Grand Jurors of the County of Kilkenny, assembled at Spring Assizes 1890, take this, the first opportunity, of placing on record our sorrow at the severe loss the County has sustained through the death of the Right Hon. Arthur MacMurrough Kavanagh. It is with feelings of pride that we look back at having been associated with him in the business of this County, and it is with unfeigned grief we mourn our able colleague. Not only for the present do we pass this resolution, but for the purpose of holding up to those who succeed us so good an example ; and we gladly seize upon this occasion to show our full appreciation of those noble qualities which made Mr. Kavanagh one of Ireland's greatest sons. W. DE MONTMORENCY, *Foreman.*"

12th March 1890.

THE END